A Thousand Li:
The First Step

A Cultivation Novel

Book 1 of A Thousand Li Series

By

Tao Wong

Copyright

A Thousand Li: The First Step

Copyright © 2019 Tao Wong. All rights reserved.

Copyright © 2019 Sarah Anderson Cover Designer

Copyright © 2019 Felipe deBarros Cover Artist

A Starlit Publishing Book

Published by Starlit Publishing

69 Teslin Rd

Whitehorse, YT

Y1A 3M5

Canada

www.mylifemytao.com

Ebook ISBN: 9781989458006

Paperback ISBN: 9781989458020

Hardcover ISBN: 9781989458327

Books in the A Thousand Li series

The First Step

The First Stop

The First War

Contents

Chapter 1

"Cultivation, at its core, is a rebellion."

Waiting for their reaction, the thin, mustached older teacher stared at the students seated cross-legged before him. Apparently not seeing the reaction he wanted, the teacher flung the long, trailing sleeves of the robes he wore with a harrumph and continued his lecture. Keeping his expression entirely neutral, Long Wu Ying could not help but smirk within. Such a statement, no matter how contentious, lost its impact after daily repetition over the course of a decade.

"Cultivation demands one to defy the very heavens itself. Each step on the path of cultivation sets you on the road to rebellion to defy the heavens, to defy our king. It is only by his good graces and his belief in the betterment of the kingdom that you are allowed to cultivate."

Wu Ying struggled to keep his face neutral as the refrain continued. Usually, he could tune out the teacher until it came time to cultivate, but today he struggled to do so. Today, he could not help but rebut the teacher in his mind. Teaching the villagers how to cultivate was a purely practical decision on the king's part. Most children would achieve at least the first level of Body Cleansing by their twelfth birthday. That allowed them to grow stronger and healthier, even on the little food they had left after the state, the nobles, and the sects had taken their portion.

"The beneficent auspices of the king allow you to cultivate, study the martial arts, and defend yourself. It is only because of his belief that each village must be a strong member of the kingdom that we have grown to the heights we have!"

It had nothing to do with the desire to begin training the villagers to be useful soldiers in the never-ending wars. Or to ensure that the village was not robbed of the grain they farmed by the bandits that seemed to grow in number every year. Or the fact that less than two hundred li[1] away, the Verdant Green Waters Sect watched over them all, searching for new recruits.

"Now, begin!"

Exhaling a grateful breath that Master Su had finally finished, Wu Ying tried to focus his mind on cultivating. That he respected his teacher was without question, but Master Su was a stickler for the rules, which required him to give the same lecture every single time. Even a saint would find it hard to listen after a while. And Wu Ying was many things, but a Saint he most definitely was not.

It didn't help that the state was obviously of two minds about cultivation itself. The three pillars of a kingdom were the government, the populace, and the cultivating sects. A weakness in any of the three would make a kingdom vulnerable. For a kingdom to be stable, each pillar needed to be as strong, as upright and firm, as the others. If any single pillar grew too high, it would eventually lead to the collapse of the kingdom.

Because of that, a wise ruler would support the development of their populace through cultivation, the surest and best form of developing an individual. But a single cultivator, if they achieved true power, could—and had, historically—overturn governments. And so, the state would always view cultivators and cultivation with some degree of distrust.

"Wu Ying. Focus!" Master Su said.

Wu Ying grimaced slightly before he made his face placid again. Master Su was right. He could think about all these thoughts another time. This was the time for cultivation. The time a villager had to cultivate was limited and precious. Stray thoughts were wasteful.

---

[1] Half a kilometer or roughly a third of a mile

Drawing a deep breath, Wu Ying exhaled through his nose. The first step in cultivation was to clear the mind. The second was to control his breathing, for breath was the source of all things. At least in the Yellow Emperor's Cultivation Method that had been passed down and used by all peasants in the kingdom of Shen.

The first step on the road to cultivation was that of bodily purification. To ascend, to gain greater strength and develop one's chi, a cultivator needed to purify their body of the wastes that accumulated. Starting the process young helped to reduce the amount of such waste build up and speeded up the progress of cultivation. That was why every villager began cultivating as soon as possible. Those children who achieved the first level of Body Cleansing at a young age were hailed as prodigies.

Wu Ying was not considered a prodigy. Wu Ying had started cultivating at the age of six, like every other child in the village, and through hard work and discipline, he'd managed to achieve not just the first level of Body Cleansing but the second. True prodigies, at Wu Ying's age of seventeen, would already be at the fourth or fifth stage. Each of the twelve stages of Body Cleansing saw the conscious introduction and cleansing of another major chi meridian. When an individual had consciously introduced and could control the flow of chi through all twelve major pathways, all the stages of Body Cleansing were considered complete.

Wu Ying breathed in then out, slowly and rhythmically. He focused on the breath, the flow of air into his lungs, the way it entered his body as his stomach expanded and his chest filled out. Then he exhaled, feeling his stomach contract, the diaphragm moving upward as air circulated away.

In time, Wu Ying moved his focus away from breathing toward his dantian. Located below his belly button, in the space just slightly below his hip line and a few inches beneath the surface of his body, the lower dantian was the core of the Yellow Emperor's Cultivation Method. From there, through the flow and consolidation of one's internal chi, one would progress.

Once again, Wu Ying felt the mass of energy that was his dantian. As always, it was large in size but low in density, uncompacted and diffuse. His job was to gently nudge the flow of energy through his body's meridians, to send it on a major circulation through his body. In the process, his body sweated, as the normally docile chi moved through his body, cleansing and scouring away the impurities of life. In time, Wu Ying's normal sweat mixed with the impurities in his body, flowing from his pores. The rancid, bitter odor from Wu Ying's body mixed with the similar pungence coming from the rest of the class, a stench that even the open windows of the building could do little to disperse.

***

Deep in the process of cultivating, none of the students noticed the rancid smell, leaving only Master Su to suffer as he watched over the teenagers. Master Su had long gotten used to the offensive odor that he would be forced to endure for the next few hours as each of the classes progressed. It was a fair trade though, for Master Su received ten tael[2] of silver and, most importantly, a Marrow Cleansing pill each month for his work.

Deep in their cultivation, none of the students moved when a young man shook and convulsed. But Master Su took action, flashing over to the boy with a tap of his foot. Paired fingers raised as Master Su studied the thrashing boy before they darted forward, striking in rapid succession a series of acupressure points along the body. After the third strike, the convulsing slowed then stopped before the boy tipped over, coughing out blood.

---

[2] A measurement of weight. Roughly 37.5 grams

"Foolish. Pushing to open the second meridian channel when you have not finished cleansing the first!" Master Su berated the boy, shaking his head. "Get up. Begin cultivating properly. You will stay here an extra hour."

"But…" the boy protested weakly but quieted at Master Su's glare.

"Foolish child!" Master Su growled as he stomped back to his station in front of the class. If he had not been there, the boy would likely have damaged himself permanently. Master Su watched as the boy wiped his mouth clear of blood before he snorted. Luckily, Master Su had been able to quell the rampaging chi flow, but the boy would likely have to spend the next few weeks on light duty at his farm. A bad time for that, considering the planting season they were in. "Stupid."

As the hour set aside for the teenagers to cultivate came to an end and the morning sun cast long shadows on the small village, the village bell rang. Master Su frowned slightly then smoothed his face as the students broke free from their cultivation trances one by one. It would never do for the students to see his concern.

"The session is over. Line up when you are done," Master Su commanded before he walked out of the small, single-room building that made up his school.

Outside, the teacher walked forward slightly, turning his head from side to side before he spotted the growing dust cloud.

"Master Su." Tan Cheng, the tall village head, came up to Master Su.

As the two individuals in the sixth level of the Body Cleansing stage, the pair shared the burden of guarding the village from external threats. It helped that Chief Tan was a lover of tea like Master Su.

"Chief Tan," Master Su greeted. "What is it?"

"The army recruiters," Chief Tan said, his eyes grave.

Master Su could not help but wince. This was the third time in as many years that the army had recruited from their village. The conscripts from the first year had yet to return, though news of deaths had trickled back. The war between their state of Shen and the state of Wei had dragged on, bringing misery to everyone.

"They're going to raise the taxes again then," Master Su said, trying to keep his tone light. Each year that the war dragged on, the taxes grew higher. He wondered how many the army would take this time and did not envy his friend. The first time the army arrived, they had filled the requirements with volunteers. The second time they came, each household that had more than one son and had yet to send a volunteer had sent their sons. This time, there would be no easy choices.

"Most likely." Chief Tan chewed on his lip slightly. As the rest of the villagers slowly streamed in from the surrounding fields, he looked around then looked down, avoiding the expectant gazes of the parents. Whatever came next, few would be happy.

***

"What is it?" Qiu Ru asked. The raven-haired beauty of the class prodded Wu Ying in the back as she tried to peer past the crowd of students who had gathered around the windows. Giving up, she prodded Wu Ying once more in the back to get him to answer.

"The army," Wu Ying finally answered.

As her eyes widened, he admired the way it made them shine—before he squashed his burgeoning feelings again. Qiu Ru had made it quite clear last summer festival that she had no interest in him. Now, Wu Ying had his sights set on Gao Yan. Even if Gao Yan was shorter, plumper, and had a bad tendency to forget to brush her teeth. That was life in the village—your choices were somewhat limited.

"Are they bringing back the volunteers?" Qiu Ru said.

"No. They're too early for that," Cheng Fa Hui said.

Wu Ying glanced at his friend, who had hung back with the rest of them. Not that Fa Hui needed to be up front to see what was happening. He towered over the entire group by a head. All except Wu Ying, who only lost to him by a handbreadth.

"If the army was returning our people, it would be before the winter," Fa Hui said. "That way the lord would not need to feed them."

Wu Ying grimaced and shot a look around the room, relaxing slightly when he saw that Yin Xue had not come to class today. As the nearest village to Lord Wen's summer abode, all the villagers dealt with Lord Wen and his son regularly. Truth be told, Yin Xue did not need to come to their village class, but the boy seemed to take pleasure in showcasing his ability over the peasants. As the son of the local lord, Yin Xue had access to a private cultivation tutor, spiritual herbs, and good food—all of which had allowed him to progress to Body Cleansing four already. In common parlance, he was what was known as a false dragon—a "forced" genius, rather than one who had achieved the heights of his cultivation by genius alone.

If Yin Xue had heard Fa Hui… Wu Ying mentally shuddered at the thought. Still, it was not as if Fa Hui was wrong. If the war was over, it made sense to make the villagers feed the returned sons rather than pay for hungry mouths over the winter.

"Are they here for us then?" Wu Ying mused. That would make sense.

After saying the words out loud, he noticed how the rest of the class stiffened. Before he could say anything to comfort them, Master Su called them out of the building.

Once the students had lined up outside, Wu Ying could easily see the army personnel, two of which were speaking with Chief Tan, while the others watched over the conscripts. As it was still early in the morning, the army had only managed to visit one other village thus far, and as such, there were only twenty such conscripts standing together. Yin Xue sat astride a horse, beside the conscripts but not part of them.

Wu Ying had to admit, the members of the army looked dashing in their padded undercoats, dark lamellar armor, and open-faced helms. But having watched two other groups leave and not return, with only rumors of the losses trickling back via the same recruiters and the itinerant merchant, much of the prestige and glory of joining the army had faded.

"Men, Lord Wen has sent his men to us once again. We are required to send twenty strong conscripts to join the king's army this year." Before the crowd could grasp the significance of the number, Chief Tan announced, "All sons from families who have not sent a child to the front, step forward."

Wu Ying stepped forward. As the only surviving son of his family, he had been safe from the recruiters beforehand. Along with Wu Ying, another six men stepped forward.

"All sons from families with more than one son in the village, step forward," Chief Tan announced.

This time, there was some confusion, but it was soon sorted out with some students pushed forward and others drawn back. By now, Wu Ying counted seventeen "volunteers."

"Why not daughters?" Qiu Ru called.

Wu Ying could not help but grimace at her impertinent words. As the local beauty, Qiu Ru had managed to get away with more impertinent comments than others. Interrupting the Chief while he was speaking was a new high.

"The army is looking for men!" Chief Tan snapped. "Qiu Jan! See to your daughter!"

"This is foolish!" Qiu Ru said.

When Chief Tan began to speak, he was silenced by a raised hand of the lieutenant, whose gaze raked over Qiu Ru. "You are quite the beauty. But our men do not need wives."

The hiss from the crowd was loud even as Qiu Ru flushed bright red at the insult.

"We are here to find soldiers. And you are, what? Body Cleansing one? Women are no use to us as soldiers until at least Body Cleansing four!"

Still flushed, Qiu Ru moved to speak, but her mother had managed to make her way over to the impertinent girl and gripped her arm. With a yank of her hand, the mother pulled Qiu Ru back. For a time, the lieutenant looked over the group, seeing that no one else was liable to interrupt, before he looked at Chief Tan.

"Tan Fu, Qiu Lee, Long Mao. Join the others," Chief Tan said softly.

Everyone knew why he had chosen the three, of course. Their families had been gifted with more than three surviving sons. Even now, their parents would have a single son left to work the farm, turn the earth. A good thing. Better than the families that were left without any. If you didn't consider the fact that now, three of their sons were fighting a war that none of them ever wanted.

"Good," the lieutenant said as his gaze slid over the new conscripts.

Wu Ying looked to the side as well, offering Fa Hui a tight smile as he saw his big friend look sallow and scared.

"Conscripts, return to your homes and collect your belongings. You will not be back for many months. Bring what you need. We will march in fifteen minutes. Gather at first bell," the lieutenant said.

The students stared at one another, looking at the few members of the class that were left, then at the other children. Wu Ying sighed and clapped Fa Hui on the shoulder, giving the giant a slight shove to send him toward his family. As if the motion was a signal, the group broke apart, the teenager's faces fixed as they moved to say their final goodbyes.

Chapter 2

"Papa. Mama," Wu Ying greeted his parents as they all arrived at their small house, having traversed through the field.

"Do not pack. I will go in your stead," his father cut in.

Wu Ying stared at his father, Long Yu Hi, as he stomped into the house. Wu Ying could see the limp in his father's steps even when he was trying to hide it, a result of his enrollment in the army over a decade ago.

"Ah Hi, don't be foolish." Long Fa Rong, Wu Ying's mother, echoed her words by pulling on Yu Hi's arm, stopping him. She met his eyes, putting subtle pressure on his arm. "Do you wish to lose even more face when they tell you no?"

"But…"

"Our son is smart and brave. He even has progressed to the second level of Body Cleansing," Fa Rong said.

But for all her brave words, Wu Ying could see the tears in her eyes, and his stomach clenched tightly with suppressed emotions. He offered her a slight smile in thanks before he turned to his father and bowed. "Papa. Please."

"You… you idiot. If you're going to go, remember what we taught you. Remember to practice every day," Yu Hi said gruffly. "Go. The seeds won't plant themselves. And the lieutenant will not wait."

"Yes, Papa," Wu Ying said, bobbing his head before hurrying to the curtain that marked his room.

He pulled it aside and quickly packed, taking the couple of changes of clothing, the single other pair of cloth shoes, and a small, softcover copy of the Yellow Emperor's Cultivation Manual. This was Wu Ying's personal copy, which he had industriously copied from the main copy in the text room, using a mixture of paper scavenged from his father's medicine and tea packages. The manual had his own notes on cultivation, notes that he used to guide his development. Next, he picked up the sword manual that contained, in cryptic terms, the steps of the Long family sword style. It was bare of much information, the details scrubbed of all but the names, a simple reminder for Wu Ying if he ever forgot. As for the details—those could only be passed down in person.

In minutes, Wu Ying was ready and, with some twine, quickly tied his belongings together. As he stepped out of his alcove, he found his mother had prepared a package of easy-to-eat foodstuff for him to take. With a twisted smile, he took it with thanks. Just before he stepped away, his mother hugged him tightly to her bosom.

Standing still and stiff at first, Wu Ying eventually relaxed and hugged her back, burying his face into his shorter mother's hair. For a moment, he reveled in the human contact. It was rare for them to touch, so this brief contact was something he intended to savor.

"Don't forget to burn a joss stick for your ancestors. Then go. Don't be late. And if you can, let us know how you're doing," Fa Rong said.

"I will. Goodbye, Mama," Wu Ying said and bowed to her one last time.

Wu Ying moved quickly to the small altar set inside the house and retrieved the joss sticks before lighting three and paying obeisance to the group. It did not take long before he was done, placing the joss sticks in the urn. Once he exited, Wu Ying looked around and found his father's back. It was in the fields once again, bent as always over the rice plants. Wu Ying's lips pursed, then he shook his head. That was his father's way—to show little emotion, to offer only the barest encouragement, and to expect the best of him. With a sigh, Wu Ying turned aside and jogged toward the village, knowing that if he did not, he would likely be late.

For all the heartache and pain in leaving, for all the likely danger they were about to encounter, Wu Ying found himself looking forward to the day. If nothing else, he would have a chance to see the world beyond their tiny village. And who knows, he might even win some glory for their family. It had happened before.

***

The trip out from the village was the conscripts' first taste of being under military rule. Immediately, the students were lined up and marched along the muddy roads, each of them forced to move in lockstep. Luckily, not only were they all cultivators, they had been taught some martial arts at an early age, ensuring that the group was fit and healthy. As such, the only concern was learning to move in unison in the weird lockstep march that the sergeant required of them.

Achieving an approximation of the march was something the disciplined students could achieve, but an approximation was insufficient for the sergeant's requirements. As such, the sergeant constantly harassed them, using a willow switch to strike at legs, arms, and backs until the group moved to his liking.

In time, the group made its way to the next village, hours away, where a similar scene as in their village repeated itself. Unfortunately, the village chief did not have as good a relationship with his own villagers. Rather than finding a justifiable or fair method of splitting the burden, the chief favored his underlings heavily, sending more than one family into tears. Yet in the face of the overwhelming strength of the army personnel and the chief's own personal cultivation strength, none dared to object.

"This… why would he do that?" Fa Hui said to Wu Ying.

"Why wouldn't he?" Wu Ying replied softly.

"He's weakening his village. Those farmers, they won't have anyone to take over their lands if their sons die," Fa Hui replied.

"Yes. And perhaps he'll take them over. Or give them to his friends," Wu Ying said, nodding toward the side where a group of villagers smirked.

"That…" Fa Hui fell silent.

Two of the biggest issues for farmers were the matters of labor and inheritance. If you were lucky enough to have most of your children survive the diseases and injuries of childhood before they achieved some level of cultivation, you then had an additional helper working your land. But when said children grew up, if you had more than a few, you faced the problem of inheritance. A plot of land could only sustain so many mouths. And no son wanted to live with his father or brother forever.

"It's still wrong."

"Maybe. But it's not our village," Wu Ying said then clamped his mouth shut when the sergeant looked over the pair.

Since they were in the square, discipline had been relaxed. But even then, the sergeant disliked them speaking too loudly. As the sergeant glared at the group, the conscripts fell silent, watching the little drama play out. In time, the new conscripts regrouped and the now larger group marched toward the next village. Thankfully, the sergeant now had a new set of volunteers to abuse, giving the older conscripts some leeway to march.

In the evening, the group found an empty clearing in the forest that spread between the farms and villages, a place where everyone could rest. Even with the amount of land needed to ensure the populace was fed, there were still areas like this—no-man's-land between villages. At this point, the conscripts learned new and interesting skills, including how to set up a camp the army way, how to dig a latrine the army way, and even how watches were to be set. In this wilderness, Spirit beasts and the occasional bandit group roamed.

"Of course Yin Xue gets his own tent," Fa Hui muttered, shooting a look at where the lord's son had his tent set up.

He and Wu Ying, along with a few others, were crouched over a boiling pot of water, waiting for the rice and vegetables to cook. Set over the pot was a small steamer where strips of meat and salted fish had been placed to cook.

Over the course of the day, Wu Ying had paid a little attention to Yin Xue, curious about the lord's son's position in the army. He was not part of the regular conscripts, evident by the fact that he was allowed to ride a horse. Yet he did not ride with the army personnel either. Even now, Yin Xue seemed to occupy a piece of land between the conscripts and the army personnel, who bunked in the center of the formation.

"Hush," Wu Ying said. "You know better, Ah Hui. You'll get us in trouble."

"Bah. We're not at home anymore. We're in the army," Fa Hui said. "The rules are different."

"Not as different as you think, peasant," Yin Xue said, speaking from behind the peasant. He set his hand on the sword hilt he carried, raising his voice. "Say that again."

"The rules are different here," Fa Hui said, standing as well.

With a wince, Wu Ying stood and put himself between his big friend and the lord's son. "Yin Xue, Fa Hui's only saying that we are all in the army now. We are just learning new rules and it's likely the rules are different." Wu Ying tried for a genial smile.

Ever since Yin Xue had gained Xia Jin's favor at the last Qixi festival, Fa Hui had been looking for ways to antagonize Yin Xue. Of course, the difference in their statuses made it nearly impossible for Fa Hui to do so safely, but obviously Fa Hui felt safe now.

"That—"

Before Fa Hui could make it worse, Wu Ying elbowed his friend in the stomach, hard enough to force his friend to shut up. Yin Xue of course noticed the interaction, but chose to say nothing of it.

"Have you eaten, Yin Xue? Our rice should be ready soon," Wu Ying said with a smile.

"No. I actually came by to speak with you, Long Wu Ying. I always heard from my father that yours was a good swordsman in the army. A man who achieved the Sense of the Sword with your Long family style. Someone who was on the cusp of the Heart of the Sword before his injury. He must have taught you a little," Yin Xue said softly, a malicious look entering his eyes.

"No…" Wu Ying automatically began to deny the statement.

"No? He didn't teach you anything?" Yin Xue said, eyes narrowing then looking over Wu Ying's shoulder at Fa Hui.

Wu Ying could not help but sweat a little internally. After all, Yin Xue was Body Cleansing 4—three whole levels above Fa Hui. And while in the Body Cleansing stage, each open meridian provided benefits, those benefits could be overcome with skill and innate strength. Unfortunately, Yin Xue had both. Fa Hui only had his innate strength. If Yin Xue kept pushing, Wu Ying knew that his friend would likely be seriously injured.

"Yes, he did. I meant, no, I would never be so forthright and say he was good," Wu Ying said, bowing his head slightly. Better to play meek and see where Yin Xue took this. If he wanted to lay down a beating, then Wu Ying would accept it. As one of the few villagers who could compete marginally with Yin Xue, Wu Ying often found himself matched with the other—in words or cultivation.

"Good, then you'll practice with me," Yin Xue said.

"I don't think we should…" Wu Ying said, casting a glance at the army personnel. They barely paid any attention to the conscripts, a fact that made Yin Xue smirk.

"I do not believe they mind. After all, practice in the martial arts is important. As is discipline," Yin Xue said, looking at Fa Hui at the end. There was even a light smirk on his face, making Wu Ying grimace.

"I don't have a sword."

"I can have one lent to you," Yin Xue said.

While Yin Xue sent a nearby conscript to pull a sword from his roll, Fa Hui had grabbed Wu Ying's arm.

"You cannot do this. He will beat you," Fa Hui hissed at Wu Ying.

"Of course." Wu Ying would not overestimate the training he had received. "But if I don't, he's going to challenge you. And you won't stand any chance."

"You don't have to do this," Fa Hui said again, but Wu Ying chuckled.

"I've been doing this since we were kids. It's fine," Wu Ying said with a wave. He nodded at the conscript who returned with the jian.

Wu Ying unsheathed the sword and did a quick check to ensure the weapon was sharp and straight before he twirled it around, gaining a feel for its weight. The jian—a double-edged straight sword—was of decent quality and weighed about a catty[3] and a half, being two and a half chi[4] long. Longer than Wu Ying was used to, but that could work in his favor in this instance.

Yin Xue watched Wu Ying's preparations with a smirk, waving the other conscripts back.

---

[3] Weight measurement. One cattie is roughly equivalent to one and a half pounds or 604 grams. A tael is 1/16th of a catty

[4] Length measurement. Three chi is equivalent to one meter. Slightly over a foot

"Are you ready?" Yin Xue said as he unsheathed his sword at his hip. The lord's son took a relaxed guard, sword held just above his lead leg as he waited for Wu Ying to take position across from him.

"This is a practice session, right?" Wu Ying said as he mimicked Yin Xue's motion.

"Of course. Just practice," Yin Xue replied. Even as his words came to an end, Yin Xue lunged forward before cutting down. Willow strikes the swallow.

Wu Ying stepped aside, shifting forms as well. Greeting the rising sun. Dragon stretches in the morning. Dragon raises its wings. Each motion led to the next, each action flowing smoothly into the other. As much as Wu Ying might protest, he was certainly not a simple beginner at sword forms, having been taught since he was little. But while he had received the Long family sword forms from his father, their training happened late at night or early in the morning, in the gaps between taking care of the farm, cultivating, and schooling. Yin Xue, on the other hand, had learned from august tutors, day in and day out, without worry or concern about a hard winter or a heavy spring rainstorm. And of course, Yin Xue was two levels higher in Body Cleansing.

"Hsss…" Wu Ying gritted his teeth as a lunge that he had been too slow to stop cut across his arm. He managed to shift the blade enough that it only scored his arm, cutting flesh and leaving a bloody wound but not harming the muscle beneath.

"Enough, Yin Xue!" Fa Hui said upon seeing Wu Ying cut.

"We have just started. Wu Ying would not stop over such a small injury, would he?" Yin Xue replied, smirking. "Or else I will have to find someone else to keep training with."

"It's fine," Wu Ying said, waving his friend down and raising the sword again. "It was just a mistake."

"Good. Very good," Yin Xue said. "Then I'll keep coming."

Yin Xue stepped forward immediately, speeding up his attacks. The pair spun and cut, thrust and blocked as they whirled around the small circle the conscripts had formed. All the conscripts watched, mouths slightly open as they exclaimed at the level of the fight before them. For the villagers, this level of fighting was an uncommon sight, even if the pair themselves knew that it was like the untrained swinging of swords in the eyes of the real experts.

In a few more passes, Wu Ying found himself pressed back as Yin Xue slowly picked up the speed and fluidity of his attacks. Wu Ying's eyes widened slightly as he struggled to keep up, his grip on his sword tightening in fear as he realized that Yin Xue had been holding back. Each motion seemed faster than the last, each attack coming closer and closer to hitting him. Wu Ying's breathing sped up, his heart rate skyrocketing. From outside the duelling ring, it would be impossible to tell, but every few attacks, Yin Xue would suddenly shift his trajectory, going for a blow that would do more than touch but kill.

"Willow strikes the swallow," Yin Xue said softly.

Wu Ying jerked his sword up to guard, his body too tired to stop its automatic reaction. Too late, Wu Ying realized that it was a trick. Yin Xue twisted the sword, dipping the blade around his own block and letting the point plunge directly into the lower right of Wu Ying's abdomen. A slight twist as the blade came out opened the wound further.

Wu Ying felt the strength in his legs give out, and he dropped to a knee. A second later, the pain hit and his breathing grew erratic.

"What is going on here!" Too late, the sergeant noticed the danger and stalked over.

As the sergeant berated Yin Xue for injuring him, Wu Ying had a hand pressed to his side to stem the bleeding.

Eventually, the sergeant turned away and looked at Wu Ying before sniffing. "Fool. Practicing with real swords. You there! You were the village doctor's son?" A murmured agreement. "Then bandage him up."

More muttered protests, but Wu Ying paid no attention to them until insistent hands had him lying down, a bandage pressed against his body. Wu Ying hissed as more pressure came down on the wound. When he focused, he saw a worried-looking Fa Hui and a thin young boy hovering over him.

"The wound is wide and open. I'll need to stitch you closed and put a paste on it. It will hurt," the boy said. "I need to boil some water and clean my instruments first."

"Thank. You," Wu Ying said.

"Don't. Idiot," the healer said with a snort and scurried out of Wu Ying's sight, Fa Hui taking over the job of keeping pressure on Wu Ying's side.

"I will kill Yin Xue," Fa Hui growled softly.

"Stop it. It was your big mouth that started this," Wu Ying said with a snarl. "I will be fine. Just avoid him."

"Wu Ying—"

"Just stop it," Wu Ying said. "Swear to me. You'll not do anything."

"I—"

"You owe me this. Swear," Wu Ying snarled.

"I swear. So long as you live, I won't touch Yin Xue!" Fa Hui said, his voice soft and urgent.

"Good."

"You, out of the way," the boy-healer said as he came back with his instruments. Pushing Fa Hui aside, he quickly threaded the silk thread through his bamboo needle. "Get some light." The healer then turned to Wu Ying, his voice growing softer and more comforting. "Now, this is going to hurt."

Wu Ying could only nod dumbly and take the cloth-wrapped piece of bamboo into his mouth. As the boy poured a handful of alcohol on his wound to cleanse it, Wu Ying bit down hard and screamed into the gag. When darkness rose to claim him as he felt the first stitch go in, he could only promise himself that he would get his own revenge on Yin Xue.

Chapter 3

Step. Another step. Then another. Pain radiated from his abdomen with each step. Even as he marched alongside the conscripts, Wu Ying felt the bandage around his side grow damper as blood squeezed out. The wound might have been stitched closed, but all this walking had probably torn at least one of those stitches. Sun An—the boyish-looking healer—had done his best to stitch everything together, but the wound had been deep.

"Drink," Fa Hui said, offering Wu Ying a waterskin.

Wu Ying took the waterskin without protest, popped open the cap, and took a mouthful of the foul-tasting drink. Sun An had woken early to boil the herbs for this drink, a tonic that was meant to help with the pain and reduce the chance of inflammation. Of course, Sun An had grumbled about the lack of proper medical supplies while doing so.

"Thank you," Wu Ying said, returning the waterskin.

"Can you last? The next village can't be that far," Fa Hui said softly as the group continued their walk.

Other than Yin Xue swinging by an hour ago to "kindly" inquire about Wu Ying's status, not even the sergeant had paid attention to Wu Ying. It seemed that Wu Ying either had to march or... well, the other options were unthinkable. The army was not known for their kind and understanding ways, after all.

"Can you?" Wu Ying said. Fa Hui had taken his gear in the morning, an act that Wu Ying had not protested. It was the least his friend could do. Quite literally.

"This? This is nothing!" Fa Hui said, hefting the pair of bags with a smile. "This is so much easier than working the fields. I can even stand upright!"

Wu Ying chuckled and regretted it, stumbling slightly. The sergeant was immediately at their sides, yelling at the pair until they caught the tempo of the march again. Once again, no mention was made of Wu Ying's obvious injury.

"Don't make me laugh," Wu Ying said once they were clear to talk once more. He had to admit though that Fa Hui had a point. Spring meant being on their hands and knees all day long, planting the rice stalks in the water-clogged fields. Marching was, for all intents and purposes, easy compared to that.

"Just a little longer. Then we'll be at the next village," Fa Hui reiterated.

Wu Ying grunted, looking at the sky and the fast looming clouds. Rain. Of course it would rain. Bending his head, Wu Ying focused on putting one foot in front of the other, riding the waves of pain with each step.

***

"Eat." Fa Hui pushed the warm bowl of porridge toward Wu Ying later that evening.

Wu Ying looked up, smiling wanly at his friend and taking the bowl before a spasm almost made him drop it. Small tarps were strung between the trees, helping to keep off the light shower, but that did little to stop his body from shivering from his damp clothing.

"Damn it," Wu Ying cursed. He had marched through the rain, soaked like everyone else, and now his body was shivering from the cold and lost blood.

"Wu Ying…" Fa Hui said worriedly, helping Wu Ying hold the bowl. "Are you okay?"

"Fine. Just pain," Wu Ying said.

Fa Hui frowned, but Wu Ying turned back to his food, head down as he slowly spooned the rice porridge into his mouth. The porridge was cold now, tasteless in his mouth. The army was stingy with their rations, barely giving them enough meat to even flavor the porridge.

"Time to change your bandages," Sun An ordered Wu Ying when he had finally finished his meal.

Moving gingerly, Wu Ying placed the bowl aside and raised his arms slightly to allow Sun An to unwrap the bandages around his body.

Sun An frowned, noting the blood and the torn stitches, as well as the newly reddened, inflamed flesh. "You have been drinking the herbs?"

"Yes," Fa Hui replied for Wu Ying, concern in his eyes. "Will he be okay?"

"It's inflamed. Possibly infected," Sun An said, running his fingers along the wound, his fingers displacing dried blood. "I can't stitch it again, not with him moving so much. And I doubt it would do any good. I'll put a salve on it, try to reduce the inflammation a bit. But he should be resting, not marching."

"I'm right here," Wu Ying said, glaring at the pair.

Sun An smiled slightly, waving in apology as he moved away to start on the salve. Fa Hui sat down next to Wu Ying, a clean bowl of water and a new bandage in hand.

"I can do that."

"I—"

"I can do it," Wu Ying said, taking the bandage and working the edges. When he saw the hurt look in his friend's face, he added, "You don't have a gentle touch."

"I do!"

"That's not what Xia Jin said," Wu Ying added.

"That—" Fa Hui looked offended for a moment before he chuckled wryly. "She was my first kiss!"

"Well, practice more."

"Like Mu Er on his sister…?"

***

Another day, another forced march. At least it wasn't raining, though the muddy roads were a pain to march in. But at the end of the day, rather than a simple clearing, the group finally caught up with the main body of the army.

Too tired, cold, and achy to pay much attention, Wu Ying marched alongside his squad as they moved along the edges of the army encampment. Even so, he could not help but notice how ordered the lamps, tents, and cooking fires were. Every single tent looked the same, with only the addition of banners hung at the edges of each cooking fire indicating the different squads. There were few men in the camp itself, though in the distance, Wu Ying heard the tramp of booted feet.

The next few hours passed in a blur as their lieutenant reported in and the conscripts were broken into the various squads they would be added to. Once that was done, the newly formed squads were marched toward the nearest quartermaster to receive their gear.

"Eh? What is this?" The quartermaster stopped the man in charge of handing Wu Ying his clothing as he eyed the new conscript. His gaze swept down Wu Ying's hunched figure, lips compressing.

"Sir?" Wu Ying asked, blinking blearily as sweat dripped into one of his eyes.

"Are you ill?"

"A little…" Wu Ying admitted.

"Idiot!" the quartermaster snarled and glared at the sergeant and lieutenant. "How dare you bring someone ill into camp!"

"But he's just—" the lieutenant protested before the quartermaster squashed his protest and pointed toward the side.

"Shut up. You! Go report to the medics," the quartermaster said, shaking his head. "Sending sick people to us! What useless garbage."

As Wu Ying stumbled away, he saw the vicious glares sent to him by the lieutenant and the sergeant. But with his feet feeling like lead itself, Wu Ying could only focus on moving in the direction he had been sent. His vision blurred slightly with each step, his eyesight narrowing as the world closed in.

In time, he found the banners flapping white in the sky. The words written horizontally on them were clear. Medical Center.

"Sir, can we help you?"

"I was... I was sent here," Wu Ying said.

He turned toward the voice, the too-fast motion making him sway further. And then shouted words as the world faded into blackness.

***

A thump. Something firm under him, his body on his back as a flash of pain shot through him, waking him briefly. Eyelids too heavy to open, Wu Ying listened.

"Fools. Sending an injured conscript here by himself."

"What do you think it is?"

"Probably another training accident."

"Har! More waste. Sending us ill-trained children. They should be at the training grounds, not here."

"Shh..."

The voices faded again as darkness consumed him.

***

"Who is this?"

"A conscript. Put him in bed twenty-nine."

"He's quite handsome."

"Don't bother. The infection has spread to his body. He won't last the week."

***

Time passed for Wu Ying in fits and starts. When he was awake, he found himself trembling, waves of cold and heat surging through his weakened body. During those moments, time seemed to slow, leaving Wu Ying with an ache in his abdomen and joints, his teeth chattering while sweat gathered all over him. When he slept, it seemed like no time at all had passed before he woke once more, shivering.

Occasionally the healers would be there, feeding him broth and medicine in equal measure. He choked down what he could, slept and shivered the rest of the time. His purgatory of rest and wake was finally broken one day when he was roughly picked up and moved aside.

"What? What's going on?" Wu Ying asked blearily as he was moved from his bed.

"The army is on its way to meet the enemy. We're going to need the beds for the injured," the attendant replied, helping Wu Ying out of the tent. Together, the pair moved toward where a small group of other patients sat on the hill.

"But I'm injured."

"So are they. It's fine. There is no rain. Here, you'll be out of the way," the attendant said, dropping Wu Ying at a clear spot. "Drink this. It will help you be a little more lucid for a bit."

Wu Ying took the medicine and felt a rush of energy enter his body. For a moment, he wondered why they had not fed this to him before. Perhaps because such medicine was only a temporary tonic, good till it stopped working. By the time Wu Ying looked up to ask, the attendant was gone.

Seated on the ground, Wu Ying looked around slowly, blinking in the sunlight. He forced himself to focus, turning his head from side to side. From their viewpoint, near where the logistic arm of the army was, Wu Ying could see little about the imminent battle. With effort, he moved his body to angle to the side, getting the best view he could of the clear fields. Better than staring at the various men moving around. Few others near him bothered to do so, most too injured or unconscious.

Even that little movement made Wu Ying pant, and he found himself curled up slightly. Grimacing, Wu Ying shook his head gently and returned to waiting. Hours passed, an attendant coming out to provide the various patients a bowl of porridge and their herbal medicine before scurrying away. Occasionally a patrol would swing by, but they grew more infrequent as the day lengthened.

In time, the cries and sobs, the panting curses and screams of men in pain reached the patients as the wounded streamed in. Wu Ying winced, tilting his head upward, but could see nothing beyond the sides of the tent. Behind the imposing black of the military tent, soldiers wailed, bled, and died, but the black façade gave no hint of the men's struggle.

Turning away, Wu Ying returned his drifting attention to the hills that spread out before the main encampment. He turned toward them to tune out the screams behind him, to remind him of the peace that existed in nature. Of the way the wind blew, the birds flew, and the sun glinted off the spearheads...

Spearheads?

Wu Ying sat up a bit more, clutching his side as it pained him again. Squinting, he stared at the same spot he had first seen the anomaly. At first, nothing. Then a glint.

"Spears." When he looked around, he saw that none of his fellow "patients" had seen anything. He frowned, waving at the nearest patient and pointing. "Spears! The enemy."

The patient could only squint at him, his long hair tussled behind him. Looking around, Wu Ying realized that none of the attendants were around either. Perhaps he was hallucinating? Once more, Wu Ying squinted, only to have his suspicions proven when the sun glinted off them again.

"I must. Must warn them." Wu Ying pushed himself up only to sink to his knees when weakness robbed him of his gains. He groaned, pain shooting through his body, the fever pulsing and sending a headache through him. "No."

Wu Ying stood with a push, screaming slightly in pain. His shrieks were lost in the shouts from the medical tent. One foot in front of the other, his teeth gritted, Wu Ying walked forward. Each step was burning pain, each motion made him cough and groan as a fire was lit in his body. Finally, finally, he made it into the tent and pushed open a flap to see a reenactment of one of the lower hells.

Bodies—mutilated, bleeding, screaming—lay everywhere. Some were strapped down, others drugged. Some clutched at open wounds, others had already been bandaged and were waiting for blessed unconsciousness. Through it all, attendants and doctors moved, doing their best in the organized chaos, stemming bleeding, sewing wounds, and planting acupuncture needles.

Stumbling within, Wu Ying grabbed the first attendant. "Spears!"

"You're not going anywhere, soldier. Just sit down, we'll get to you," the attendant replied without even looking. With a jerk of his shoulder, he pulled his garment from Wu Ying's weak grip.

Wu Ying stumbled, almost losing his footing.

"No! Spears are coming," Wu Ying said but realized he was talking to the air. Forcing himself to walk deeper inside with a miserable grunt, Wu Ying dragged his body onward, feeling a hot wetness at his side as his wound once again bled freely.

"What are you doing back here?" A doctor appeared before Wu Ying, frowning.

Wu Ying stared at the face, realizing it was one that had attended to him before. "An attack. It's coming. From the other side." Breathing forcefully, he turned, pointing in the direction where he had seen the spears.

"What? Impossible. The scouts would have seen it."

"I saw it!"

"You're hallucinating," an attendant replied, taking hold of Wu Ying's arm.

Wu Ying snarled, calling up the dredges of his cultivation, of the last of his strength, and shoved the attendant away as he stared at the doctor. "Please! Just look. Look."

The attendant, angry, strode back and put Wu Ying in a lock, shoving him down and eliciting a scream of pain.

But still, he muttered as the attendant shoved him around, bringing more pain. "They're attacking. Just look…"

The last sight Wu Ying caught before he once again fainted was the frowning doctor's face.

Chapter 4

"Is he the one?"

"Yes."

"Wake him."

"But…"

"Wake him."

A pungent-smelling herbal ointment was rubbed under Wu Ying's nose. Then a hand pushed against his shoulder, slowly pulling him upward. Wu Ying blinked as he woke, realizing he was once again in a soft canvas bed, staring at a quartet of individuals.

The first was a face he recognized—the doctor who had treated him and the one he had warned. The other three, Wu Ying had not seen before. One was a glowering, middle-aged, bearded soldier with full-body armor and headgear that Wu Ying could not recognize at a glance. Before he could puzzle it out, Wu Ying's attention was drawn to the other two—individuals in colorful silk civilian clothing, a sharp contrast to the uniformed individuals all around. Both wore swords and had long hair and the best skin Wu Ying had ever seen. Even the male of the pair was so fair and smooth that Wu Ying would have thought he was a teenage girl if not for the masculine jut of his chin. As for the woman behind the man, she was a peerless beauty who put Qiu Ru to shame, her slender figure swelling with just the right amount of curves.

"You are awake," the man said.

"Yes." Wu Ying struggled to sit up further with the help of the doctor, his body refusing to listen to his orders. He frowned, feeling sweat pouring down from his brow and swiping at it with his hand. His movements were sluggish, uncoordinated, but the pain from his abdomen seemed remote at the moment.

"Is that how you speak to your betters?" the soldier growled. "Greet Elder Cheng Zhao Wan and Fairy[5] Yang Fa Yuan properly."

"And General Chao Keli," the doctor quickly added.

"General Chao, Elder Cheng, Fairy Yang," Wu Ying said, looking between the group.

Elder Cheng looked bored, impatient with the formalities, while Fairy Yang continued to look on imperiously.

After Wu Ying greeted the group formally, Elder Cheng spoke up. "You are the one who gave the warning?"

"Yes. Yes, Elder," Wu Ying replied. He bobbed his head low, doing the best he could to bow before finding himself almost falling off the bed.

"What is wrong with him?" Fa Yuan said. For the first time, Wu Ying heard the melodious tones of the fairy, her voice cultured and gentle.

"Infection of the blood from a stab in his abdomen. It missed his major organs, but he was marched here in the rain afterward," the doctor said.

"Ah." Elder Cheng stared at Wu Ying quietly, his eyes raking the cultivator. Whatever he saw made him frown before he fished within a pouch by his side. With a flick of his hand, he tossed a jade bottle to Wu Ying, who missed the catch and let the bottle fall on the bed cloth. "You did well. The attack was headed by three in the Energy Storage stage. If we had been caught unawares, we would have lost many of the generals."

"Tai Kor[6]!" Fa Yuan exclaimed in surprise. She jerked her head to the bottle, eyes wide. "That…"

---

[5] Fairy is an unofficial title given to women of exceptional beauty. Mostly as a form of respect to indicate the level of beauty and grace – akin to a fairy / goddess.

[6] Big Brother. Often used as a term of respect and also to denote a subordinate relationship.

"Is appropriate. The Meridian Opening Pill will help him cleanse his body." Elder Cheng nodded one last time at Wu Ying before walking away, stopping when he was a few feet away. "If you survive, come seek me again."

Huffing, Yang Fa Yuan followed Elder Cheng with her face frozen. The general stared between the two groups before hurrying after the pair, his head bent slightly.

"If I survive…?" Wu Ying said to no one at all, staring at the pill.

"Cultivation when you are so ill is not advised. But…" The doctor looked at the pale and sweating boy. "Well. If you are not going to use it, you should make sure to inform me. I can buy the pill off you and have the fee sent to your parents."

"My parents." Wu Ying gulped then fumbled for the jade bottle. Within, a single pill sat, glistening white and pearlescent. Even the smell when the cork had been removed cleared up some of his mind, allowing Wu Ying to breathe and think better. With it came the pain and knowledge that he was dying, truly dying.

"Good luck," the doctor said softly, squeezing Wu Ying's shoulder before walking off.

Wu Ying pushed himself up further, breathing slowly as he attempted to clear his mind. As he looked around, he noticed the amount of attention he had attracted. Or more accurately, the amount of attention the Meridian Cleansing Pill had attracted. As a spiritual medicine, its quality was clear to everyone. Such a piece of medicine would have been impossible for commoners like them to acquire. Even a lord's son like Yin Xue had to make do with herbal concoctions made from the dregs of the herbs used to make such pills. Only those within a powerful sect had any chance of acquiring such a pill.

Gripping the bottle firmly, Wu Ying resolved to make full use of this opportunity. If he did not do so, Heaven itself wouldn't be able to help him. Tossing his head back, Wu Ying quickly downed the pill and focused his mind on his body.

***

Wu Ying's chi was turbulent, unstructured, and dispersed through his body from the infection. Even the brief moment he had taken to reorganize his mind and meditate had allowed Wu Ying to gather a little in his lower dantian. But it was insufficient for his purposes. If he were to break open a meridian, he needed to harness significantly more chi.

The Meridian Opening Pill that he swallowed had, at first, a cooling effect on his body, clearing his mind. Taking the opportunity presented, Wu Ying directed more of his chi into his dantian, concentrating the gathered energy further. A change in the pill startled Wu Ying, the body of the pill growing warm now as it sat in his stomach. As it dissolved, pulses of energy were sent out through his meridians, rushing through his body. Rather than a comfortable warmth, the heat was like live coals under his skin, the energy a raging thunder compared to the gentle flow of his own chi.

Grunting, Wu Ying pulled at the energy, attempting to corral it around his dantian. He focused on channeling the energy, driving it around his meridians, where it cleansed and opened blockages, flooding back into his dantian where he focused it in a swirling ball of chaos. Of course, it was impossible for any human to have any of their meridians actually closed—but there was a difference between the fully cleansed, open meridians of a cultivator and a normal human. This process of cleansing was taxing on the body, however, and as such, it was often taken in slow increments. Typically, a Meridian

Cleansing Pill was only taken when one was fully healed, for the risks otherwise were too great.

In this case, Wu Ying had had no choice. Done right, the cleansing process would drive the infection out in his sweat and, yes, his puke, snot, and potentially blood. Holding on to that truth, Wu Ying focused his mind through the pain, through the constant and ever-increasing surges of chi the pill provided him. He channeled all he could through his dantian, sending the chi into a spiraling ball of energy. Finally, when Wu Ying could hold on no longer, he guided the energy to the first of his uncleansed meridians.

On the outside, Wu Ying was trembling uncontrollably, his body flinching and twitching as the energy from the pill coursed through his meridians unceasingly. Eyelids twitched, his hair shook, and even his toes clenched and released uncontrollably. Black blood slowly escaped Wu Ying's skin, only to run down his body as it mixed with foul-smelling sweat. But through all that, Wu Ying's breathing stayed consistent as he worked to regulate his chi. In a corner of the medicine tent, unseen by others, Fa Yuan watched.

Finally, Wu Ying could no longer hold on to the ball of chi within his stomach. Like every other Body Cleanser in the Yellow Emperor's Style, he had cleansed his lung and then heart meridians. Now, he reached inward and pushed the energy along the next meridian, the pericardium[7] meridian. The flood of power that coursed through his body wrapped around the muscle and tissue that protected his heart. The flood of faint yin energy as well as the fire element hosted within the pericardium helped to cleanse him further. But as his chi passed through his meridian toward his hand, he felt the pain of blockages being blown away by the sheer power of it.

---

[7] Traditional Chinese medicine pericardium meridian is different from the Western anatomical pericardium

Each exhalation led to a groan, each inhalation a second of release from the encompassing pain. Again and again, energy flooded his body, cleansing it of the infection, of the built-up impurities of life. The borrowed energy pushed his cultivation at an astounding rate, but his formerly strong body's stored energy was used as well, thinning out the once-muscular peasant. In time, Wu Ying felt the difference, the ease that the chi flowed. But the energy from the pill had yet to subside. Without a choice, Wu Ying moved on to the next meridian, the kidney meridian. Even as his body flagged and his will ached, he pushed on. To give up now would be the end of it all.

∗

Hours passed before Wu Ying came to. When he did, he found himself drenched in a sticky black substance, his clothing and hair so foul he struggled not to retch. In fact, around him, Wu Ying realized, was a gap, as even the gravely injured had been moved away from his bed. Yet for the first time in days, Wu Ying felt clear-headed, though extremely weak.

"Ah! You are done," the doctor said, smiling. "Good. Get washed. Outside please."

Wu Ying complied with the doctor's orders, helped along by an unhappy attendant. As he washed himself in the provided barrel of water, as the gunk from his cultivation slowly peeled off his body through repeated scrubbing, Wu Ying could not help but marvel at his body. Even though he felt weaker and hungrier than ever before, his senses were sharper, his proprioception—his sense of his own body and balance—better than ever. And as weak as he felt, Wu Ying could not help but note that he was able to stand and clean himself without the help of the attendant. Even if it did require a significant number of rests on the convenient footstool.

When he finally returned, Wu Ying was grateful to note that his bedding had been exchanged for something cleaner. Thankfully, someone had dropped off the clothing he had brought with him, so Wu Ying had a set of clothes to wear. Even his frugal nature could not stand to wash and wear the thoroughly soiled clothing he had cultivated in. It was much better off as fuel for the watch fire.

"Eat!" the doctor ordered Wu Ying, pointing at the piles of food set on his bed.

When Wu Ying moved to speak, the doctor shook his head and pointed at the food. As his stomach growled, Wu Ying could not help but agree to the doctor's suggestion, digging into the food.

"Is good!" Wu Ying commented around a mouthful.

The doctor, having come back to check on Wu Ying, smiled slightly. In truth, Wu Ying knew the taste had as much to do with his hunger and his expanded senses as the cooking skill of the chef. But still, it tasted like heaven itself after days of bland broth and porridge.

"When you are done, pack your things. As you are no longer sick, we need your bed back," the doctor ordered.

"Thank you for your care," Wu Ying said, bowing to the doctor around a mouthful.

The doctor waved the words away and gave Wu Ying directions to not only his squad but his benefactor. Wu Ying left quickly, debating what to do as he hurried into the camp. In the end, Wu Ying decided to see Zhao Wan first. Better to speak with the Elder and not let him wait. From the way the general had acted, Wu Ying knew that the Elder was significantly more important than anyone in his squad.

It did not take him long to find the tent. Unlike the tents of the army, this one was colorful and bright. After announcing himself and being invited in,

Wu Ying stepped into the opulent tent. The duo from the Verdant Green Waters Sect were seated in chairs around a tea table. Both turned to stare at Wu Ying as he entered, their gaze raking over his form.

"Fourth level?" Yang Fa Yuan said.

"Fifth," Zhao Wan corrected.

"Not bad," Fa Yuan said.

"You saw through my cultivation already?" Wu Ying said with a blink. At the Body Cleansing stage, each growth in cultivation was small, its external effects minor. To see through his cultivation in so short a time, their eye of discernment must have been significantly higher than anyone Wu Ying had ever met.

"Of course," Elder Cheng said. "It seems you have taken full advantage of the opportunity presented. In that case, I shall present you another opportunity. Join the Verdant Green Waters Sect as an outer sect member."

For a moment, Wu Ying could not believe what he had heard. In a large sect like the Verdant Green Waters, disciples were split into numerous levels. Someone joining the sect would either be a direct, core, inner, or outer disciple, with varying benefits given to disciples at each level. As the largest sect in the kingdom, even an outer disciple of the Verdant Green Waters held a higher status than a regular inner disciple in any other sect in the kingdom. It was rumored that the benefits offered to outer sect members put other sects to shame. If he worked hard, Wu Ying might even become an inner disciple and be given a chance to learn the core teachings of the sect.

But...

"I thank you for the offer, Elder Cheng," Wu Ying said, bowing with gratitude. The truth was, the offer was better than anything a simple farmer's son could ever expect to receive, no matter their past lineage. The offer was so much more that Wu Ying did not even know how to react.

"Are you not going to accept Tai Kor Cheng's offer?" Yang Fa Yuan said angrily.

Wu Ying could not help but wince at her tone. Not accepting immediately was certainly an insult to Elder Cheng. But...

"I have never considered being a true cultivator," Wu Ying said, bowing slightly. "It is not something that was ever an option. And I have a mother and father, a farmland..."

When Fa Yuan opened her mouth, Zhao Wan raised his hand, stilling further words of condemnation. "It is good that he is considering it slowly. Once you enter the martial arts world, the world of cultivation, there is no turning back. Our lives are filled with both opportunity and danger, as you well know, Little Yang."

Fa Yuan sniffed but quieted down.

"Thank you, Elder," Wu Ying said.

"Go back to your squad. Think about the matter. If you decide to join us, speak with Little Yang again. I have to leave soon, but she will take you to the sect." Elder Cheng waved, an obvious dismissal that Wu Ying took with grace, bowing as he left, his head spinning.

Him? A cultivator? The Heaven sure had an amusing sense of humor.

***

It did not take Wu Ying long to find his squad. It only cost him a few questions to better-oriented soldiers. When he found the squad, his eyes widened to see that many were cleaning and caring for weapons and armor that obviously had recently seen use. Spotting his big friend among the other conscripts was easy.

"What happened?" Wu Ying said to Fa Hui when he managed to make his way over.

"Wu Ying. You're alive!" Fa Hui exclaimed with good cheer, standing and clapping Wu Ying on the shoulder. "I'm so glad."

"As am I. But what happened to you all? Were you in the battle?" Wu Ying said.

Well, perhaps he shouldn't have been that surprised. After all, the entire army had clashed but a day ago. Still, to add untested and untrained conscripts to the fight seemed foolhardy. And certainly not something the army would normally do, if his father's stories were to be trusted.

"We were!" Fa Hui said with a grin. "At first we were placed with the reserves. But about halfway through the day, a lot of our reserves were sent back to the camp to deal with a disturbance there. Soon after that, the army of Wei pushed our lines hard and even managed to break through!

"Of course, they sent us in then, along with the Elder from the Verdant Green Waters Sect. You should have seen Elder Pang when he fought! One slice of his blade and dozens of soldiers fell. Those cowards from Wei would have run if it wasn't for the Elder from the Six Jade Gates Sect showing up."

"Rubbish. It was only a dozen with each strike," Sun An said, peering closely at Wu Ying with a puzzled look in his eyes.

"Then?" Wu Ying said as he prodded Fa Hui to continue his talk.

"Well, after that, Elder Pang and the Wei Elder fought above us, running along our shoulders and striking at one another with their swords. Not that I had much time to see them fight —we had to push them back ourselves," Fa Hui said. Fa Hui then proceeded to regale Wu Ying with tales of the fight, of the chaotic scene that accompanied the push of the spears as each army attempted to shove the other back. In the end though, even Fa Hui ran out of ways of saying things were chaotic, bloody and deadly. "I hate to say it, but Yin Xue was actually quite brave. He charged the Wei Elder and managed to exchange a single blow with him. It allowed Elder Pang to launch an attack that the Wei Elder could not block, injuring him. After that, the Wei coward ran off and we pushed the army back."

Sun An snorted. "Brave or idiotic? If his horse had not balked, he would have lost his head. As it was, he's lucky all he received was a cut across his chest."

"That kind of luck, I would take. Elder Pang was so grateful, he even offered Yin Xue a chance to join the sect as an outer discipline!" Fa Hui said.

"Him too?" Wu Ying muttered.

At the exclamation of shock from his friends, Wu Ying found himself having to explain what had happened to him over the past few weeks. Luckily, it did not take long for him to relate his side of the story.

"And you turned the Elder down?" Fa Hui said, shocked.

"I didn't turn him down," Wu Ying said defensively. "But my parents—"

"Would understand. You are being offered the chance to become a cultivator! To gain immortality, or at least a long life. And if you become an inner disciple, you could easily pay for extra help for your father," Fa Hui said. "You cannot be hesitating over them!"

"I can," Wu Ying said. "They are getting old. And you know my father cannot work that long in the fields. I do most of the work as it stands. And it's only an offer to be an outer disciple."

"But you could still afford to send something back to help, could you not?" Sun An said. "I hear that even outer disciples receive three taels of silver a month. On top of not having to feed or house themselves."

Wu Ying could only nod in agreement. When Fa Hui prodded him, literally, Wu Ying shook his head and stood. "I best report in to the sergeant. I'm sure he has something more to say to me. Perhaps with the fight over, we'll be sent back?"

"You're funny," Sun An said, smirking.

Wu Ying could only offer a wry grin. They all knew that this was but a skirmish. The war had dragged on for years. It was unlikely that it would end over a single fight.

As Wu Ying reported in to the sergeant—and received latrine duty for his lack of participation in the earlier battle as punishment—he found himself wondering what, exactly, had him hesitating. Sure, life as a cultivator was significantly more dangerous. Everyone had heard about the fights between sects, the constant battles between cultivators as they searched for spiritual herbs, for weapons, for cultivation manuals. Of the feuds that grew between individuals.

Was it fear? Wu Ying dug into himself and the latrine, cleaning the sides and moving the refuse to the wheelbarrow, where another unfortunate would take the fertilizer to be deposited elsewhere. No, Wu Ying decided, it was not fear. It was uncertainty and the unknown. All his life, he had known what would happen. Even being conscripted had not been particularly surprising. He knew what to do in the army, or what was expected of him at least. Life as a peasant might have been boring, but it was predictable. The calamities they faced were pedestrian, common.

But a cultivator? That future was more uncertain. What would he do with a hundred, two hundred years of life? With the strength to fight a dozen men? With the respect of others? For the first time, Wu Ying found that his horizons did not end at the back of an ox or behind a plough. Perhaps...

Perhaps that was enough. A chance. An opportunity for something more. Something better. It was not a declaration of wanting to become the number one under heaven. Or gaining immortality like one of the eight immortals of Daoism. But it was all he had. And for a farmer's son, it was enough.

For now at least.

Chapter 5

The next morning, Yang Fa Yuan was waiting for him at the exit to the camps. After completing all his tasks yesterday, Wu Ying had returned to inform them of his decision. After brief greetings, the pair joined up with the rest of the individuals who had been chosen to join the sect—a sparse four others who waited beside the gates with their horses. Wu Ying had to admit, if nothing else, the look of astonishment and doubt that Yin Xue shot him when he arrived with Fairy Yang made his initial doubts about his choice seem trivial. Already this new life was paying out.

"Come. We will go to Er-cheng, where we will take the boat the rest of the way." With that said, Fairy Yang led the group to the edge of the camp. At the road, she turned her head toward the group and said simply, "If you fall behind, you fail."

Having passed on her ultimatum, Fa Yuan mounted her horse and set it to a slow trot. Each step of her horse took her farther from the startled initiates, before Wu Ying woke himself up from his surprise and took off jogging. Immediately, the rest of the group followed, though Wu Ying knew that this was an unfair challenge. As the only one with humble beginnings, he was also the only one on foot.

Once Wu Ying had caught up, he slowed down to keep pace with Fairy Yang while silently marveling at the chi coursing through his body. A significant amount of food and a good night's sleep seemed to have restored his body to a state that was even better than before. Moreover, Wu Ying knew that he was still not at his peak state either. Given more time and sufficient food, he would be able to reach heights he had never known.

With those thoughts, Wu Ying ran alongside Fairy Yang. Occasionally he glanced over to see the back and side of the young woman escorting them and noted how no matter how far they had gone, neither her clothing nor her physique was stained with sweat or dust. It was partly the visage of the curves of her body, pressed tight by the wind of their passage, that drove him on. Not that he ever had a chance with such an august personage, but he would not be a man if he didn't admire her form.

"How are you able to keep up?" Yin Xue said with a frown, looking down at Wu Ying, who continued to run alongside them even after they had crossed a number of li.

"Good eating," Wu Ying said with a flash of a smile.

He then ignored Yin Xue, trying to focus on his breathing as he ran. Running, in truth, was not something he had much experience with, beyond races around the village among his friends. All of which Fa Hui had won. Long distance running like this was a different game altogether, and his initial surge of enthusiasm waned as the li went by, replaced only by the stubbornness that lay in his core. He refused to fall back, not now that he had chosen to go down this path.

Hours passed, Wu Ying's only break the times when the horses were slowed down to allow them to rest. Even then, the slower plodding of the horse required the cultivator to jog or be left behind, but the break was gratefully taken. When the sun was high overhead, Fa Yuan finally called a break for lunch. Thankfully, Wu Ying was not designated as cook, allowing him to slump next to a tree and rest. Exhaustion swept through him, almost taking him to sleep as his body ached with the recollection of his recent sickness and his long run. Stubborn or not, one night's rest or new cultivation level, the run ahead of him would have challenged him even at his peak. Which he was not at.

When Wu Ying sensed a presence near him, he let out an inquisitive grunt without opening his eyes or raising his head. The silence took a sudden chilling effect, one that made Wu Ying's eyes shoot open.

"Fairy Yang!" Wu Ying scrambled to his feet and bowed, flushing red in embarrassment. "My apologies!"

"Resting?" Fa Yuan said coldly.

"Yes."

"You are at Body Cleansing 5. That should have been a simple run for you," Fa Yuan said.

"I… I was just sick. And I'm new to it," Wu Ying said, desperate to explain his position.

"Excuses. Are you circulating your chi at all?"

"My chi? But…" Wu Ying shook his head. "Is that not dangerous while moving?"

"Only for the inexperienced and the addle-brained," Fa Yuan said with a sniff. "Learning to cultivate while moving is just another method of cultivation. You breathe while you cultivate, your heart beats. Why should you not be able to cultivate and run?"

Wu Ying wanted to protest that those were things he did unconsciously. But that wasn't exactly true either—breathing through his nose and via his stomach was something he'd had to learn to do for cultivation. It seemed easy at first, but ensuring that he breathed in and exhaled fully with each breath in a constant rhythm, no matter the distraction, was a learned skill.

"How do you start?"

"With your breathing of course," Fa Yuan said, gesturing for Wu Ying to stand.

After that, she gave an impromptu lesson, detailing the breathing rhythm, the flow of his chi through his meridians, and most importantly, which areas to be wary of. By the time food was ready, Wu Ying had grasped the basics—now he would need to practice it before he could come up with new questions.

Barely twenty minutes later, the group was back on the road. For the last five minutes of their rest, Wu Ying had been cultivating, allowing the chi within his body to flow through his meridians, reinforcing his body and energizing it. Now, he restrained the greater portion of the chi flowing through him, allowing only a trickle out of his dantian before he slowly stood.

Each movement threatened to derail the delicate balance he had established between his body, his chi, and his concentration. Carefully, so carefully, he took a step. The first step sent a shudder through him as he nearly stumbled, but an instinctive shove of his own chi brought him upright. Still, he felt the searing flow of his chi through his body, the slight tearing in muscles that were suddenly triggered. Gritting his teeth, Wu Ying forced himself to take another step, trusting that he would find his balance. And then another.

In a short while, he found himself on the paved road, grouped with the rest. A portion of his attention noted that Yin Xue and the others were looking at him strangely as he drunkenly stumbled around. Fa Yuan only offered Wu Ying a single glance before she kicked her horse, starting their journey once more.

In silence, Wu Ying joined them, his initial stumbling run sending pulses of agony through his body as his meridians stretched and twisted with his chi flooding through them. His dantian, under assault from the contained chi and the erratic movements as he attempted to manipulate and cultivate at the same time, burned, making Wu Ying feel as though a dozen needles were piercing his body.

But still, Wu Ying refused to stop. It was obvious, at least to his mind, that he would not last the rest of the run. Not in his previous state. And so he cultivated, sending energy through his meridians, feeling the chi rush back in with each step. In time, he found a rhythm to his breathing, the pulses of energy, and his steps as Fa Yuan had mentioned. In that rhythm, running itself was effortless. Even cultivation, drawing in chi from the surroundings and collecting it in his dantian to be sent through his body, seemed easier. Perhaps it was that he was moving through new regions of energy, tapping into new environments with each step. For the first time, Wu Ying found that cultivating was less like drawing air through a ten-foot straw and as simple as breathing.

When the group finally halted for the evening, Wu Ying found a new challenge. Having been caught up in the act of cultivation, he found himself almost reluctant to let the feeling go. But with the group having arrived at the city's south gate, continuing cultivating would have been bad form. A glassy-eyed stare to questions would just engender bad feelings. And Wu Ying had to admit, he was a filthy, sticky mess. If not for the presence of Fairy Yang, Wu Ying had a feeling that the gate guards would not have allowed him through the tall, roofed city walls.

Inside, the town of Er-cheng was a revelation to Wu Ying. Due to the immense amount of work planting, caring for, and harvesting rice three times a year involved, he had never had time to travel farther than the next village. If not for Lord Wen's men coming by every few months to pick up the tax rice, what little free time they had would have been taken up delivering it too. As such, Er-cheng, the major township of their little county, was the largest settlement he had ever seen.

"So large," Wu Ying said, turning his head from side to side.

In the short time since they had walked in the city, he had seen more people than in the entirety of their village. The buildings that made up the town were also, generally, better made, with a mixture of wood and earthen walls used with the predominant, dark clay tiles on the inclined roofs. In the town, Wu Ying noted that the slate-covered flagstone ground was even better repaired, with space enough for four carriages to move side by side.

"Peasant," Yin Xue said with a sniff. He glared at Wu Ying, looking ashamed at how the village yokel turned and stared at every single thing, from the roadside merchants hawking their wares to the open shops. If not for Fa Yuan's presence, the various hucksters, beggars, and pickpockets would have taken advantage of Wu Ying already. Obviously, as the lord's son, Yin Xue had been to Er-cheng numerous times. His father even had a residence in the city.

"We rest on the boat," Fa Yuan said impatiently, clicking her tongue and speeding up her horse.

Forced to follow, Wu Ying's attention was brought back to the task of ensuring he did not step on anything untoward. In time, the group managed to make their way around the central courtyard where Yin Xue's father lived and worked to the port. Leading the group unerringly, Fa Yuan brought them to a sleek craft at the edge of the docks.

"Captain."

"Fairy Yang." After scrambling to his feet and setting aside his fishing pole, the erstwhile captain bowed low. "Your quarters are ready."

"Prepare space for these five. They are new outer sect members. I wish to leave as soon as possible," Fa Yuan said as she blew past the captain to walk into the ship.

"Of course, Fairy Yang," the captain said before whistling loudly to alert his people.

The other sailors scrambled onto the boat or up from what they were working, guiding the horses into the hold while rigging the sails and oars for sailing. In the meantime, the captain was shouting at a nearby tug, who began maneuvering to draw out the ship. During the entire process, Wu Ying and the nobles stood to the side, out of the way. In a few minutes, the initial chaos had resolved and a short sailor came up to the group.

"Captain says you're staying with us? Only have one room free," the sailor said and looked the group over. Having made a judgment of their various social statuses, the sailor gestured to the group of four nobles. "Come. I'll show you the room."

"Wait. Four of us to a room!" Yin Xue said, his eyes wide. "That—"

"Only three rooms. One for Elder Yang, one captain, one yours," the sailor said, his face flat. "Cook gave up room too."

There was a long pause as the group realized they had displaced the cook. That dire warning was enough to make even the spoiled Yin Xue pause as he contemplated the horrors of an angry cook. Protesting further could result in the worst possible revenge—bad food!

"We're coming," one of the nobles said.

Wu Ying sighed, watching the group head off, then frowned, considering where he could store his bag.

"Over there," a sailor said, pointing. "Cupboards. Mark your bag. Don't touch anyone else's."

Nodding in gratitude, Wu Ying made his way over to put away his bag. After a moment, the villager grimaced and went to see if there was anything he could do. Spending all day working in the field meant that standing around and watching someone else work made him feel somewhat useless. However, the ex-farmer was sent to the bow of the ship, out of way of the sailors who did their best in the failing light.

"I wonder if it's dangerous?" Wu Ying muttered. As night encroached on the town, lanterns were lit on the boats, revealing their forms and locations. Even the small tug had a pair of lanterns on it, the hard-working rowers pulling as they guided the ship out.

"Not as much as you think," a sailor said to Wu Ying, making him jump. Beside him, the sailor idly held an axe. At Wu Ying's concerned look, he chuckled. "For the tug rope. In case we need to part with them quickly."

"Oh."

"No one would be foolish enough to attack Fairy Yang. Or a boat of the Verdant Green Waters Sect," the sailor said proudly, nodding toward the simple flag that flew above their ship. "As for danger, the port is so busy that leaving and entering the city at night is common. Once we reach the deeper channel in the river, we will break out the oars and row upriver."

"Not sail?" Wu Ying said, glancing at where the sails were still furled.

"Wind going wrong way," the sailor said, snorting at the peasant. "Later in the evening, the wind will change and we'll lower the sails."

"Ah," Wu Ying said.

Curious, the ex-farmer fell into a languid conversation with the sailor, who was happy to explain the ways of the river. Their conversation was only broken briefly when the pair coiled the rope when it was released by the tug and the ship surged ahead as the rowers got to work. In that time, Wu Ying learned that the boat they were on had been specially designated for Fairy Yang and their potential recruits. During other times, the captain and his crew would run messages, pick up smaller packages, and wait for other Elders for the sect. It was a good life for all involved, since the sailors managed to see their land-bound families often, the upkeep of the boat was taken care of by the sect, and nearly a quarter of the time, they did nothing but wait.

Wu Ying waved goodbye to his new friend as he went to receive his dinner. As for the sailor, he continued to hold a wooden pole as he scanned for potential debris ahead of them. With the pole stationed at the front of the ship, the sailor would have only a little time to push away any obstacles. It was no wonder that the Captain had chosen one of the higher-leveled Body Cleansers to do the job.

***

For the next four days, life for Wu Ying was rather indolent. Fairy Yang spent most of her time in her cabin, cultivating. The four nobles imposed on the sailors, indulging in long tea sessions while discussing the finer points of life and cultivation. As for himself, Wu Ying chose to follow Fa Yuan's example, taking a turn on the oars while practicing the moving cultivation method. Learning to channel his chi through his body, to slowly cleanse his meridians even when he was undertaking regular, simple tasks like these was still a challenge, but it came with certain side benefits.

"Wu Ying, have another bowl. You are still too skinny!" the sailors called, teasing him.

Wu Ying could not help but chuckle, accepting both their good-natured ribbing and a third serving of food. The fare provided was simple, consisting mostly of fish, fresh vegetables, and heapings of rice. Still, with the liberal application of garlic, ginger, wild onions, and soya sauce, combined with a dash of exercise, it was as good a meal as any Wu Ying had ever eaten.

"If you are kicked out of the sect, you should join us," a bushy-eyebrowed sailor said.

"Yes. We could use another strong Body Cleanser," added another.

"Idiots," a third said. "If he is kicked out of the sect, do you think they will let him work here? No. My cousin could use you on his boat."

"That drunk? He'll be lucky to keep sailing till the next eight moon! No. My sister-in-law's brother has a twelve-foot ship, newly bought, that is much better!"

"Don't listen to these scum," Er Gu, the captain butted in, snorting at his crew good-naturedly. "They know nothing but boats. If you are kicked out, you best leave the county. Better to leave the province. Hanshu down south has a big port. You could certainly find work there."

The captain's sober reminder made Wu Ying freeze. For the first time, he realized that his choices had consequences that reached further than he had thought. In the back of his mind, he'd always considered that he could just return home if he failed. But the captain's words were a sober reminder that while the Verdant Green Waters Sect was overall a good sect, it would not likely be a good idea to continue living in an area they controlled. If nothing more than to avoid the loss of face and mocking that would inevitably result from such a banishment.

"Eh, now you've said the wrong thing again, Captain!" the sailors scolded their boss before slapping Wu Ying on the shoulder, rousing the teenager from his thoughts.

"Forget it. You won't fail. Don't think we've not noticed you cultivating every time you can in the evenings. A dedicated student like you will definitely do well," the sailors said even as they pushed more food onto his bowl.

Wu Ying could only smile helplessly and consume his meal until he was too full to eat. But their words once again woke the worry in his chest. What neither Elder had informed Wu Ying about when they recruited him was the way membership in the outer sect was handled. Wu Ying had known that all members of the outer sect had an opportunity, via a test, each year to join the inner sect. What Wu Ying had learned from the sailors was that outer sect members who failed miserably in the test or were in the lowest portion of those tested would be kicked out. This ensured that the Verdant Green Waters Sect always had a place for new, promising candidates.

"Captain, how much longer?" Fa Yuan asked as she came up onto the deck.

The presence of the august Elder put a damper on the jovial mood of the sailors, who quieted down immediately.

Er Gu bowed. "A few more hours, Fairy Yang."

"Let me know when we have arrived," Fa Yuan said. "And send a meal down to my cabin."

"Of course."

Fa Yuan turned to stare at Wu Ying, looking him up and down. "You have reinforced your rise in cultivation. There is still much to be done, but it seems you have been working hard."

"Thanks to Senior," Wu Ying said, standing and bowing to Fa Yuan. "Your pointers have allowed me to progress much faster than normal."

"As they should," Fa Yuan said with a sniff. "Make sure to bathe more often though."

"Oh. Yes. Sorry!" Wu Ying flushed red while nearby sailors snickered slightly.

They all fell silent when Fa Yuan swept her gaze over them before they came to rest on the lounging quartet of nobles. They, in turn, stood and bowed to Fa Yuan. For a time, the cultivator stared before she turned and walked back down the stairs.

"Interesting," Er Gu muttered softly.

"Captain?"

"Ah. Sect politics," Er Gu said, looking at Wu Ying for a second. He shook his head when Wu Ying moved to ask. "No. I do not get involved."

"But I'm—"

"A member of the sect." Er Gu cut Wu Ying off before stomping off to chivvy his rowers.

***

Hours later, the ship finally pulled up to the small town at the base of the cliffs. It was there that the horses for the sect were stored and where rice, vegetables, and other necessities were off-loaded and carried up the mountain to the sect. Fa Yuan strode off the ship's plank with barely a glance behind her, while the nobles hastily placed instructions with the captain for the care of their animals. Because of this, Wu Ying found himself standing behind Fa Yuan as she finished speaking with one of the supervisors. Rather than inadvertently eavesdrop, he looked around the small town. All around them, dock workers unloaded ships while other workers packed five-feet-by-five-feet canvas bags held together by a simple bamboo structure. The moment a bag was packed, waiting coolies slipped the bags over their shoulders and took off.

"We made good time because of your help," Fa Yuan said, glancing at Wu Ying as she waited impatiently for the group.

"Thank you."

"Being helpful is dangerous in the sect," Fa Yuan finished, shutting Wu Ying's mouth with a flat look. "Watch yourself."

"I—"

"Finally," Fa Yuan said, cutting off Wu Ying as the nobles arrived. A moment later, five large canvas bags were deposited by their feet by coolies directed by the supervisor. "On the sixth street to the east, you will find the gate leading to the sect. You will each take a bag, climb the stairs, and deliver your bags." Fa Yuan looked upward before smiling slightly. "As it's your first time, I will be generous. You have until sundown."

Together, the group turned their heads. A short distance away, a waterfall blocked off the entrance to the higher peaks of the mountain, the distant thunder of the waterfall muted. Still, even in the river, the expansive greenery that surrounded the waters gave life to the sect's name.

High above, the group glimpsed the start of the sect's outlying buildings among the lush greenery. Many of those buildings dotted the roadway that led upward, lying among the water and untouched forest, stretching to the peak. At the edges of their vision, they could just barely catch glimpses of the green-trimmed roofs, decorated with the wisps of clouds, that marked the start of the sect proper.

Together, the group gulped and looked at the bags by their feet. At this point, they realized that Fa Yuan had left. Quickly looking around, Wu Ying's jaw dropped when he spotted the cultivator skipping across the water toward the cliff face. In seconds, she arrived and was lightly jumping upward, directly ascending the mountain beside the waterfall.

"No wonder she left us…" Wu Ying muttered.

Climbing the way she did, Fa Yuan had a significantly shorter journey than if she had taken the "normal" route. Of course, her path required a certain level of expertise in qinggong. Turning back to the task set before him, Wu Ying blinked at the others.

"What are you doing?" Wu Ying exclaimed.

"Lightening the load," Yin Xue replied calmly. With a last tug, Yin Xue finished knotting up his bag, the bag of rice that he had extracted now on top of Wu Ying's bag.

Following his lead, his friends had added another bag of rice to Wu Ying's bag, reducing their burden. Wu Ying glowered at the group as they took off running, laughing at the prank they had pulled.

A single bag of rice was not much of a reduction and could easily be blamed on bad packing by the dock workers. However, the additional four bags would mean his trip up would be significantly tougher. For a moment, Wu Ying considered discarding the rice bags there. After all, it was not his job to carry theirs. But—what if he was punished for leaving the items? Certainly, Fairy Yang had not been the kindest of mentors.

"I'll just consider it more training," Wu Ying said after a moment.

It didn't take him long to get rope to secure the rice bags, which allowed him to heft the now extremely heavy contraption to his shoulders. Together with the five original bags, he now carried nine rice bags—each weighing twenty jin[8]. Breathing deeply, Wu Ying started at a slow walk to get used to the weight.

By the time he had reached the gate and the slate-covered staircase up, Wu Ying was moving at a slow jog. Nowhere near as fast as the coolies who brushed past him, their long, wiry legs pumping with the ease of constant practice. Still, having achieved a rhythm, Wu Ying concentrated and began the process of cultivating while moving. After all, he was just climbing a mountain.

***

An hour and a half later, Wu Ying caught up with the first noble. Having overheard their conversation, Wu Ying knew that this particular recruit had only just achieved Body Cleansing 4 before the army arrived. Furthermore, from the snide remarks passed between the group, Wu Ying was pretty certain the noble had achieved the majority of his development from spiritual herbs, rather than hard work. And while such methods worked, they left gaps in one's cultivation, in his body.

"You. How are you walking with all that?" the noble panted, hands on his legs.

---

[8] 20 jin = 10 kg = 22 lbs

Wu Ying mentally tutted. His teachers and father would have beaten his back till he straightened up. Still, after calming down his cultivation and sending the threads of chi back into his body, Wu Ying replied. "Because I have to, no? After all, we have come this far. To go back now, it would be a shame."

Discarding the noble from his mind, Wu Ying took another step. Even that momentary stop had taken its toll on his strength and stamina. Perhaps stopping was not the wisest idea after all.

"Idiot peasant. I can't let him beat me," the noble muttered behind Wu Ying, who ignored him as he strode upward. As a coolie jogged down the trail past Wu Ying, he heard a question that intrigued him. "Hey, you, yeah. Coolie. How far is it up?"

"For us? Two hours. For you… six."

Six. Grimacing, Wu Ying did the math quickly. There was, perhaps, another four hours before the end of the day. And while he was faster than the noble, he was not that much faster. To be safe, he should try to double his speed. Leaning forward slightly, Wu Ying pushed off his back foot, speeding up. Once he'd established a new pace, Wu Ying let his conscious mind slip into his body once more, touching his dantian and the core of energy that sat in it.

A gentle push, and his chi flowed through his meridians. He absently noted how the coolies who came up from behind him sped up their steps to pass him faster, the stench of his impurity-laden sweat lingering in the air. Thankfully, deep in his cultivation, Wu Ying could not smell himself.

Forty-five minutes later, Wu Ying came across the next pair of nobles. This time around, Wu Ying found no reason to stop, no desire to speak with them. A glance toward the setting sun informed him that he might have another couple of hours left before it set. Floating in that languid place of movement and cultivation, it took a long time for Wu Ying to realize why his initial estimation was wrong. In the mountains, sunsets happened much faster. There was no slow lingering on the horizon.

Discontent rushed through him, forcing Wu Ying to stagger and grip the rock wall for a second as his concentration broke and his chi rampaged. Wu Ying breathed hard, trying to calm down the pain that shot through his body. He coughed slightly, tasting blood from burst blood vessels in his chest and throat before he wiped his mouth. No. No time for this.

Focus.

His legs ached from overuse, his lower back throbbed with each motion, and his shoulders, his shoulders were on fire. He could barely feel his arms anymore. Even circulating his chi had only helped so much. And still, he had to carry all of this. For a moment, Wu Ying considered discarding the extra rice, but he shook it aside. No. Leaving the rice bags on the trail would be even worse than leaving them at the docks—who knew what would happen to the bags? Animals and other creatures could easily break the bags open.

And pain. Well, when wasn't life painful? Working the fields every day, planting and caring for the rice stalks, digging and reinforcing the canals that flooded the rice paddies, harvesting the grain and starting all over again. Life was pain. But if you chose only that to focus on, then you forgot to enjoy the rest of your existence. A fresh breeze blowing by, carrying the smell of cooked lunch and fresh water. The lanterns that covered the village during the festival in early spring. His first kiss, stolen just before they had to go to class.

Small things, all the sweeter because of the pain. Perhaps for the nobles, this was excruciating. A true test of character. But it was no harder than working in a thunderstorm, trying to save as much of the harvest as possible. Or the times he had tilled the soil by pulling the tiller himself because the ox had been lent out to someone more in need.

Pain was a constant companion if you were a peasant. And this? This was just another Tuesday.

A step, then another. In time, he found his rhythm again. Then he picked it up further. At some point, he stopped cultivating consciously. A thread of chi rolled through his body, flooding his meridians and empowering him. But never did he stop.

***

"Is this it?" Wu Ying said, blinking slightly at the small gatekeeper's hut. Beside it, the paifang, the traditional three-arched structure that denoted the entrance to the sect, stood before him. The paifang was washed in lush green paint, the circular pillars decorated with jade and gold. And at the top was the banner that named the sect.

"Don't leave your bags there. Take it to the storeroom behind the kitchen," the gatekeeper growled when Wu Ying looked as though he wanted to collapse.

"Where…?"

"Straight up the hill. Third road on the right, go to the back of the building."

Groaning, his legs trembling uncontrollably, Wu Ying struggled forward. A part of him noted that he hadn't seen Yin Xue since the docks. As much as he disliked the other, Wu Ying had to admit Yin Xue's cultivation at Body Cleansing 4 had been well reinforced with both herbs and practice. In either case, Wu Ying would not let his failure to be the first up the mountain stop him.

"Just a little more," Wu Ying muttered as he staggered up the hill. He swiped at the sweat that collected on his brow, reaching for the water pouch at his side and finding it empty. After all, he had not expected to climb a mountain. "Why are the roads so far apart?"

The paved roadway before him was wide, so wide that it almost felt as if he was back in town. The shrubbery and trees beside the pathway were carefully managed and trimmed, while the pathway itself was swept clean by hard-working sect members in simple, dark green clothing with verdant green stripes. But the roadway stretched on and on, the incline gentler but seemingly never-ending. Ten minutes of staggering and he finally found the second road that branched to the right.

"Just one more," Wu Ying panted. He flexed his fingers, trying to force blood flow through his dead arms as he staggered forward.

Various sect members who were on their way back, now that night was falling, stared at the weaving boy, muttering among themselves at the insanity. After all, his bag bulged with rice bags, some strapped to the sides and top.

The corner. Finally. Wu Ying staggered to the right, almost bowling over a young lady as she came walking out. He twisted his body desperately, attempting to dodge her and stay balanced. He partially succeeded, leaving the young lady unmolested but himself on the ground, facing the sky. A wave of exhaustion ran through him as he watched the last rays of sunshine fade.

Fade.

Why was that important?

"Are you okay? Do you need help?" the woman asked.

"Fine. I am fine," Wu Ying said. Except when he tried to stand, he could not do so.

"Lying down on the job," Yin Xue said mockingly as he strolled up. "How typical of a lazy peasant."

Wu Ying groaned as he tilted his head backward and sideways, spotting Yin Xue strolling forward. Even the normally kempt noble looked slightly bedraggled after the long walk, though Wu Ying knew he likely neither smelled nor looked as bad as Wu Ying. Yin Xue's words were enough to ignite what little passion was left within his body and forced Wu Ying to roll sideways and struggle to his feet, his head going light as he reached halfway. As he began to fall, a hand gripped his arm and pulled gently but firmly, supporting his weight and the bag's with ease.

"You?" Wu Ying said, blinking as he stared up the slender arm to spot the woman.

She smiled at Wu Ying demurely. "Lee Liu Tsong. You should take care better care of yourself."

"Thank you, Senior Lee," Wu Ying said.

It was no stretch to imagine that she was his senior in the sect. Liu Tsong had a beautiful, heart-shaped face and long hair that had been collected in the back in a simple bun, held together by a jade comb piece. As a Body Cleanser, she had extremely fair skin with nary a spot, but the strength she exhibited obviously indicated she was higher than Body Cleansing 4—at least 5, if not 6.

"Go. You should deposit that soon, otherwise Elder Huang will be upset," Liu Tsong said.

"Thank you." Wu Ying bowed his head then stumbled forward.

Yin Xue shifted his foot slightly, almost as if he would trip the other, but stilled his body when Liu Tsong turned her attention to him. The noble forced a smile before letting it widen as darkness overtook the mountain. Even Wu Ying in his exhaustion noted the change in lighting.

"Nooo…" Wu Ying whimpered. But he could not change the heavens. Not yet.

As Wu Ying staggered to the back of the building, he finally saw the end of the journey. Standing at the kitchen, lips pursed, was a middle-aged man in dark robes and a simple headdress of the Elders. This must be Elder Huang that Liu Tsong had mentioned.

"Elder," Wu Ying greeted cordially.

"Put the bags there. And what kind of foolishness is this, carrying nine bags?" Elder Huang said. "What cultivation level are you at?"

"Body Cleansing 5," Wu Ying answered as he dumped the bags aside.

Kitchen workers quickly moved to help the exhausted Wu Ying, who slumped to the ground, his body burning. When he realized what he was doing in front of the Elder, Wu Ying attempted to stand.

"Do not bother. It is obvious you have overdrawn your ability," Elder Huang said with a sniff. "So you are one of Elder Cheng's, are you?"

"Yes, Elder. I am Long Wu Ying," Wu Ying said as he bowed. A part of him trembled, wondering if it was Elder Huang who would inform Elder Cheng of his failure. After all, he had not reached the building in time. Or would Fairy Yang speak with him directly?

"Interesting," Elder Huang said.

Before he could speak further, a boy ran up to Elder Huang with a bamboo slip.

The Elder gave it a quick glance before he nodded. "You and three others have passed the test."

"Three?" Wu Ying said with a frown. Yin Xue was the only one who had been ahead of him.

"Yes. The other two stumbled to the paifang just in time," Elder Huang said. "Useless. Even when they carried less. It is a waste to let them stay, but I guess I have no choice or else Elder Lin will complain again." The last was said with a mutter. Realizing Wu Ying was still there, Elder Huang pointed. "Wash yourself at the well then come inside. As you have just arrived, you will eat here for now. I am sure someone will show you the way."

Wu Ying smiled gratefully, though he found he could not even move to do as Elder Huang said.

As the Elder turned away, he glanced back at Wu Ying. "Come back tomorrow morning. Since you like carrying bags so much, I will make use of you. We need to increase our stock with the new arrivals."

Once the Elder was gone, only then did Wu Ying let out a groan. More bags. His aching body was definitely going to hate him. Why had he had to carry all nine bags? It seemed that the Elder did not care.

Muttering about the unfairness of it all, Wu Ying rolled onto his side and worked himself to his feet. He might as well get cleaned and fed. As he slowly made his way up, he noted one of the others who had started the journey with him just coming around the corner.

Chapter 6

Another day, another bag. Over the last two weeks, Wu Ying had spent every day from morning to evening running bags of rice, wheat, mung beans, and other sundries up the mountain. Once he had achieved the same timeframe as the other coolies, the dock supervisor had started loading Wu Ying with even more bags. When he protested, the cultivator had been informed that this was under orders of Elder Huang. At that point, all his objections faded away.

After that evening when Wu Ying had basically crashed on the floor of the dining room, Senior Liu Tong had found him the next day and shown him to his quarters. That it was but a small room with barely space for the wooden bed and a wooden chest for his clothing was testament to how low he stood on the totem pole. Of course, to Wu Ying, that amount of space was more than sufficient—it might be a little smaller than the room he'd had at home, but not by much.

From that day on, Wu Ying had been left to run errands for Elder Huang, with even less on-going guidance on his cultivation than when he was a villager. Admittedly, Wu Ying found that the guidance Elder Huang did provide was much more pointed and insightful, helping him reinforce his current cultivation significantly.

Still, Wu Ying thought as he eyed the fading sunlight and trotted up the stairs, seven bags of vittles on his back, it would be nice to receive some form of formal guidance. As he passed another poor recruit, Wu Ying could not help but smile slightly at the exclamations of surprise when they caught sight of his burden.

To Wu Ying's surprise, the particular chore set by Fairy Yang had actually been part of the recruitment requirements. Conversations with his Seniors had enlightened Wu Ying further. Politics within the sect was even more convoluted than he had expected. Every Elder—every cultivator who had achieved a Core—could nominate up to three recruits for the sect. But because the actual number of slots available varied from year to year, the recruits were put through various tests. Luckily, this year, a higher-than-normal number of injuries and lazy or slow cultivators had been trimmed, leaving only a small number required to be cut. Elder Huang, as the least senior Elder, had been tasked with the work of cutting all those who did not meet the sect's standards.

"Hurry up. I don't want to be late," a new sect applicant said, his voice dripping with scorn. In front of him, a trio of coolies struggled under the added weight of the rice bags the noble had placed on their backs. Wu Ying idly wondered what he had paid the coolies – or even if he had. Few commoners would dare object to such a request from a cultivator.

Wu Ying said nothing as he leap-frogged the group, keeping to his slow jog as he let his chi churn through his body. The sect's standards were different than what he had expected. Cheating was expected, even encouraged to some degree. Each guide's initial order to bring the bags up were worded vaguely enough that cultivators could—and did—find ways around it. After all, cultivation required not only discipline but insight, craftiness, and luck. So long as the cultivator managed to make his way to the sect with his bag, he passed. Well, so long as he did that and had a strong enough backer.

"Wu Ying. Fifth load of the day. I expect you'll be getting another bag tomorrow." The gatekeeper chuckled.

"Elder Lu. Please don't joke about such things," Wu Ying said as he slowed down and released his cultivation. Perhaps the greatest progress he had made was the speed with which he could shift from cultivating on the move to normal interactions.

"Who is joking? Elder Huang is a real believer in hard work." Seated cross-legged on his stool, the gatekeeper drew on his long pipe again.

"This is for you, Elder," Wu Ying said as he reached behind him and untied the bag. He handed the roll of tobacco to Xi Qi that he had been entrusted to carry from one of the ship's captain. Xi Qi smiled upon receiving the package, stroking the wrapping like a lover.

Once again, Wu Ying wondered about the gatekeeper. Even to his new senses, Wu Ying could tell that Xi Qi was more than a lazy old man. Yet he never cultivated and insisted on constantly polluting his body with smoke. But as Wu Ying was learning, everyone in the sect had their own secrets. And vices.

"Chen family tobacco. Only two catties are ever sold to outsiders." Xi Qi sniffed at the package reverently. "Well? You best be off."

"Yes, Elder." Wu Ying bobbed his head and took off running once more.

When Wu Ying had set down his bag and was stretching tired muscles, Elder Huang found him.

"Wu Ying. I heard you did five loads today," Elder Huang said.

"Yes, Elder."

"Good. Very good. Pity that I have to give you up, but today is the last day I'll have you for the whole day," Elder Huang said. "Tomorrow, you'll begin your studies in the mornings. But I expect you here in the afternoons. Understand?"

"Yes, Elder Huang," Wu Ying replied, trying desperately to keep his face smooth.

"There should be enough time for one more load. Go," Elder Huang said, pointing.

Wu Ying winced, knowing there was no way he would make it back before dark. And climbing the hill in the dark was a painful experience. Obviously he had *not* been successful at keeping his elation hidden.

***

There were more newcomers than Wu Ying expected. Sure, he had seen the various recruits arrive over the last two weeks, but seeing them all gathered in the large courtyard, the amount of them struck home in a way that seeing them dribble in had not. There were easily at least fifty recruits in the courtyard, some socializing, others going through a slow stretching routine.

"Damn. All these nobles," a voice muttered behind Wu Ying, causing him to turn to stare at the speaker. He blinked, seeing a bald, short individual in bright orange Buddhist monk robes. Seeing Wu Ying looking at him, the monk returned Wu Ying's scrutiny by looking him up and down. "You're not one of them, are you?"

"No. But what are you doing here?" Wu Ying said with incredulity. It made no sense for a monk to be in the sect—their objectives were rather different.

"Oh, my Teacher sent me here after I was kicked out," the monk said, rubbing the top of his head. The baby-faced monk flashed Wu Ying an innocent smile, one without an ounce of deceit in it. Clasping his hands in front of him, the monk bowed. "Liu Tou He."

"Long Wu Ying," Wu Ying said, offering a palm over fist greeting in return. Still, he looked slightly askance at Tou He. A monk who was sent out but still wore his robes? Suspicious.

"Ah. Don't worry," Tou He said, waving as he tried to dismiss the topic. "I just liked eating meat too much. My father was a hunter, see? And until he died, we used to hunt and eat meat all the time. When he died, my uncle sent me to the temple, but... well. I snuck out to hunt all the time. My Master said I was a bad influence on the rest of the acolytes."

"That…" Wu Ying fell silent, shaking his head. Really, he knew nothing about the inner workings of a monastery, so it sounded possible. "But why are you still dressed like that?"

"It's more comfortable. The Elder said I could wear this," Tou He said.

Wu Ying raised an eyebrow but shrugged. Well, it did not matter to him, but Tou He's orange robes set him apart in the sea of grey, black, and green. As it was, the pair of peasants were already ostracized. If you were already on the outs, did it matter if you were further different? Wu Ying mulled the thought over, never having been in such a situation. Tou He seemed happy to stand in companionable silence until the clapping of a pair of wooden boards drew all their attention.

Standing at the head of the stairs leading down to the courtyard, a young man stood with his hands clasped behind his back. Unlike the outer sect members in their uniform robes, the man stood in pale-green-and-blue robes, staring at the group.

"I am Cheung Chi Sing," Chi Sing began.

"Greetings, Senior Cheung," the new recruits bellowed as a group.

"I shall be your martial arts instructor." Chi Sing flicked his hand to his right, where a small trail left the courtyard. "To begin with, follow the trail. The last five to arrive will be required to spend another hour training." When the group made no move to go, Chi Sing harrumphed. Even that small exhalation of breath sent a gust of wind down the steps to swirl leaves and sticks. "Go!"

Like a colony of rabbits, the group exploded into action, rushing for the pathway. Caught at the back of the group, Wu Ying growled slightly as he moved to overtake the others. His movements were brought to an abrupt halt when Tou He placed a hand on Wu Ying's arm.

"That path leads around the mountain. Wait. There will be time to overtake them all," Tou He said.

Wu Ying glanced at the pile-up at the entrance to the pathway, the shoving, elbowing, discreet and not-so-discreet blows, and slowed down with Tou He. No point in getting injured just yet.

"How do you know?" Wu Ying said.

"Ah. I have spent many hours cleaning the paths," Tou He said with a slight smile. "I was assigned to the path-clearing detail when I arrived."

"I was running goods up the mountains," Wu Ying offered.

The pair of them finally broke into the path, going at a slow jog behind the others. As all the recruits were at least Body Cleansing 4, the initial pace the group set was quite good.

"I saw," Tou He said. "You were cultivating too, were you not?"

"I was," Wu Ying said, surprised at Tou He's insight.

"It is very similar to how some of our—the monks—were taught to meditate while moving." Tou He's lips twisted in a wry smile. "I was never good at that."

"If you can talk, you should be ahead," Chi Sing said, appearing next to the pair.

The pair jumped, turning their heads to see their senior easily keeping pace by tapping on the ground with his foot every once in a while, bounding multiple feet with each step. It looked as though he was out for a casual stroll.

"Yes, Senior," the pair chorused.

The two sped up, nearing the nobles in front of them. As they attempted to pass though, the nobles swerved in front of them, blocking their path.

"Is this how you want to play this?" Wu Ying growled, anger flaring. "Fine. Tou He?"

"Right."

Wu Ying swerved left as Tou He went right, forcing the nobles to choose who to block. When the nobles chose to block him, Wu Ying grinned and waited a moment to allow Tou He to pass before he went right as well. When the nobles attempted to block him again, Tou He slowed down in front of the nobles, forcing them to stumble or crash into the monk. As the nobles broke their rhythm, Wu Ying darted to the side. Together, Tou He and Wu Ying put on a burst of speed.

"Good work."

"Easy," Tou He said.

"Next?"

"Of course."

Grinning wide, Wu Ying sped up even further. Too bad all this overtaking meant he had no chance to cultivate. But this kind of training was good too. After all, while it was possible to cultivate without studying martial arts or relying on one's body, the sect had little use for those who could not defend themselves. Well—at least ones without special skills.

Once the pair had overtaken another two groups of nobles, they watched as Chi Shing passed them with the greatest of ease. Obviously disinclined to provide any further motivation to those at the back, the senior was on his way to the front. Exchanging looks, Tou He and Wu Ying picked up their pace again. Somehow, they knew if they did not put on a good showing after that talking-to, they would face even more sanctions.

***

An hour later, the pair jogged into the courtyard, breathing deeply. Some heaven-blessed individual had placed a series of water barrels in the courtyard where the leaders had already congregated. Without a word, the pair headed for an unpopulated barrel to drink their fill before the others arrived.

True to his word, Chi Sing noted the last five outer sect members to arrive before he guided the entire group through another punishing workout that involved wind sprints, burpees, clapping push-ups, squats, crunches and more. At the end, Chi Sing demonstrated the sect's most basic martial art form—the Seven Diamond Fist. It was categorized as an external martial art, one that focused on the strength of the body rather than internal strength and, as such, was perfect for the Body Cleansers.

At the end of the two-hour repetition of the form, the group was lined up and forced to enter the most basic of cultivation and martial art stances—the horse stance. Legs spread wide, feet facing forward, the group squatted until their thighs were parallel to the ground, and their arms were held akimbo as if holding a giant urn. There, they were forced to stand and cultivate while a gentle wind blew through the courtyard.

It had been weeks since Wu Ying had cultivated standing still. Ever since Fairy Yang had shown him the way of moving cultivation, Wu Ying had exclusively practiced it. Considering how much of his life had involved running physical errands, it made sense. Moving cultivation allowed him to cultivate for more hours than most, which had progressed the opening of his sixth meridian significantly.

Now, he was standing still, sending his chi through his body, and Wu Ying found it more difficult than he had ever thought to stay still. Drawing chi through his breath, into his body, and circulating it to enter his dantian before it could enter his meridians to do good was difficult. It was very much like pushing mud with one's hands in a flooded field, an endeavor that was as tiring as it was fruitless. The dregs of chi that he managed to corral and send to his dantian were tiny, especially compared to the amount that he needed.

Part of the problem with progressing to each new level in Body Cleansing was the need to store ever more chi in one's dantian. Without adding to the chi a body held, keeping fully opened meridians clean and unsullied was impossible. Wu Ying often imagined his meridians were like the canal system in the village—if you added another field with its own canals, you needed more water. Too little water and none of the fields were properly submerged, resulting in little to no crops.

Cultivating to his next level was very much like that. First, he had to draw in more chi. Moving allowed him to tap into the chi of the world more easily, though Wu Ying had to admit his ability to retain the energy that he absorbed still left a lot to be desired. He might only hold three parts in a hundred. Which was better than many of his contemporaries in the village, but was far from the one-in-ten that the true prodigies were rumored to be able to achieve.

In either case, right now, he was attempting to draw more chi into his dantian. At the same time, he could send what little chi he had through his body, diverting a slightly larger than normal amount to the currently clogged sixth meridian, the kidney meridian. In time, Wu Ying knew he would gain enough chi that he could force the issue and break through. Or he might be like Fa Hui and suddenly realize that his next meridian had cleared.

That was the thing about cultivating in the Body Cleansing stage. So much of it was the slow, gradual cleansing of the body and meridians that sudden jumps in levels were possible. As the process was more of a case of cleansing the body instead of reaching a significant new threshold, it was not unheard of—though uncommon—for individuals to progress in multiple levels.

The tolling of the mid-day bell woke Wu Ying from his cultivation, drawing him back to full awareness of his body. He drew a deep breath, sending his chi back into his dantian and slowly letting it subside. As he stood, he noted the low ache in his knees, hips, and arms from holding the horse stance for so long. All around him, he saw others slowly shaking themselves out. A few nobles were standing up from seated positions. Surprisingly enough, Senior Chi Sing dismissed them to go for lunch without a further word.

"We can sit?" Wu Ying muttered as he eyed the seated nobles, many of whom had even found mats for their bottoms.

"They can." Tou He inclined his head again. "Their sponsors came and gave them permission."

"Sponsors?"

"The Elders who allowed them in."

"Of course. I understand now," Wu Ying said as the pair walked toward the dining halls. Wu Ying then realized something and frowned, looking at Tou He. "How were you able to see all that? Weren't you cultivating?"

"Two minds," Tou He said, holding up his fingers. "It's a technique they taught us at the temple. Though my Master says he wished he never taught that to me. Perhaps I would not have gotten into as much trouble."

"Sounds like an amazing technique," Wu Ying said.

"At my level of insight of the technique, it's only marginally useful. It lets me fully perceive the outside world while cultivating," Tou He said with a shrug. "It's similar to what you do when you cultivate while moving."

"Really? You think I could learn it?" Wu Ying said, perking up. He immediately froze, realizing how gross a breach in etiquette he had made. Asking someone to teach their techniques was just not done.

Tou He nodded. "Of course. Just find me sometime and we'll try."

"Really?" Wu Ying said, wide-eyed.

"Of course. I am no Taoist to discard knowledge or Legalist to think it should be restricted," Tou He said with a sniff. "If you ask, I will teach."

"Thank you!" Wu Ying said, dumbfounded and grateful.

Together, the pair moved off, chatting about what they had learned and their afternoon tasks, leaving behind the five sect members who had been late to begin another workout. Unlike inner sect members, all outer sect members had tasks they had to do each day. It was only in the morning that they had time to cultivate and train. Still, considering the abundant food and the coaching they received, Wu Ying was grateful. He would be more grateful if he didn't have to carry so many damn bags of groceries though.

After chuckling to himself, Wu Ying found himself explaining his thoughts to Tou He, his first new friend in the sect.

Chapter 7

"Still ascending the mountain?" Yin Xue mocked Wu Ying at the paifang that lead into the sect.

Beside them, Lu Xi Qi, the gatekeeper, watched while drawing on his pipe.

"Yes," Wu Ying said with a grunt. He shifted slightly, the bag that weighed him down digging into his shoulders. Two months since they had started proper training and he had managed to increase the weight he carried to ten bags. He could have carried more, but there were physical limits to how many he could carry without the bags falling as they became too awkward.

"A perfect role for a peasant," Yin Xue said.

"Oh? And what are you doing?" Wu Ying said with a frown.

"I am working the library," Yin Xue said.

At his words, Wu Ying started slightly. Of course. He had been so caught up in his own cultivation that he had forgotten the sect had numerous facilities outside of the kitchen and his quarters.

"Forget it. A peasant like you would never be able to gather enough contribution points to read anything worthwhile."

Wu Ying frowned. "Contribution points?"

"Har. Peasant," Yin Xue said, shaking his head as he walked off.

Wu Ying frowned, staring at the lord's son and wondering how it was the pair of them had grown so antagonistic. They were from the same county. Should they not, at least, be acquaintances?

But life was never that simple. Envy. Pride. Regret. It all got in the way of human interaction. And so, the pair stood, opposing each other. Yet seeing Yin Xue made Wu Ying realize that he had forgotten his reason for being there. In the routine of his everyday life, the comfort of good food and clear orders, he had lost sight of his original objective. Inner sect member. Not to while away his days working on his cultivation at a leisurely pace.

"Thank you," Wu Ying found himself muttering to the retreating back of his nemesis.

"You are more and more interesting every day," Xi Qi commented. When Wu Ying looked at him, the gatekeeper chuckled and pointed with his pipe. "Best deliver your goods."

"I will. But, Elder, may I ask a few questions?"

"Ask away. Not as if I'm going anywhere."

"Then, if Elder will tell me, how do I get contribution points?" Wu Ying said.

"By contributing to the sect of course." When Xi Qi saw the discontented expression on Wu Ying's face, he cackled. "It's the usual. Money. Spiritual herbs. Rare manuscripts. Service."

"Thank you, Elder," Wu Ying said, bowing to Xi Qi. Or as much as he could, considering the weight he carried.

It looked as though he needed to find some other way to serve the sect. Carrying the produce of the sect—while important—likely would not result in much of a contribution.

Over the next few hours, Wu Ying turned over ideas of what he could contribute to the sect. Truth was, he knew little about how the sect actually worked. That was just another advantage the nobles had over the peasant-born. They had knowledge of the sect, its inner workings and politics, that he didn't. He would consider it unfair, but in the end, he didn't have the energy to do so. It was just the way the world was. A man's only choice when he learned of the great inequality of the world was to decide if he would break under that knowledge or go on.

"Elder Huang," Wu Ying said as the day came to a close.

Elder Huang was once again out the back of the kitchen, overlooking the produce that had come in that day. "Wu Ying, is something on your mind?"

"I was wondering about my contribution points. Do I get any?" Wu Ying said after working up his courage.

"Two months. Not the slowest I've ever seen, but close," Elder Huang said.

"You were expecting me to ask before this?" Wu Ying said.

"So easily distracted," Elder Huang chided, making Wu Ying wince. "But yes, it should have been your first question to me in the first week."

"And…?"

"You have received a considerable sum. For this kind of work. You're a hard worker and have brought up more goods than any other sect member. That has saved the sect some money, which has added to your contribution."

"Oh." Wu Ying grinned. "How do I tell how much I've received?"

Elder Huang snorted slightly, reaching into his robe and pulling out a small jade stamp. He palmed it for a second before tossing the jade stamp to Wu Ying, who caught it deftly. "Bring it to any of the services you wish to use. They will let you know your total. Do not lose the stamp, or else you would lose all your points. You may have tomorrow afternoon off."

Wu Ying bowed once again, lower than ever this time. The Elder snorted, shaking his head as he turned around, muttering about idiot teenage boys. Once Elder Huang was gone, Wu Ying found himself dancing a little. An afternoon off! And contribution points! Now the question was, who to ask about what he could spend it on?

***

Tou He unfortunately was as ignorant as Wu Ying. But unlike Wu Ying, his ignorance was based on a conscious decision to ignore the entire issue.

"Don't you want to be an inner sect member?" Wu Ying said with a frown as they spoke over lunch.

As usual, the pair was sitting together after martial arts and cultivation training. By this point, their martial arts training had progressed to studying forms for different weapons and repeating those forms till they had each memorized. However, Senior Chi Shing had indicated that they would begin the sparring portion of their training very soon.

"I do. But there is no rush," Tou He said.

"Yes, there is," Wu Ying said.

"Why?"

"Because you might be kicked out otherwise!"

"They only remove the bottom hundred. So long as our cultivation level is high and has progressed and we consistently contribute to the sect, we are safe." Tou He inclined his head slightly, looking at Wu Ying curiously. "I thought all your work with Elder Huang was for that purpose."

"No. I just forgot about the library." Wu Ying scratched his head. "And I didn't really get a briefing on my options when I came."

"Really? Your sponsor offered nothing?" Tou He looked pityingly at Wu Ying. "Well, as I have the afternoon free, shall we work on your knowledge lapse?"

"Sure. But who do we ask?" Wu Ying said.

Really, Wu Ying only knew a few people. Senior Chi Sing had no desire to spend time with them. Wu Ying could not bother any of the Elders he knew with such a trivial matter, especially Elder Cheng. After all, Elder Cheng would have already spoken to him on this if he intended to. As for Fairy Yang… well, he had heard rumors that she had entered secluded cultivation to break into the Core Formation stage. At this juncture, it was impossible for her to speak with anyone. And really, Wu Ying remembered the cold, beautiful woman who had led him here and shuddered. No. Not her. That left...

"Senior Lee?" Wu Ying muttered to himself. She had been nice that time he bumped into her. They had even exchanged greetings when they had seen one another around. She seemed, unlike so many others, accessible at least.

"You know someone?" Tou He said with a smile.

"Maybe."

"Then let us go! I'd rather not see Elder Yun again if possible."

"Eat first!" Wu Ying said, jabbing his chopsticks at Tou He, who had risen.

The ex-monk flushed and sat back down, rubbing his bald head apologetically. Wu Ying rolled his eyes but suited action to words.

Finding Senior Lee was easier than expected and only required them to interact with two other seniors and run one extra errand. It was a good result, considering how most inner sect members liked to make outer sect members who bothered them run random errands. Senior Lee herself was actually at home at the time, seated in the inner courtyard of the small house she had been provided as an inner sect member.

"Wu Ying, was it not?" Senior Lee greeted Wu Ying after the pair had entered and made their own greetings.

"Yes, Senior."

"Why did you look for me?" Liu Tsong asked.

Her hand absently came up to brush a stray lock of hair behind her ear, distracting Wu Ying for a second. One of the dangers of joining the sect was the sheer amount of distraction the women in the sect provided. Cultivation cleared the skin, perfected the body, and made one more "true" to who they were meant to be. In most cases, that meant making said person more beautiful. But like any good thing, constant exposure had increased the boy's resistance and he quickly shook off his enchantment.

"We were hoping Senior Lee would be willing to provide some guidance," Wu Ying said.

"Guidance? Well, you'd normally speak with the Elder—or the Senior they assigned—for that," Liu Tsong said doubtfully.

"I have not seen Elder Cheng since he offered me this position months ago," Wu Ying said with a bob of his head. "And Fairy Yang is in seclusion."

"Oh, Elder Cheng!" Liu Tsong exclaimed, as if his name explained everything. When Wu Ying and Tou He looked at her blankly, Liu Tsong smiled. "Elder Cheng is known for his eccentricities. He believes in the Dharma of Fate and expects that those picked by him are either fated to progress or not. As such, he does not believe in providing further help. Of course, all that means is that the other Elders and Seniors take up the burden of helping his recruits. If they wish, of course."

Wu Ying groaned slightly before he stopped, glancing fearfully at Liu Tsong. Liu Tsong just offered a sympathetic smile. Sometimes, actions like his audible groan could be considered a major loss of face for his benefactor. After all, Wu Ying was complaining about him in public. Such actions could be punished, if Senior Liu Tsong felt the need for it. As his initial reaction faded, Wu Ying realized that it was quite possible no other Elder would have chosen him. So perhaps Elder Cheng's whims were a form of good fortune as well.

"Then will you help us?" Tou He said, getting right to the point.

"Well, I guess so. If it's only questions," Liu Tsong said, casually brushing hair out of her eyes with a graceful sweep of her hand. Sadly, her actions were lost on the innocent Wu Ying and had little effect on the ex-monk.

"What kind of facilities do we have access to as outer sect members?" Wu Ying said.

"For now, you have access to the first level of the library, where basic martial arts techniques and some less rare cultivation techniques are available.

Of course, you should stick to the Yellow Emperor's Cultivation System for now, but it is possible to supplement his cultivation system with others if you're insightful enough. And there are scrolls on the cultivation methods available for the next stage—Energy Storage," Liu Tsong said, ticking off items on her fingers. "You'll want to begin practicing those battle techniques soon, if you intend to learn any. When the tournament begins, you'll want to be well versed in them."

"Thank you. I was thinking the very same," Wu Ying said with a nod. "You should train too, Tou He."

"I have my own techniques," Tou He said with a shake of his head.

Wu Ying frowned then shrugged. Tou He was particularly cagy about the name of the temple he had come from, though Wu Ying had at least gotten him to admit that it was not the infamous Shaolin or Wudang Temples. But whatever temple it was, Tou He had been practicing for years, which probably would put anything Wu Ying learned in this short period to shame. Anything except for his own sword technique.

"Next, there's the apothecary. You can trade in your spiritual herbs and minerals, if you have any, for contribution points. But I warn you—they're very picky about the quality of the herbs, so if you do not know how to care for them, I recommend you just mark the location and sell that information. You can also borrow books about herb gathering there, if you're interested," Liu Tsong continued. "In addition, if you're facing a blockage in your cultivation, you might speak with the apothecaries about a suitable pill. Of course, it's quite expensive. Truthfully, at the Body Cleansing level, there should be no blockages that time and dedication cannot fix.

"Then there's the blacksmith and armory. You can purchase weapons and turn in rare metals if you find any. Obviously, those metals that are suitable for smithing are rarer, but they're less picky about the state the ore is in."

Wu Ying nodded slowly, taking in all this information. It seemed he had been missing out on much of the sect. Though in some ways, it didn't matter, since he'd had no contribution points to spend anyway.

"Is there a way to get more contribution points?" Tou He said as he glanced at Wu Ying.

"Oh! There's the assignment hall of course. But did you not go there?" Liu Tsong said with a frown. "Surely that's how you got your current assignments."

"No. Elder Huang just told me to come by the next day," Wu Ying said.

"Oh. Oh dear." Liu Tsong frowned.

"What?"

"Nothing. Nothing," Liu Tsong said, waving. "I'm sure it's nothing."

"Really?" Wu Ying said.

"Sure…" Liu Tsong smiled sweetly. "Well, that's all I can tell you about the facilities. Did you have any other questions?"

Wu Ying considered then said, "Are there any cultivation methods or items I should buy? Or not?"

"That I should not speak about," Liu Tsong said firmly. "That is something your own Senior or sponsor should discuss with you. Or those in the appropriate departments."

Wu Ying grimaced, but no matter how he pushed, Liu Tsong refused to budge. After his third request, she politely but firmly escorted them out of her house, leaving the pair standing on the doorstep.

"That was rude," Tou He said.

"Yeah. I was just asking—"

"Not her. You." Tou He waved a finger in front of Wu Ying's face. "She already refused you once. Why did you ask her again?"

"But how am I supposed to progress?"

"The same way we all do. Through hard work," Tou He said.

At that point, a group of cackling noblemen walked past. They were clad in the same green robes of the outer sect members, but their station was clear through the sheer variety of expensive items they wore. An embroidered gold-edged fan, a belt with a jewel-set sword, and a jade-and-gold hairpin were among the many expensive items the group showcased.

"You were saying?" Wu Ying said as the group walked past them.

"Well, those of us not born with their advantages," Tou He muttered.

Wu Ying rolled his eyes but clapped his friend on the shoulder. "Come on then. Let's visit the library."

"I must decline. I have learned what I needed and should continue my own cultivation," Tou He said. "But I wish you well."

"Uh huh," Wu Ying said with a snort and waved as his friend left him.

At least Wu Ying had directions to the building now. Setting his feet on the main trail, the cultivator took a light jog to head up the mountain. One of the reasons he had not known about all these important facilities was due to their location. As important buildings for the sect, they were not located at the lower edges of the mountain like the outer sect members' residences and the kitchens but secured within the inner sect portion of the mountain. Of course, there were rumored private collections reserved only for Elders farther up, but those were of little concern to Wu Ying.

The mountain that the Verdant Green Waters Sect occupied was one of the highest in the province and stretched for numerous li upward. The one main road up the mountain branched off along the way to residences, halls, and other locations for training. In fact, Wu Ying lost count of the number of halls available just for the outer sect members. As it was, the new recruits all trained in one courtyard and ate together in one hall, while older, more established outer sect members stayed at other residences according to their results in the tournament.

Wu Ying actually had little interaction with those outer sect members. A large portion of those sect members were like Tou He—lacking any real ambition to progress, they were content to work the menial jobs and while their life away slowly progressing in their cultivation. It was, Wu Ying had to admit, not a bad life. Compared to a peasant's life, it was downright luxurious. A small number of outer sect members—the few who had just missed out on promotion the year before—spent most of their time cultivating and training. With their goal missed the previous year by such a small amount, most worked hard to ensure they entered this year. None wanted to be another infamous story in the sect like the thrice-touched Lee.

Because of all this, most of the outer sect members had little time for those who had just arrived and had yet to undergo the tournament. Who knew which one of the sect members would last the year and which would leap over the dragon gate[9]? In the first case, one would waste their time, and in the second case, one might inadvertently insult a soon-to-become Senior. For those outer sect members who desired a quiet, peaceful life, neither option was desirable.

Jogging up the mountains, the lush vegetation of late spring all around him, Wu Ying listened to the distant rumble of water down the river and the minor falls throughout the mountain. He could not help but wonder how his parents were doing. The one thing he had made sure to take care of—with the help of his friends at the docks and Xi Qi—was to ensure that the majority of his allowance was sent to his family. Since he received his payment directly from Elder Huang, that had been a simple matter to set up through the use of promissory notes and the merchants in town. A letter should be coming soon, Wu Ying hoped.

---

[9] The full saying is "The carp has leaped over the dragon gate" and is an old Chinese saying. The image of a carp jumping over the Dragon's Gate (atop a mythical waterfall to become a dragon) symbolizes courage, perseverance, and accomplishment. In this case, it's the cultural equivalent of "sprout wings and fly to the heavens."

Finally, Wu Ying found himself at the library, its designation splashed across the front in large, beautiful calligraphy. Even from his position a few feet back, Wu Ying could feel the pressure of the spiritual energy imbued into the calligraphy.

"Right place. Now, where…?" Wu Ying said softly as he walked toward the main doors.

Within, a desk attendant sat, watching over entrants.

"Purpose of visit?" the attendant asked, his tone bored.

"Greetings, Senior. I want to browse the martial arts manuals for outer sect members," Wu Ying said.

"Browse, or do you want a consultation with the Elder?" the attendant asked.

"Consultation?" Wu Ying said hesitantly.

"Place your sect stamp on the jade plate." The attendant pointed. "I will verify your total."

"Yes, Senior." Wu Ying placed his stamp on the plate. After a moment, he spoke up. "Could you tell me how many I have?"

"You don't know?" the attendant said with scorn in his voice before he looked down and muttered under his breath, "Idiot nobles." The attendant looked up. "It'll cost a hundred contribution points to see Elder Ko. I had a slot open up earlier today, so you can see him in an hour if you wish. I will send him to you if you wish to browse the stacks until then. And you have a hundred forty-seven contribution points."

"So many!" Wu Ying yelped. He even ignored the attendant's spurious accusation of him being a noble, so great was his surprise.

"Of course. It is not worth the Elder's time to speak with you otherwise. But the price of the consultation also includes one manual recommended by the Elder," the attendant said. "Or you can browse the stacks and look for yourself."

Wu Ying looked behind the attendant at the shelves that made up the library. He frowned at the disordered mess the numerous scrolls and books seemed to make, never mind the sheer volume. And truth be told, Wu Ying had little confidence in finding a martial art that suited him. Not yet, at least.

"I would be grateful for whatever guidance the Elder may impart," Wu Ying said.

After the cultivator had stored his sect stamp and the attendant had provided Wu Ying a brief summary of the library's rules and layout, the attendant waved Wu Ying in. All the necessary bureaucracy taken care of, Wu Ying took a deep breath and stepped into the library to take the next step on his cultivation journey.

Chapter 8

Within the library, Wu Ying moved to the left, starting at the shelves which the attendant had indicated were for martial arts techniques. Quickly, Wu Ying realized that these techniques were not haphazardly shelved but set aside by the kind of technique. In his hands were techniques for the spear, a weapon that Wu Ying had some knowledge of but no significant formal training in. Wu Ying set the book aside and moved down, searching through the stacks.

Spear. Ji[10]. Dao[11]. Bow. Mace. Rope. Greataxe.

One after the other, the manuals ran on and on. There were eighteen traditional arms[12], and it seemed that the sect had manuals for all of them. Some, like the crossbow, only had a few manuals, while other more popular weapons, like the axe or jian, had significantly more. Out of curiosity, Wu Ying stopped at the area where the jian[13] manuals were kept.

He flipped through the manuals, scanning the instructions and forms. As he flipped through manual after manual, his frown grew greater and greater. At times, Wu Ying would stare at a particular passage before shaking his head and moving on to a new manual.

"You find our work on the jian inadequate?" a deep voice said, startling Wu Ying.

Turning, Wu Ying realized that an Elder stood beside him, dressed in the iconic green-and-grey robes that the Elders all wore around the sect. A quick

---

[10] Also known as the dagger halberd. It's a weapon with a spear tip and a spike-axe-like protrusion traditionally. The Song dynasty version actually added a more axe-like head to the weapon

[11] Dao—Chinese sabre. Single-edged sword, often with a slight curve.

[12] The exact list is contentious, with varying sources. I'm using a mix of the Wuzazu and Water Margin listing.

[13] Jian—double-edged sword. Shorter, thinner, and lighter than the European longsword. Meant for single-handed use normally, though two-handed jian exist

look at his headdress was enough to inform Wu Ying that whoever spoke to him was high up on the ladder. Piercing black eyes bore into Wu Ying, seeming to weigh him even as a suffocating pressure filled Wu Ying with trepidation.

"I would never dare say something like that, Elder," Wu Ying said, bowing deeply.

"Interesting. What style did you learn?"

"Long style jian," Wu Ying said. "My father never mentioned the style name."

"Long family jian. If I'm not incorrect…" The Elder looked down the shelf and stepped past Wu Ying, who shrank back automatically. He pulled a small manual from the shelf and handed it to Wu Ying. "Is this it?"

Wu Ying took the manual hesitantly then, under the eyes of the Elder, scanned through it slowly at first. Moving more quickly, he flipped through page after page, skipping toward the end. The Elder said nothing, watching Wu Ying read till he was done.

"I'm sorry!" Wu Ying said when he realized he had been making the Elder wait. At the Elder's wave to dismiss the apology, Wu Ying finally answered the question. "Yes, this is it."

"But you seem unhappy."

"I…"

"Speak."

"It is a very poor copy of our style," Wu Ying said finally. "There are finer points that are missed, as well as numerous transitions that are missing or out of order."

"That is no surprise," the Elder said with a sniff. "If it was complete, it would not be in this section. Whoever collected this must have done so from watching your family practice. The work itself is sub-par."

"Oh," Wu Ying said, his hand clenching slightly.

At the Elder's clearance of his throat, Wu Ying relaxed his grip on the manual and set it back on the shelf. To think that some outsider had dared to steal their style—and then sell it! It burned, even if that sale had come with significant mistakes. But of course, that was why so much of their style had not been written down but passed orally, from father to son.

"Yes. Now, if you are the rightful heir of this style, if you would pen corrections or a new manual, I could see my way to ensure you are properly compensated," the Elder said.

"You would?" Wu Ying said, surprised.

"Of course." After a brief pause, the Elder chuckled. "Ah. I never introduced myself, did I? I am Elder Ko. I am in charge of the library for the inner and outer sect members."

"Greetings, Elder Ko. I am Long Wu Ying," Wu Ying said. "But I must decline your offer. I am not authorized[14] to pass on the art as yet."

"Are you sure? I could provide a significant number of contribution points for an authentic Long family jian manual."

"I am sure."

"Humph." Elder Ko fixed Wu Ying with a glare that Wu Ying astutely avoided by keeping his gaze lowered. Still, he felt the Elder's attention on the back of his head, making him grit his teeth. The silence stretched for minutes, allowing Wu Ying to hear every single turn of the page, every scuffed footstep in the library. Or so it seemed. "Good."

"I'm sor—wait? Good?" Wu Ying exclaimed.

"Yes. I would have banned your use of the inner sect library if you were so cavalier with such secrets," Elder Ko said.

"That was a test?"

---

[14] Traditionally, students were not allowed to teach other students until they received permission from their original Master.

"Everything is a test. Now, your sect stamp?" Once Elder Ko had received it, he touched his own sect stamp to it, transferring the cultivation points to himself. "Now, do you have any other training?" After Wu Ying finished listing his small list of skills, the Elder sniffed. "Basic training at your village. Garbage."

Wu Ying winced but bent his head in acknowledgement. It was, sadly, a fair assessment. Even the basic martial arts they were learning in the morning was better than what he had learned in the village. He thought that they were taught the barest basics to make them effective, but not enough to ever make the peasants a threat. Not that peasants, with cultivations in the low digits, could ever be a threat to a Core Cultivator.

"And what level have you achieved with your swordsmanship?" Elder Ko asked.

"I have only achieved a novice level with the style thus far," Wu Ying said with a grimace. It was one of his personal shames.

"Really?" Elder Ko said with a frown but sighed. "Show me."

"I—" Elder Ko twitched his hand and handed Wu Ying the sword he drew from his side, cutting short Wu Ying's excuse. "Thank you, Elder."

Wu Ying stepped back, eying the distance around him before setting the sword at his side. He drew another deep breath before releasing it, relaxing his body. In the tight quarters, Wu Ying truncated much of the strikes and steps of his form, doing his best to showcase his minor knowledge.

There were five major levels of understanding of a martial art. At the initiate level, one could be considered to have memorized and grasped, at the lowest level, the movements and essence of the art. Novices had grasped more than the set movements and could apply them in a more fluid format, while those with intermediate understanding of the art could fight smoothly using the forms without hesitation. In addition, at the intermediate level, practitioners had grasped the basic understanding of the martial art. As for peak understanding, that was the level most practitioners achieved after a decade or two of study, with the ability to combine the martial art style with others in a combative stance. Generally only geniuses or those who came up with the Style itself could achieve the stage of perfection, grasping both the basic and underlying means of each movement as well as the potential within each action.

Of course, all of that was a fuzzy concept in some ways. A simple, less complex style would be simpler to grasp and grow into higher levels of achievement than a complicated style like the Long family sword art. It was because of this, and the wide gaps between each level, that Elder Ko had requested Wu Ying to showcase his grasp of the style.

All this, of course, was outside the basics of swordsmanship—the Sense of the weapon itself. That was a different form of understanding.

"A pleasure to watch," Elder Ko said, tapping his lips. "And for your age, a novice level understanding is understandable. If disappointing. You are no martial genius, that is clear. Nor have you grasped the Sense of the Sword either."

Wu Ying winced slightly but could not help but accept Elder Ko's blunt assessment. It was true enough. Fa Hui, that big ox, had managed to win as many matches as he lost when they sparred sword against spear. Even if Fa Hui had never received any particular additional training, size, strength, and weapon choice made a big difference.

"No protest?" Elder Ko smiled. "Good. You have the correct mindset at least. Now, do you understand what the process is for choosing the correct martial art?"

"Uhh... one that suits you and your inner strengths, yes?" Wu Ying said. That much, at least, he understood.

"Of course. But that is not all. Suitability is one criteria, but you must also consider compatibility with your other styles and, at your level, growth!" Elder Ko said, wagging a finger at Wu Ying.

"Growth?"

"Of course. You are just starting on your cultivation journey. A martial art that suits a Body Cleanser might be useless when you achieve Energy Storage, never mind Core Formation. As a Body Cleanser, you have no ability to project your chi outside of your body, as you have not opened the energy storage meridians in your body. Only at the Energy Storage stage will you begin such a process," Elder Ko said.

Wu Ying nodded quietly. That information was not unknown to him, but he had not truly considered the implications, since it had never mattered to him before. But obviously, Elder Ko was right.

"Many of the works in this section are only suitable for practitioners in the Body Cleansing stage."

Of course, many practitioners would never know better until it was too late—unless they sought Elder Ko's guidance. Or received such guidance from their families. Which, come to think of it, they probably did.

"I look forward to Elder Ko's guidance," Wu Ying said with a bow.

"Har. A sweet-talker," Elder Ko said. "Now, considering your sword style, you are actually well placed for further levels in cultivation. While the Long style jian art provides significant benefits at the lower levels, it is when you have achieved Core formation stages that its strength will truly be shown."

"Elder is very knowledgeable."

"Your great-grandfather's brother once fought my master," Elder Ko said with a sniff. "A pity that he fell during the war."

Wu Ying bobbed his head. He vaguely recalled that story, but it was such a long time ago that the matter for their family had faded. Still, it was due to his contributions that their family held what little prestige it did in their village.

"Considering its slow growth and your lack of development in the jian, if you do not improve significantly, you should avoid taking challenges using weapons in the tournament if the format allows it." Elder Ko walked down the stacks, leading Wu Ying to a portion of the shelves that took up one entire row. Even a quick glance was enough to inform Wu Ying that this entire row contained fist arts. "It is better for you to study a fist art that is compatible with what you have learned but which you can make use of in the Energy Storage stage too."

"Yes, Elder."

"Good." Elder Ko walked among the shelves, pulling manual after manual before tossing the majority back. He did not even look deeply at those he picked up, only checking to verify the name of the manual before moving on. In this way, in a short time, the Elder had accumulated three manuals he was happy with, which he passed to Wu Ying. "Study the introduction, principles, and first stance for all these. Then make your choice."

"Of course, Elder Ko," Wu Ying said with another bow. "I was hoping the Elder might recommend a cultivation method too."

"Already?" Elder Ko sniffed but nodded, leading Wu Ying to another section of the dimly lit library.

Along the way, Elder Ko stopped to adjust some manuals, giving Wu Ying time to view the burnished wooden shelves and the manuals in detail.

"Did the Elder not want me to show my cultivation?" Wu Ying inquired as they walked.

"I have already seen it," Elder Ko said. "When you were showcasing your forms, your chi moved through your meridians on its own accord."

"It did?"

"Of course. The reason the Yellow Emperor never recommended movement while cultivating was due to the propensity of cultivators to inadvertently activate their chi during practice and, eventually, normal movement. While that allows you to cultivate faster, it also allows those with the proper training to grasp another's cultivation level," Elder Ko said. "Were you not informed of this?"

"No."

"Hmmm…" Elder Ko turned down the stacks and walked along the manuals for cultivation, repeating his earlier actions. When he was done, this time, Elder Ko offered Wu Ying half a dozen manuals and held another one. "All these would be suitable for you. Of course, we do not recommend shifting from the Yellow Emperor's style as yet. While the style provided to you is slower than some others, it has the benefit of not aspecting your chi. The vast majority of the cultivation methods in your hands will, unfortunately, force an aspect onto your chi. There is no help for it, but that is what we have at this level.

"As for this"—Elder Ko waved the simple scroll in his hand—"this is a cultivation exercise."

"An exercise?" Wu Ying said. This was the first time he had heard of a cultivation exercise.

"Yes. Exercises are unlike full styles—they focus upon one aspect of cultivation and force an individual to repeat it constantly. It is uncommon for cultivation exercises to be used these days, as cultivation styles have progressed sufficiently that many exercises are included in most styles," Elder Ko explained patiently. "But in this case, this exercise focuses on awareness and containment."

"Why would I need awareness?"

"Greater awareness of one's chi and when it flows will allow you to understand when you are activating your chi. Containment will help you reduce the external signs when you are cultivating. It will also dampen the signs of your passing in general," Elder Ko said. "Do you understand?"

"It'll stop people from reading my level as easily?" Wu Ying said, a light bulb going off.

"Good. And unlike those manuals, this you can afford."

"Oh. Oh…" Wu Ying ducked his head. Well, yes. Cultivation manuals would be expensive. How expensive, he was not certain. Still, he took the last manual from Elder Ko, intent on studying all his options.

"Good. Then we are done."

Elder Ko turned and walked away, leaving Wu Ying clasping the many books and staggering off to find a quiet corner to read.

***

Hours later, Wu Ying leaned back in his chair and rubbed his eyes. As he lowered his hands, he stared at the lamps that had been lit all around the library, giving off flickering light. His stomach rumbled, reminding Wu Ying that he had not eaten anything since that morning, an uncommon occurrence as he always managed to grab an afternoon snack from the kitchens. Never mind the dinner that he had missed too.

Still, the day had been productive. He had finished reading through the documents the Elder had provided. As Elder Ko had said, all the cultivation manuals aspected his chi, ensuring that his chi would resonate with one of the five elements[15]. It was, of course, quite common for individuals to have their

---

[15] Traditional Chinese culture has five elements instead of four—Fire, Water, Earth, Air, and Metal

chi resonate in that manner—in fact, Wu Ying was certain most of the Elders were aspected in one form or another. However, his level of cultivation and insight were insufficient to sense that as yet.

However, Wu Ying was certain that changing his cultivation right now was a bad idea. For one thing, the cultivation techniques he had read were not that much of an improvement over the Yellow Emperor's. And while he only had the manual for the Body Cleansing stage, the Yellow Emperor's guide was sufficient for now. If he managed to actually achieve a position in the inner sect, he would have access to better manuals. Still, reading the manuals did offer him one benefit—they had expanded his view on cultivation and enlightened him on certain aspects of the Yellow Emperor's style. Wu Ying knew, given time to experiment and digest the information, he could progress even faster now.

As for purchasing the cultivation manuals, he could not afford a single one, so he put the entire matter aside.

Wu Ying focused on the three martial art styles he had been given. Reading those had taken most of his time. Even though he had been instructed to only read the principles and first stances, understanding and grasping the details of each style required concentrated attention.

The first book was a fist art, the second a palm art, and the last a kicking art. Of course, those weren't the only differences between each martial art style. Styles could be differentiated by both internal and external arts—that was, whether a style required significant understanding of chi or just a powerful body. Of the three, the palm art was the only internal art. And while the Long family jian style was an internal art too, his father's warnings resounded in his head. *Avoid studying too many internal arts until you become proficient with our family style. Till then, you are only likely to confuse yourself.*

Considering that, the palm art, while easier to understand from the looks of it, probably had numerous traps he had yet to see. Better to set it aside. In that case, Wu Ying's options were the fist style and the kicking style.

Falling Stars Fist emphasized long strikes and quick movements, using a flurry of blows to stifle an opponent's ability to defend themselves. The Falling Stars Fist originated from the north, so it required a focus on deep stances to begin and the ability to explosively change directions. As a pure fist style, it was easy to learn and would provide Wu Ying with a fighting style he could quickly master—giving him new explosive power. As a fist style, compared to the basic style they learned as an outer sect member, the Falling Stars Fist was significantly better and would improve so long as his cultivation and strength improved.

On the other hand, the Northern Shen Kicking Style emphasized footwork and fast kicks at a short distance. Unlike what he had assumed, it actually contained a significant amount of grappling techniques as well, since the style focused on disrupting, grappling, and locking joints before finishing off the opponent with kicks.

Both styles suited his current understanding of the Long family jian style. Explosive lunges and quick footsteps were part of his original martial style, along with the extended use of the jian's reach to keep opponents at the maximum range. Wu Ying knew that at later stages, projected chi would extend his attacks with the jian even further. As such, the footwork that he'd learn with either style would be beneficial, with the Falling Arts expanding on explosiveness and the Northern Shen on evasiveness.

However, the Northern Shen Kicking Style had less in common with the actual use of his sword since it focused so much on kicks and grappling. Right now, the Long family style focused on the longest range, so Wu Ying's options when an opponent got within his effective range were reduced. In other words,

107

if an opponent chose to box or grapple with Wu Ying, his only chance was to run away.

In the end, the question for Wu Ying was simple—did he want a quick boost to his strength, which the fist art would provide, or was he looking to patch a hole in his defenses? With only eight months left to train, he would only be successful at studying one new style. Especially since he was going to be purchasing the cultivation exercise.

Wu Ying leaned back, staring at the flickering shadows on the ceiling. This was perhaps the first and most important decision he would make on his cultivation journey. Thus far, everything had been provided directly, but this decision would begin the process of differentiating him from all the other cultivators in the Verdant Green Waters Sect. A strong martial background would help Wu Ying in all endeavors in the future. Strength, personal strength, would go far in helping him deal with his lack of background.

So.

Wu Ying sighed and dropped his head, staring at the manuals. He tilted his head to the side, staring at his right hand, which had rested on the kicking style. He traced the title again then chuckled, shaking his head. What was that story? About how one could never tell the future? Better to accept that the future was unknowable and that all choices were equally good or bad and choose.

A kicking style that patched a hole in his defense sounded like a better choice in the end. His cultivation journey was long. Better to work on building a firm foundation now than push for a short-term gain. When the earth moved, only the houses with a firm foundation would stand.

Nodding firmly, Wu Ying stood and took the manuals in hand. First, to return all but the Northern Shen Kicking Style. Then to purchase the cultivation exercise. Lastly, and most importantly, dinner!

Chapter 9

Having found new areas to study, Wu Ying found himself modifying his daily schedule. In the morning, Wu Ying woke up an hour earlier to study the Aura Strengthening cultivation exercise. After breakfast, he had the group martial arts and cultivation practice, then Wu Ying had lunch and worked for Elder Huang. Rather than spending the entire afternoon working, Wu Ying worked only for five hours, giving him an hour in the evening and the time after dinner to work on the Northern Shen Kicking style.

This morning saw Wu Ying seated on his bed, expanding his awareness as he cultivated. The awareness portion of the exercise was actually somewhat easier than he had expected. Between the lessons that Tou He had imparted on the Two Minds process and his practice while moving, Wu Ying found that he had inadvertently learned how to split his consciousness sufficiently that he could feel and sense his chi as he cultivated. As he cultivated, Wu Ying finally began to understand what the manual had actually discussed about the chi field and dispersal.

To Wu Ying, it was like a canal system fielding a series of fields. His meridians were the canals leading from the river—his dantian—while the chi was the water. Right now, his canals were made of packed earth. A simple and functional method of directing chi to the fields. But because they were made of packed earth, some water escaped, soaking into the earth around the canals.

This "soaked earth" could then be noticed and sensed by other cultivators who had the requisite skills. The cultivation exercise basically taught Wu Ying how to strengthen his canals to reduce the amount of chi that soaked out. Of course at this point, the entire metaphor broke down.

Because the exercise focused more on strengthening the aura around his body—not strengthening his meridians—while restricting his aura to his skin itself. By doing so, he kept more of his chi within his body, rather than radiating it out like most others. This ensured that others could not sense his cultivation when it ran—or even during normal times. It had the additional advantage of decreasing the speed with which he lost the chi his body stored. While the amount of improvement was minimal, Wu Ying had to admit that the amount of chi he needed to progress was tiny—at least in comparison to old monsters like the Elders. So any gain was important.

Perhaps the greatest frustration for Wu Ying was that while he could slowly develop the strength of his aura while cultivating at a standstill, it was a completely different matter when he did so while moving. Added to his frustration was now, Wu Ying could sense the way his chi continuously leaked from his body. He felt as though he were waving a beacon each time he cultivated while moving. Thankfully, the ability to sense such changes was something only the most astute Seniors and the Elders had on a conscious level. Otherwise, Wu Ying would have died from embarrassment.

The toll of the bell indicating the start of breakfast time interrupted Wu Ying's slow, meandering thoughts. The cultivator slowly exhaled and stopped cultivating, consciously releasing the lock he had placed on his aura. He held still for a few seconds as he watched his body unconsciously take up the slack of holding his aura tight. Satisfied that his efforts were holding—at least for now—Wu Ying stood and stretched, allowing blood to flow back into his peripheries, before departing his room for breakfast.

The rest of the morning exercises were routine, almost boringly so. By now, the entire group could lap the mountain in half the time it had taken them to do so the first day. Chi Sing, the sadist that he was, had just doubled their running. All of their exercises had increased significantly to balance out the group's increasing competence.

Halfway through the time that would normally be allotted to studying forms, Chi Sing called a halt to the activity. When he had everyone's attention, the cultivator spoke.

"Good. Now that you all have the basics down—and have been religiously practicing the forms I've taught you—you are ready for the next, most important, portion. The sect has no use for those who cannot fight. To preserve our morality, we must have the strength to do so. As such, from this day onward, you will spar with your sect-mates. At the end of this coming winter, you will take part in a martial tournament which will determine your ranking in the sect," Chi Sing said. "Now. Pair up."

Tou He and Wu Ying blinked then grinned at each other awkwardly as they automatically sought each other out. Standing a short distance from Tou He, Wu Ying could not help but wonder how good his friend was. As a monk who had studied martial arts since he was young, he certainly had had more time to devote to the development of his ability.

"Good. Found someone you're comfortable with, have you?" Chi Sing's grin widened. "Now look to your left. Switch with them." As everyone looked around, slightly confused by the change, Chi Sing added, "The last pair to find a new partner will be the first to demonstrate their grasp of the martial arts."

His words jolted everyone into movement. No one wanted to be the pair forced to showcase their abilities. After all, it was a duel. Someone was going to lose—and thus lose face in front of everyone. Wu Ying found himself paired up with Yin Xue.

"I heard you visited the library. Hoping to stay in the sect?" Yin Xue sneered.

Wu Ying grunted and turned away from Yin Xue, his attention drawn to the poor couple who had been instructed to move toward the first landing to showcase their fight.

Once they were ready, Chi Shing raised his voice. "All right, even though you are dueling, we do not need any deaths. So no fatal strikes. Fight at seventy percent of your strength. Do not speed up just to land an attack. You are dueling to gain experience—cheating now will not allow you to learn anything properly. And most importantly, if I or your opponent calls stop, you stop immediately. Any blow landed after a stop is called is liable to be punished. Understood?"

"Yes, Senior," the group answered.

"I said, *understood?*"

"Yes, Senior!" the group roared.

"Good. Ready yourself."

The two opponents faced off against each other, falling into stances. The larger of the opponents, standing just over six feet tall and well built, took an orthodox position with one hand in front and the other behind, resting his weight on both feet. His opponent, a young lady whose head only reached her opponent's chest, took a different stance, dropping lower with one foot extended before her and a palm upward as she waited.

"Begin!"

The man rushed the girl, a looping overhand punch coming in to crush her light defense. Rather than take the attack straight-on, the girl dropped her extended foot and shifted forward blindingly fast, her hand folding as she struck with her elbow as she entered the man's guard. A loud "oof" resounded through the courtyard as the pair met, the air within his chest driven out.

The girl twisted in that low position, using another elbow strike as she spun around. The attack sent the man spinning, a motion that the girl exploited to strike him again and again with short, sharp attacks. But it was not all going her way. The man shrugged off the blows and pushed back against her, shoving her aside and sending her spinning away with sheer force.

Resetting themselves into stances, the pair dashed forward again and exchanged another series of blows. Wu Ying watched, his eyes narrowed as he gauged their ability. The large man had little technique, his style a mixture of what the sect and the kingdom had taught and something very similar to both—all of which focused on large, powerful attacks. While he did not connect often, when he did, his greater strength blew past the girl's defenses.

On the other hand, the girl had an interesting and unique short-range style that required her to get within her opponent's reach. It featured a low stance, sharp blocks, and power generated from the twists and turns that she used to evade and close in.

The battle raged on the platform, the pair working to exploit each other's weakness. In time though, a punishing blow caught the girl on the top of her head, sending her sprawling. Before she could recover, a kick came, taking her in the stomach and sending her sliding along the ground.

"Hold!" Chi Sing said as the man rushed forward. "Rest, then begin again. Here or below, I do not care." When he confirmed the pair had understood him, Chi Sing turned and glared at the gathered group below. "Well? What are you waiting for?"

Everyone turned to their opponent. Before Wu Ying had fully turned, a punch caught him on his cheek, sending him sprawling backward. Before he could recover, strikes came one after the other, forcing Wu Ying to cover up and ride out the flurry of attacks. He groaned slightly as a punch caught him on his cheek, another his exposed lower ribs, then a solid punch to his stomach. As he fell backward, a kick sent him to the ground.

"Useless."

"You cheating hún dàn [16]..." Wu Ying snarled as he scrambled to his feet, his body throbbing.

Yin Xue had stepped back, smirking at his opponent. "Cheating? Senior said start. But come. See if you can land a blow against me. Peasant."

Wu Ying gritted his teeth and strode forward, falling into his newly learned Northern Shen stance outside of Yin Xue's reach. Drawing a deep breath, he calmed his emotions as he had learned to do and considered what he knew of Yin Xue's style.

Fast.

A quick slap-and-retreat allowed Wu Ying to deal with Yin Xue's sudden attack. The follow-ups were dealt with in similar manner, though Wu Ying circled so as not to run into others. Wu Ying quickly found himself pressured, Yin Xue's strikes coming from multiple directions, switching forms within seconds. Unfortunately, not knowing Yin Xue's forms, he knew not the names or the rhythm that he fought in. Forced to rely on his intuition, Wu Ying stepped forward, letting a straight punch skim across his shoulder.

Wind steps got Wu Ying in. A low crescent kick, focused on his raised knee, looped around Yin Xue's front leg and kicked it on the back. Balance disrupted. Then Turtle takes the Leaf to grab the exposed neck with a striking hand. After that, finish by turni—

Before Wu Ying could complete his attack, his hand was stripped from Yin Xue's neck. A second falling palm struck his nose, forcing Wu Ying back and making his eyes tear up. Before he could recover, multiple attacks fell on him, pushing Wu Ying backward. Again, Wu Ying found himself defending, attempting to dodge and position himself. But this time around, the strikes

---

[16] Literally, mixed egg but used pretty much as "bastard"—except worse than modern day usage. Think 1960s context of calling someone a bastard.

were harder, stronger. If not for his new Body Cleansing Level of six, he would have been seriously injured.

"Enough!"

Suddenly, the onslaught stopped.

"What is the meaning of this?"

Wu Ying looked up, blinking around an eye that had turned red from dripping blood. He spat blood, lips cut open as Chi Sing held Yin Xue in a casual arm lock.

"That peasant dared touch me!"

"And so you broke my rules by speeding up," Chi Sing said, disdain in his tone. "You there. Change with this idiot. And you, pass me your sect stamp."

"Why?"

Chi Sing casually slapped Yin Xue's face at his question. When Yin Xue stared at Chi Sing, he received another slap, making his face grow redder.

"Hurry up."

"Here!" Yin Xue offered his stamp from within his robes, anger making his entire face and neck flush red.

His disrespectful tone earned him another casual slap. As Yin Xue finally learned his lesson and ducked his head, he glared daggers at Chi Sing from under his brows. Finding Chi Sing entirely ignoring him, Yin Xue turned his ire on Wu Ying, who was openly smiling.

"I am removing twenty of your contribution points. Any objections? No. Good," Chi Sing said, tossing back the sect stamp. Chi Sing looked around at the group staring at Yin Xue's punishment. "Go ahead. Please. Break my rules. I do require more contribution points."

With a rustle, all the watchers turned back to their opponents to continue sparring. Those who had begun to speed up slowed down, some doing so even further than the recommended amount as fear of losing their precious points pervaded the courtyard. Chi Sing smirked before he turned to look at Wu Ying, who still sat on the ground, with disdain.

Wu Ying scrambled to his feet and bowed. "Senior!"

"Useless. Learn to guard better." Chi Sing turned away, leaving Wu Ying to face his new opponent.

The tubby cultivator who stared at Wu Ying offered him a half-smile, though a little malicious light glinted in his eyes.

Of course the nobles were going to blame him. Forcing himself not to sigh, Wu Ying readied himself for another round.

***

"Well, that could have gone worse," Tou He said as he found Wu Ying lying on the ground after class had finally ended.

Thankfully, Chi Sing wasn't a complete sadist and had allowed everyone to actually sit during this morning's cultivation. If not, Wu Ying would never have managed to make it through the day. As expected, his next five opponents had taken the opportunity to lay into Wu Ying for his presumptuous behavior of getting beat upon in front of Chi Sing. The only reason he was not further bruised was due to the nobles taking care to only hit him at full strength when they were sure Chi Sing could not see.

"Really?" Wu Ying said as he took the offered hand and stood stiffly. Thankfully, cultivating had the side effect of refreshing his body, reducing the injuries that had accumulated over the last couple of hours.

"You could have lost all your duels," Tou He said with a chuckle.

"You are not as funny as you think," Wu Ying said as he limped toward the dining hall. "How did you do?"

"Adequately."

116

"Senior monk, will we see you later for training?" another cultivator said, looking at Tou He imploringly.

"Yes, of course. I promised."

At his words, the cultivator bowed low and hurried off to join his friends.

"Just adequately, eh?" Wu Ying said.

"You could join us," Tou He offered.

"I need to work on the style I purchased." Wu Ying rubbed his ribs. "I've got a long way to go before it's useable in sparring practice."

"Yet you used it," Tou He said.

"I learn faster that way," Wu Ying said. Balancing the use of what he knew, what he was trying to apply, and not getting hit had taxed Wu Ying's mental processes to the maximum. Which obviously meant that he was slower than ever to react to attacks. "At least when I kick their ass in the tournament, they'll be surprised."

"Good," Tou He said, clapping his friend on the shoulder and eliciting a wince. "Perseverance is important for a cultivator."

"As is a high pain threshold," Wu Ying added.

***

That evening, Wu Ying stood in a small clearing halfway down the hill. It was one of many small parks that dotted the mountain, but this one was rarely used due to its location. Between the distance from the residences and the lack of sect-provided lighting, few outer sect members felt the need to visit. For Wu Ying though, the privacy was a boon. It allowed him to practice the Northern Shen martial style without interruption and, as importantly, without embarrassment.

"Four inches." Wu Ying groaned out loud as he dropped lower. The damn stance with the leg outstretched hurt. That he was meant to be able to lower his body all the way to the ground with one leg extended and the other tucked beneath him before shifting smoothly and twisting was ridiculous.

The footwork in the Northern Shen Kicking Style was both esoteric and angular, requiring him to shift his body with each step to evade attacks. Unlike some styles, the focus was more on evasion than blocking attacks, allowing the fighter to close the distance on evaded strikes before countering. It also meant that, among other things, it required a greater degree of flexibility than any other style that Wu Ying had ever practiced.

"Then... Swallow Greets the Crane." Transfer weight and kick. As much as Wu Ying would prefer to complete this portion slowly, he had neither the strength, flexibility, nor balance to do so. Yet. The front kick flashed upward before he pivoted and dropped his foot to the side, landing to the side and shifting his body again.

Hours of practice. Each step followed by a movement. Sometimes a block, sometimes a punch. A warding gesture, a gentle plucking motion. Kicks. So many kicks. And interspersed, the locks, throws, and upsets that made up the core of the style.

In truth, Wu Ying knew, at a certain point, his lone study would have to end. Grips, locks, and throws just couldn't be practiced well without a partner. The question was, who could he work with? Thinking back to his humiliating defeats, Wu Ying knew that he would need to keep at least a portion of his form hidden if he were to have any chance in the upcoming exams.

Deep in thought, Wu Ying spun and turned, the guttering flame of the lanterns he had brought slowly darkening as the night faded.

Chapter 10

A week later, Wu Ying found himself standing before Elder Huang once again, his work done for the day. Wu Ying offered the Elder a tentative smile while he gestured to the sect stamp in his hand.

"Rubbish! You think I'll spend my time filling your contribution points for you every day? What do you think I am? So free to do this kind of work?" Elder Huang scoffed. "Go see the administrative office and do it yourself, you lazy trash. And run another delivery for me for wasting my time."

Wu Ying bowed low even as he took Elder Huang's chiding in good grace. The Elder was not incorrect—he should have known better than to bother the Elder with such a trivial thing. No one in power wanted to be questioned over minor things. Turning around, Wu Ying took off down the mountain, a portion of him daydreaming about the kinds of things he might purchase with his new contribution points.

Hours later, Wu Ying found himself outside a large administrative building that was but a stone's throw from the library itself. While Wu Ying had seen it before on his—only—visit to the library, he had not paid much attention to it. Now, washed and clean, Wu Ying found himself dreading his visit to the administrative building as he recalled Liu Tsong's earlier vague comments. Thus far, most of his interactions with others had been less than stellar.

Built on a slope on the hill, the building required one to ascend a series of stone steps to reach the door. The building itself showcased the wealth of the sect, with its intricately decorated columns and carved edging along the sloped, tiled roof. Even the pair of large, double-doored entrances were carefully decorated with mother-of-pearl inlays highlighting memorable acts by the sect's founder. Within, a series of long counters faced the entrance, where severe-looking attendants worked. Small, discreet plaques indicated the locations that outer, inner, and core members were to line up. Not surprisingly, the line for outer sect members was the longest, with the fewest attendants waiting on them. Seeing the line continue to grow as he looked around, Wu Ying hurried to get into line and wait his turn.

"Nature of business?"

The attendant's bored voice cut across Wu Ying's contemplation of the cultivation exercise he had indulged in while waiting. The wait itself had not been as bad as he had expected—just over an hour.

"Collecting my contribution points, Senior," Wu Ying answered as he offered his stamp.

The attendant took it without even looking up, passing the stamp over a jade plate on his table. As new words floated upward on the jade tablet, the attendant frowned and stilled.

"Problem, Senior?"

"Wait here," the attendant said. Taking the stamp with him, the attendant walked away into the inner recesses of the building.

Wu Ying stood still as he struggled to keep his face smooth, a growing sense of anxiety gathering in his stomach.

When the attendant came back, he did so with an older man with a long, wispy beard, a headdress that indicated a middling status as an Elder in the sect, and a sneer that seemed permanently etched onto his face.

"Elder Mo, this is the student I spoke of," the attendant said, bowing deeply.

"Long Wu Ying," Elder Mo said as he tossed Wu Ying's sect stamp in his hand. "You bypassed the assignment hall to take work with Elder Huang directly. What do you have to say for yourself?"

"Elder." Wu Ying offered a low bow. Out of the corner of his eyes, he could tell that everyone's attention had been drawn to him. After all, this kind of entertainment could not be bought. "I ask your forgiveness. Elder Huang asked me to see him directly."

"And you did not report here immediately?" Elder Mo said with a sneer. "You think your sponsor is enough to ignore our rules?"

"No, Elder."

"Useless. I should take back all your contribution points," Elder Mo said, tapping the stamp.

"But I've used some already…" Wu Ying said softly.

"Yes. That is why I have come up with another assignment for you. Which you will complete," Elder Mo said and tossed Wu Ying a simple wooden slip. Wu Ying caught it and looked at the words, before looking up as Elder Mo continued. "Finish the assignment successfully or do not come back."

Elder Mo dropped the sect stamp on the table and walked away. All around, the volume of conversations increased as the audience discussed Wu Ying's punishment. Many wondered what kind of task he had been given, a few going so far as to crane their necks to read the slip. Wu Ying quickly slid the slip into his robes, along with the newly retrieved sect stamp, before he scurried out. Even before he left, he heard the growing hubbub of conversation.

This would certainly not do his reputation any good.

***

After reporting on the events to Elder Huang, Wu Ying retreated to the park where he always trained before he finally found the time to look at the wooden assignment slip. Any hope of Elder Huang intervening had died at the Elder's simple grunt of affirmation, which left Wu Ying with only the choice of completing this task.

"What did he send me to do?" Wu Ying wondered.

From overheard conversations and gossiping with Tou He, Wu Ying had expanded his understanding of the kind of assignments that the sect normally tasked their members with. A large portion involved the acquisition of necessities for the sect—gold, produce, horses, lumber, and the like. Wu Ying termed those assignments noble bait—perfect assignments for rich nobles to gain contribution points. In fact, thinking back, Wu Ying could recall more than one instance when his village had been randomly assigned to new tasks to aid their lord Wei.

The next level of collection assignments were normally assigned to inner sect members—those resources were not something a low-level cultivator could expect to get. Everything from spirit stones to spiritual herbs were common gathering tasks, but rarer manuscripts, beautiful paintings, or even exotic tea could be among those assignments. Most of those assignments were issued by the Elders of the sect directly, brokered through the assignment hall, rather than a sect requirement. In this way, the Elders could gather resources and personal objects of interest without disturbing their own cultivation.

Next were bounty quests. At the lowest level, bounty quests were sent out by the local lords and the kingdom for bandits, thieves, and other riff-raff who refused to live within the bounds of society. While the local lord would often send his men to deal with them, due to the constant war in the last few years, the number of such bandits had increased. Wu Ying knew that how dangerous the roads had become was a common refrain among the merchants. In general, most bandits were peasants—individuals with low or no cultivation levels. On occasion though, famous outlaws had—through fate or fortune—received training and raised their cultivation levels. Those types of bounty quests were given by local lords or the kingdom itself to the sect. Such difficult quests were often assigned to inner sect members.

On top of that, the sect had their own enemies. Most of them were other-sect members, enemies who had higher cultivation grades than Body Cleansing. Assignments to deal with such enemies paid significantly more, but were obviously something only those with the appropriate cultivation levels could handle. Thankfully, as the largest sect in the kingdom, the Verdant Green Waters Sect had no "marked" enemies in the kingdom itself, meaning that sect members needed to leave the kingdom for such assignments.

Lastly were the miscellaneous assignments, those which were uncommon enough that their difficulty ranged significantly. Diplomatic and teaching assignments were part of this category, where experienced sect members would journey to the outside world to spread goodwill among the populace or other sects. Occasional bodyguarding requests also made their way to the assignment hall. Guarding assignments—of merchant caravans or towns—were even more rare, as few merchants had the funds to request such work from the sect, while local lords often used their own people. If there was such work to be done, it was often done by itinerant wanderers and smaller sects.

Wu Ying sighed as he stared at the plaque in front of him. A simple request for plum blossom wine—three jars[17] of it. Somehow, Wu Ying doubted the request was as simple as it appeared. Tapping the wooden slat, Wu Ying debated who could be relied upon to provide illumination on this matter.

"Told you he would be here." Tou He's voice cut into Wu Ying's contemplation.

"Tou He? And Liu Tsong? Sorry, Senior." Wu Ying stood and bowed to the Senior when he realized his lapse in propriety.

"Wu Ying. You're becoming increasingly famous," Tou He said with a smile. "First, you manage to make all our peers hate you. Now, you've managed to even make the Elders notice you."

---

[17] In China, wine was traditionally stored in crockery jars

"This kind of fame, I can do without," Wu Ying said as he recalled the scene in the assignment hall.

"It's true though. Even I heard of Junior Wu Ying and how he angered Elder Mo. Quite amazing. So what kind of quest did he give you?" Liu Tsong said, eyes twinkling with amusement.

"Senior, please, don't trouble yourself with such a small matter," Wu Ying said, holding the wooden slat to his body as he bowed again. "We have troubled you too much already."

"Oh rubbish." Liu Tsong stepped forward lightly. In the space of Wu Ying's blink, she was in front of him and effortlessly pulling the wooden slat from his fingers. "Now, let's see. I have to have something to tell the other Seniors…"

Wu Ying groaned, having already guessed her real objective. But since she was there and it was too late to hide the matter, he might as well make full use of Liu Tsong.

"Do you know of this wine, Senior? I have never heard of it myself," Wu Ying said.

Beside him, Tou He winked at his friend.

"Three Stone Plum Blossom Wine?" Liu Tsong muttered, tapping the slat against her chin. "I think… yes! Oh. Ohhhhhhh."

"Senior?"

"Mmmm, this is difficult. Three Stone Plum Blossom Wine can be bought at Yi County—three counties away," Liu Tsong said. "But there is a problem. You see, the Zhong family that makes it, they only release a hundred jars a year. And the time for it to release is coming very soon. Worse, to go there, you'll need to go through Li County."

"What's wrong with Li County?" Wu Ying said with a frown.

"Even I know that," Tou He said. "It's filled with bandits."

"Especially Chao Ji Ang," Liu Tsong said. "He's reputed to be at least Body Cleansing 9. Some rumors even put him at Energy Gathering stage. He and his men have killed all the constables sent to apprehend him, and he always burns the ships he takes."

"Ships?" Wu Ying said.

"He mostly stays on the river and canals that connect the counties," Liu Tsong said. "Some say that he burns the bodies to hide his defilement of their corpses."

"That's horrible!" Wu Ying said, his eyes wide with shock. To do that to a corpse? Wu Ying could not imagine how he would meet his ancestors if that happened to his body. What kind of creature did that? How could he ever face his parents when they met in the heavens later on? "Is there no other way around?"

"Of course there is, but if you want to be there to buy the wine on time, you'll have to journey there on the most direct route. The only good news is that the proprietor never raises his price—he only sells on a first come, first serve basis. If he did not limit people to three jars, there would be none for anyone," Liu Tsong said. "This is going to be a difficult journey for you."

"Yes." Wu Ying fell silent as he considered the dangers of the trip.

"You practice that Long family sword style, but you don't have a sword, correct?" Liu Tsong said with a frown.

"No. It was not something we could afford," Wu Ying said.

It was not as if he could have taken his father's—that weapon had been granted to him by the army on his leaving. Using it while his father was alive was a breach of propriety and law. Of course, his father had been granted that weapon for breaking the family heirloom. In the end, they were too poor to purchase a proper sword for Wu Ying. There had been discussion about picking up something cheaper—shoddy work from an apprentice smith perhaps—but both his father and Wu Ying found the prospect of such a weapon distasteful. And then, of course, the army came and it became moot.

"Come with me," Liu Tsong said and promptly exited the clearing.

Wu Ying frowned, looking at Tou He, who shrugged. The pair hurried after the young lady whose swift steps and greater cultivation ate up the distance with ease. When they reached Liu Tsong's residence, the Senior was nowhere to be found. They frowned, standing in the inner courtyard as they looked around, curious to where she could have gone. When Liu Tsong came out, she was carrying a sword and a roll of paper.

"Take this," Liu Tsong said, shoving the items into Wu Ying's hands.

"I cannot—"

"The sword is of no use to me anymore," Liu Tsong said with a sniff. "And the map is nothing. You can get it yourself for a single contribution point."

"Thank you, Senior. I am grateful for your words and items. But if you would, why are you helping me?" Wu Ying said with a pensive frown.

"Whim. And because Elder Mo and his kind have been doing this kind of thing forever," Liu Tsong said. "They pick on those who have no real backers just because they can. I—and my sponsor—we do not think that is right. And so we do our best to help against it."

"Oh. If that's the case, can you speak of who your sponsor is, Senior Liu?" Wu Ying said.

"Of course. You actually impressed him when you met with him at the library. Elder Ko is also sometimes allies with Elder Cheng, your own sponsor. Though Elder Cheng is a little too fickle to be considered a real ally," Liu Tsong said with a half-smile.

"I thank you, Senior Liu." Wu Ying once again bowed his head.

"As for me, I have something for you too. Give me your sect stamp," Tou He said, making a beckoning gesture.

Wu Ying did not move to do so. "Why?"

"You're going to need to buy provisions for the trip. And since Elder Mo didn't give you funds, you'll need to take funds from the sect for your purchases. For three jars, the amount you have is insufficient, no?"

"Uhhh… probably," Wu Ying answered. Truth be told, he had no idea how expensive this trip would likely be. It would be a real tragedy to travel all the way there and find himself short of funds. But to borrow Tou He's contribution points seemed wrong.

"Come. Don't waste time. This is a small matter between friends," Tou He said, gesturing again. Reluctantly, realizing he had no real choice, Wu Ying handed over his sect stamp. "You know I would come if I could."

"I know," Wu Ying replied.

As sect members, none of them could just leave as they wished. Even Wu Ying would need to apply for a permit to leave the sect, though obviously with his current assignment, it would be automatically approved. And for most inner sect members, experiential training was a common thing. This restriction on external travel was due to a few factors. Each sect member was an investment for the sect, and as such, the sect would review recent contributions by each member who applied for an external trip permit. Those who had not contributed sufficiently would be gently advised to shape up. In addition, by restricting and tracking where each sect member was, the sect was able to head off potential reputation problems. As an outer sect member, there was no way Wu Ying or Tou He would normally be allowed out at this stage in their training.

"I do not know how to thank you both," Wu Ying said, his voice filled with gratitude.

"Make sure you come back," Tou He replied as he handed back Wu Ying's sect stamp.

***

After that, preparations were simple enough to complete. Thankfully, the assignment office placed no further roadblocks on Wu Ying and happily exchanged out all his contribution points for funds and provisions. They even helped Wu Ying arrange for a place on a merchant ship traveling downstream. When Wu Ying finished packing all that he was to carry, he once again realized how little he actually had. Yet, looking within himself, Wu Ying could find little to regret about that. Money, a sword, food, and clothing. That was sufficient for a true cultivator.

"Off for experiential training already?" Xi Qi said when he saw Wu Ying walk through the pifang with his bag and sword.

"Elder Lu. I have an assignment from Elder Mo. This is my pass," Wu Ying said cordially as he handed over the required pass for leaving.

Xi Qi frowned, looking over the simple wooden slat that detailed Wu Ying's right to leave the sect and the reason for it. As he handed back the slat, he looked Wu Ying up and down slowly. "Continue working on your aura strengthening. You've progressed far. And at your stage, it is best not to travel as a cultivator. Turn down any challenges you find. Losing face is better than losing your life."

"Yes, Elder Lu," Wu Ying agreed.

"Also, please give this to Old Man Li when you collect the wine. That old cheat owes me one bottle still," Xi Qi said as he tossed over a stamp infused with his chi. "Bring it back undamaged."

"Of course, Elder," Wu Ying said, bowing low after storing the stamp safely with the rest of his money.

Since he was going to be going to the location anyway, doing a favor for Xi Qi was a small matter. Furthermore, he was better off having a favorable reputation with at least one Elder, even if he was nothing more than the gate guard. As it stood, while Elder Huang looked favorably upon the efforts Wu Ying had put into the kitchens, he was the one who had caused all the trouble for Wu Ying. As for Elder Cheng, his supposed sponsor? Well, the less said about him, the better.

"I shall take my leave then." Wu Ying said, bowing goodbye again and receiving a languid wave from Xi Qi.

With that, Wu Ying trotted down the stairs, stopping only long enough to turn around and stare at the pifang and the sect's signboard. To think that he would be leaving after only a few months. Would he ever see the sect again? What kind of experiences would he have had by the time he came back?

Turning away, Wu Ying took the familiar route down the mountain, a little spring in his step. Well, it was time for this farmer's son to see more of the world.

Chapter 11

"Time to stop, Wu Ying." A hand came down on Wu Ying's shoulder, shaking him from his stupor.

For most of the afternoon, Wu Ying had been at the oars, taking up an entire bench by himself as he worked an oar alone. A part of him had paid attention to the steady drum beat that kept the rowers in time, orders that were punctuated occasionally by the vocal orders of the captain. But mostly, Wu Ying focused on his cultivation, slowly gathering more and more chi into his dantian and reinforcing the small pool of energy within. Lastly, a very small portion of his attention was sent to his aura as he worked to contain the overflow of his chi.

The entire process was difficult enough that he'd had no time to pay attention to anything outside of those things. If the act of rowing was not so repetitive, Wu Ying would have had to give up on extending his consciousness to his aura or cultivating. As it was, the difficulty in separating his mind across these component parts had progressed his understanding of both Two Minds and the Aura Strengthening exercises significantly. While he could not personally tell how well he was doing, he was sure he achieved at least a novice understanding of both.

"Uncle[18]," Wu Ying said as he finished storing the oar. He slowly stretched as he turned to the man speaking to him. "Have we arrived?"

"We have. The tugs will guide us the rest of the way in," the sailor said with a grin. "Exactly on time. And my men are more rested than ever, thanks to

---

[18] While traditionally there are numerous ways of addressing someone, for ease of reading and use, I'm going to use the more modern equivalent of Uncle / Auntie. This is generally used for strangers who are not related but older than you as a respectful form of address.

you. If all my passengers were willing to work the oars like this, travel would be so much easier!"

"Har, Uncle, it's true." Wu Ying chuckled. "Is dinner ready then?"

"Ah, you are terrible. Eating so much, you'll eat away my profits," the boat captain said with a pained smile.

Together, the pair ascended the steps to where the crew was already busy eating. Before he joined them, Wu Ying begged off to wash himself clean at the stern of the boat, as was his usual routine. After cultivating all day, even Wu Ying found his stench unacceptable, never mind the poor sailors who would have to sit next to him.

Shucking his robes, Wu Ying stood at the stern with only his pants on and pulled water from the river up with the bucket, washing himself and cleaning off his long hair as he did so. Idly, he glanced down at his body and the scar along his torso from the injury caused by Yin Xue. After all this time, the injury had fully healed, leaving only a diagonal scar.

What surprised Wu Ying more was the state of his body. Having spent so much time cultivating and working on technique, Wu Ying had not really paid attention to the changes. He no longer had a mild layer of fat across his torso, all of it burnt away by constant activity and revealing chiseled abdominal muscles, thighs that were as wide as a young girl's waist, and calves that had doubled in size. In fact, looking downward, Wu Ying was surprised to note that his pants were riding a little higher than normal—barely covering his ankles now.

"Did I grow taller?" Wu Ying muttered, shaking his head. Well, he was still growing, barely having crossed sixteen years of age. But all this muscle was unsightly. He would certainly never be mistaken for a refined scholar if he looked like this. "Then again, what would I do with one of those scholarly women? It's not as if I have much to speak with them about."

Laughing, Wu Ying quickly dried himself and moved back to the group of sailors. He might have spent a little more time reading the classics than his classmates, but that did not make him a scholar. Far from it—he still had not finished the four books and five classics[19].

A week of traveling had taken them across one county entirely. In town, Wu Ying would have to find another ship to ride on, as this one headed east now. Hopefully that task would not be too difficult. After all, the town was bustling with activity. Surely a boat or two would be going in the direction he needed.

***

"What do you mean there are no boats?" Wu Ying said incredulously as he stood before the administrative office the next morning.

While boat captains did not need to register where they were going, it was beneficial for them to do so. In this way, both correspondence and additional trade deals could reach the boats when necessary. Of course, most boats ran a fixed course—going back and forth on fixed schedules—but itinerant traders also made up a portion of the traffic on the rivers.

"You heard of Bandit Chao, yes?" the attendant said tersely.

"Of course," Wu Ying replied.

"Well, he's been very active lately, as all the river guards have been withdrawn west due to the war. Now, few merchants dare run that route unless they're traveling together. You missed the last convoy by two days," the attendant said.

"When will the next one leave?" Wu Ying said.

---

[19] The four books and five classics were the required reading (and quoting) material for the Chinese imperial examinations and are such, considered "must reads."

"Not for at least another week," the attendant replied. "Many of the captains have already shifted their routes to other locations. It might be less profitable, but it's better than losing your life."

Wu Ying sighed and rubbed his head in frustration. He could not afford to wait two weeks for the ships to leave. Even though he had a little extra time, it was only a few days at most.

"If that is all, you can leave. Others are waiting!" the attendant snapped at Wu Ying, who apologized and left, frowning.

His only choice was to travel over land. But overland travel, especially if he went with a merchant, was slower. Much slower. Then his only choice...

"I'll go myself!"

***

Saying and doing were obviously two different matters. For such a long journey, Wu Ying would need provisions. After all, he had not attained the state where he could subsist only on morning dew and sunlight. At this stage of his cultivation, Wu Ying needed food and a lot of it. Better then to purchase more and plan to buy even more at each of the villages he would pass.

In truth, Wu Ying would prefer to purchase everything he needed in one go and then cut across the land, using smaller trails and roads to speed up his travel. But strong as he was, carrying too much would slow him down. And he could not afford a horse. Never mind the fact that he had never learned to ride a horse.

Because of this, it took Wu Ying nearly the entire morning to purchase supplies, pack, and ready himself. Leaving through the east[20] gate of the town, Wu Ying once again marveled at how easy it was to travel as a sect member. He only needed to show his sect stamp, and formalities like the travel pass and the entrance fees were waived.

Still, Wu Ying considered, it was best if he hid his allegiance soon. Elder Lu's advice resounded in Wu Ying's mind. A cultivator could never be too careful, as those cultivators who had something to prove and those who wished to acquire unique knowledge or riches would target others of their kind. Violence in the martial world was a given. As such, once he was a decent distance away from the gates, Wu Ying found an empty clearing to exchange his robes for his peasant clothing. After hoisting his backpack and hiding his pouch inside his tunic, Wu Ying jogged.

Even though he was running, Wu Ying chose not to use this time to cultivate. For one thing, he no longer had the protection of Senior Yang. For another, the area around him was new and unknown, forcing Wu Ying to check his map and the directions each time he came to a crossroads. Rather than risk getting lost or being interrupted or attacked while cultivating, Wu Ying focused on improving his control of his aura.

Li after li passed as the hours turned, Wu Ying only breaking to drink water and chew on the travel food he had purchased. Simple meat and vegetable buns and soya sauce-soaked glutinous rice balls with pieces of chicken made up the majority of the food he had bought. Smaller packages of vegetables and rice lay in his bag, awaiting the evening when it was time to cook. Since it was

---

[20] Traditionally, Chinese cities were built with four main gates along the compass points and the city lord's mansion situated in the center. Cities were generally walled as well to increase security.

nearing the end of the moon phase, there would be little light to run at night, even if Wu Ying was willing to risk that kind of danger.

That evening, Wu Ying found a small clearing a distance from the road. Rather than the usual rest stops which he could ill afford, Wu Ying preferred sleeping outdoors. Even if animals and spirit beasts roamed the countryside, he should be relatively safe. After all, it would require significant bad luck to draw one to him in the vast wilderness.

"Cook the meat and the vegetables first. Stir it in with the rice with the sauce afterward," Wu Ying muttered as he set the small pot he had brought along on the fire.

All settled, Wu Ying stood and stretched, considering his next steps. "Ah! I haven't actually tried the sword yet."

Speaking out loud seemed like a strange thing to do, but considering he had been running for the entire day without speaking to anyone, the sound of a voice—even his own—was comforting. Pulling the blade out of its sheath, Wu Ying inspected the weapon.

The sword Liu Tsong had provided was a simple iron sword, made by a serviceable craftsman but not anything of note. Still, it was the first sword he had ever owned and it was, for his purpose, perfect. A simple straight blade, edged on both sides and slightly longer than his father's sword. The hilt was wrapped with leather to reduce slippage. There was no tassel on the end of the sword, but that was fine with Wu Ying. He knew certain flashy fighters enjoyed adding them, but he found them annoying.

"Let's try this out," Wu Ying said after glancing at the pot. He should have just enough time to finish the basic form before his meal was ready.

Stepping away from the fire, Wu Ying resheathed the sword and entered a neutral stance. The first step of the Long family jian style forms all started with a neutral stance, as the first act was always the drawing of the sword. It was rare, in the style's viewpoint, for a practitioner to start with the sword drawn, so obviously the first thing one must learn was how to unsheathe the sword.

Step. Draw. Twist the hips and tuck the shoulder slightly. Roll upward even as the blade came free from its sheath. Each motion followed the other, each action a continuation. One of the intrinsic aspects of the form—of the style— was the continual motion that it required. In addition, the style was domineering, incisive, and penetrative, focusing on long steps and quick strikes that required the practitioner to commit fully then retract immediately. Unlike some other styles, the Long family style focused on dominating the battlefield with each action, such that feints and attacks blended into one another seamlessly.

As Wu Ying moved, the air around him rose, kicked up by the swift movements of his feet and the whirl of his blade. Yet the wind sputtered and died, rising and falling as his movements hesitated or his attacks cut but were unable to generate sufficient strength. Twenty minutes later, Wu Ying finally came to a stop, the sword sheathed with a flourish.

"Cao. Still missing by a half-inch," Wu Ying said as he looked around at the kicked-up dirt. He sighed and shook his head, walking over to his pot of food. "I'll need to practice more to get used to this blade. But first, dinner!"

When dinner was nearly over, Wu Ying straightened his back, an errant sound alerting him. Turning away from the fire, he peered into the darkness and frowned as he carefully set aside his bowl.

"Who is it?" Wu Ying called.

Instead of an answer, a snuffling came from the undergrowth. Standing warily, Wu Ying let his hand land on the sheathed blade, eyes narrowing. A pair of eyes three feet off the ground appeared, glowing red in the firelight.

Wu Ying winced as he stared at the boar. A flame-spirit demon boar, it seemed. One that had achieved some degree of strength over the years. Even a normal boar was a menace. Their greater weight, their low-slung body, and the thick layer of fat that covered their vitals made them difficult to injure and kill with normal weapons. Add in the boar's naturally aggressive nature and most farmers preferred to deal with wolves—at least those animals had reason for their aggression. A spirit-enhanced boar was just the same, except multiplied by ten.

Lowering his stance, Wu Ying eyed the boar, who snorted and snuffled. A sudden bunching of its muscles telegraphed its charge. The creature crossed the space between them in a breath, hooves sending clods of dirt into the air. Exhaling, Wu Ying stepped sideways even as he drew and cut. The attack slashed across the boar's neck, cutting deep and parting skin, fat, and muscle. But such was the size of the boar's neck that the attack failed to hit a vital spot.

"Damn it," Wu Ying snarled as he spun around, lashing out even as the boar turned.

His next attack scored its back, leaving a shallow cut across its tough hide. As Wu Ying jumped back, the boar let out a squeaky oink and released a wave of fire at Wu Ying. An additional jump backward allowed Wu Ying to avoid the majority of the attack, leaving his face and exposed skin red and hot.

More cautious now, Wu Ying fell back into his guard as he waited for the boar to attack him again. The boar rushed Wu Ying, who stepped aside as he lashed out in a series of quick wrist cuts that opened the boar's skin. Better to focus on a slow fight, one that wore the monster down, than attempt another decapitating strike.

As he fought, Wu Ying focused on controlling his breathing, knowing he needed to keep it regular and calm to control his body. Yet the thrill of battle ran through him, his heart speeding up and his vision narrowing as he fought for his life, alone, for the first time. Oh sure, spirit beasts had attacked the village before, but he had never been at the forefront. Nor had he been alone.

Together, the pair fought, the boar relentless in its aggression while Wu Ying moved smoothly in circles. Luckily, the monster could only use its fire attack once in a while, allowing Wu Ying to focus on cutting the monster apart. As time wore on, the pair grew increasingly tired. As the boar charged Wu Ying once again, he neatly side-stepped the monster and cut again. Wu Ying's blade sliced deeper into the exposed muscles on the boar's back, making the monster snuffle in anger once again. However, this time, as Wu Ying landed, his foot trod on an overturned piece of earth and he lost his balance for a split second. The boar twisted around as it took the opportunity to charge Wu Ying again.

"The Sword's Truth," Wu Ying shouted as he regained his balance.

Without time to back off, Wu Ying could only trust in the first major attack form of his style. The Sword's Truth was a lunge, but a lunge filled with the intent and conviction of the cultivator. It required full commitment, as it gathered all the strength in a cultivator's body, requiring the cultivator to completely believe that nothing could withstand the attack itself.

Facing the monster head-on, the blade was directed slightly off the line of the monster's charge, aimed at the exposed wound on its neck. Braced in a perfect line, the sword bucked in Wu Ying's hand as the weight of the monster pushed down on him. The impetus from both of their attacks pushed the sword deep into the creature's body even as Wu Ying's feet dug up the earth as he was pushed back. Thankfully, the attack was sufficient to pierce something vital in the monster's body. It stopped thrashing finally, leaving Wu Ying with some light wounds on his arms and an aching hand.

"Finally," Wu Ying said and leaned against a nearby tree.

His once-pristine clearing was now trashed, the ground riven with holes from the boar's striking feet, burnt grass sputtering, and the boar's blood splashed everywhere. Only Wu Ying's decision to hoist and secure his bags of provisions above the treeline earlier had kept them safe.

"This will not do for tonight's rest." Never mind how uneven the earth was now, the smell of blood would bring insects and bigger monsters. "Better find another clearing."

Shaking his head, Wu Ying moved to pull down his bags. Rather than unhook the rope once he'd collected his bags, Wu Ying tied it to the boar's body and hauled it up, allowing the monster to bleed out as Wu Ying bandaged his arms. Briefly, Wu Ying considered storing some of the boar's blood but then shook it off. He had not brought a container for it. More's the pity. Better to take the meat and be grateful that he had that much.

"Oh!" Wu Ying smacked himself on the head. "It's a demon beast!"

Grinning, Wu Ying stared at the carcass. Somewhere in there, the monster had a spirit stone. His very first. While it was likely small and dim as befitted the smaller demon, it was still a demon stone. When he returned to the sect, he could trade it in for more contribution points. Worst-case scenario, it was still worth a decent amount of coin.

Smiling, Wu Ying settled down to wait, more content with the disturbance. He almost wished he would be attacked again.

Almost.

Chapter 12

As the rest stops along the road system were spaced roughly a day apart, Wu Ying decided to carry the meat from the boar to the nearest stop and sell it there. Since he managed to arrive around mid-morning, the owner of the stop was more than happy to purchase the meat to feed the lunch and dinner crowd. As Wu Ying stared at the taels he had been provided, he could not shake the feeling that he had been cheated. Certainly, paying the same price per cattie for spirit-infused boar meat as for normal pork seemed wrong. But in the end, Wu Ying took the funds and the hot meal gratefully. It was not as if he could actually carry all the meat with him, nor did he have the salt or time to smoke the boar properly. Better to sell it and earn a little coin than to worry about the matter.

Having properly consoled himself and eaten a warm meal, Wu Ying took off once more at a leisurely jog. While he received more than a few strange glances over the fact that he was running with a big bag slung over his back, since none of those individuals managed to overtake him, it was of little concern to Wu Ying. And really, while his cultivation and body were strong, that was only in comparison to the base ranks of the populace. Older and more experienced cultivators were able to do what he did with ease, and even among the commoners, the occasional gifted genius cropped up. As such, Wu Ying's actions, while unusual, were not entirely uncommon. Especially since Wu Ying had yet to study or master any qinggong[21] skills to move lightly at superhuman speeds.

Along the way, Wu Ying paid attention to the traffic on the road. Even if travel by the canals was both faster and more convenient, many locations were

---

[21] Literally "light skill." Comes from baguazhang and is basically wire-fu—running on water, climbing trees, gliding along bamboo, etc.

not connected that way. As such, everyone from merchants, beggars, scholars, monks, government officials, cultivators, and more used the roads. The conveyances used varied depending on the individuals' stations. Everything from simple wagons to carriages, horses, and rickshaws were seen on the road, though just as many were like Wu Ying, making do with nature's most popular form of transportation.

Even though Wu Ying found himself surrounded by people, he spent no time talking to them. And while there were numerous kinds of travelers, the roads weren't packed. More often than not, he saw people at clearings resting, or he would pass another group as he ran. On a few rare occasions, he was passed by those on horses or in carriages.

Wu Ying found the entire scene endlessly fascinating. This was a life that he had never been exposed to, and the traveling community seemed to have a series of mores that he was slowly gleaning. Many of these wanderers seemed happy, free from the social and economic restrictions that kept farmers locked to their land. It was an eye-opening sight for the young man, much like his first city. Once again, Wu Ying was forcefully reminded that the world under heaven held marvels and wonders galore.

***

Day after day, Wu Ying found his life repeating the same pattern. Run, eat, train his aura strengthening techniques and his martial art forms, eat, get attacked by spirit beasts. Not that he was attacked every night, but the attacks were more often than common sense would have suggested. On one particular day, Wu Ying found himself leaning on a shop counter, nursing a sore rib while talking to the rest stop's proprietor.

"Are there a lot of demon beast attacks on the road?" Wu Ying asked, somewhat exasperated. If not for the fact that his body required less sleep due to his higher cultivation, there would be no way for him to keep to his current pace.

"Attacks? No more than usual," the owner said, twirling his long white mustache. The old man cocked his head to the side, considering Wu Ying and his dirty peasant garb. "The weather has been good, so the berries and fruits should be blooming. But I did hear that a new spirit beast took residence on Mount Heng. Might have driven down a few more demon beasts."

"A few?" Wu Ying said, shaking his head. "This is the fourth demon beast I've killed!"

"You're staying alone in the wilderness, aren't you?" When Wu Ying nodded, the proprietor snorted. "Of course you're being attacked. The beasts know to watch the trails for people. They might not be intelligent, but demon beasts are cunning—and peasants with low to no cultivation are the best prey. Especially when they're alone."

"Alone..." Wu Ying blinked, realizing what the owner was saying. Between supressing his cultivation with his aura strengthening techniques and camping alone, Wu Ying was basically placing a giant sign above his head that said "easy prey."

"Well, you're obviously very skilled with that sword. But a young man like you, you should work on your cultivation more," the owner said kindly. "It's not seemly for one so young to have so little presence."

"Presence?"

"I might not have the eye of insight of a real cultivator, but I've served enough of them in my time. The real ones have a presence. If you pay attention, you'll realize that all cultivators have that too," the proprietor said, smiling. "The stronger the cultivator, the stronger their presence. And yours is, well..."

"Weak," Wu Ying acknowledged.

Of course it was weak. He was suppressing his aura! But thinking on the matter, Wu Ying frowned as he tried to sense the proprietor's aura. After a time, Wu Ying shook his head, having failed. Perhaps he should do as the old proprietor recommended and test his sensing ability on an on-going basis, especially when he went back to the sect. His ability to read cultivations would naturally grow when he achieved the Energy Storage stage, but there was no reason not to practice it now.

"Thank you, Uncle," Wu Ying said with a bow.

"Not at all. Now, for this wolf meat, it's not the most popular. Especially the heart. But I can buy it for six taels," the proprietor said, gesturing to the meat arrayed across his counter.

Wu Ying rolled his eyes but got down to haggling, while a portion of his mind continued to go over their conversation. Presence, eh?

***

Another day, another long run. Days blended together, the only change for Wu Ying the progress he marked on his map. What should have been a two-week journey by boat had become a two-week marathon trip through hills, forests, and plains with no end in sight.

As the sun crept toward the horizon, Wu Ying chewed on a stick of sugar cane as he ran. As a child, he had always loved the treat, and having found a grove of unattended sugar cane earlier in the day, he had chopped a plant down to take with him. It made the entire run more manageable. When a scream resounded through the low hills, Wu Ying dropped the piece of cane with surprise.

"What is that?" Wu Ying said with a frown. He slowed down as he looked about but saw no danger in his proximity.

Of course, the scream had originated from a distance ahead of him. Wu Ying considered shifting directions or just slowing down, but he shook his head. Those thoughts were not something a cultivator should have. Having resolved to help, Wu Ying sped up.

The first thing Wu Ying noticed was the crowd. Next was the merchant's wagon that the crowd surrounded. Wu Ying quickly realized that the crowd was no ordinary crowd but a group of bandits, all of whom had swords and other weapons as they threatened the merchant. He frowned, seeing no women. But that high-pitched scream should have come from a female.

"What's going on here?" Wu Ying said as he arrived. Eying the group, he exhaled and untied the knots around his bag as he readied himself. Best not to be encumbered if things went as he expected.

"This is none of your business," one of the bandits said, turning around and sneering at Wu Ying. The balding bandit wielded a simple spear, which he leveled at Wu Ying. As Wu Ying looked at the group, he noticed that many of these bandits wielded hooked spears, nets, and daos. "Just wait there. We're collecting our fee."

"Your fee? It looks like you're attempting to collect their lives," Wu Ying said, eyeing the bruised and bloody merchant on the ground, a bandit straddling the prone body.

The employees stood pressed up against the wagon, fear in their eyes. A quick sweep of Wu Ying's gaze told him that there were a half dozen bandits, plus the one speaking with him. Of those six, one held the horses still, leaving only the one beating the merchant and four others an immediate threat.

As he confronted the group, Wu Ying found his heartbeat speeding up and his palms growing sweaty. It took all his hard-won self-control to keep his breathing low and slow as the group moved to surround him. Faced with the bandits, Wu Ying realized he might have to actually kill another person. Was this how Fa Hui felt when they had clashed with the army? Somehow, the way Fa Hui had described the event to him, Wu Ying kind of doubted it. Perhaps he wasn't...

"Are you listening to me?" the balding bandit snarled as he jabbed his spear toward Wu Ying's face.

It was not an actual strike, just a threat, but the spearhead came so close to Wu Ying's face, he reacted without thought. Wu Ying sidestepped, and the sword in his hand unsheathed in the first move of the Long family style.

"You dare!" the bandit leader who held the merchant in his hands snarled.

All around the bandit, his comrades recoiled in surprise as their friend staggered back, the spear falling to the ground as his arm separated from his body. A moment's shock, before the formerly belligerent bandit screamed. Clutching his arm, the bandit fell backward as blood spurted from his arm, coating the area around him in scarlet droplets.

"Move," Wu Ying whispered. Whether it was said to the bandits or himself, even he was not sure. But now that blood was drawn, this was no time to stop.

Another spear jabbed toward him and Wu Ying blocked it with his forearm, catching the blade as it slid above his shoulder before he pulled its wielder toward him. A quick kick and twist of his arm as he grabbed the spear sent the bandit stumbling into another, giving Wu Ying time to spin toward the last bandit. A quick clash of blades and a failed attempt at a wrist cut forced Wu Ying to fall backward as the three bandits recovered.

"Finish him, damn it!" the bandit leader growled as he kicked the merchant toward his servants and stood up. "And you people, move and I'll kill you."

Wu Ying stepped back lightly as the group continued to attempt to encircle him. He dropped his bag with a shrug, letting it land beside him as he moved backward constantly. As the bandit on his left moved around the discarded bag, breaking up the formation, Wu Ying acted.

A single quick step took him close while he spun. Clearing the vermin from the doorstep, followed by greeting the rising sun. Then the dragon stretches to back off as the bandit on his left collapsed on his newly injured leg while the one in the middle blocked Wu Ying's retreating cut. Another quick forward step, a kick to the temple of the downed bandit before Wu Ying twisted, his blade blocking the attack while positioning itself to allow Wu Ying to gently extend his hand. The blade plunged into the attacking bandit's neck, sliding in with such ease that Wu Ying almost believed he'd missed—until the sudden explosion of blood as his jian exited. Then, close, grapple and upset, kick and stab.

As quickly as it started, the fight was over. Wu Ying's hand trembled slightly as blood dripped from his jian. Around his feet, the bodies of the badly trained bandits lay, slowly bleeding to death. After kicking aside a weapon a dying bandit scrabbled for, Wu Ying walked forward to where the bandit leader looked on in fright. The rest of his opponents were either injured enough that they were dying or in shock as they stared at Wu Ying's retreating back. The bandit leader stared at his fallen men then Wu Ying, who no longer hid his cultivation. The pressure of his advanced cultivation made the bandit leader's lips tremble.

"You'll pay for this. When Boss Chao finds out, he'll hunt you down!"

"Only if you survive," Wu Ying said as he stalked forward. Internally, Wu Ying marveled at the dispassionate calm within him. Unlike his fight with Yin Xue, where he had been a bundle of nerves, or even in his struggle against the boar, Wu Ying found himself casually analyzing the bandit leader. He noted the way the bandit's throat bobbed as he swallowed, the cold sweat and darting eyes, the way the bandit's feet were angled away from him and the hostages. It all added up to…

"Go!" Wu Ying shouted.

Startled, the bandit leader's eyes widened before he darted off, followed soon after by his remaining follower from the front of the wagon. Wu Ying smiled slightly in satisfaction. Good. He had no desire to kill if he did not have to. And with the leader being so much closer to the merchants, if he had chosen to take a hostage, Wu Ying would have been unable to do anything. Though as Wu Ying turned around to stare at the injured bandits who slowly bled out, he found his respect for the bandit leader reaching a new low. Abandoning his own people. Despicable.

"Benefactor!" The merchant and his servants quickly scrambled to bow to Wu Ying. "Thank you so much."

"It's fine. It was nothing," Wu Ying said, waving his free hand casually. As he did so, Wu Ying realized how heavy his jian felt, the way blood dripped from the newly christened blade. Wu Ying casually waved the weapon, sending the majority of the blood sliding off, before he turned to his pack for a spare cloth. Best to clean it before it rusted.

"You're hurt, benefactor!" a voice exclaimed, making Wu Ying pause.

He frowned, looking down and seeing a slowly growing spot of blood on his left side. As he stared at the spot, Wu Ying's body finally allowed the full extent of his injuries to make themselves known. Pain flared in his side, the way a fire ant's bite did. "Oh."

It hurt, but not too badly. For a second, he debated what to do, but considering the wound did not seem to be bleeding quickly, Wu Ying decided to finish what he'd started. A few moments later, he had cut off a piece of cloth from one bandit's clothing and cleaned his sword, then he returned the blade to its sheath.

"Please, benefactor, let us see to it. My servant has some small skill in healing. And we can carry you with us to the next stop!" the merchant said, wringing his hands as he eyed Wu Ying.

Wu Ying opened his mouth to reject the advances then reconsidered. Beyond gratitude, the merchant probably figured it was safer to have Wu Ying with him. And while Wu Ying could travel faster than the slow wagon—that was, if he was uninjured—right now, he needed to treat his wound and cultivate to speed up his recuperation. In this case, still cultivation was obviously superior. If he was going to cultivate, he might as well do so while traveling toward his destination.

"Thank you," Wu Ying finally answered, agreeing to it.

"No, thank you, benefactor!"

The merchant waved to a servant, sending him to pick up Wu Ying's bag, while the others helped Wu Ying to the wagon. Servants sent off, the merchant collected the coin purses and weapons of the bandits, a small dagger making an appearance in his hand as he finished off the injured. In short order, the group was ready to travel with Wu Ying seated on the wagon back, cross-legged and his chest bare. The servant applied a poultice and wrapped a bandage around Wu Ying's chest.

"I will be cultivating to recuperate. Inform me if there's an issue," Wu Ying said softly.

At the merchant's quick nod, Wu Ying closed his eyes, his attention turning back to his dantian. In the churning sea of chi, he slowly exhaled and focused. Best to start.

Chapter 13

Power. Enlightenment. Skill. All of that was required for a cultivator to progress. At that moment, Wu Ying was finding that he had, inadvertently over his journey, accumulated a little enlightenment. Through the struggles with the demon beasts, through his grasp of the bandit's demeanor, through watching the world as he ran, his world view had widened. And in so doing, his ability to draw more chi expanded as the heavens itself approved.

Chi flowed into his body in growing torrents, entering his dantian and swirling in the growing pool. Even as he leaked some of this chi from his body and exhaled even more, it accumulated. Chi swirled, circulating through his body, and raged through his open meridians. Afraid that if he did not act, his meridians would break under the new stress, Wu Ying pushed against his sixth meridian. Already mostly cleansed, the impurities within gushed out as black blood from his open wound.

"What is that?"

"Is something wrong?"

"Should we do something for him?"

"Don't disturb our benefactor while he is cultivating. Don't you know any better!"

Words swirled just outside Wu Ying's conscious thoughts. But none of it had any killing intent, no bodies moved toward him, so he sat, undisturbed, as Wu Ying felt the sixth meridian break open. Another push, and the chi within his body gushed through the newly opened meridian, bringing a moment of ecstasy and release for Wu Ying as the pressure within his dantian lessened. Even his aura trembled, his newly achieved level straining the seal on it.

Wu Ying had no time to focus on that as the chi, rushing through his dantian, continued to build up. He groaned slightly as his wound throbbed and impurities were pushed out even as his muscle and skin knit under the influx of new energy. In the meantime, Wu Ying did the best that he could to corral the energy within his dantian, sending it spinning in circles as it flooded in and returned from his meridians. Rather than attempting another breakthrough immediately, it was better to allow the raging water of his chi to balance itself. In either case, the newly increased flow would cleanse his other meridians anyway, helping him ready himself for the next step.

Hours later, Wu Ying finally opened his eyes to note that the wagon had long ago come to a stop. Now, they were no longer on the road but in the stables of a rest stop. Tilting his head, the cultivator squinted in the wane light of the lanterns that hung in the stables, spotting a dozing servant a short distance away.

"Where are we?" Wu Ying called as he stood, stretching tired muscles. A slight pain in his side informed Wu Ying that the injury still existed, though a quick internal check showed it was significantly less dangerous.

"We are at the Fuxi rest stop. We passed the other one mid-day, but because you were still cultivating, my master pushed on to this one," the servant said, scrambling to his feet and bowing. "Congratulations to benefactor for breaking through."

Recalling the matter, Wu Ying quietly reached out toward his aura, sensing the difference. He mentally groaned, realizing that he was once again "leaking" chi. As Wu Ying attempted to seal the leaks, his stomach rumbled, reminding the cultivator that he had not eaten since this morning.

"My master has paid for your room and board, benefactor. If you'll follow me, I'll show you within," the servant said, bowing once again.

"Thank you," Wu Ying replied and followed.

Thankfully, dinner was quickly served and the patrons within the rest stop were willing to allow Wu Ying to eat his dinner in peace. Even so, the young man spotted the inquisitive looks and whispered conversations directed at his presence as he ate. Perhaps his actions against the bandits had been a little impetuous. But what else could a cultivator do when faced with such a situation?

"Sir cultivator, do you mind me joining you? I have some great wine here," an older merchant said, smiling as he placed a wine jar on Wu Ying's table.

"Certainly. Though I'm not sure I will be able to appreciate your wine to its fullest," Wu Ying said. After all, it was not as if they indulged in expensive wines at home.

"There is no better time to begin learning than now. Let me introduce myself. I am Dong Yi Ru, a small-time merchant of no real name," Yi Ru said.

"Long Wu Ying, cultivator." Normally he would add his sect, but Wu Ying decided to leave it out at this time. While he was out on official sect business, he also was too weak to properly carry the sect's name. If he were to be defeated or otherwise caught in a shameful situation, if Wu Ying survived, he would bring even more trouble for himself in the future.

"A pleasure, Cultivator Long. Come, let us drink." Immediately, Yi Ru opened the wine jar and poured a drink. As he was about to hand a glass to Wu Ying, a hand came down hard on the table, surprising the group.

"What is this? Why are you bothering my benefactor?" the merchant from this afternoon snarled, leaning over to glare at Yi Ru.

"Your benefactor? Have you even asked his name? Or given yours? How ill-mannered," Yi Ru said with a sneer.

"There was no time!" the merchant protested. But having been reminded of the matter, he turned and bowed to Wu Ying. "Benefactor, this one is Ou Xi Rang."

"Long Wu Ying," Wu Ying replied. When Xi Rang gestured toward a seat, Wu Ying nodded, dismissing Yi Ru's slight tightening of lips. This was Wu Ying's table after all. "Thank you for bringing me here."

"It was the least I could do," Xi Rang said. "But I wanted to ask, what are your plans after tonight?"

"I'll be continuing my journey." When the pair looked at him inquisitively, he sighed and added, "To Yi County."

"Really? How coincidental. So am I," Yi Ru said.

"As am I," Xi Rang added. "Would benefactor be willing to journey with us?"

"For free. Of course a cheap, unscrupulous merchant like you who cannot even afford guards would suggest that," Yi Ru said with a sniff. "Cultivator Long, I would be honored if you will allow me to hire you."

"Hire?" Wu Ying said, tilting his head curiously. Not that he would take them up on it. He still needed to make it to the city in time.

"Yes. How about five taels for the journey?" Yi Ru said.

"Five! You call me cheap and offer my benefactor only five tael. I never mentioned money because such a hero would not lower himself to such a thing. But, benefactor, I once came across this pill. Perhaps it could be of use for you," Xi Rang said, pulling forth a small pill bottle. He pushed it toward Wu Ying, who automatically took hold of it but stopped himself from opening it.

Wu Ying left the pill bottle on the table. "This… thank you for your offers. And your kind thoughts. But I fear, I cannot take either request on board. I need to arrive before the twenty-third of this month at Hinma city."

"The twenty-third?" Yi Ru said slowly as he leaned back, a frown tightening on his face. He looked at Wu Ying then sighed, standing. "Well, enjoy the wine.

It is a pity. It would have made the trip safer with a cultivator of your ability, but I will not be traveling to Hinma till later."

"Of course. Thank you for the wine," Wu Ying said with a bow. The action also allowed him to hide the slight quirk of his lips as the merchant abandoned the conversation. Yi Ru was obviously not one to pursue losing conversations.

"Har. Yi Ru is always like that," Xi Rang said as he watched the man walk away. He smirked, shaking his head before he turned back to Wu Ying. "Keep the pill. You saved my life and my servants. It is the least that I can offer."

Wu Ying paused, then nodded and kept the bottle. Rather than insult the man and open it now, he stored it away to check on the contents later. "Thank you then. It seems you and Yi Ru are well acquainted."

"We work the same circuits," Xi Rang said. "Though lately it has grown significantly more dangerous. My wife kept pestering me to hire more guards, but I never got around to it. Remember, always listen to your wife!" Wu Ying offered the older man a strained smile while Xi Rang continued. "As for the ones we hired, they all left, the damn rat bastards, when the rumors started that Ji Ang and his people had stopped raiding the river."

"They did?" Wu Ying said. That was not what he had heard.

"Ever since the merchants started running convoys, the pickings have been slim. Of course it was only a rumor till now," Xi Rang said. "Now all of us on the road will either have to risk running with fewer guards and being attacked or turning around."

Wu Ying winced slightly, sipping on the cup of wine as a tinge of guilt flashed through him. Not that he could protect all the merchants. And if he tried, he would definitely be late. The merchants would travel at the slowest pace. Once again, Wu Ying felt the helplessness of his position, of his inability to alter the world or choose what his heart desired. Once again, he was forced to choose between his own future and the well-being of others.

"Do not worry, young man," Xi Rang said, clapping Wu Ying on the shoulder. "Some things we can only leave to our fate."

Wu Ying looked at the smiling man then nodded. Too true. Some things only the heavens could dictate. It was not his place to choose for Xi Rang or any of the merchants. He could only live the life he had, doing the best he could. To cut short his own journey now for others would be a betrayal of his destiny.

"Come. Let us drink, rejoice at new friends, fateful encounters, and a brighter future tomorrow!" Xi Rang said, waving to the barkeep. "I will order us some good wine."

Dismissing the deep thoughts, Wu Ying gratefully accepted Xi Rang's words. Yes. Drink now, worry tomorrow.

***

Wu Ying set off early the next morning, intent on making up for the lost time yesterday. A part of him worried as well that the bandits would find their boss. Even if he had progressed to another tier in his cultivation, Wu Ying had to admit that his actual martial arts proficiency was not up to par. Only time and practice would take him to the next stage. For a moment, Wu Ying lamented his inability to be a genius—an individual who could glance at a single performance of a form and grasp its fine points. No, Wu Ying was a plodder, someone who could only develop through repetition and hard work.

As he ran, Wu Ying touched the pouch inside his robe. That morning, in the privacy of his room, Wu Ying had had the time to view what he had received from Xi Rang last night. The simple seal that denoted Xi Rang's favor had been quickly viewed and put away. In the future, it might be of use if Wu Ying ever needed the merchant's help. The pill, on the other hand, was surprisingly another Marrow Cleansing pill. This one brought less of a refreshing fragrance, a simple indicator that its quality was lower than the previous one. Of course, Wu Ying knew the real pill-makers, the alchemists, would have better ways of telling the quality. But that was another area of study he had no access to.

Even then, the fact stood that the pill was free—a gift. And a single pill would have cost at least a month's contribution points if Wu Ying had purchased it. Even if the efficacy of the pill was not as high, he would need to consider carefully how best to use it. After further thought and more li, Wu Ying came to a simple conclusion—use it later. The hardest time for a cultivator to progress was not in the beginning but during the process of breaking through to another level. The cleansing process required sufficient chi within an individual's body. However, the process of breaking through was wasteful and spent the gathered chi within a cultivator's dantian like water in a dry field. Rather than use it now, Wu Ying would wait until he was ready to attempt another breakthrough. In that way, he would guarantee his progress and make full use of the gift.

Pill issue settled, Wu Ying settled more comfortably into his run. The only concern for him now was to cover the missed distance, which meant he needed to run one and a half times farther than before this day. That way, he would be able to find a place to camp during the night, letting him skip the expense of staying at a rest stop. Thankfully, the increase in his cultivation had led to a corresponding increase in his physical strength and endurance. As such, the harder pace he was setting was viable.

Once he'd settled into his new running pace Wu Ying turned his attention to his aura. While having a reduced presence had some disadvantages, Wu Ying still felt that practicing the cultivation exercise was important. As he studied the cultivation exercise, Wu Ying further understood some of the implications of its ability. Being able to suppress all information about one's cultivation could provide significant benefits during a fight. Of course, there was some slight concern that such activity could be considered inappropriate for a martial artist—after all, at the apex level, the goal was a complete suppression of his aura, making him effectively invisible to spiritual senses. That was something only an assassin would do.

Then again, Wu Ying chuckled to himself, the idea that he could ever achieve an apex understanding of any cultivation method was inconceivable. He was but a rice farmer from a small village. That kind of training, of ability, was something only the heroes, the geniuses, and the carefully guided members of sage clans could expect.

But at least, Wu Ying thought, he had one thing and that was the discipline, the earth-deep stubbornness that made up the caretakers of the land. Drought, flood, pestilence, and sun, you worked the earth. Day in and day out, because there was no other choice. And so, Wu Ying worked the exercise, trained himself as he ran. Even if he only was half, a quarter as gifted as those heaven-blessed individuals, he could still move forward. And that, in itself, was sufficient.

***

Day. Then night. Then day again. Wu Ying ran, covering li after li of ground, his feet pounding flattened earth, worn cobblestones, and sometimes even wooden planks as he crossed the numerous streams and rivers that dotted the countryside. He covered the ground he needed and made up the lost time. That moment of enlightenment and a single good deed had done wonders for Wu Ying. It would almost make up for the trouble it brought to him right now.

"This the one?" The bandit who asked the question was, surprisingly, small. Barely over five feet tall, he moved with a limber litheness and a predatory grace that set Wu Ying's teeth on edge. Wu Ying also noted that he wielded a jian, as well as the deference the bandit group showed him.

"Yes, leader," a familiar-looking bandit said as he eyed Wu Ying. The last time Wu Ying had seen the bandit, it had been holding on to the merchant's horses. The bandit ex-ambusher sneered at Wu Ying, his lip curling up as his mustache trembled. "He's the one who killed our men."

"*My* men. Which you uselessly got killed," the short man said. "You did well, guessing he'd go ahead."

"Thank you, honored leader Ji Ang," the ex-ambusher said with a relieved smile.

The smile stayed on his face even when the infamous bandit spun around, his sword unsheathing before it slashed across the ex-ambusher's neck. The smile stayed until frantically firing nerves and reality hit and the ex-ambusher staggered backward, clutching at his bleeding neck. The bandit's mouth moved, as if trying to ask why, but no words came from his destroyed throat.

"But you lost my men. After I told you not to take them," Ji Ang said. "Failure after disobeying orders is not acceptable."

Wu Ying watched Ji Ang's ruthless action silently, flicking his gaze around the group that surrounded him. There were easily over twenty bandits, more than enough to deal with a cultivator like him. They had come out of the woods on the trail as he turned a corner, surrounding him before he could escape. Now, all Wu Ying could do was wait with his hand on his sword, hope to take as many as possible if he was forced to fight, and search for a way out.

"Well, now, what do we do now?" Ji Ang walked forward, his eyes raking over Wu Ying's body. "You're not bad. Well built. Decent cultivation." Wu

Ying shifted uncomfortably, waiting. Ji Ang's smile grew wider. "Ah! I have it. I have a newly opened position. Join me."

Wu Ying's jaw fell open slightly, the offer the last thing he had expected. A way out was mildly tempting. When he glanced at the former occupant of the position, what little temptation there was disappeared. Better to die now, honor intact, than at the whims of an insane, corpse-loving bandit. Even Wu Ying knew that the chance of him running away if he agreed to join was highly unlikely. More likely, they would watch him closely and give him a "test" soon after.

As Wu Ying's jaw firmed and he settled into a stance, Ji Ang's smile widened. "I thought so. You cultivators are all the same. Always concerned about your honor. Well then. Die."

At the bandit's command, his men surged into action. Bows which had been pointed at Wu Ying twanged, loosing a trio of arrows at the already moving cultivator. Since there were two bows pointed at him from the right and one on the left, Wu Ying went left. In the time Ji Ang had taken to show off, Wu Ying had pulled his bag off both his shoulders so that he could sling it in front of him as he rushed forward. Stuffed full of hard food, his clothing, bedroll, and his cooking implements, the bag managed to stop the single arrow coming from the left. Of the other two, one missed entirely while a second scored his back, tearing a line of blood.

No time to worry about that as Wu Ying threw the bag at the first bandit that came at him, side-stepping around him as he blocked a spear thrust from another with his forearm. That action brought another spike of pain as skin and cloth tore. Yet Wu Ying refused to slow down, knowing that he stood no chance if he did not break through. Block finished, he stabbed the sword at the bandit's face as he ran pass him, barely scoring his opponent and not caring.

A dao came cutting down, fast and savage. Wu Ying spun out of the way, kicking once he'd finished. The attack threw his new opponent off balance enough that Wu Ying could grab him by his throat and shove him backward. His sword sliced at the bandit's flailing hand, cutting off fingers and forcing the dao to drop aside even as Wu Ying rushed to the edge of the treeline. There might have been twenty bandits in all, but they had circled him at a distance, ensuring there were only a few in any one direction.

"Kill him!" Ji Ang snarled.

Acting on his command, spears lashed out. One caught the hapless bandit in the back, pulling the bandit out of Wu Ying's grip. An axe cut into Wu Ying's side while a dagger halberd cut into his leg. Focused on the archer ahead of him, Wu Ying ignored the injuries as he ran forward. Instinct made him cut upward, catching an arrow that he barely saw release and deflecting it high. Other bows twanged behind him, but a scream of pain from another bandit indicated how successful firing into the melee was for the bandits.

And then Wu Ying was in the trees, running past the archer who threw himself out of the way. Behind, free to shoot at Wu Ying now, the other archers launched more arrows.

"You won't get away," Ji Ang called, anger lacing his voice.

In the distance, Wu Ying heard the man running, the tramp of his feet surprisingly loud even amidst the clatter of weapons, harsh breathing, and grunts of the other bandits.

"I'll try," Wu Ying muttered as he ran, weaving between tree trunks. Thankfully, the same undergrowth that had hidden the bandits so well in their surprise of him proved a blessing for Wu Ying now as the archers fought to see the disappearing cultivator.

As the initial rush of adrenaline faded, Wu Ying felt the pain from his numerous injuries. He gritted his teeth as he ran, feeling his blood fall beside him. He couldn't outrun them all, not injured. But having no other choice, Wu Ying kept going. Behind him, the howls and shouts from the bandits slowly changed from surprise to glee as they began to have fun.

"Come on, boy. Run."

"Oooh, you're bleeding. Bleeding real good."

"You should have stood and fought. Better than to run and die tired."

"Don't worry, we'll give you a head start."

Wu Ying's breathing grew ragged as he grew tired. The pain in his body expanded, encompassing his world even as the bandits behind closed in on him. A stumble sent him sprawling, desperately grasping for something to hold him up even as an arrow flashed overhead to slam into a tree. Pushing with all his might, Wu Ying stood again and staggered forward.

"Almost got him!"

Of course, whether it was true or just another taunting shot, Wu Ying didn't know. Thunder drummed in Wu Ying's ears. Thunder from the labored beating of his heart. Thunder from the footsteps coming for him. Thunder from the falls ahead.

Falls?

Wu Ying's head came up as hope sprang in his chest. It was insane. It was cliché. How many heroes threw themselves from the falls to come back later, stronger than ever? But, perhaps… well. It was better than running aimlessly. Wu Ying found his feet picking up as he angled toward the waterfall. Perhaps knowing what he intended, the bandits sped up behind him.

Faster. Wu Ying ran faster, heading for the loudest parts of the falls. Faster. He could even hear the water running now.

A hand fell on his shoulder, twirling Wu Ying around. Wu Ying reacted automatically, using the spin to lash out with his jian. The light double-edged sword caught the bandit high on his head, tearing off skin and sending him sprawling backward. But not before he planted a knife in Wu Ying's stomach.

Back.

Wu Ying gripped the dagger in his body with one hand, his sword in the other, and turned back around to run. The fleet-footed bandit staggered around, blocking his friends as he screamed. If not for Wu Ying's higher cultivation and their earlier playing, he would have been caught already. But Wu Ying knew he was slowing, slowing.

The water was his only chance, so Wu Ying ran. Another ten feet, then suddenly, he was there. At the banks of the river. The river and the waterfall that crashed down into it, generating the thunder in his ears. With a groan, Wu Ying stumbled forward, realization hitting him. Of course the loudest part of the river was where the falls fell.

Hope disappeared as Wu Ying stared at the water. In the foaming white beneath the waterfall, directly beneath the thundering cascade of liquid, he thought he saw something. But another shout made him turn around to face his assailants. Tired, bleeding, and bereft of hope, Wu Ying raised his weapon. Better to die standing.

"Sorry, Papa. Sorry, Mama."

Chapter 14

The bandits slowly exited the dense undergrowth, no longer feeling the need to run as they cornered the bleeding cultivator. Wu Ying slowly looked across the group, his chest heaving as he sucked in air and his blood slowly mixed with the water lapping in the river.

"Finished running, have you?" Ji Ang said when he sauntered over. "I told you there was nowhere to go."

"Leader! He blinded my brother. I ask that you let me kill him," a particularly tall and gangly bandit snarled, showing the hooked sword that he held. "I'll kill him slow for making us run."

"You're not his match, Ko Yan," Ji Ang said, shaking his head. "I'll finish him myself."

"No! He hurt my brother. I will kill him," Ko Yan said, moving forward with a snarl.

Ji Ang rolled his eyes and flicked his hands, allowing the other bandit to go forward.

Ko Yan grinned as he stalked forward, leering at Wu Ying. "I'm going to make you hurt and cry."

"You said that already," Wu Ying said softly. "At least your brother was better at getting things done. When he could see."

The goading worked, making Ko Yan rush forward, his sword rising above his head. Wu Ying waited, watching, then moved, his sword speeding forward as he used the Sword's Truth. The strike took Ko Yan in the throat, tearing through cartilage and bone and nearly decapitating the man. The next moment, as Wu Ying's weight came fully down on his leg, the cultivator stumbled, nearly falling from a sudden lack of strength. He pushed himself upward with the help of his sword, his head spinning.

"One more," Wu Ying breathed, offering the group a bloody smile.

"I told him," Ji Ang said with a roll of his eyes. He raised his jian before he shook his head. "Let's end this farce. Archers!"

Wu Ying blinked, straightening and trying to gauge the distance between him and the rest of the bandits. Too far. Even as the creak of bows being drawn reached his ears, he desperately considered his options. The dagger. If he pulled and threw it, perhaps…

"Who dares disturb me?" The voice roared through the riverbank, making pebbles dance and leaves shake.

An arrow, newly drawn, accidentally loosed into the ground. The group froze as a suffocating pressure enveloped them.

"What… who is that?" one of the bandits blathered, his hands shaking so badly he could barely hold his spear.

"Senior! I did not see you there. I apologize," Ji Ang quickly recovered, bowing to the speaker behind Wu Ying.

Taking a gamble, Wu Ying turned his head carefully to look behind him and caught a glimpse of the speaker. A vivid-blue-and-white-robed man with a long, lustrous beard strode out from underneath the waterfall. As he walked lightly on the churning water, steam rose from his body as the water that soaked him evaporated.

"Your killing intent has disturbed my cultivation. How dare you bring your petty squabbles here?" the cultivator snarled.

Even tired as he was, Wu Ying could tell that the presence of this cultivator was far above any of them. He reminded Wu Ying of the senior Elders in his sect, those who had formed their cores. In other words, they were but bugs to the waterfall cultivator.

"We did not know Senior was using this waterfall. We would not have dared follow that cultivator here otherwise," Ji Ang said, quick to push the blame onto Wu Ying.

"I... I was trying to get away, Senior." Wu Ying wanted to raise his voice, to speak stronger, but he was finding it hard to even stay standing and conscious.

"Go. All of you. This one is about to die as it stands. And your killing intent is disturbing me," the Senior said, looking between the group.

"But we have to kill him!"

There was no warning, no indication, just a twitch of a hand, and suddenly a spray of water flung itself at such speed that it tore apart the speaking bandit. The attack left a bloody mess and torn leaves behind, covering those bandits who stood beside the outspoken bandit with blood and viscera.

"Our apologies, Senior. You are correct. We will leave now," Ji Ang said and bowed, waving his group back. He glared at Wu Ying, who could only offer a bloody smile before Ji Ang turned around.

As they left, Wu Ying slumped to the ground, willpower finally running out.

"I would begin cultivating once you've drawn out that dagger and bandaged your wounds. If you survive, that would be your fate," the core cultivator said, almost disinterestedly.

Wu Ying turned to stare as the man walked back toward the waterfall. "Thank you, Senior."

Receiving no reply, Wu Ying began the slow process of bandaging his wounds. He started with the ones that were easy to get to, doing his best not to jar the dagger in his stomach. When he was finally ready, having torn apart his clothing for bandages, he gritted his teeth. Gripping the dagger tightly, he pulled it out with a surge of strength then stuffed the cloth around the newly revealed wound. Not daring to disturb the Senior, he had gagged himself beforehand, so his cries were muffled. As he fell over from the pain, Wu Ying blanked out, only coming to minutes later.

Blood. So much blood lost. And his body still bleeding. Worse, Wu Ying knew that he had internal damage—muscles, veins, and innards torn apart from the jostling knife. Only the fact that the knife had been mostly blunt at the edges—more a shiv than a knife—had saved Wu Ying from receiving even more damage. Still, Wu Ying knew from his previous experience that infection would come soon.

There was but one solution. If he could cultivate and cultivate well, he could drive the impurities and the infections out from his body, keeping it clean and clear. To do that though, he would need a lot of chi. Grasping within his robe, Wu Ying levered himself to a sitting position and popped open the pill bottle.

One chance.

Wu Ying was exhausted, in pain from his injuries, and woozy from blood loss. Even with the pill, Wu Ying knew his chances of success were low. There was one way—to overdraft his chi from his dantian. To use it all, not leaving a single ounce in reserve. If it worked, he would break through the next level and heal a significant portion of the damage. If he failed, he would die on the spot.

Wu Ying swallowed the pill and waited in lotus position. In seconds, he felt the warmth from the pill enter his stomach, pulsing through his body as it drew power toward him. The tendrils of chi it sent through him made Wu Ying grit his teeth as it woke up his wounds. For a moment, his concentration wavered, then Wu Ying pushed the pain aside with a surge of will. His entire focus drew down deep into his torso, into his dantian, as he worked to collect the chi surging through his body.

First step, collect the chi, letting it run through his current meridians as needed, but mostly keeping the majority swirling within. Keep drawing the power in, from both the surroundings and the pill. The water, flowing a short distance away, refreshed the chi in the surroundings constantly and improved the flow of chi much the same way his movement-based cultivation did. It was part of the reason why cultivating in such locations was so common.

Wu Ying drew upon this external chi as well as the chi from the Marrow Cleansing pill, letting it swirl around the core of his dantian. He felt his dantian strain as it battled to handle all the new pressure. Pain radiated from Wu Ying's wounds, nibbling at the edges of his consciousness even as Wu Ying struggled to keep the energy together. Wu Ying knew he was taking part in a careful balancing act—pull in as much chi as he could hold and channel before he lost his concentration entirely, before he lost consciousness. Eyes closed, darkness wreathed his inner world, nibbling at the edges of his mind. Slowly, Wu Ying felt his consciousness fade.

Time.

He set loose the energy, where it thundered down his meridians. The chi forced them open, burning his nerves and deep in his body as chi ran rampant through it. He plunged deep into his dantian and forced the energy out, pushing and shoving at the pool as he emptied it. It felt as if he was inverting the pool of chi within his body, blocking the flow of chi back to it even as he poured out the remaining energy. The pain increased as the energy, unable to move freely, burnt him from within.

Wu Ying coughed once then again, blood flying from his lips as blood vessels within him broke. Blood dripped from his nose, delicate vessels torn asunder. Wounds that had stopped bleeding broke open again, vicious black and green sludge mixing with his heart's blood. Pain, so much pain that Wu Ying was in no danger of losing consciousness now, consumed him. But perhaps because it was so great, it stopped mattering.

Now.

He released his grip on his dantian, allowing the chi to flow again. It thundered back into the center of his stomach, pounding the walls of the container, and it was all that Wu Ying could do to hold it together. As more flooded in, Wu Ying worked to guide the chi out, restoring the circulation circuit. Seven meridians now thrummed with power, though even Wu Ying could tell that the seventh's was barely broken open. Insufficient chi to properly facilitate its use.

But with seven open meridians, his body was healing and fixing itself at a rate that was more than ten times the speed of a non-cultivator. Infection that had threatened to take root was pushed out, burnt away by the chi that soared through his body, while his wounds slowly scabbed over. In the blink of an eye, the Meridian Opening pill was used up and his body's acupuncture points opened, sucking down chi as fast as they could. Without thinking, Wu Ying let his hand dip into the water nearby and sipped water from a cupped hand to replace his lost fluids. The entire movement was unconscious, driven purely by instinct.

Under the waterfall, where water pounded his body, strengthening it and drawing additional chi toward him, the core cultivator sat. An eye cracked open, staring briefly at Wu Ying's silent figure before it closed again, and the lightest traces of a crooked smile crossed the cultivator's face.

Under the pounding thunder of the waterfall, the gurgling brook, and softly swaying leaves, the pair of cultivators sat, drawing in the world's chi as they grew stronger.

***

When Wu Ying finally consciously opened his eyes, days had passed. Cultivation, true cultivation, always passed in the blink of an eye. For powerful core cultivators and beyond, cultivation could easily take months or years. At that stage, the cultivator was not only processing additional chi but also the insights, the minor moments of enlightenment that the cultivator had accumulated. For those advanced cultivators, the chi they drew in was more than sufficient to sustain their bodies.

Wu Ying was nowhere close to that stage, and by now, his body had processed all the normal stores of energy. If he continued cultivating, he would seriously hamper his body's healing as it took even more resources from his body, eating away flesh and nerves. For now at least, his body had patched over the majority of his wounds.

"Thank you, Senior, for your earlier help and for letting me stay," Wu Ying said as he stood. When he finished speaking, Wu Ying bowed low in the direction of the waterfall.

If the senior cultivator had not intervened, Wu Ying would have died for certain. Even then, he almost did. A part of Wu Ying wondered why, but he dismissed the question. Whether it was completely altruistic or there was another reason, Wu Ying would pay the debt when needed.

Having paid observance to formal courtesy, Wu Ying walked farther down the river. During his flight, Wu Ying had lost his pack. His clothes were torn, tattered, and blood-stained. Not that the peasant tunics he wore were a great loss, but without his sect robes that were in his pack, he had nothing to change into. Rather than walk through the woods with blood-stained robes, Wu Ying decided to move downstream before he attempted to wash himself clean. In that way, he would not be disturbing the senior. Or at least, he hoped so.

There was, of course, a certain amount of hesitation in leaving the vicinity of his erstwhile protector. He had no guarantee Ji Ang was not waiting for him to do that very thing. Then again, Wu Ying also dared not stay too long and potentially anger his benefactor. Better to leave and risk being attacked again.

Still, Wu Ying cautiously checked the forest edges and the surroundings before he waded into the water to wash and find a meal.

An hour later, Wu Ying had a fire and just under half a dozen fish roasting on sticks. He was looking at the food impatiently, his stomach growling at even the hint of freshly cooked fish. Thankfully, the fish in this particular river were both trusting and nowhere near fast enough to avoid the cultivator. Even so, the light exercise of catching his meal had informed Wu Ying that his wounds were still in need of healing. At least in this life-and-death battle, he had come out ahead.

As fat sizzled and dropped onto the fire once again, Wu Ying lightly poked the edge of the fish with a whittled stick, watching as the wood slipped into the cooked flesh with ease. Lips pulled wide into a grin, Wu Ying took the fish off the fire and placed them on a washed, flat rock.

"That smells good."

The words made Wu Ying jump, a hand dropping toward his sword before invoked memory told him who the speaker was.

"Benefactor." Wu Ying bowed to the senior cultivator, dropping his hand away from his sword. That the cultivator had managed to sneak up on Wu Ying was not surprising, if somewhat ego busting. "I'd be honored if you joined me."

"I will," the cultivator said, sitting down and taking the proffered stick of fish.

In silence, the pair ate, Wu Ying's aching stomach only slightly mollified by the tender white flesh. That he had to give the majority of the fish to his benefactor was painful.

"Thank you for the meal. I am Dun Yuan Rang," Yuan Rang said finally.

"A pleasure to meet you, Senior Dun. Long Wu Ying at your service," Wu Ying said with a slight bow of his head.

"You have interesting enemies, Wu Ying," Yuan Rang said.

As Wu Ying flushed and opened his mouth to protest, his stomach rumbled again. "My apologies!" Wu Ying bowed immediately.

"It seems I have taken your lunch." Yuan Rang stood then looked at the water before he shook his hand. A sword dropped into it, seeming to appear from nowhere.

Wu Ying's eyes widened as he realized that Yuan Rang carried a storage ring—an enchanted object that could store objects in a hidden space. Wu Ying had heard of them in tall tales spoken of cultivators, but had never expected to see one in use himself.

As Wu Ying was getting over his surprise, Yuan Rang drew his sword from its scabbard. A gentle flick of his hand made the sword dart out and plunge into the water. Finger held before his face, Yuan Rang swirled it around for a few moments before he jerked the fingers back to himself. Following his gestures, the sword flashed back out of the river to land in Yuan Rang's hand. On the sword, still wriggling slightly, were seven large and exquisite-looking river carp.

"Here." Yuan Rang gestured as he dropped the carp onto the stone Wu Ying had used. He also absently tossed a small pack on the ground. "Salt."

After thanking Yuan Rang, Wu Ying quickly cleaned, gutted, and pierced the fish before setting them around the fire. Yuan Rang stood a short distance away, staring at the flowing water without moving.

"Come," Yuan Rang called to Wu Ying when he was done and had washed his hands clean of the offal.

"Yes, Senior?" Wu Ying said, trotting over obediently.

"You practice the Long family jian style and are at the seventh layer of Body Cleansing, yes?" Yuan Rang said.

"Yes, Senior." Wu Ying was not surprised that his secrets were exposed—his attack, his cultivation, it had all been in the presence of this Elder.

"Good. I will suppress my cultivation to your level then," Yuan Rang said and walked a short distance away.

When he turned back, he had drawn his jian, the scabbard disappearing into his storage ring. Yuan Rang's breathing slowed down and an unseen pressure faded as his breathing evened out. Even Wu Ying could tell that Yuan Rang had actually done as he had said he would.

"Senior?" Wu Ying said, puzzled. Still, with a naked sword pointed at him, Wu Ying automatically drew his own. Against such a strong opponent, a draw strike would be too slow.

"I have been contemplating a new martial skill for my jian. It is time that I tested it out," Yuan Rang said. "Try not to die too fast."

Wu Ying's eyes widened as he raised his sword to block the sudden lunge. Even with his cultivation suppressed, Yuan Rang was blindingly fast, the lunge he had used covering the ground between them in a blink of an eye. Wu Ying stumbled backward, his back foot spraying pebbles as he finally regained his footing. His left hand landed on his right, steadying it and stopping the shaking in his weapon's blade even as the ache in Wu Ying's hand subsided. A single strike and Wu Ying had almost lost his jian and his head.

"Decent. But you have not achieved the Sense of the Sword fully yet, have you?" Even as he spoke, Yuan Rang circled Wu Ying, his sword lazily dipping and circling.

"No, Senior," Wu Ying said as he automatically moved in the same direction as Yuan Rang, keeping the distance open with the footwork he had learnt. The Sense of the Sword was the first true level of understanding the sword—or any weapon really.

At the most basic level, anyone could use a sword by picking it up. But at that stage, most users saw the sword as a tool—a powerful, deadly, sharp tool. But they would not be able to use it to the full extent and would, in effect, treat the jian in their hand the same as they would a dao or a hooked sword or even an axe.

Those who used a jian long enough—or any weapon—would gain a Sense of the weapon. Not just its weight and reach, though obviously that was important, but an understanding about the jian as a weapon. Its advantages and disadvantages compared to other weapons, the most common attacks for the weapon and its true benefits. At this stage, minute differences in each weapon no longer bothered the wielder. The next level was the Heart of the Sword, where a wielder no longer felt the sword was a weapon, an external tool, but a portion of their body. As for the reputed Soul of the sword, the wielder would no longer need a jian to replicate the weapon itself.

"Long family jian style. And some other footwork." Yuan Rang hummed then smiled thinly. "Let us find out."

Once again, Yuan Rang crossed the distance between them in a second, his sword flashing. Wu Ying met the attack as quickly as he could, battling the stronger opponent with everything that he had. Yet deep within, Wu Ying knew he was going to lose. Even with his cultivation suppressed, Yuan Rang's body was strengthened significantly through the cleansing and opening of all his major meridians. On top of that, Yuan Rang was at least at the Heart of the Sword. Even his own father had barely touched the edges of that realm.

In a half dozen more blows, Wu Ying knew with sick certainty that Yuan Rang was holding back. And not just a little. In his fight with Yin Xue, Wu Ying had known that Yin Xue had achieved the Sense of the Sword already. Even so, Wu Ying had had the feeling he was only slightly behind the other, close enough to see Yin Xue's back. A figure he could reach, if he practiced hard enough.

Yuan Rang was a peak that he could not see. His skill and understanding of the jian, the esoteric movements of his blade and the casual strength each of his blows generated sent Wu Ying constantly stumbling back. In those half dozen blows, Wu Ying was certain that Yuan Rang was actually fighting outside the "normal" distance his style specialized in.

All this thinking came at a cost, as Wu Ying quickly found out. Another block, a quick wrist twist, and his sword flew from his hand, leaving Yan Rang's jian resting against the hollow of his throat.

"Eight passes," Yuan Rang said, shaking his head. "Pitiful. Pick up your sword. Let us begin again. Try to last until the fish are ready."

"Senior." Wu Ying bowed and scrambled to grab his fallen sword. He quickly checked it over before Wu Ying turned and took his guard again.

"If you do not improve, I cannot actually test my move properly," Yuan Rang said scornfully. "Do try not to disappoint me again."

"Yes, Senior."

Yuan Rang's only answer was a thrust, and the ring of blades once more erupted in the clearing.

***

It was late afternoon when the nearly non-stop sparring came to an end. If not for the frequent breaks that Yuan Rang allowed for eating and prepping and cooking more fish, Wu Ying was certain he would have fallen over already. The constant pressure of battle, the fast tempo of the fight, and the unceasing routine had combined to tire out Wu Ying's mind, relaxing the tight control he had placed on his moving cultivation. Unconsciously, Wu Ying had begun to cultivate while moving and fighting. Not a lot, and it only helped boost his fighting ability a little while drawing in just a touch more chi than normal. Yet that was not the only gain Wu Ying received in the hours of sparring.

His Sense of the Sword had grown, expanding in leaps and bounds such that his initially shaky grasp of the Sense of the Sword had firmed and progressed. Wu Ying knew that he had reached a greater mastery of the sword and had perhaps even touched the peak mastery of the Sense. In effect, Wu Ying from now on would be able to pick up any jian and, within moments, use the weapon well—perhaps not to the peak of its ability but close to it. In a fight where inches and micro-seconds counted, Wu Ying would intuitively understand both the weight, heft, and strength required to wield the weapon.

"Rest and cultivate. We will fight one last time after that," Yuan Rang said sternly.

Wu Ying's eyes widened before he slowly nodded and went over to the water's edge to do as ordered. As he cultivated, Wu Ying considered Yuan Rang's style. Over the course of the afternoon, Yuan Rang had slowly exposed more and more of his native form, rather than using generic strikes that pressed Wu Ying. As such, Wu Ying now had a much broader understanding of Yuan Rang's style. Yuan Rang fought upright, often staying within his opponent's measure and using quick wrist motions to block attacks and land blindingly fast wrist cuts. When an opponent pulled back or left an opening, Yuan Rang would step forward in quick, fast lunges whose target shifted positions at the last moment. In effect, Yuan Rang's was similar to the Long family style, though it used less footwork to create openings, instead relying on flexible wrists and arms and a high level of perception.

Of course, Wu Ying knew that what he was seeing was only a shallow depth to the style. It was obvious that the style and its usages changed when chi was projected through the weapon. As Yuan Rang was suppressing his cultivation,

Wu Ying knew he would not have a chance to experience that particular portion of the style yet. For which he was extremely grateful.

"Ready?"

"Yes, Senior," Wu Ying said and stood.

Wu Ying looked down at his sword, grimacing slightly. Truthfully, he would have preferred a few more minutes to work out some of the chips in the sword, bring back its sharpness. But Yuan Rang was not really asking, so Wu Ying set himself for another round of sparring.

The moment their blades clashed, Wu Ying knew this time was different. The speed that Yuan Rang was moving, the certainty in his attacks gave hint that this time, he was serious. For the first time, Wu Ying had a glimmer of understanding of why Yuan Rang had spent time sparring with him earlier. If Yuan Rang had unleashed his full potential at the start of the day, Wu Ying would not have even managed to last three passes.

As the pair fought, blood blossomed around Wu Ying. Lunges and light cuts scored his body. His already tattered tunic became even more frayed, his shirt finally giving way to reveal his slim, muscled, and bloody torso. Again and again, Wu Ying had to sacrifice portions of his body to light cuts to avoid exposing himself to deeper, more dangerous follow-ups. That was Yuan Rang's style—forcing the opponent to either choose to block quick attacks at the edges or to swing too wide, block too hard, and open oneself to a lethal strike.

Wu Ying's breathing grew ragged, his eyes squinting hard as his view of the world shrank to the tip of the jian, the edge of the blade, and the tap of feet on soil. There was no conscious realization, no particular action that Wu Ying could point to, but suddenly, he knew. Throwing himself backward, Wu Ying desperately brought his sword sweeping across his chest and face even as Yuan Rang exploded into a blindingly fast lunge. Flat of the sword directed toward

Yuan Rang, Wu Ying adjusted the angle ever so slightly as Yuan Rang dropped the tip of his jian, the point directly aimed at Wu Ying's heart.

Wu Ying sacrificed the flat of his blade to protect his heart, placing his palm to reinforce the weapon even as the explosive attack smashed the jian into Wu Ying's chest. The pair flew backward, crossing half the lake before the explosive impetus of Yuan Rang's attack faded, sending Wu Ying's body continuing to fly across the river and smash into the other bank. The senior cultivator landed on the raging waters, tapping on the water lightly to fly backward to the dry shore. With a dismissive wave, Yuan Rang shook out his sword and returned it to his sheath.

"Minor achievement. I have a long journey yet," Yuan Rang muttered, disappointment clear on his face. He turned away, not even offering Wu Ying's prone form a second glance before he took off running across the treetops.

On the other bank, Wu Ying lay still and unmoving until a cough erupted from his chest. Groaning with pain, Wu Ying rolled over as the shattered remnants of his blade fell to the ground. Shaky fingers moved toward his chest and tugged at the shards of metal that had embedded in his chest. Wu Ying stared at the remnants of his weapon. If he had not blocked the attack with the flat of his blade… The sheer strength of that attack…

Too tired to take in the implications, Wu Ying let his head fall back onto the ground and stared at the slowly darkening night. Drawing a deep breath, Wu Ying decided to once again cultivate and heal his newly gained wounds. This constant abuse of his body, healing and being injured, was bound to leave him with scars. Once again, Wu Ying chuckled. Good thing he was no precious scholar.

Chapter 15

As the morning sun greeted Wu Ying two days later, he stood up from his cultivation. Clad only in tattered pants and dried blood, Wu Ying made his way into the river to wash and find some breakfast. It did not take him long to start a fire, his flint always stored in his coin pouch. A peasant's wisdom that, but one that stood him in good stead. Thankfully, the summer weather meant that even the evenings were nicely warm.

As Wu Ying supped on his breakfast, he stared at the map and sighed. The map was relatively barren of the geographic features, but at a guess, Wu Ying had two choices from his current position. Head back to the road and follow it, risking the possibility of running into Ji Ang and his bandits again. Or strike out through the wilderness. Though he might save some distance, the direct route was also more arduous and dangerous. While there might be fewer monsters that lay in wait, there would definitely be more powerful spirit creatures in the hinterlands.

On top of that, Wu Ying knew that he was late. Not actually late yet, but he had spent too long cultivating and healing. Even if he used the road, he wouldn't make it on time. Even so, Wu Ying was determined to at least try. Perhaps some other purchasers had been delayed or dissuaded due to the increased danger.

"Through the woods," Wu Ying finally said to himself.

Going by the road made little sense. He was almost certain Ji Ang would be waiting for him there. Or if not the bandit leader himself, his people. Better to cut through the backcountry. But before he left, Wu Ying took the time to cut down a couple of bamboo shoots and sharpen their edges with the remnants of the sword. Even though it was broken, Wu Ying took the sword and its remnants in his scabbard. Perhaps a good blacksmith might be able to fix it.

Decisions made and now armed, if not dressed, Wu Ying took off at a slow jog through the woods, away from the river. Thankfully, he had enough backwoods knowledge to guide himself in a mostly straight line. With the way roads worked in the surroundings, he was sure to hit another one if he kept going in the same direction.

As he ran and worked on suppressing his new cultivation level, Wu Ying also found time to muse about his most recent experience. Yuan Rang was a bit of an enigma. While it was obvious that Wu Ying had been used as a sparring partner, Yuan Rang did not necessarily need to use a beginner like him. If Yuan Rang had been willing to wait even a day, he could have visited any city and found a martial arts school or arena to do the same.

Then again, Wu Ying mused, Yuan Rang might be a lone wanderer. They were common—independent cultivators who had no sect or school to back them. They were rumored to be extremely paranoid about showing their cultivation and martial secrets to others. The use of an arena or even challenging a school would be public matter, no matter what was promised. In the end, rumors would circulate. Picking on Wu Ying was safer. And if Wu Ying had failed to sacrifice his sword, Yuan Rang would have been guaranteed to end any talk about his style.

Which, Wu Ying wondered, led to the question of why Yuan Rang had not ended his life when the attack failed. He had no doubt Yuan Rang knew he had survived. Was it, like his sponsor in the sect, a belief in fate? Certainly his earlier actions when he saved Wu Ying from Ji Ang had indicated the same. Then again...

Then again, perhaps Yuan Rang did not care. Wu Ying had already angered the bandits, had been grossly injured, and in the end, was only a Body

Cultivator. What could a novice cultivator like him actually understand of Yuan Rang's style, of his final attack?

Lips pursed, Wu Ying considered the question, replaying the last fight in his mind. Yes, what could he learn from it?

***

The green spirit snake lunged, and only a swift side step and a cross-body block with his improvised spear kept Wu Ying safe. Emerald scales and a slitted yellow eye the size of a dinner plate passed by inches from Wu Ying. The snake had overgrown its normal brethren, being nearly as wide as an oxen and easily thirty feet long. The creature had attempted to ambush Wu Ying and had only managed to spike itself on a spear, forcing this intense battle.

Moving too fast to stop, the snake smashed into a tree, shaking the boughs and sending a cascade of leaves and fruit falling. For a moment, the snake stopped, dazed. Wu Ying snarled, spinning the spear and jumping high before thrusting forward as he fell, using the combined weight and thrust to punch the sharpened edge of his spear into the snake's body. As the spear sank through meaty flesh, Wu Ying felt the momentum of his fall halt for a second.

Previous passes with the snake had already informed Wu Ying that that was the only way to pierce the monster's tough scales. Perhaps if Wu Ying had a proper spear, he would have more options. Thankfully, the spot he had targeted had been scraped a little raw after repeated strikes, leaving the sharpened tip to plunge into the meat.

The next few minutes involved the most terrifying ride of Wu Ying's life as the snake bucked, twisted, and attempted to throw Wu Ying off even as he worked the spear deeper. Eventually, the bamboo shattered, leaving a gaping wound that bled profusely while throwing Wu Ying off.

After that, it was only a matter of running and hiding until the snake grew bored enough to leave. When Wu Ying finally found the monster again, it had laid down to rest and was easy prey. If not for the fact that the snake had left in the same direction Wu Ying was traveling and his want and need for a spirit stone and meat for dinner, he probably would have let it go. After all, he had let off a couple of other monsters thus far.

Or been let off. Thankfully, the higher-level spirit beasts were happy to do the calculation of damage and survivability. As they gained greater strength, they also gained greater sentience and understanding. Trading his death for damage that might leave them prey for other spirit beasts was a bad trade, and so after testing him, most left.

Having finished skinning the snake, Wu Ying cut off a large portion of the meat, placed it in the skin, and tied off the ends to form a bundle. Wu Ying glanced once more at the beast before pulling out the fangs. The green snake wasn't venomous, but its fangs would make a nice tip for a new spear. Wu Ying briefly debated then resolved the debate by placing down the meat and lashing together a makeshift spear, one tipped with the snake's fang. Having finished his hasty construction, Wu Ying replaced his broken sword in its scabbard and took up the bundle before jogging away. Better to leave before any scavenger decided to fight him for the remains.

It was a good thing that most powerful spirit beasts had little interest in humanity and were, naturally, cautious. Wu Ying could imagine the kind of calamity a spirit beast that had developed a core could bring to a small village like his. In fact, the occasional story that surfaced of such a tragedy, of near total destruction of entire villages before the local army or lord put a stop to it, was enough. Whether it was a five-starred brown bear or a blood-mist red deer, those animals were generally content to grow and seek enlightenment in the depths of the forest. After all, their road to enlightenment and cultivation was different from humanity's. Their dao, at the end, was constrained by their nature. And while some might find enlightenment and grow to be like humanity, few would transcend if they followed that path. As such, it was safer and better to follow the dao of nature.

Of course, that did not necessarily hold true for demon spirits. Among the many lectures that Wu Ying had managed to attend in the sect, one had discussed the classification of demon beasts. At the simplest—and most common—level, demon beasts were spirit beasts that attacked humans. Of course, that inadvertently lumped predator spirit beasts in with "demon beasts," though those beasts were not necessarily directly antagonistic against humans. They would hunt and eat humans if they were sufficiently weak, but no more than any other predator would.

Real demon beasts were different. There were two major kinds. The first were native demon beasts, creatures whose core had been tainted by poisons or toxins or had acquired demonic characteristics due to influence from the demon plane. In rare cases, the most powerful spirit- and dao-seeking monsters might even have followed a demonic dao. The second kind were actual demons from the demon planes. Those were much rarer, since breaches between the planes were major incidences and something the sects and the government watched out for.

As such, while attacks in the deep backcountry happened, the attacks were less frequent—though more dangerous.

***

Nearly three days. Two of which were spent in the backcountry and half of the other traveling on the blessed road Wu Ying had finally stumbled upon. That he even managed to trade one of the smaller demon cores he had collected for clothing and a bag was fortunate, in his view. Of course, on a pure value basis, he had been cheated to the high heavens, but when you were wandering around the countryside with nothing but a pair of ragged shorts, a sword, a coin purse, and a roll of snakeskin filled with spirit beast meat, well, value changed.

Perhaps that was the truth of things, Wu Ying mused. The world that each person saw was but a shadow of the truth, one that changed as the illumination cast by their enlightenment changed. Each individual was a seer of shadows, a blind man groping his way through a fully lit room.

And if so, what was enlightenment? Was his own understanding of the world but a candle in the darkness, an insensitive fist wrapped around a cornerstone of the world? Perhaps that was why no one grasped the Greater Dao of the universe and looked for the smaller daos when seeking enlightenment. Because it was impossible for the human soul to understand anything but a small portion of the universe. And so, cultivators sought the smaller daos of the sword, of fire or water, or the virtues.

Thoughts like this were in some ways too early for a cultivator like him, having just left the starting line with the marathon finishing line of cultivation so many li away. But at the next stage, when he started cultivating an energy-gathering method, he would need to consider this deeply. He'd heard a few apocryphal stories of those who had found themselves following an elemental dao then learned, too late, they were unable to progress further due to their cultivation. Some shattered their cultivation, devolving to the start, to begin again. Most such unfortunate souls found themselves stymied, unable to truly ascend.

No. If he were to search for a dao that would suit him, he should start thinking now, Wu Ying determined. At the very least, he should consult a sage or two if possible, and at the worse, an Elder. Their guidance could help forestall any issues in his cultivation.

All that, of course, was dependent on Wu Ying actually avoiding being thrown out of the sect. Which, considering he was now two days late to the sale of the plum blossom wine, was not looking good. Staring at the city gates, Wu Ying sighed. Dressed in peasant clothing, with his cultivation suppressed, he had been waiting in line for the last hour in an attempt to enter the city.

Hinma was one of the larger cities Wu Ying had ever visited, the town walls that surrounded the city four times his height. From idle conversations with those waiting with him, Wu Ying had learned that these were the outer walls. A set of inner, older walls separated the old city from the new. And of course, in the center of the city, the magistrate's administrative center and mansion was located. At each barrier, another set of security checks were conducted. And of course, the entrance fee was taken.

Even so, as a city established at the confluence of a pair of rivers, Hinma had more than sufficient traffic. It was why Wu Ying was still waiting for his turn to enter. He knew that if he showed off his sect stamp, he would likely be able to bypass the queue, but he still found it a bit strange to do so. Never mind the fact that he was actually enjoying his conversations with the commoners around him. Talk about the city interspersed with gossip about locals brought a nostalgic pang. But eventually, all good things had to come to an end.

"Number in the party?" the guard asked, his voice laced with boredom.

"Just one, sir," Wu Ying said.

"Five coins."

"Of course." Wu Ying bobbed his head and handed over the round coins with their centers cut out in squares.

When the guard gestured him through, Wu Ying walked in blithely.

"Wait!"

Wu Ying stopped, frowning as he turned toward the speaker. Standing just inside, overseeing the group, the guard lieutenant raked his eyes over Wu Ying's form before stopping at the bag slung over the cultivator's shoulder.

"What's in that bag?"

"My bag? An extra set of clothing, my provisions, and a bedroll." At the lieutenant's loud harrumph, Wu Ying swung the bag around toward the guard. As he did so, he noticed that the flaps had fallen open, showcasing his major treasure as well. "Ah, some snakeskin from a green spirit snake I encountered."

"I thought that was what it was," the guard lieutenant said with a sniff. His voice was filled with haughty disdain as he walked forward to tug open Wu Ying's bag without asking. "I want this."

"Uhh…" Wu Ying said, startled by the sudden change.

"Come. Show me the quality. I'll give you a good price," the lieutenant said again.

"This, I, well…" Wu Ying took a deep breath before gesturing around him. "Perhaps somewhere more private?"

The lieutenant took a quick look around before he nodded firmly and gestured for Wu Ying to enter the guardhouse. Soon enough, the roll of scales and skin that Wu Ying had harvested was laid out on the table within. The few guards clustered within on their break had gathered around too, whispering among themselves.

"Look at the size of those scales!"

"Beautiful. The shimmer is amazing."

"Perfect. Must be the choicest cut."

"Where is the rest of the skin?" the lieutenant asked as he stared at the roll.

There was enough there to make a full tunic. Maybe even a pair of gloves on top of that, if the armorer was skilled and wasted little. But with his experienced eye, the lieutenant could guess at the size of the creature. The amount showcased here was miniscule.

"Left behind," Wu Ying said with a shrug. It hurt his coin purse to think about the waste, but he had not had either the time to do a full skinning job nor the ability to carry all of it even if he did.

"What a waste," the lieutenant said. "Is it close?"

"No," Wu Ying said, shaking his head. "It's likely all eaten and damaged by now."

"Truly a waste. I, Lieutenant Tung Zhong Shei, will buy this for twenty taels," the lieutenant said, finally getting around to introducing himself.

"Twenty!" The other soldiers gasped at the lavish display of wealth. After all, they each only earned about five taels a month—and that had to cover all their expenses.

"That's very generous," Wu Ying said, his hand lightly tracing the skin.

It was a superb piece of material and would, once worked, provide significant coverage and protection. The scales of a spirit beast were high quality material and would provide great protection while being extremely flexible, a must for martial artists. It, of course, helped that the material itself was beautiful as well, with rippling shades of emerald and seafoam green.

Even though Wu Ying had taken the time to stretch the hide out and secure it using broken branches and salt on the inside, if it had been a normal animal, the skin would have been ruined by now. Luckily, spirit beasts were filled with qi, including their bodies, allowing a greater level of abuse in their preservation. Still, Wu Ying knew that Zhong Shei was being somewhat of a spendthrift. Yet the man's family name was very familiar.

"But…"

"Twenty-five." Zhong Shei upped the price without hesitation.

"It's not the price, honored Lieutenant," Wu Ying said. "I just arrived at the city and have yet to get my bearings."

"Do you doubt that I am offering you a better price than any *merchant* would?" Zhong Shei said with scorn.

"I meant nothing like that. I came to the city to purchase the famed Three Stone Plum Blossom Wine," Wu Ying said hurriedly before the lieutenant grew any angrier. The man could easily "confiscate" the skin if he was pushed too far. "But because I'm late, I fear there might be no more. If there isn't, I was hoping to trade this with someone."

"Wine, wine, wine!" Zhong Shei sounded exasperated. "It's always about the wine. You know this city is known for more than just wine? We have some of the best pottery in the country. Master Wu's paintings are reaching spirit-awakening levels. But all you cultivators care about is the wine."

"My apologies, honored Lieutenant, but it is a request from an Elder in my sect," Wu Ying said, deciding to reveal his affiliation. While he did not want to use it to get into the city, this seemed like a good time to do so, especially if his initial guess was right.

"Another greedy Elder," Zhong Shei said. "Fine. The wine sells for one tael per jar. Right now, they're sold out, so the aftermarket price is about five tael— if you can find someone to sell them. I can release a total of three to you though. Is that sufficient?"

Wu Ying blinked, the entire matter moving slightly faster than he had expected. While he had guessed from Zhong Shei's family name that he might be connected to the wine producer, he had never thought that Zhong Shei would be able to sell him the wine directly. At most, Wu Ying had expected an introduction, a door opened. Now, he had to decide how desperate he was to get the wine. Returning without the wine was almost a guarantee of being sent out from the sect. But… perhaps being a wandering cultivator was not so bad. Or, as he had improved his cultivation, perhaps he could return to the village.

Okay, perhaps not the last. After all, it was likely that any such action would bring the displeasure of the sect and certainly send the army calling again. Without the sect's protection to keep him from being conscripted, he would be back at where he started, just a little stronger.

And realistically, he was getting the equivalent of fifteen taels' worth of wine. Even if Wu Ying wanted to buy the wine, he might not be able to find a supplier as had been pointed out to him.

"Well?"

"Sorry, honored Lieutenant." Wu Ying bowed again when he realized he had been standing there in silence, thinking. "If the lieutenant can provide me with three jars, then I would be grateful."

"I'm still on duty, so wait here," Zhong Shei commanded, waving to the surroundings.

When one of the guards opened his mouth to object, the glare the lieutenant shot him was enough to shut him up. Zhong Shei strode out of the guard building to take up his duties, leaving Wu Ying to roll up the skin and offer apologies to the men within.

"It's fine. It's fine. The lieutenant is always like that," one of the guards commented.

"That's right. Because he comes from the merchant's family, he has a lot of money and privilege. But he sometimes forgets about our rules."

"But he's a good leader. Always makes sure our weapons and armor are up to standard. And he works all day too with us. Better than most of the noble brats who take up the job." A slight pause as the guard looked at Wu Ying, who offered an encouraging nod. Realizing that Wu Ying was not insulted, he continued. "They're always strutting around, acting like they're the favored sons of heaven. Even if they're nothing more than lieutenants."

"Useless third sons," the first guard said with a sniff before realizing that Wu Ying had finished packing. "Well, sir cultivator, we don't mind you here, but if the captain comes…"

"The captain's a real stickler."

"Yes. She's horrible. She'll put us all on report."

"So if sir cultivator is willing…" The guard gestured to a side room.

When Wu Ying walked over with his bag, he realized it led to holding cells. When Wu Ying looked back at the guards, they all looked uncomfortable, but Wu Ying chuckled.

"I'll cultivate within. Just let me know when it's time to go," Wu Ying said as he walked in, taking his bag with him.

Chapter 16

A quiet knock on the door brought Wu Ying's attention back to the external world. He drew in a deep breath then exhaled slowly, allowing the turbid air within his lungs to escape. Thankfully, as he was mostly reinforcing his cultivation, the sweat and stink of this process was muted. As Wu Ying stood and caught a whiff of himself, he grimaced. For definitions of muted at least. Another polite knock on the door brought Wu Ying's attention back to the present.

"Coming," Wu Ying called.

He slowly stretched, checking his body over after being seated cross-legged for so long. While he preferred to cultivate while moving, pacing in such a small space was not much more beneficial to him than sitting still. And truth be told, Wu Ying was a bit tired from all the travel. Sometimes, moderation was best. Not that you could tell from the sudden jumps in his cultivation in the last few weeks.

Thankfully, being in the Body Cleansing stage, Wu Ying was much less likely to harm his future potential by increasing his cultivation so fast. Still, if he could, he would prefer to spend more time reinforcing and cleansing the opened meridians before he attempted the eighth level. If nothing else, it would help him control his aura better.

"Sir cultivator, the lieutenant's shift will be over soon," the guard on the other side of the door said when Wu Ying finally opened it. A moment later, the guard's nose wrinkled slightly. "We do have a wash area as well."

Wu Ying stared at the guard, who looked uncomfortable, probably belatedly remembering that Wu Ying was actually a cultivator.

"Show me, if you will," Wu Ying said, keeping his face stern. He had to admit, he was a little miffed but also somewhat amused.

The guard relaxed, quickly guiding Wu Ying toward the back, where a bucket and an urn of fresh water waited. A few minutes later, Wu Ying was clean and refreshed and walked out to see an impatient-looking lieutenant. Zhong Shei's tight gaze relaxed slightly when he spotted Wu Ying, almost looking approving when he noticed the formerly dusty and dirty peasant had cleaned up. Somewhat.

"Come. My uncle's house is this way," Zhong Shei said, gesturing for Wu Ying to follow.

Wu Ying hurried after the man who did not slow down as he strode through the streets. All around, pedestrians moved out of the way of the uniformed and armored soldier, paying the customary respect for authority. What was not customary were the murmured words of praise and admiration coming from the women whose eyes followed Zhong Shei's figure.

Looking out of the corner of his eyes, Wu Ying mentally compared himself to the soldier. Okay, so Zhong Shei's hair was a little longer, a darker black, and much glossier. And yes, his skin was fair too, free of any pockmarks, blemishes, and scars, unlike the weather-worn visage Wu Ying held. Even with his improved cultivation, the fact stood that Wu Ying had been running for the last few weeks in the blazing sun. Improved cultivation—at his level—could only do so much. And Zhong Shei might be a touch taller. But Wu Ying's shoulders were broader, his chest wider, and arms and thighs bigger!

Well, okay. Perhaps too big. Wu Ying knew he was stockier than most of the effete noblemen and merchants' sons. After all, he had spent his growing years working the fields and not lounging around, reading books and drinking tea. His mood darkening slightly, Wu Ying moved behind Zhong Shei in silence. It seemed that even as a cultivator, he was doomed to stand in the shadow of the nobles and merchants.

"We're here," Zhong Shei announced without preamble. He gestured to the doors. "Be mindful of my uncle if you see him. He is touchy and hard to get along with, but remember, it is his wine."

"Of course. I am already grateful at my fortune to meet someone so well-connected."

"I am, aren't I?" Zhong Shei preened as they entered the mansion. They turned to move around the wall that blocked the view into the house before the pair were met by a servant. "Ah, Ah Kong! I'm headed to the cellar with an acquaintance. No need to tell my uncle."

"Yes, sir," Ah Kong said, bowing.

"Actually…" Wu Ying said hesitantly before he pulled out the seal provided to him by Elder Xi Qi. "I was also entrusted with this to show to your uncle. Elder Lu said your uncle would recognize it."

"This…" Zhong Shei's lips pursed before he let out an exasperated breath. "Fine. Ah Kong, take it to my uncle."

"Of course."

The seal was quickly taken by Ah Kong, who left while Zhong Shei stomped along without a word. Wu Ying hurried to catch up, looking at the well-appointed house with wide eyes. The mansion was the largest he had ever been in personally, potentially even larger than the lord's mansion back in the village, and was built in a U shape. Wu Ying assumed Zhong Shei lived there, since the guard was unlikely to have married yet.

Even if the building was significantly larger, the basic architecture was similar to most other residential buildings, with half-exposed wooden beams interspersed between the doors and white-painted plaster. Of course, in Wu Ying's house, they'd used packed earth and had not bothered to paint the walls. Nor did they have any of the various scrolls and paintings that hung conspicuously throughout the building.

"Don't dawdle. I'm not here to show you the house," Zhong Shei snapped at Wu Ying, who flushed slightly with guilt.

Of course, he was not an actual guest, so taking the time to peruse the works there was not allowed. More the pity too, as the works were all better than anything Wu Ying had seen except in the sect.

"Here we are," Zhong Shei said. From wall to ceiling, the storeroom was filled with wine jars, so crammed full that the shelves were nearly overflowing. Zhong Shei strode in without a care and looked through the numerous wine jars, reading the scribbled notes hanging off the necks of the jars before he set three aside. "This should be it."

"Thank you, honored Tung. Here is your snakeskin," Wu Ying said, offering the skin.

The pair did a quick switch, one that involved a little more juggling than either would have preferred, as the room had no convenient table. But finally, Wu Ying had the jars of wine in his bag, packed with donated rags and hay to increase their survivability.

"Good. Time to go," Zhong Shei said and waved Wu Ying out.

Wu Ying frowned, wanting to remind Zhong Shei about the Elder's seal, but a crotchety old voice cut him off.

"Taking from my personal collection again, are you? What did I say about that?" the voice said.

Wu Ying turned, spotting a short, older man who exuded a presence that made Wu Ying's breath catch. A part of him analyzed this new presence, trying to decide on how it "felt" compared to the Elders in his sect and benefactor Dun. The rest of him was busy bowing low and sweating internally.

"Uncle[22]! I was just finishing a trade," Zhong Shei said with a wide and innocent smile.

"You brat." Uncle Tung strode forward and smacked Zhong Shei over the top of his head. "Always taking from my collection. That snakeskin, it's for that Ong girl, isn't it?"

"Yes, Uncle. It really suits her eyes, don't you think?" Zhong Shei's quick and enthusiastic reply was met with another smack.

"Idiot boy. All of you chasing after one girl." Uncle Tung then turned to Wu Ying, who had stayed bowed, preferring to keep his head down—literally—than get involved in what sounded like a favorite nephew and uncle bickering. Never get involved in family disputes. Any smart Chinese knew that one. "You're the one who brought this?"

Straightening, Wu Ying glanced at the seal Uncle Tung was holding up. "Yes, honored Elder."

"So he's still alive. And out of wine again. Fine..." Uncle Tung walked inside the room and rooted around the back. Eventually, he came back with a dusty wine jar.

Zhong Shei's eyes widened as he stared at the jar before looking between it and Wu Ying incredulously. As Wu Ying held out both hands to take it, Uncle Tung pulled his hands back.

"Elder?"

"I have a better idea." Uncle Tung turned to Zhong Shei, holding the wine bottle in front of him. "You'll guard and deliver this for me. Along with a letter."

"Uncle, I have a job."

---

[22] Traditionally, Chinese families use a much more exact form of address which would immediately denote an individual's relation to another. For example, this would be "Oldest uncle on my father's side." For ease of reading and familiarity, I'm going to stick to "Western" denotations when something like this comes up.

"I'll deal with it," Uncle Tung said with a casual wave. "This one does not look strong enough to guard this properly. Not alone. And you need tempering. A good trip might open your eyes."

"But Lady Ong—"

"Will get her armor. When you're back," Uncle Tung said sternly. "How long have you been stuck at the eight level?"

"A year."

"With the amount of spirit pills and meat you ingest, you should already have broken through," Uncle Tung said. "You need more experiences. More enlightenment. And discipline. This trip will be good for you."

"But Father—"

"Will agree with me," Uncle Tung stated flatly.

"I can't just leave…"

"Three days," Uncle Tung said, glancing at Wu Ying. "A fleet of boats is leaving in that time. I will arrange for passage for you both." Uncle Tung's eyes raked over Wu Ying, taking in his peasant clothing and his bag. "I will send Ah Kong with you to find accommodations, and he will pass word of which boat later."

"Yes, honored elder," Wu Ying said agreeably.

Since Zhong Shei would be looking after the other jar, it was of no concern to Wu Ying. Though the trip might be somewhat uncomfortable, especially with the way the other man was glaring at him. At the dismissive wave of Uncle Tung's hand, Wu Ying scurried out of the room and met with the aforementioned servant.

Wu Ying and the servant left while Uncle Tung's slowly rising voice grew behind them as he scolded his nephew, who continued to attempt to wheedle his way out of the trip. As he left, Wu Ying could not help but consider that perhaps it was for the best that his family was small.

***

Ah Kong, the servant, was taciturn and quiet but knowledgeable of the city. Wu Ying's attempts at dispelling the distance between them could not make the other open up to casual conversation, but at the end of their short trip to a clean, well-priced, and convenient travelers' inn, Wu Ying had garnered the information he required. After paying the fee for a private room for a few days, Wu Ying made his way back out to look for the recommended merchant.

While it might have been convenient for there to be a single location to sell his beast stones, real life did not work that way. As such, finding an honest and trustworthy merchant was important. Luckily, Ah Kong knew of a few, one of whom had a shop close to the inn. While he was a little concerned that Ah Kong might be receiving a kickback for his recommendations, it was unlikely to be an issue. A servant of such a powerful and famous merchant easily made more money doing his job than any little kickback someone like Wu Ying could create—even if the merchant completely scammed him.

And thankfully, Wu Ying was not a complete greenhorn in the sale of beast cores. While there were numerous things he did not know, the occasional appearance of those creatures in the vicinity of the village was a fact of life. As such, most children grew up watching and learning the basic pricing for such items.

In general, demonic beast cores held significantly lower value than normal spirit beast cores. Due to the corruption in these cores, alchemists and doctors needed to purify the cores before they could be used. Most demon cores were, at best, a fifth of the price of a spirit core of the same type and size.

Along with type, the originating animal, size, element, and cultivation level all mattered. Animals from predators were generally more expensive, due to their overall rarity. Those kinds of cores were used by cultivators and were best sold to merchants who dealt with cultivators since they had the higher demand. Alchemists and doctors were more likely to buy herbivorous or prey spirit beast cores since their gentler natures made for better pills and medicine.

All of which explained why Wu Ying was visiting a merchant rather than a doctor with the demon beast cores he held. After all, the vast majority of the cores he had came from predators who'd felt that Wu Ying would make a decent snack.

"Good day. How are you doing? How may we help you today?" the merchant called to Wu Ying the moment he entered, his eyes raking over Wu Ying's poorly dressed form without judgment. His smile did not even waver. Definitely a man who was successful at this business.

"I would like to sell some demon and spirit cores," Wu Ying said as he approached the counter.

Wu Ying surveyed the contents of the store. It was very much as Ah Kong had described—a medium-sized store whose primary stock was geared toward cultivators. On this floor alone, Wu Ying saw scrolls filled with cultivation manuals, martial art styles, and battle techniques, swords and other weapons of varying quality, an assortment of pills and herbs which Wu Ying mostly could not recognize, and of course, the ubiquitous labeled and prepared spirit stones. Each of those stones had been carefully prepped to allow cultivators to draw in the stored chi, with its attendant element, and—if a cultivator was lucky—the creature's enlightenment. Of course, unprepped stones could be absorbed raw, but cultivators would find the process more difficult and less efficient.

"Of course. One moment," the merchant said, walking to the side a bit and reaching beneath his counter.

He came up with a simple wooden tray with a white cloth placed upon it before he gestured for Wu Ying to showcase the stones. After they'd tumbled into the tray, the merchant picked up a nearby stick and pushed them around, separating the stones by color and size with quick flicks. The merchant held a hand over each location, humming softly to himself.

"Eight cores. Five demon cores of small size from various predator animals. Three spirit beast cores of intermediate size, one of which comes from the rare green spirit snake," the merchant said with a smile. "I can offer… hmmm… five taels for the demon cores. The spirit beast cores are worth five and a half tael each, but the snake's rare. I can sell that one immediately after processing. Call it seven tael for that one. The offer is only if you sell all of them here though."

Wu Ying did the math in his head quickly. Twenty-three tael for all his cores—much better than he had expected to receive. Selling prices in the city were higher than when the traders came to his village, which, come to think of it, made sense. After all, those traders had to transport the cores to the cities or sects, running the risk of being robbed.

Keeping his features smooth, Wu Ying considered the matter before sweeping his gaze over the shop. "If we traded for some items, I assume there'd be a better rate?"

"Of course." The merchant nodded. "If you wish to look around, I will cover the stones and place them back here. When you are done, inform me and we can complete the deal."

"Good," Wu Ying said with a smile.

The merchant quickly did as he suggested, placing the beast cores and tray behind the counter while Wu Ying seriously perused the goods. As he walked around slowly, he considered what he needed.

Most importantly, a sword. The one he currently wielded was broken, and even if he managed to sell it or have it fixed, it would still be fatally flawed. Better to sell the metal and buy a new, untarnished sword. Cultivation manuals and styles were probably too expensive for him. In addition, he had so much still to learn that adding more styles would be foolish. Still, Wu Ying knew he was fast closing in on the Energy Gathering portion of his cultivation, so a quick perusal of those manuals might make sense. As for cultivation resources, those were important. Wu Ying was tempted to look into another Meridian Cleansing pill, though a snide portion of his mind pointed out that perhaps some healing pills or concoctions might be better.

Mind made up, Wu Ying moved more determinedly through the store. The weapons were stacked in three distinct locations—those that were piled in a barrel on the floor, those that were carefully displayed but still in easy reach of the shoppers, and those placed behind the counters, carefully displayed and out of reach without aid. A quick glance at the pricing of the jian within reach showed that Wu Ying could forget about the better weapons. Each of the displayed jian cost forty to fifty tael each—or put another way, the full price of a single good harvest. Even if they could harvest three times a year, that money had to go into buying the sundry requirements of the farm, from additional feed for the horse, farming equipment, clothing, firewood, and more.

Turning away from those swords, Wu Ying dug into the pile of swords in the barrel. Those swords were similar to the one given to him by Liu Tsong—made of poor steel or iron and forged by an apprentice blacksmith. On the other hand, they had the advantage of being cheap. In truth, Wu Ying was surprised to find such a barrel here—after all, most cultivators would be richer than him, right? Or perhaps not. Cultivation resources were expensive. Spirit cores were expensive. Cultivation manuals were expensive. And weapons from bandits and the like were plentiful and easy to collect, especially if they attacked you.

That thought made Wu Ying's hands pause as he considered that he might be pawing through a dead person's belongings. Then the practical youth shrugged. Not as if it was the first or last time he had used someone's discarded or relieved possessions. And…

"This looks good," Wu Ying said as he drew a sword fully from its scabbard.

He eyed the weapon along its edge, checking its line, and pursed his lips when he saw the nicks. Nothing a good file and a few hours' work could not fix. Slapping the flat of the blade a few times, he watched the weapon wobble before he balanced the blade on his finger to find its center. A little too far forward and the steel was poor, having slightly too much of a spring for Wu Ying's liking. But the scabbard was functional, the hilt tight, and it still held a good edge. Best of all, it only cost nine tael.

Next up was the cultivation manuals and styles. A quick perusal over the various names and the introductions informed Wu Ying of that most important of facts—he just didn't have enough knowledge to be perusing the information. More time spent learning would be better. As he turned away, Wu Ying saw the title of a familiar style out of the corner of his eye.

"Yellow Emperor's Cultivation Style—Energy Gathering stage?" Wu Ying muttered as he picked up the book. The cost was only five tael, which was surprising. What was even more surprising was that there were another four copies right underneath the one he'd picked up. He turned to the merchant. "Why is this so cheap?"

"Why wouldn't it be? It's the Yellow Emperor's style. Every family of note has a copy already. Though mine is an exact copy. Guaranteed. I also have cultivation notes from Tsifu Liu and Tsifu Teck in there."

"Is it still elemental-free?" Wu Ying asked. There were a number of cultivation styles like that, though few decided to pursue that course of cultivation after Body Cleansing. Each stage after Body Cleansing took more and more chi, time, and enlightenment. Sticking to an elemental-free style was hobbling oneself in the long-term. But still…

"Of course. The Yellow Emperor was the emperor of all. How could he be that if he constrained himself to a single element?" the merchant said with a snort.

"Is there a Core cultivation method for this style then?"

"Yes. Though that's where it stops. To grow your nascent soul, you'll need to find your own path. The Yellow Emperor famously never left a cultivation manual for that, saying that there could only ever be one emperor."

Wu Ying nodded slowly. Growing the nascent soul was important, since it basically allowed a human to restart, developing a portion of them that was untainted by the world. With a fully-grown nascent soul inside their body, a cultivator could touch upon the dao, achieving immortality. If there was a stage after one broke through the nascent soul stage, the gods were not speaking. Still, this information made clear that while dithering on what to do for his cultivation was possible in the short-term, it was not possible in the long-term. Still… Wu Ying placed the scroll alongside the sword and moved on.

Potions, pills, and pastes. No poisons—but that kind of thing wouldn't be sold in a merchant's shop. Few cultivators would ever want to be known to be a poison user. As for medicines, while there were numerous medicines that were particularly useful for any specific ailment—over-drafting of chi, meridian healing, internal injuries, and more—Wu Ying was no doctor. Better to go with something a little more generic. He picked up the bottle of pills that promised to speed up healing before he turned to the cultivation resources.

The various cultivation resources could roughly be divided into three areas: those that directly helped within any single cultivation grade, like the Meridian Cleansing Pill; those that aided the development of one's affinity to a specific element; and those that helped with enlightenment. Of course, Wu Ying recalled his father's derisive tone about those who sought enlightenment via drugs. His father had famously characterized those cultivators as dung-rolling, goat-loving slackers.

With those words ringing in his mind, Wu Ying looked at the cultivation boosters. Even the basic Meridian Cleansing pill by an apprentice alchemist was worth nearly twenty taels for a full bottle. Setting the pills aside, Wu Ying eyed the various jade adornments clustered next to the pills. Those made no sense to him.

"What are the jade pieces for?" Wu Ying asked.

"You know how jade can protect and collects chi? Most of these have been worked to collect ambient chi. When placed on the body, it speeds up cultivation as they provide another source of chi. Of course, in time, you might need to recharge the jade," the merchant said, walking over and pointing at a pale bracelet. "Take this one for example. This is moon jade, charmed to draw chi from moonlight. When placed out in the open during the full moon, it absorbs and cleanses the chi of the moonlight. When you next cultivate, you will be able to draw that chi into your body, speeding up the process. Of course, it's more effective for fire-aspected cultivators. Air cultivators find it good too."

"Thank you. Are there any you could recommend?" Wu Ying said, curiosity aroused.

"For you?" The merchant eyed Wu Ying and the cores before sweeping his gaze over the bottle of healing pills, the sword, and the cultivation manual in Wu Ying's hand. "Perhaps this bracelet. It's unaspected and unworked, so it's only marginally effective. But if you find a charm-maker or blacksmith, you could have it fixed. The quality is quite good after all."

"Thank you."

Since Wu Ying looked to be done with asking, the merchant walked back to his counter and continued to clean his wares. Wu Ying browsed through the cultivation aids a little longer, briefly eying the various protective talismans before discarding them and picking up the jade bracelet.

After placing the bottle of healing pills and the bracelet on the table in front of the merchant, Wu Ying unhooked his sword. "I'd like to see if I can trade this in too."

"May I?" The merchant gestured.

"Of course. It is broken, but the iron could be reused," Wu Ying warned.

"Ah." Taking his hand back, the merchant shook his head. "I'm sorry, we don't deal with broken weapons at all. There are a few blacksmiths you could see about this. But for the rest, we can certainly talk."

Wu Ying sighed but took back the sword, strapping it back to his belt. He leaned forward, a smile crossing his lips as he got ready to haggle.

***

A half hour later, Wu Ying walked out of the store with everything he'd wanted and an additional two tael. Whistling, Wu Ying made his way to the recommended blacksmith, where another short period of bargaining commenced. Afterward, Wu Ying walked out with a simple belt knife, one that could be used for cutting bread, chopping meat, or stabbing enemies as needed.

Having completed his errands, Wu Ying made his way back to the inn while musing about the remainder of his free time. A nagging guilt informed Wu

Ying that he had placed his training to the side in the last few days in his attempt to hurry to the city. A couple of days of dedicated practice could do wonders. But as Wu Ying walked through the city, he knew that he would be remiss in leaving without seeing some of the sights. There were palatial buildings, temples, cultivated parks, and martial arts centers to see! And, most importantly, new cuisine to taste.

As Wu Ying resumed his walk with a baked, stuffed bun in hand, he pondered his options. As Uncle Tung had pointed out, cultivation and training without enlightenment was a surefire way of stalling oneself. Guilt was another hindrance in cultivation. Guilt and regret would hinder him if he did not see the city, but so would it if he did nothing but waste his time.

Wu Ying quietly plotted out his next few days as he entered the inn's bottom floor and took a seat at one of the many dining tables. Training tonight, then rest. Then more training in the morning, followed by sight-seeing in the afternoon. He would spend a few hours in the mid-afternoon on more training, then more sight-seeing and snacking before returning to the inn for dinner. Or eating out, if he found some place reasonable. Then training again.

That should satisfy his guilty conscience. And if not... well, Wu Ying would adjust his schedule until the nagging guilt and regret balanced themselves out. After all, that was part of living too.

Chapter 17

Days later, Wu Ying found himself standing on the bow of a ship, watching as Lieutenant Tung Zhong Shei said goodbye to Ah Kong and his gathered friends. No family, Wu Ying absently noted, but it was not as if Zhong Shei was leaving forever. Just a short trip before he came back. That Zhong Shei's friends included a bevy of pretty young girls was not surprising—but from the way the guard constantly searched the crowds, it was obvious that a particular young lady was not there.

Not that Wu Ying particularly cared. Beautiful or not, the lady Ong was obviously out of his reach. For that matter… Wu Ying rubbed his nose, considering. In the past few months, his interest in the fairer sex had waned somewhat. A side effect of all the cultivating? Or more likely a side effect of the sheer amount of training and work that he had faced. Who had the time to look at romance when you spent entire days running up mountains?

"Why are you laughing?" Zhong Shei said as he stomped over, his bag still slung over his shoulder.

The captain had yet to inform them—or send anyone over to inform them—where they would be staying, leaving the pair of passengers to wait at the bow of the ship.

"Just an idle thought. Your friends are gone?" Wu Ying said, his demeanor more relaxed now that they were mostly out of the city. That he was a sect member—even an outer sect member—had raised his social standing in Zhong Shei's eyes. Enough so that the merchant's son was willing to talk to him voluntarily.

"I sent them off. The captain wanted me on board," Zhong Shei said grumpily. "Well, so long as you're not insane. Though if you came from the Verdant Green Waters on foot, that's arguable."

"How...? Ah Kong, right?" Wu Ying said, remembering the dinner invitation on the second night and the conversation the pair had held. "You sent him?"

"My father," Zhong Shei said. "He was quite interested in the news about the roads and the bandit Ji Ang. That news will do his merchant firm a lot of good. Spread some goodwill among those he tells and save him some money too."

Wu Ying nodded slowly. "I'm not sure if Ji Ang would stay in that area."

"Of course. We'd already heard some rumors, but confirmation is important," Zhong Shei said. "But the bandit is a real problem. He's smart. He cultivates a style that lets him sense the strength of others at a distance, and he and his group avoid targets that are too strong. Which means he picks on all the individual merchants and runs from everything else. Every group we send out..." Zhong Shei grew visibly frustrated before he relaxed, shaking his head. "We'll get him. They never last."

"Of course not," Wu Ying said with a nod. Glancing at Zhong Shei's slim bag, he leaned over. "I don't see the bottle."

"In my storage ring," Zhong Shei said with a half-smile, especially when Wu Ying's eyes widened. He smirked before touching the bag. "This is just for clothing. And some small keepsakes to keep the thieves busy."

Wu Ying could not help but look at Zhong Shei with envy. Ah, to be young, handsome, and rich.

"You two, come along. I'll show you your cabin."

"Cabin?" Zhong Shei said.

"Yes, cabin. You are sharing one." The sailor who had been sent to guide them gestured again. "Well, come on."

"Damn it, Uncle! Forcing me to share..." Turning around, Zhong Shei glared at Wu Ying. "You better not snore!"

***

"Can't sleep?" the sailor asked Wu Ying later that evening as the youngster walked up from belowdecks. Since they were heading downwind and downriver, the boat had its sail fully out, leaving the oars docked and Wu Ying nothing to do.

"Snores like a tree cracking in winter."

"Well, don't bother the others," the sailor cautioned before he turned back to darning his pants by the light of the lantern he sat beneath.

The deck of the boat was quiet, only the slow creak of the deck and sails, the lapping of waters, and the occasional raised voice from below breaking the silence. Few sailors were up at this time of night, just the lookouts, the helmsmen, and a few others, like the sailor who spoke to him, catching up on their chores. In the silence, Wu Ying moved to the bow and found a clear portion of the deck.

If he could not sleep, he might as well practice. Sliding into a resting position, Wu Ying took a deep breath and exhaled. Light flashed as he surged into motion, the sword drawn from his hip with a flash. Each motion was sharp, incisive. A twist, a turn, the jian catching the lantern light and flickering like a firefly.

Step by step, form by form, Wu Ying trained in the sword style passed on to him by his family. Even if he had practiced it for years before, there was an impetus, a need that drove his actions now. Before, even in the sect, the knowledge that he would need this style to fight for his life had been academic. Now, Wu Ying understood in his flesh, his muscles, his bones, that to survive this world, he needed strength.

Sense of the Sword gave his actions perfect distance and timing. But it did nothing for how smoothly he moved, how he chained each action together. Only practice, only conscious practice, would do that. As he moved, Wu Ying paid minute attention to his body, judging his balance and weight distribution, the speed of his thrust and the integration of his muscles. He had replayed that final attack from Benefactor Yuan Rang over and over in his mind, seeing each motion, each turn of the body and exertion of muscle.

There was no way for Wu Ying to replicate the attack, not really. He knew not the chi flow, the theoretical underpinnings of the attack. It was one of the fundamental truths of styles—you could copy the motions, but it left behind the understanding of when, where, and how to use the motion. You could not copy the multiple variations of the attack that were never shown—or the way the attack might block off specific retaliations because of subtle positioning.

Still, Yuan Rang's attack had been carried out in the Body Cleansing stage of cultivation, one whose major impetus was the use of the cultivator's body. As such, while he might never be able to replicate it, Wu Ying could take some wisdom from the attack and integrate it into his understanding of the Long family style.

When he was done with the first sword form, Wu Ying moved to the second. Time passed as his body sweated, a small thrum of chi running through him as he unconsciously circulated it, cultivating as he moved. When he was finally done, the moon was high in the sky and the shift had changed.

Bringing his legs together, Wu Ying stared at the passing night sky and the wisps of clouds, thinking over what he had learned. For a time, he stood there, letting the knowledge settle before he sheathed his sword.

Enough for tonight. Perhaps Zhong Shei had quieted down.

***

"Why are you up already?" Zhong Shei said as he came up from belowdecks, running a hand through his hair to ensure it was properly coifed.

"It's ten in the morning," Wu Ying said, shaking his head slightly as he finished the movement he had been in the midst of when Zhong Shei had spoken. It involved a cut kick followed by a stomp and what could either be a block or grab, which would result in a hip turn to upset and destabilize. Back leg would then come up as weight came forward and the form itself followed with a sweep. Of course, depending on the strength or location of the attacker, it could also be a simple kick to the foot.

"Exactly! We're in the middle of the river. There are no shifts to wake up for, no captain complaining about you being late or patrols to be done. It's freedom."

Wu Ying did not deign to answer Zhong Shei as he continued to practice. Crane stretches in the water followed by waterfall splashing saw Wu Ying land on the sweeping foot and drop into a low stance. After which Wu Ying had to stand, using an axe kick at low range even as he twisted. It was a weird combination, and he, as yet, did not understand its use. It also hurt—quite a bit—to do. His body had yet to adapt.

"I thought you were a jian-wielder," Zhong Shei said, interrupting Wu Ying again.

The cultivator sighed and landed lightly, holding the pose to let his body memorize the position. "I am. I'm also studying this."

"Huh," Zhong Shei said, watching Wu Ying go back to practicing. With a wave, the guard ambled off to find his breakfast.

An hour later, when Wu Ying had finally finished his daily practice and was taking a moment to rest, Zhong Shei plopped down next to him, a white bun in each hand. "Bun?"

"Thank you," Wu Ying said, taking the proffered food.

The pair ate in silence for a time before Zhong Shei spoke up. "What are you doing next?"

"Cultivating."

"Seriously?" Zhong Shei said with a roll of his eyes. "We're out. Free from the city. And you're going to cultivate?"

"Yes," Wu Ying replied, wondering why Zhong Shei was even speaking to him. Then he realized the guard had no one better to talk to. He was the closest one to Zhong Shei in station on board and, even more importantly, the only one free. At Zhong Shei's impatient gaze, he relented and explained. "At the sect tournament, I intend to win a spot in the inner sect if possible. At the least, I don't intend to be sent back."

"What are you? Body Cleansing Five? Six?"

"Seven."

"Damn. For a peasant…" Zhong Shei looked at Wu Ying when he realized that perhaps his surprise could be considered insulting. When he saw that Wu Ying did not react, the guard relaxed. "You're pretty good. If you fail, you can always join our town guard. Or hell, any guard. You aren't horrible with your leg form, and with that cultivation level, you'd make squad leader soon enough. Maybe even lieutenant like me."

"That's good to know," Wu Ying said noncommittally. "How long have you been a lieutenant?"

"Nearly two years now. I was promoted when I reached my eight opening," Zhong Shei said before his face darkened. "Not that I've progressed since then."

"Well, perhaps if you tried cultivating more…"

"But it's so boring!" Zhong Shei complained, shaking his head. "It's always cultivate this, practice that. I want more than that. I want love. Romance. The feel of a good woman in my arms, delicious wine, and better conversation. I'll break through soon enough. I just need to buy another Meridian Cleansing pill when my next paycheck arrives."

Wu Ying looked at the rich merchant's son for a time as he chewed on his bun. A part of him knew he should be angry or jealous at the casual way Zhong Shei discussed buying pills to improve his cultivation. It really wasn't the best way to do it and not something the son of a farmer could ever hope to do. But Zhong Shei wasn't arrogant about it. Just matter-of-fact. He seemed to understand the risks involved and took the liabilities on with full understanding. And really, getting upset because the rich could buy what the poor couldn't was... well, foolish. Or perhaps just tiring. Better to focus on what he could do than burn with jealousy all the time. Wu Ying stood and walked away from the guard.

"Where are you going?"

"To cultivate," Wu Ying replied with a smile and slight bob of his head, swallowing the last of the bun as he walked to the prow. "Thank you for the snack."

***

For the next couple of days, life on the river boat grew quiet. When Wu Ying was not training or cultivating, he spent his time fishing over the side of the boat and talking to the sailors. It had taken all of three hours on the first day before Zhong Shei, bored with the lack of entertainment, joined him in silent cultivation and, later, training. Admittedly, the merchant's son was as likely to take time off to rest, talk, and eat as he was to train, but Zhong Shei did train.

For all that, today was different. Halfway through the morning, the sails were furled and the oars taken out. Wu Ying frowned as Zhong Shei joined the cultivator with a grin.

"Finally! We've made it to Ping Zhu," Zhong Shei said. "We can walk, eat, find some local beauties!"

"We are only here for half a day. Maybe less."

The ship was only staying long enough to unload their cargo and pick up more for the trip farther downstream. They also had to wait their turn for when the river was clear. The following part of the river was extremely turbulent, filled with small rapids that made it difficult for boats going upstream to travel via oars. As such, river traffic was closely regulated, the ships coming upstream pulled on ropes. Luckily, the vast majority of upriver traffic came at night, when the sides of the river would be illuminated with lanterns and dangerous boulders marked with white paint.

"Ah, but what a half day. I know the perfect restaurant," Zhong Shei said. "Close to the docks and perfect."

"This isn't a good idea. If we're late…"

"I'll tell the captain where we're going. And promise him a meal from the restaurant if he informs us before he has to leave. It'll be fine," Zhong Shei said, already ambling over to talk to the captain.

Wu Ying rolled his eyes, though he had to admit the captain was likely to agree to Zhong Shei's offer. After all, not only were they paying passengers, but Zhong Shei was an important personage. It was unlikely that the captain would leave him.

"I can't really afford an expensive meal," Wu Ying admitted when Zhong Shei finally made it back. His purse was quite bare, especially after spending all his funds at the store. While he had a little money left—mostly from his original stash—that was not all his. If he could, Wu Ying would trade it back for cultivation points and return what he owed to Tou He.

"It's my treat," Zhong Shei immediately offered.

Wu Ying made a slight face but thanked the man, who waved the matter away. While Wu Ying hated to owe anyone, Zhong Shei had offered. And truth be told, getting off the ship and onto dry land would be lovely. As would food that was not overly laced with salt and soya sauce.

Together, the pair disembarked when the boat docked and they headed into the city. Zhong Shei walked in front, happy to show off his knowledge of the city, detailing little facts about the place. Of course, most of his facts revolved around the guards, the young nobles and scholars who hung around the city between the imperial examinations, and the chasing of various beauties and delicious food. Wu Ying found most of the information bewildering, as Zhong Shei was not a good storyteller, forgetting to provide context or to follow the thread of his own story.

"You should try the duck here… not right now! We're going to eat fish and prawns at Uncle Mo's restaurant," Zhong Shei chided Wu Ying. "Don't spoil your appetite. We'll get one on the way back.

"Young master Lu over there is the third child, so he's actually penniless but with a heavy gambling addiction. Don't ever play mah jong with him though, he's very good.

"The rice candy there is famous. I used to buy them when I was younger.

"Miss Peng! You're looking beautiful as always. Those earrings are perfectly sized for your delicate ears. Are you interested in joining us for lunch?"

In this way, Wu Ying and Zhong Shei made their way to the restaurant. When they were finally neared the restaurant after a good thirty minutes— mostly punctuated by Zhong Shei's frequent stops—Wu Ying caught a glimpse of a familiar face walking into a side street. He frowned, staring at the figures that streamed in after.

"What?"

"Bandits," Wu Ying said.

Having made up his mind, Wu Ying turned away from the restaurant and moved toward the side street the bandit group had disappeared down, all the while craning his neck in search of additional members on the main road. Not seeing any, Wu Ying sped up before coming to an abrupt halt when Zhong Shei's hand landed on his shoulder.

"You can't just say things like that and disappear!"

"I saw Ji Ang walk into that side street," Wu Ying said as he shrugged off the hand.

As he turned the corner, Wu Ying spotted the last of the figures that had followed Ji Ang step into the doorway of a bar. Frowning, Wu Ying stared down the street.

"Are you sure?" Zhong Shei asked when he caught up once again.

"Mostly," Wu Ying said. Even though he'd only caught a glimpse, Ji Ang's face was not one that was easy to forget. At least, not for Wu Ying.

"And he was walking around in broad daylight?" Zhong Shei's face grew grim. "Then the rumors are true. He has paid off the guards and magistrate. Come on."

"Wait. What?" Wu Ying said as Zhong Shei started down the street, hand on his sword. Automatically, Wu Ying followed his companion.

"How many were there?"

"Seven others."

"Good." Zhong Shei stopped when Wu Ying gripped his arm, dragging him to a standstill.

Wu Ying dropped his hand when Zhong Shei shot him a cold look, never removing his hand from his sword's hilt. "What do you think you're doing? There are seven of them. You aren't even a guard here."

"I don't intend to arrest him."

"That's even worse! You can't go about killing people."

"Not people. Ji Ang and his crew. They're all wanted bandits. They all have a bounty on their heads," Zhong Shei said. "I will not let him escape. The blood on his hands could wash away Mount Tai[23]! Together, we can take them. His bandits are all trash but him."

"I never agreed to this," Wu Ying said, shaking his head. "I've got a mission to complete, and fighting him again isn't part of it."

"Don't you want revenge? Does your blood not boil?"

"No," Wu Ying said.

Zhong Shei snorted, reading the lie in Wu Ying's clenched jaw.

But the cultivator turned away, moving to the exit before he stopped as a familiar trio of figures blocked it. "How did…"

"Told you I recognized him." A voice behind Wu Ying made him turn as the remainder of Ji Ang's group came out with their leader.

"Cào[24]," Wu Ying cursed while drawing his sword. He eyed the edges of the alleyway and grimaced even further. The Long family style revolved around movement, so this was a really bad place for him to display his swordsmanship. Luckily, the Northern Shen Kicking style he had been studying actually had footwork that worked well in such tight spaces.

---

[23] Mount Tai is the eastern mountain of the Five Great Mountains of China and one of (if not the) most famous.

[24] It's a swear word. Starts with an F. Yes, I even added the intonation here. 😊

"I'll take him. You watch our back," Zhong Shei said, the usual light-hearted merchant's son gone. The lieutenant who had stopped Wu Ying at the gate had returned, all stern-faced and serious. "Wish I'd brought my armor…"

"Don't we all," Wu Ying muttered. Damn his curiosity. Damn Zhong Shei for slowing him down. All he'd wanted to do was confirm matters before he reported it. "Stay alive."

Ji Ang and his men didn't seem content to talk or posture much either, already dashing forward to meet the pair from both directions. Only Ji Ang held back, content to let his men deal with them first.

Wu Ying had no more time to glance back as the first bandit arrived, holding a shortened sabre overhand. Reacting on instinct, Wu Ying threw a stop-lunge, catching his opponent in the throat. Immediately, Wu Ying recovered and the bandit fell, gurgling and clawing at his wound. As the pair behind the bandit stumbled around their fallen friend, Wu Ying pressed his sudden advantage, landing a few light, cutting blows.

Only when the pair had retreated out of his range, over the top of their dying friend, did Wu Ying have a moment to think. In the momentary stillness, Wu Ying realized what had happened—his day of intense fighting with Duan Rang had seen his battle sense grow sharper, his sense of openings firmer. Since the only chances he'd ever had of landing a blow on Duan Rang had been fleeting moments, the resolution in his attacks had grown sharper.

The grunting and clash of blades behind Wu Ying reminded the cultivator that a more desperate battle was going on behind him. Ji Ang was a cultivation level above Zhong Shei, so the fight behind him would be significantly more dangerous. Considering the bandits before him had stopped moving, Wu Ying decided it was time to finish this.

Dragon steps was the basic movement technique in Wu Ying's sword fighting style. It taught the stylist how to cover ground explosively with no windup or tell-tale movement. In a flash, Wu Ying bounced forward, appearing before one of the bandits even as he executed the Sword's Truth. The straight lunge sought the bandit's heart, and only a last-minute twist allowed the bandit to escape the immediately lethal attack. Instead, the blade tore through the bandit's ribcage, puncturing a lung and tearing out of the bandit's chest. For a moment, Wu Ying's blade was stuck. The other bandit took full advantage of the opportunity.

Crane stretching in the water saw Wu Ying drop and weave, dodging the cut before he threw a rising knee, catching the inside of the remaining bandit's thigh. The strike buckled the bandit's body before Wu Ying continued the twist and rise, striking with his elbow as his leg landed. The bandit staggered backward and was finished off by a simple cut to the throat.

Moving away from the corpses—or soon-to-be corpses—Wu Ying approached the fight between Zhong Shei and Ji Ang. Zhong Shei had already maimed one and killed another bandit, but was now hard-pressed as Ji Ang joined the fight with the remaining bandit. Anger radiated from the bandit leader at the loss of his men. A hard strike caught Zhong Shei's jian, sending the guard to his knees, where the other bandit's sword stabbed into his shoulder.

"You damned cultivators. I'll kill you all!" Ji Ang growled as he raised his weapon over his head.

"No, you won't," Wu Ying said as he blocked the fatal blow.

Shoving with his body, he pushed Zhong Shei back, using his scabbard to strike the other bandit across the face peremptorily as the pair tumbled away from the bandits. Hopefully Zhong Shei would have enough time to recover.

"I should have killed you when I had the chance," Ji Ang said as the pair fought, their blades flashing down the shaded alley.

Feet pounding, Ji Ang finally caught a break as Wu Ying's initial momentum faltered, sending back a riposte that had Wu Ying retreating for defense. Silently, the pair observed one another over the tips of their weapons.

"You've gotten better," Ji Ang complimented.

"You're still as bloodthirsty as ever," Wu Ying replied, his eyes narrow.

It was, in its own way, a compliment. Ji Ang's killing intent, the focus that he brought to the fight, was amazing. The subtle pressure of an opponent who had taken lives, one after the other, was like nothing that Wu Ying had ever faced—except once, briefly. If not for that final strike by Yuan Rang, Wu Ying might have found himself seriously unnerved. But having faced death again and again, Wu Ying was no longer the novice he had been. Now the likelihood of death was less worrisome.

Introductions complete, the pair clashed once more. Quickly enough, Wu Ying realized that like him, Ji Ang maneuvered his sword with grace and understanding. Not too surprising that the older bandit had achieved the Sense of the Sword. In fact, it seemed as though he was on the cusp of finding the Heart. But thin line or not, the line still stood.

Dragon turns in slumber. Greeting the rising run. Blades flashing, the pair exchanged blows over and over. Sparks flew from the swords, such was the force of their clashes. Each blow rang through the narrow alleyway, which intensified the noise until it seemed as if an entire band was there. A momentary slip, a twist, and Wu Ying fell back, his left arm bleeding from a shallow wound. On the opposite side, a light cut marred Ji Ang's cheek.

"Wu Ying! I'm here," Zhong Shei said as he came forward, having dealt with the last opponent. He leaned against the wall slightly, one arm hanging uselessly by his side as his shoulder bled. "Let us finish this monster."

"You two…" Ji Ang's lips curled. "One a new cultivator. The other a spoiled, injured brat. Do you think you can beat me?"

"Yes."

"Justice will prevail!" The silence after Zhong Shei's pronouncement made the guard look between the pair, who stared at him incredulously. "What?"

"What are you? Six?" Wu Ying said.

"Even my son doesn't say things like that," Ji Ang added.

"Well, your son wouldn't," Zhong Shei said.

"How dare you. My wife brings him up to be an upstanding citizen. He'll be a scholar one day!" Ji Ang growled.

Wu Ying stood there, dumbfounded, as his sheltered world was broken open once again. Ji Ang raised his sword and charged the pair while Wu Ying was still getting his head around the idea of the bandit having a wife and scholar of a son. Caught by surprise, Wu Ying threw a hasty block and was saved only by Zhong Shei's quick aid. Ji Ang cursed, jumping back to dodge Zhong Shei's attack, and blocked the next cut contemptuously. The three stood at a standstill, breathing slowly as they eyed the other party for the next attack.

"Naïve." Ji Ang eyed Zhong Shei and Wu Ying before his smile widened. "I'll show you how far a distance there is between us though. Watch my Formless Blade!"

Immediately, Ji Ang executed his attack. Eyes thinning in concentration, Wu Ying focused as the bandit's blade swirled. In moments, the single blade became a dozen, each seeming to flicker and disappear in the shadows of the alleyway. Cursing, Wu Ying and Zhong Shei wove their swords in their respective defensive patterns in an attempt to deflect the real blade among the illusory ones.

Again and again, the clang of blades resounded through the alleyway. Both of the cultivators were forced backward as the bandit pushed them, blood blooming around their bodies as attacks slipped past their guard. Thankfully, the defense patterns kept their vitals safeguarded, forcing Ji Ang to bleed them slowly.

"Bodies!" Wu Ying called as memory tickled his mind. He hopped backward with a powerful thrust of his legs, jumping over the bodies that lay on the ground from their earlier fights.

Zhong Shei landed beside him a second later, the pair raising their swords as Ji Ang carefully moved around the corpses. Given a break, the pair breathed deeply, feeling the sting of cuts across their body.

"Can't win if we defend," Zhong Shei said weakly.

Glancing at his friend, Wu Ying was startled to notice how pale Zhong Shei had grown as he continued to lose blood. The wound in his shoulder was deep and dripped a steady stream down his hand.

"Can you hold?" Wu Ying asked worriedly.

Ji Ang sneered at the pair as he tested their defenses, but the quick probes of his sword were sent back with light blocks. Wu Ying could tell that the man was still testing the pair, waiting for Zhong Shei to bleed out.

"Not much. Follow me," Zhong Shei replied.

Suiting actions to words, the guard surged forward, batting aside Ji Ang's weapon. Yet the attacks were so weak that the bandit's lips curled up even further as he focused his attention mainly on Wu Ying and his attacks. It would be a fatal mistake.

Twisting with the next block, Zhong Shei used the momentum to pull up his injured arm, forcing himself to move it through the pain. Blood, collected in a loose cupped hand as it dripped down his arm, was tossed at Ji Ang's face. The brief blindness distracted the bandit, and he stumbled back. Right into the bodies of his comrades. For a moment, Ji Ang's hands opened as he unconsciously attempted to regain his balance.

A moment was sufficient for Wu Ying to execute the Sword's Truth. The singular attack of the Long family style was a powerful lunge that threw everything into a single attack. Yet this one had been modified slightly by Wu Ying, a result of Yuan Rang's attack. The attack became even sharper and more explosive. In that moment of vulnerability, Wu Ying's jian punched through Ji Ang's chest, through his heart, and out the back, all the way to Wu Ying's hilt.

Surprised by the effectiveness, Wu Ying stood stock-still, eye to eye with his opponent. Ji Ang stared at Wu Ying in surprise as blood dripped down his face, giving him a crazed look. His sword clattered to the ground and his now-free hand moved to grab Wu Ying, who contemptuously pushed the hand away. A second later, the light dimmed from Ji Ang's eyes and he collapsed, sliding off the sword.

It was only then that the clamor of guards outside the alley could be heard. Wu Ying groaned, looking backward and forward around the alleyway before rifling Ji Ang's body. He took the bandit leader's coin purse and scooped up the scabbard and Ji Ang's sword. He quickly sheathed the sword before thrusting the weapon at Zhong Shei.

"What...?"

"Put it in your storage ring," Wu Ying snapped. Even as he said that, he was emptying the coin purse into his own before tossing the empty, bloody purse aside. He then slid his purse back into his robes before bending to clean his weapon.

It was crouched, bleeding, and wounded, cleaning his sword on the corpses of his enemies, that the guards found him.

"We're not going to make it to the boat, are we?" Wu Ying muttered even as Zhong Shei swayed, bloody and fumbling for a healing pill while speaking with the guards.

The only good thing was that Zhong Shei had taken his advice and hidden the bandit leader's sword in his storage ring before the guards arrived. Wu Ying hid his smile while he sheathed his blade and waited quietly, his sect seal held out for all to see. Not as though any of the weapons or coin purses on the corpses were ever likely to make their way to him if he had waited.

Chapter 18

As Wu Ying had expected, the fight between themselves and the bandits had resulted in quite a bit of chaos. If not for his liberal usage of his sect seal and Zhong Shei's ruthless use of his own standing as the son of a prosperous and well-known merchant and the favored nephew of an even more famous and rich wine maker, along with his position as a lieutenant of a neighboring city, the mess would have been even worse.

As it stood, the pair were frog-marched to the nearest guard post, where a doctor treated their wounds before they were subjected to questioning separately. For the most part, Wu Ying told the truth, only omitting details about the famous bandit's sword and coin purse when asked. After a vigorous two hours of questioning, the pair were finally released back to a holding room, where they found their belongings from the ship. Thankfully, the precious jars of wine were untouched—the shield of wealth, position, and martial prowess keeping the pair's belongings safe, even in their absence.

"They asked about the sword. And his coin purse," Zhong Shei said to Wu Ying, who was storing his clothing and other belongings once again.

"I'm sure they did." Wu Ying glanced around slightly, curious where the listeners were.

Zhong Shei followed Wu Ying's eyes and tilted his head toward a small hole that could barely be seen in the mud wall. "I did ask them about the bounties and the rest of the bandits' belongings, but I never got an answer."

"Oh? I'm sure they'll get around to getting the bounty. Don't they have to report it to the appropriate authority first?" Wu Ying said. Not as if he had any clue how bounties actually worked.

"Yes. I'm sure they will." Zhong Shei's voice took on a tone of mock sadness. "I have a feeling that the bandits probably spent all their coin though.

I doubt they had a tael between them all. Probably why Ji Ang had nothing either."

"Really?" When he met the nobleman's son's knowing gaze, he sighed and added, a little louder and more theatrically than needed, "Yes, I'm sure you're right."

Zhong Shei covered his mouth, stifling a snort of laughter. After a time, he continued, his voice straining to keep serious. "And I bet the weapons we found aren't very good quality. Really, what are we going to do with a bunch of rusty swords? It would be better if they just took them and gave us the value for them, rather than make us carry that trash around."

"Trash. Right," Wu Ying said, trying not to wince too much.

He knew what Zhong Shei was doing now. Bribes were a fact of life, and by refusing the true value of the weapons, they'd grease the wheels for their exit. Still, he hated the idea of giving up all that money. But Wu Ying was also clear how precarious their position was. While rumors would have spread by now about the pair of cultivators who had fought and killed the infamous Ji Ang, the pair might still "disappear" or "succumb to their injuries" before they were released, allowing the guards to take their goods and the bandits. It was not as though either of them had their powerful patrons present. Better to give a little and appease the guards' greed than be too greedy themselves and disappear.

"That's good. I'm going to cultivate now. Let me know when dinner is here," Zhong Shei finally said, closing his eyes and taking the lotus position.

Wu Ying watched him sit down and, to his surprise, actually cultivate. After a moment, Wu Ying shook his head. Why was he surprised? The man was injured. Cultivating would allow him to speed up his healing.

And perhaps being in the best shape possible was important. After all, they had yet to meet or deal with the bandit's backers. Though Wu Ying would be surprised if they made their move. While they might be unhappy that their cash cow had disappeared, acting against the pair wouldn't change that fact. But corrupt officials were not necessarily known for their humble nature and logical reasoning.

After a moment, Wu Ying set a chair in the middle of the doorway before moving over to a corner of the room to cultivate. All he could do was get ready and wait.

***

"Told you it would be fine," Zhong Shei said with a smirk the next morning as they walked out of the guard station.

Their promised bounties would make their way to Zhong Shei's residence, where half would, eventually, be transferred to Wu Ying—once everything had been confirmed. After their battle, Wu Ying found himself trusting the guard. A man who would shout "Justice will prevail" unabashedly in a fight would be unlikely to stoop to stealing his reward.

And if he did... well, Wu Ying shrugged. That money had only been earned because Zhong Shei had dragged him down that alleyway. By himself, Wu Ying would have turned around and enjoyed a nice, quiet lunch once he had confirmed his initial suspicion.

"You did no such thing," Wu Ying said as he squinted in the mid-day light. "Now, how are we going to head downriver?"

"Leave that to me!" a chubby merchant cried. Walking forward, he grabbed and shook their hands enthusiastically. "Tang Kei Chan. I am a friend of your father, Zhong Shei, and I would be happy to host you on my boat."

"I—" Wu Ying started to stall the man.

"For free," Kei Chan said as he looked at Wu Ying. "It's the least I can do for the heroes who took down Ji Ang. The bastard already burned one of my ships and slaughtered the crew on another."

"Ships…" Wu Ying fell silent while Zhong Shei stepped forward and bowed to Kei Chan.

"Oh, I remember now! It's Uncle Tang. You always brought those red sweets with you when you visited Father during New Year," Zhong Shei said, smiling. "We would be in your debt."

"No, no, no, we are in your debt. Come. I have prepared a feast first. Many want to thank the heroes of the hour. And then we will take you down," Kei Chan said as he brought the pair to the waiting rickshaw.

Once again, the pair glanced at one another before they climbed in, giving in to the inevitable. It would be a huge loss of face for Kei Chan if they turned him down, especially as he seemed to have organized all this on his own. And while Wu Ying was willing to do that to an enemy, doing that to someone Zhong Shei knew and had good relations with was just wrong.

***

Hour later, Wu Ying stood on the prow of the boat as it pulled out from the port. It had only taken them all of the morning—including multiple drinks and dishes—before the pair could extricate themselves from the banquet thrown in their honor. Wu Ying absently touched his hand, looking at the biggest surprise of the day—a jade band that hid its true worth behind its simplicity. His first storage ring. The ring could only store about a small chest's worth of items, but it was still a priceless artifact. Or well, not priceless. Just very expensive.

Once more, Wu Ying cast his mind into the storage ring. It took a little effort, a little chi, but as he had spilt his blood onto it and sealed the ring to himself, the ring woke to his request. A constellation of items appeared within his mind, little blobs of energy and matter that Wu Ying intuitively knew to be the items he had stored. He even knew, via that same rough guide, how much more he could store. And what he could not—chief among them, living creatures of any kind.

"Nice view, is it not?" Zhong Shei said as he joined Wu Ying. "Though not as nice as the young ladies at the restaurant."

"You could have stayed longer," Wu Ying said.

"And leave you to go alone? What kind of friend would I be then?" Zhong Shei said with a snort.

"Friend?" Wu Ying said, cocking his head to the side as he stared at the guard lieutenant. Zhong Shei looked uncomfortable, and Wu Ying found himself battling off a smile. Eventually he relented and gave a simple nod.

Zhong Shei relaxed, watching the blue-green water flow by before he leaned in and murmured, "So. Do you just not like women?"

"Why'd you ask that?" Wu Ying said, somewhat annoyed. Not that there was anything wrong with a preference for men, but it was not for him[25]. Certainly, certain sects were even known for encouraging that practice among their sect members, to create stronger in-house bonds.

"You didn't seem particularly interested at the banquet. The women—especially lady Pai—were throwing themselves at you. And there you were, being all quiet."

---

[25] For those curious, prior to the start of the Ming dynasty, homosexuality in ancient China was not considered wrong, and most religions and philosophies were "neutral" on the matter. It is only in the Ming dynasty onward that opposition to homosexuality increased.

"Oh. Oh…" Wu Ying fell silent. Eventually, he looked at Zhong Shei and admitted the truth. "I was uncomfortable and trying not to embarrass myself. And the people they were speaking of—the musical pieces and literary works, I did not know half of them."

"You don't? But…" Zhong Shei nodded. "Of course. You didn't get our education. I bet you hadn't ever eaten at a restaurant like that either, have you?"

"No." Wu Ying lips twitched up. "The food was quite good."

"Quite good? That was the best restaurant in the city."

"Really?" Wu Ying rubbed his nose, embarrassed. "My mother cooks better."

"Oh, your mother. Of course she does," Zhong Shei said with a roll of his eyes. He did not openly contradict Wu Ying though. That would be a huge insult, one strong enough that it would likely shatter their newfound bond. "Well, I have few of those books with me if you're interested."

"That would be good," Wu Ying said.

Zhong Shei smiled and reached out to the railing, making a small pile of books appear before adding a familiar sword.

"I almost forgot about that." Wu Ying swept the books up into his own storage ring. He took the sword and tugged on the weapon, realizing only then that it was stuck tight. "Damn. Cleaning the blood out is going to be troublesome."

"Well, let's see it. We lied to the guards to keep this," Zhong Shei said impatiently.

Wu Ying chuckled and used more force to pull out the stuck weapon. The pair marveled at the weapon. If nothing else, they could safely say that Ji Ang had had good taste in jians. This one was slightly longer the weapon Wu Ying wielded, and a touch thinner too. Instead of the common diamond-shaped edges, the sword was actually made with an octagonal-edged pattern to increase its thickness and strength. All across the blade, a waterfall pattern could be seen—the mark of a highly skilled forging process.

"Wǒ kào[26]."

Wu Ying could only nod as he got a good look at the sword. He knew, from the fight, that the weapon was good—amazing even. But this, this was far above what he had expected. This was the kind of weapon that sat behind the counter, out of reach of the grubby hands looking to grasp it. This was the kind of weapon that could start fights—or end them.

Wu Ying looked back to where the sailors moved around on the deck, and he quickly slid the sword into the scabbard and made the entire thing disappear. At first Zhong Shei was startled, but seeing the worried look in Wu Ying's eyes as he stared at the others, he nodded.

"I'm tired. I want to sleep in some place quiet. How about you?" Zhong Shei said artfully.

"A good idea."

The pair ambled down the stairs, doing their best to look inconspicuous until they reached their cabins. Zhong Shei gestured to his, and Wu Ying nodded. Inside the tiny room, Zhong Shei held up a hand, quickly inspecting the passageway before he slid the door shut firmly and nodded.

Once again, the sword made an appearance, and the pair carefully inspected and marveled over it. In silence, the pair pored over the sword, checking its fittings and the scabbard itself. Yet no matter how they looked, the sword was as expensive and lethal as it seemed on first viewing. With their inexperienced eyes, they could not find a single flaw. Wu Ying pointed at a small mark near the handle on the blade, drawing Zhong Shei's attention to it.

"I don't recognize it," Zhong Shei said.

---

[26] Basically "holy shit"

"Neither do I," Wu Ying agreed with a sigh, the worm of dread that had coiled around his intestines at his first realisation of what they held had grown even bigger, fed by the nightmares of what-if. "I was hoping it was something you'd seen in the city."

"I never paid attention," Zhong Shei admitted. "But I don't think it's anyone in town. No one does this level of work. Even I'd know that."

"So what do we do?" Wu Ying said. "This isn't something Ji Ang would just have. He must have taken it off someone. Someone important."

"Well, no one knows we have it." At Wu Ying's flat, incredulous look, Zhong Shei snorted. "Fine. We're the best suspects. But I don't want to give this up…"

"Neither do I," Wu Ying said then blinked, realizing another problem.

Zhong Shei realized it at the same time, and the pair stared at each other in concern. There was only one jian after all—and both of them desired the weapon.

The standoff was broken by Zhong Shei, who reached out with two fingers and pushed the sword toward Wu Ying. "You killed him. It's yours."

"I couldn't have done it if you hadn't distracted him. It was your idea to go in too. And you got injured," Wu Ying said and pushed it back.

"I can't take it. It's too much," Zhong Shei said, shaking his head.

"You think I can? That sword is worth more than the entire harvest of my family's farm since I was born! I couldn't even sleep holding on to that."

"You really have messed up expectations of the kind of life those richer than you have," Zhong Shei said, shaking his head and tapping on the sheathed blade. "This is so far out of my experience that I might as well be you."

"We're both impressed. But you should still take it. I already took the money. You deserve something from him." As Zhong Shei opened his mouth to protest, Wu Ying continued. "And whatever you think, I'm still just a peasant. An outer sect member peasant, but a peasant. If the owner—or whoever wants the sword—comes, you'll have a better chance of talking them down from killing you outright."

"You think I should give it to them?" Zhong Shei said, his eyes widening.

"If it's between your life and the sword? Definitely."

Wu Ying's eyes widened when Zhong Shei looked like he actually had to think about it. As much as the guardsman thought their differences were not that great, at times like this, Wu Ying knew the differences were as large as heaven and earth. No farmer would value a thing over his life. The weather, the government, the army—they all took from the common people every day. But so long as their lives and their dignity were intact, everything else could be recovered.

"Maybe I should keep this," Wu Ying said as he saw Zhong Shei's continued reluctance to do the smart thing.

"No." Zhong Shei snatched the sword, making it disappear into his storage ring. "I'll give it up. I promise. But I'll take it."

"Good." Wu Ying could not help but feel a little heartache at giving the weapon away. But at his strength, a weapon of that value was more calamity than fortune. He did not have the strength to wield it, not in public. And if he could not use it, then what was the point? A horse left to graze all year round was not a horse; it was a useless egg. "Good. I'll be going to cultivate now."

"I will too," Zhong Shei said, seemingly motivated by Wu Ying's words. When Wu Ying had exited the room, just before closing the door, Zhong Shei called, "Thank you. Brother."

Wu Ying looked back at Zhong Shei and nodded. The motion made Zhong Shei grin before he closed the door, leaving Wu Ying to head into his room to cultivate. In a corner of his mind, Wu Ying wondered if Zhong Shei would actually cultivate.

Probably. Nearly dying from being too lazy had a great motivational effect.

Wryly smiling, Wu Ying took a seat on his bed and closed his eyes.

Very motivational.

Chapter 19

"Is this it? The Verdant Green Waters Sect?" Zhong Shei asked Wu Ying.

Wu Ying almost rolled his eyes but finally deigned to nod. As if there was anywhere else for the boat to go, never mind the fact that Zhong Shei had asked that question but a few hours ago.

Still, Wu Ying pushed away the irritation. It had little to do with Zhong Shei and mostly revolved around his own uncertainty. He had been away so long—nearly a month and a half after all the delays, waits, and fights. And even if the mission had no stated time limit, Wu Ying could not help but remember that Elder Mo had not exactly assigned the entire quest with the purpose of being fair.

"Glad to be home?" Zhong Shei asked.

"This isn't my home," Wu Ying corrected the man automatically. "But it'll be good to have the mission completed." Wu Ying absently patted the bag on his back. Rather than flaunt his newfound wealth, Wu Ying had moved the bottles and his everyday wear into the bag for now. The rest of the precious gifts—expensive clothing, wines, a couple of decent jian, and a dao—and the majority of his funds sat in his storage ring. "What are your plans after your delivery?"

"Well, I was hoping to see the sect a bit. I hear the sect women are to die for."

Wu Ying rolled his eyes at his lustful friend. The movement made his gaze catch on a nearby ship unloading some familiar bags. His lips quirking, Wu Ying turned to Zhong Shei as he asked innocently, "Hey. You wanted to know what I did at the sect, right?"

"Of course. But you told me it was very boring."

"Sure, sure. But why don't I show you? That way you can experience a little of the life of an outer sect member."

"Is that allowed? I do not want to cause trouble."

"No trouble, no trouble. We'll call it part of your experiential training."

"If you say so."

Wu Ying was very proud of himself that he did not cackle there and then.

***

"You. Are. More. Despicable. Than Ji Ang," Zhong Shei panted as they climbed the mountain.

"Oh, come on. That's only three sacks!" Wu Ying said as he bounded ahead of Zhong Shei, four sacks and Wu Ying's own bag on his shoulders. "This is a light run."

"You huài dàn²⁷."

Zhong Shei fell silent as he pushed himself to follow Wu Ying. Over the last few weeks, the pair had worked hard on practicing to pass the time. Even now, Zhong Shei felt the churning morass of chi in his dantian ready to break out into his meridians. After being stuck for so long at level eight, he was ready to open a new meridian. It was due to all that training that Zhong Shei found the strength to keep up with Wu Ying, who bounded up the steps like a mountain goat.

Though the huài dàn could at least sweat a little.

---

²⁷ A very mild curse. Literally "bad egg" or "wicked." Yes, I'm having fun adding Chinese curses.

***

"Elder Lu," Wu Ying greeted the gatekeeper when the pair finally made their way up the mountain. He bowed low to the Elder while keeping the bags on his back, balancing the entire affair and himself perfectly.

Behind him, Zhong Shei had collapsed on his knees and was breathing deeply, sucking in thin air.

"You've been practicing the Aura Strengthening technique," Elder Lu said with approval. "And improved your cultivation too."

"Not as well as I should have," Wu Ying said as he straightened, a trace of disappointment in his voice. He had hoped to keep the increase in his cultivation secret for a time.

"You are still leaking at your kidney eight, heart eleven…" Elder Lu proceeded to list out the rest of Wu Ying's failings in his aura.

Quickly, Wu Ying memorized the points, even going so far as patching a couple. Immediately, he felt the membrane that kept his aura contained strengthening.

Elder Lu looked at the recovered Zhong Shei. "And who is this?"

"This is Tung Zhong Shei, Elder Lu. He was sent to safeguard your wine jar," Wu Ying said.

"Junior Tung greets Elder Lu," Zhong Shei said as he stood and bowed low. He then stepped forward and twitched his hands, making the wine jar appear as he offered the gift to Xi Qi. "My uncle sends his greeting and a letter. He also asked that you consider sending a letter next time, instead of a sect member."

Xi Qi waved in dismissal of the last portion, taking the letter and wine jar. A moment later, he had the wine jar stored and the letter open, the crease between his eyebrows deepening as he read. Finally, he closed the letter and looked at Zhong Shei. "You may enter the sect. Understand that you are a guest. Wu Ying, take him to the entrance hall. Tell them I have authorized his stay as a guest."

"Yes, Elder," Wu Ying said, bowing again.

Taking the dismissal, Wu Ying steered the pair to the kitchen, where they deposited their load. Wu Ying smiled a little, even knowing that he was unlikely to get any contribution points for this, not having reported in yet. Watching Zhong Shei pant up the hill was gift enough.

"Come, let's get you settled. Then I should turn in this assignment," Wu Ying said. Better to get his friend settled immediately—it was unlikely that Zhong Shei would be allowed into the deeper regions of the sect.

Luckily for Wu Ying, once Zhong Shei had been introduced as a guest, the attendants at the hall were more than happy to take over. The pair made arrangements to meet up for dinner later that day before Wu Ying broke off, headed for his room. In it, he set aside everything but the wine jars, which he kept in his bag, and took the time to wash himself of the dirt and sweat of traveling. Luckily, he had an extra pair of sect robes, allowing Wu Ying to dress himself appropriately.

Dressed and cleaned, Wu Ying was as ready to deal with Elder Mo as he ever would be. The administrative hall itself was the usual hub of busyness, sect members flowing in and out of the building. As an outer sect member, Wu Ying took his place in the long line that served them and waited patiently for his turn. When it finally came, he stepped forward while drawing forth the assignment slip, swallowing the dry nervousness in his throat.

"Junior Long Wu Ying completing his assignment," Wu Ying said firmly. "I have the wine jars here."

"Wu Ying?" The attendant frowned, obviously recognizing the name from somewhere. After a moment, his eyes widened and he looked at Wu Ying more closely, as if he was seeing a two-headed monster. "Please hold. I must have a Senior verify the wine. Please place them on the table in the meantime."

As the attendant scurried away, Wu Ying sighed. Obviously it would not be so easy. Wu Ying quietly pulled the jars out of the bag, setting them aside and checking them once again for cracks. Relieved to see that everything was still fine, Wu Ying stepped back and waited. He did not have to wait long before Elder Mo himself came striding out, hands behind his back.

"You finally came back. And you claim that you have brought the wine?" Elder Mo said with a sniff. "Even though the sale would have been completed long ago and all the jars were taken up by others. Do you think we are fools?"

"No, Elder," Wu Ying said, bowing low. "These really are the jars of plum wine."

Elder Mo glared before he strode forward and looked at the wine jars. His eyes swept over them for a moment, stopping on the labels and the seals before he picked up one. He frowned, inspecting the jar before placing it down with a light thump.

"Well, the forgeries are quite good. But there is only one way to tell." Elder Mo gestured to the waiting original attendant. "Bring a cup."

Once again, Wu Ying waited as the attendant left his post.

Elder Mo, on the other hand, fixed Wu Ying with his gaze. "Failing an assignment is shameful and will see you banished. But attempting to trick the assignment hall will see your cultivation crippled. Do you still dare say that these are Tung family plum wine?"

"I do, Elder," Wu Ying said.

Once again, Wu Ying felt the gazes of the sect members locking onto him and the Elder, happy to have some entertainment to lighten up their lives. Elder Mo snorted and left the conversation at that until the attendant arrived.

As the Elder took the proffered cup and reached for the jar, Wu Ying decided to speak up again. "Elder, if the jar is opened by you and it is the plum wine, I will not be able to complete my mission. You have not accepted them as yet."

"You need not worry about that. If this is the plum blossom wine, I will bear the consequences of opening it," Elder Mo said dismissively. With a flick of his finger, he popped open the cork. The moment he did so, the enticing aroma of the plum blossom wine washed through the hall. Along with the smell came the flood of chi the wine had contained, awakening the cultivators' senses and expanding their awareness.

"Good wine."

"This smell reminds me of plums and spring."

"Very good wine."

"Could it be the real thing?"

"Impossible. That assignment has been there for two years already. Even getting into the merchant's hall is hard. All the previous assignees were beaten up by the other buyers' people when they tried to get in."

"So that's why Elder Mo assigned it to him."

The hubbub of conversation behind Wu Ying enlightened the cultivator. A touch late, Wu Ying mused, but at least he now understood things better. And he'd thought the entire hindrance was Ji Ang and the timing. It seemed there were even more hidden traps.

Finally extracting himself from the surprise that the smell had brought upon him, Elder Mo poured the wine into the cup. Still, his actions had a little hesitation now as the Elder frowned at the wine. For an Elder like him, it was as simple as breathing to grasp the fact that the wine before him was no simple libation. It was a masterful work, one that layered multiple scents.

Elder Mo brought the full cup to his face, swirling it and releasing the aroma near his nose. His eyes narrowed again as the unmistakeable smell of plum blossoms filled the room, doubly confirming his initial impression. Hesitating no longer, the Elder tossed the wine into his mouth and froze. When he finally unfroze, he smacked the cup down with force and exhaled a breath, one that brought with it a flow of turbid chi.

"Good wine. Very good wine!" Elder Mo said, pouring another cup.

"Then I have completed the assignment?" Wu Ying said, relief flowing through him. But that relief was dashed by the next pronouncement.

"Good wine. But it's not the Tung family plum blossom wine. This is too good." Elder Mo sipped on the wine more carefully now. "Their wine has never been this good."

"Elder Mo—"

Elder Mo sipped on the cup as he stared at Wu Ying. Tapping his chin, he offered magnanimously, "Tell me where you got this wine and I'll make the crippling quick."

"This is Tung plum blossom wine. I got it directly from the winemaker himself." A slight pause, then Wu Ying added, "Well, from his storeroom via his nephew. But Uncle Tang saw it all."

"Really. The kind of stories children will make up," Elder Mo said, shaking his head. With a flick of his fingers, Wu Ying's feet were swept out from under him as a wave of force took him to his knees. "Kowtow[28] and beg for forgiveness for making up such lies."

Wu Ying's chest burned with anger as he struggled to his feet with numb legs. Elder Mo gestured again and Wu Ying slammed into the floor, catching

---

[28] Traditional method of bowing where one gets on their knees then places their head against the ground. It's a very subservient form of obeisance.

himself with one hand while the Elder tsked. All around, conversations ceased as they watched Wu Ying being disciplined.

"You dare to continue this farce? You do not know how high are the heavens, do you?"

"I have done nothing wrong," Wu Ying said as he tried to force himself onto his feet. Yet he found it impossible as a formless pressure pushed down on his body.

Those nearby felt it too, the use of chi pressuring them all. Wu Ying struggled to keep his body upright, mostly via stubborn will, as he felt his muscles strain and bones creak under the pressure. As Elder Mo's face darkened further, a light cough broke the deepening silence in the admission hall. The sect members blinked and turned their heads to be greeted by the sight of a younger Elder with dark hair and a light smile.

"Elder Cheng!" Wu Ying gasped in surprise at seeing his sponsor for the first time in months. For a second, hope flared in his chest—then he recalled Liu Tsong's comment. There was no way Elder Cheng was there to save him.

"Are those the jars I requested?" Elder Cheng Zhao Wan said. He walked forward, sniffing the air. "That smells amazing. But why is one open?"

"Elder Cheng." Elder Mo looked at Elder Cheng and shook his head. "I'm sorry you've been bothered about this. This despicable person was attempting to pass off this wine to fulfill your assignment. But while it is good wine, it is not the plum blossom wine you once shared with us all."

Elder Cheng frowned as he walked over, tilting his head. As he neared the group, his eyes widened when he actually noticed Wu Ying, then he returned his attention to the smug Elder. "This wine smells very familiar though. May I?"

"Of course." Elder Mo gestured to one of the attendants.

When Wu Ying tried to stand back up, Zhao Wan shook his head and Wu Ying stayed where he was, on one knee with his teeth gritted as Elder Mo's formless pressure exerted itself on him. A short while later, the attendant was back with a clean cup. Elder Mo poured for Zhao Wan.

Elder Cheng repeated Elder Mo's actions, sniffing, tasting, then slamming back the entire drink. His eyes widened before he too exhaled a turbid breath. "Good wine. It sends the chi in my core singing. I can feel my chi purifying."

"It's true. But it is not the Tung plum blossom wine," Elder Mo said, his lips thinned.

"It is," Wu Ying growled.

Another flick of his finger sent Wu Ying sprawling, his face stinging from an unseen, chi-driven slap.

"You sick dog. You dare speak when your betters are speaking." Elder Mo raised his hand to strike again, but Elder Cheng spoke up.

"Junior Long is correct though. This is Tung plum blossom wine," Elder Cheng said.

"What? No. This is much stronger than what was provided before," Elder Mo said, shaking his head. "Elder Cheng, you are not trying to cover for your sponsored member, are you?"

"Have I ever?" Elder Cheng said, raising a single eyebrow.

Elder Mo's face grew taut as he slowly shook his head in acknowledgement of Elder Cheng's well-known proclivities.

"This is Tung plum blossom wine, but it is the family's own collection. They only sell the dregs to the public. The failures. Even that, as you know, is rare enough. This is worth much more. It's no wonder that Elder Mo does not recognize the taste though—only a few outside of their family have tried it. I would be interested to know how Junior Long managed to get three such jars. Even the single jar I had the pleasure of trying was hard to come by."

"Personal collection?" Elder Mo's face paled as he clearly recalled the implausible story Wu Ying had related. Eying the bleeding Wu Ying, he sniffed. "Well. It seems you have completed the assignment."

Wu Ying pushed himself to his feet once again, but this time, no formless pressure or strike robbed him of his footing. Reaching into his pouch, Wu Ying pulled out his sect stamp and handed it to the attendant, who tapped it against the sealing block. The sweating attendant handed the sect stamp back with the assignment marked complete.

"Well, go. Unless you intend to take another assignment?" Elder Mo said.

Slowly, the hall broke into life again as most considered the free show over.

"No, Elder. I am content with my assignment with Elder Huang, if that is still available," Wu Ying said, keeping his head down. He burnt with the injustice of the accusation, of the blows he'd received, but he could not act out. The difference in station between the two was too wide. Any disrespect would put his own standing in jeopardy.

"It is. Go."

Wu Ying was turning around when Elder Cheng's voice cut in. "Wait."

"Yes, Elder?" Wu Ying turned back.

"Give me your sect token." Wu Ying frowned but handed it to Elder Cheng, who passed his own token over it before tossing Wu Ying's back to him. "It is customary to provide a higher remuneration for work that is completed over the specifications, and this is far and above my request." Zhao Wan smiled, looking Wu Ying up and down carefully. "It seems I was right and you do have some fate with me."

"Elder." Wu Ying bowed after storing his seal, unsure of what to say. Better to be polite and say nothing.

"Now, Elder Mo, I recall hearing that you would compensate for the open jar," Elder Cheng said, his eyes glittering with malice. "This jar cannot be stored any longer. And you know that I always serve three such jars during the autumn festival. How am I to do so with one jar open now?"

Elder Mo's eyes tightened as he looked at Elder Cheng's wide, smiling face then down at Wu Ying, who was slowly backing away. Elder Mo's lips twisted into a sneer before he controlled it and smiled back at Zhao Wan.

"Well, Elder Cheng, I never expected something like this to occur…"

Once out of the nearby orbit, Wu Ying took off at speed. Better not to be seen while Elder Cheng extracted the maximum advantage from Elder Mo's mistake. It was obvious to Wu Ying that Elder Cheng must have been present long enough to hear the entire thing and could have put a stop to the farce. Rubbing his face, Wu Ying made a mental note not to put any trust into any of the Elders. They were all playing their games of politics, and minor sect members like him were nothing.

Chapter 20

Later that night, after a dinner with his only friends in the sect—Liu Tsong, Tou He, and Zhong Shei—Wu Ying stumbled back to his room, slightly inebriated after a joyful celebration. At the room's entrance, his hand paused as he noted the formerly locked door was now unlocked. Drawing his sword, Wu Ying readied himself to charge in.

"Enter, Wu Ying," Elder Cheng called from within.

"Elder," Wu Ying said, sheathing his sword and entering. If Elder Cheng wanted him dead, he did not need to break into his room to do that.

Soon afterward, Wu Ying found himself detailing his adventures while Elder Cheng listened impassively, seated on the only chair in the tiny room.

"So. You survived your journey. Made friends with the nephew. Killed an infamous bandit. Managed to complete your assignment. And helped me gain an important favor from Elder Mo," Elder Cheng said as he stroked his beard.

"Yes, Elder."

"Quite a busy half year." Without another word, Elder Cheng stood and walked toward the door. Wu Ying automatically stepped aside, allowing the man to walk past him. Only when Elder Cheng had turned the corner of the door did he speak again. "Coming?"

"Yes, Elder!"

Wu Ying hurried out of the room, locking his door before following his superior. As he jogged to keep up with the fast-moving Elder, he found his inebriation burning away. To Wu Ying's surprise, Elder Cheng led him up the mountain, higher than he ever had been, before they entered a private courtyard. By the time Wu Ying stumbled within, Elder Cheng was standing in the center of the carefully manicured location, waiting with one hand behind his back.

"Elder?" Wu Ying asked.

"Show me your cultivation."

Wu Ying released the seals on his aura, allowing the chi that would naturally leak out to do so.

Elder Cheng watched for a short period before he gestured to Wu Ying's belt where he carried his sword. "Show me."

"Where?" Wu Ying said, looking around the courtyard for something to hit. Or did he mean his forms?

"Against me. Hurry up."

Wu Ying blinked then drew his sword, shaking his head at the whiplash of commands. But as he stared at Elder Cheng, a slight shudder ran through him. Something, a deep instinct, told Wu Ying not to take the demonstration lightly.

Drawing himself to his full height, Wu Ying eyed Elder Cheng one last time then stalked forward. When he was within range, he started with light, quick stabs. Elder Cheng swayed slightly, dodging the attacks. The Elder did not even need to say anything to showcase his disappointment. Eyes narrowing, Wu Ying sped up, giving up on easy, probing attacks and committing to the fight.

Only when he did that did Elder Cheng move his lead hand. Surprisingly, a light glow surrounded it, condensed chi that he wielded like a sword to block Wu Ying's attacks. Again and again, Wu Ying spun around the Elder, who twisted, blocked, and leaned away from the attacks, never moving from his starting spot. Occasionally, he idly attacked Wu Ying, his attacks carrying a weight that sent Wu Ying staggering back whenever he blocked.

Falling into the rhythm of the sparring match, Wu Ying's earlier reticence disappeared. He sped up as he utilized everything he had practiced, everything he had learned in his sparring with the wandering cultivator Yuan Rang and the life-and-death struggles he had experienced. His blade grew keener, his attacks sharper as the killing intent behind his strikes evolved.

Wu Ying tried everything, from straight lunges, wrist cuts to feinted blows that became strikes, using the myriad forms of the Long family style. When that failed to move Elder Cheng or land a blow, he shrank the circle and fought closer, adding in kicks from the Shen style to confuse and hamper Elder Cheng. Most of those were casually dodged, others blocked with the light lift of a leg or twist of the arm. No matter what Wu Ying did, he could not make the man move. And still, Wu Ying fought on as he searched for the moment.

There.

A moment's gap, an opening in the way Elder Cheng blocked a kick then leaned back from a subsequent cut, leaving him slightly off balance. Wu Ying threw himself forward, taking full advantage. The Sword's Truth—that deceptively simple lunge that was not simple at all. It streaked toward Elder Cheng's throat at an angle to his body, intent on tearing out the side of it. For the first time, the Elder moved, taking a single step back. His hand came down almost lazily, slapping down the blade as it reached the end of its momentum, the attack sending tremors of power through Wu Ying's hand.

"Decent." Elder Cheng lowered his hand, the chi sword disappearing as he allowed the energy to disperse. Wu Ying slowly lowered his sword, breathing hard. "We can work with this."

"Work with…?" Wu Ying's eyes widened as understanding dawned. "Are you going to train me?" Unsaid was the "at last" that he desperately wanted to add.

"Yes. I do need to repay your help. That will balance our karma. You'll also need it, if you are to survive Elder Mo's ire."

Wu Ying winced, knowing what Elder Cheng said was true. Elder Mo might not be able to do much to Elder Cheng, but Wu Ying was the perfect target.

"Do not concern yourself yet. Until the sect examinations are over, you are safe. Sending an outer sect member on an external assignment was already unusual. Sending him out twice would be too much for the sect to ignore." Elder Cheng assessed Wu Ying's condition then gestured for him to raise the sword. "Now. Try again. And this time, minimize your motions more. You are wasting time with too many movements."

Wu Ying hid a groan, raising his sword as instructed. Somehow, he knew that this training session was going to last a while.

***

Hours later, Wu Ying shuffled home, exhausted and aching. Even with the boost his increased cultivation had provided and the release of his chi from his dantian, Wu Ying's body hurt. And unlike his training session with Yuan Rang, not once did Elder Cheng lay a hand on him directly. But, Wu Ying thought as he raised his right hand and watched as his fingers trembled uncontrollably, that did not mean the Elder did not feel free to attack his weapon.

Even so, Elder Cheng's training was as good as Yuan Rang's. Better in some ways. More guided, for Wu Ying realized that the Elder had constrained his defenses to a certain number and types of forms. Once Wu Ying became aware of the fact and worked a solution to Elder Cheng's defenses, the Elder changed the pattern, forcing Wu Ying to start again. It was exhausting, both physically and mentally, since Elder Cheng still forced Wu Ying to constantly move at full speed. But the training also lacked a certain "edge," a bite that Yuan Rang's brutal methods had used.

Training was going to be hell, Wu Ying knew. Every third night, Elder Cheng intended for Wu Ying to return and train again. Over the next four months—the time before the end of autumn, when the sect festival would be held—he would be trained by Elder Cheng. When Fairy Yuan returned, she would take over the classes.

In the meantime, Wu Ying had been provided specific pointers for his martial arts training. He would need to enlist the help of others, since the majority of it involved evasion, timing, and movement drills—none of which the constant repetition of forms could help.

Luckily, Wu Ying smiled to himself, there were a few people he could call on.

***

Legs apart, body lowered slightly. Hands by his sides, though a slight amount of tension was still carried within them. Wu Ying stood, focused on Zhong Shei's body. The punch came from the left this time, a looping overhand cross. Wu Ying shifted and twisted without moving his feet, even as another punch moved immediately after. For the next couple of minutes, Wu Ying ducked, bobbed, and weaved as best he could, patching together forms, perception, and intuition as he dodged. There was an art and a science to evasion—duck under an arm that punched at you and the next attack could only come from a few angles. The forms he studied taught the next motion, the best angle to shift to to reduce the chance of being hit. But they only reduced it—and that was where perception and intuition came in.

When a nasty uppercut caught Wu Ying by surprise, he staggered backward and rubbed his chin, looking at the smirking Zhong Shei.

Once the pair had regulated their breathing, Wu Ying smiled. "Your turn."

"I hate you," Zhong Shei complained even as he got into stance.

This time, Wu Ying would get a chance to work some combinations to hit Zhong Shei. Lightly, of course, but his job was to learn movement patterns, to understand angles and how to mix up his attacks.

The pair traded off three more times before they proceeded to a moving evasion pattern, one that was "encouraged" through the use of a sharp sword. Not extremely sharp, but sharp enough to make them bleed.

Evasion. One of the first skills he had been given to improve.

***

The spear flew toward his face, stopped only by a wrist-driven block. Jian held in front of him, his body turned toward Tou He, Wu Ying watched as the spear was retracted swiftly before being stabbed forward again, the spearhead dipping at the last moment in a feint attempt. Wu Ying blocked the attack, but this time, the spear did not withdraw all the way, and it cut forward and upward, leaving a thin slice of blood along Wu Ying's blocking arm.

"Damn it," Wu Ying snarled.

"You always turn your wrist too much when you block," Tou He said.

"I know. I told you to watch for that," Wu Ying groused, flexing his hand. Already, the chi in his body had collected around the wound, helping it clot.

"Ready?"

"Go."

The spear came shooting forward again, this time as an overhand chop. Wu Ying moved to block with the lightest touch possible.

Defensive practice. Another skill to work on.

***

"You need to catch me when I'm moving back," Liu Tsong said, grinning as she held the rice bowl perpendicular to her body.

"I'm. Trying," Wu Ying said as he thrust with his back leg into a lunge then recovered forward and spun his back leg into a kick. After that, he dropped his body onto the outstretched leg to chase after the dodging Liu Tsong.

"No, you're just charging me. Remember, this is timing training," Liu Tsong said.

"There is no such training!" Wu Ying howled as his stomach grumbled.

"Well, there should be."

Laughing, Liu Tsong continued to tease him, forcing Wu Ying to try to catch her as she taunted him with his meal. The other two laughed, watching. It was an entirely unfair matchup, considering the inner sect member was both an entire cultivation level higher and more skilled. But then, good training always meant pitting yourself against your betters. And Liu Tsong was purposely pausing at times, giving Wu Ying the opportunity to catch her when she came to a rest—if he could judge and use those breaks properly.

***

Another night and Wu Ying stood before Elder Cheng. The cultivator slowly pivoted on one foot into a drop lunge before a cross-body block and recovery followed by a pair of wrist cuts. Also known as dragon catches the rainbow. The moment he had finished the cuts, Wu Ying pivoted on his foot and repeated, moving in a slow circle.

"Focus on those cuts. They should originate from the wrist only. Do not move your elbow!"

"Drop. Drop. Let the earth take you. Do not push."

"Faster! Your back leg must recover immediately."

"Lower your weight. Bend your knees and relax your stomach. Remember, keep your weight centered around your dantian."

Again and again. Each iteration an improvement, building on the last. Sometimes, Elder Cheng would spar with him. Other times, it was form work or drills that focused on a single area of improvement. Over and over again.

***

Days passed like that, the last dregs of summer fading, turning over with the cold winds of autumn. As much as Wu Ying trained, so did his friends. It seemed as though the sect itself had caught a training fever. Every day, the courtyards filled with sect members, each of them practicing their martial styles or cultivating in a desperate bid to increase their standing. It was not just the newcomers; even those who had been around for a while worked hard. After all, those sect members who showed no improvement from year to year were in danger too—if in nothing but a decrease in the resources the sect would dedicate to them.

The library grew busier as sect members browsed the books in search of a solution or a quick fix. A magic pill that would give them an edge over the competition. The assignment hall grew busy as well, since a few sect members had given up on winning a decent position at the tournament and were looking to bolster their standing via contributions. Demon subjugation assignments were quickly snatched up, the experiential training and additional funds from such activity highly popular.

For the second time in his life in the sect, Wu Ying found himself indulging in the routine of training and cultivating. In the blink of an eye, the leaves on the trees had turned color and dropped, signaling the start of a longer, colder season. Only the occasional letter from home, finding its way to him via merchants, broke the monotony of his life.

That, and his friends. Surprisingly, Zhong Shei stayed, spending the months in training and cultivation. Whether it was the atmosphere or his newfound determination after their fight with Ji Ang, Zhong Shei's cultivation and martial prowess soared, breaking through two meridians. Of course, even with his newfound discipline, Zhong Shei would still pay regular visits to the brothels and inns at the base of the mountain.

Two days from the start of the sect tournament, Wu Ying's eyes opened in his room as he exhaled a turbid breath. His nose wrinkled as he stood, grateful for his forethought of stocking up on clean cloth and buckets of water. A few minutes later, Wu Ying had cleansed his body of the filth and grey impurities that had coated his body.

Body Cleansing 8. Four more meridians to go before he was ready to progress to the next stage. It was remarkable growth for someone who had been at Body Cleansing 2 a bare eight months ago. Of course, Wu Ying knew that it was as much due to a few fortunate encounters and the support of his friends. While it was possible to grow and be enlightened by doing nothing more than staying in a single place all one's life, most people—and perhaps most importantly, him—needed stimulus. Impetus. Experience.

Rubbing his chin, Wu Ying grimaced and reached for his knife. Better to clean himself up while he pondered if, perhaps, he had found the beginning of his dao. The Dao of the Restless Feet? The Dao of Unfortunate Circumstances? The Dao of the Uncultured Wandering Farmer?

Laughing, Wu Ying nicked his chin and had to stop and dab at the wound until the blood stopped running. Still, he couldn't help but let out a low chuckle once in a while as he dressed. A glance out the open window allowed Wu Ying to check on the angle of the sun. Time to get moving if he did not want to be late.

A part of Wu Ying wondered how Yin Xue had done. The nobleman's son had been at Body Cleansing 4 before they arrived. The last time they'd met, he had progressed to Body Cleansing 6. Could he have progressed further? Easily—with the support of his father and the sect.

Body Cleansing 8. Wu Ying let out a tired breath. It was not enough to achieve a place in the inner sect. Most of those who entered the inner sect were in the 10s, if not at Energy Gathering stage, when they finally achieved that honor. Now that the tournament was days away, Wu Ying faced the truth of his ambition. As much as Wu Ying desired otherwise, he could only hope to stay in the sect for another year.

Perhaps Tou He was right, Wu Ying sighed. Perhaps all this struggle was in vain. But if man did not endeavor to better himself, then what use was he? Even the farmer wanted a better harvest every year, or a larger field. Ambition was intrinsic to the human condition—but tempering that ambition was the course of the wise.

Shaking off the morose thoughts, Wu Ying closed the door of his room. Better get going if he did not want to be late for training. If he could only ensure he stayed, then that was all he could do.

Chapter 21

Once a year, the sect's main bell was used. Once a year, to mark the time for the outer sect members to gather and again to mark the start of the Verdant Green Waters Sect's annual tournament. The tournament was always held at the end of autumn, as the weather turned toward winter but before the snow fell. It was the perfect time to test what the students had learned during the busy period of the year—or so the sect said. In truth, Wu Ying believed it was to save the sect the cost of winter's rations—but that was, perhaps, the cynical farmer within him. After all, you always had to think about the harvest and winter stores.

In either case, the members of the sect were gathered in a courtyard higher on the mountain, one so large that it was easily three times Wu Ying's family's fields. Even then, the crowd was gathered like sheep, with barely enough space for all the outer sect members. Thankfully, the inner sect members were scattered on the slope and buildings around, watching the proceedings. For now, the outer sect members would do the fighting. Most were gathered for a good show and a chance to see the rising stars of the sect, those who would replace the members who had fallen out of favor or left.

Of course, the number of inner sect members naturally decreased each year. Being a cultivator was a dangerous job, and the various external assignments took their toll with death, injury, and missing members a fact of sect life. Sometimes inner sect members left on multi-year assignments or for experiential training, freeing up space in the sect compound. It was up to the Inner Hall Master to decide how many spots he had that year—taking into account loss of sect members, those away for experiential training or secluded cultivation, and the gifted—or wealthy—few who would be elevated directly.

In the crowd, Wu Ying craned his neck, desperately searching for Tou He. He knew that Liu Tsong and Zhong Shei were above, watching the proceedings in comfort. That, of course, left Wu Ying with only Tou He—but neither had thought to arrange to meet up earlier. Threading through the crowd with occasional pushes and apologies, Wu Ying growled in exasperation and considered giving up on his fruitless quest.

"Well, look who has survived," a familiar mocking voice rang out.

Wu Ying turned to meet the voice and spotted Yin Xue and his usual entourage. The entourage itself consisted of five individuals, two of which were commoners like him. Wu Ying was slightly ashamed of them, by how quickly they felt the need to grab onto the coattails of another. Of course, flanking Yin Xue were a pair of noblemen's sons who were part of the entourage, the "main players." From what Wu Ying recalled of the pair, neither had the talent or discipline to elevate themselves from the outer sect. Which, as much as Wu Ying hated to admit it, Yin Xue did.

"Yin Xue," Wu Ying greeted, mostly politely.

"You dare use the Lord Wen's name directly. How dare you!" One of Yin Xue's barking dogs stepped forward, snarling.

Wu Ying looked at him, extending the sense he had worked on, and sighed. Probably no better than Body Cleansing 4. Maybe a poor 5. His actions once again reminded Wu Ying of one of his more recent frustrations. All that time spent learning how to judge other people's cultivation by their presence, only to learn that it was a skill Tou He and the rest of the outer sect members had been taught by the sect during his absence. It was frustrating at best, though his own exploration of the skill had given him a better "feel" than most. Few of the outer sect members could judge beyond "low, mid, and high" levels in each stage.

"What. Have nothing to say?" the dog snarled, and Wu Ying rolled his eyes.

"Not to a dog like you." Wu Ying turned to Yin Xue and nodded before he turned to go back to looking for his friend.

"Don't bother with the peasant. We'll take care of him later," Yin Xue said a little too loudly behind Wu Ying.

Wu Ying shook his head as he pushed away. Damn idiot. After all this time, he still seemed to have it out for Wu Ying. Which really puzzled Wu Ying in a way. Was Yin Xue's ego so small that he felt the need to stomp on Wu Ying even now? Was he that insecure in his place in the sect, insecure in who he was, that the existence of a peasant that he knew was considered an insult to his ego?

Perhaps. But in either case, Wu Ying could not fix him. All he could do was look for his friend and do his best in this exam. Yet a fruitless half hour of searching for Tou He later, Wu Ying found himself lost in the crowd with nothing to show for it but a slightly sweaty back. Exhaling a tired breath, Wu Ying looked up as the sect's main bell rang once more.

Too late for anything else now. The crowd fell silent, all the outer sect members turning to face the main landing, where the Outer Hall sect master had walked forward. This was the first time Wu Ying had seen the august personage, Elder Khoo Yang Min.

"Sect members, we welcome you to the annual tournament. Here, you will vie with your fellow cultivators to ascertain your standing in the sect. While martial prowess is only one of the factors that decides your continued presence in our sect, the Verdant Green Waters Sect has always stood firm in its obligations to the state of Shen. We are its guardians against other sects, the sharp jian and the unbowing dao of their defense. As such, your standing in this tournament will greatly influence your overall standing in the sect." Elder Khoo's voice carried across the courtyard with ease, empowered by chi so that everyone within the courtyard and those watching could hear him.

Hands behind his back, the long-haired, white-bearded Elder stared at everyone with piercing eyes over his long, hooked nose. "For all that, we have little reason to judge you individually. Your sect trainers have all assessed you over the course of the year. If you look at your sect seal now, your current standing in the sect will be displayed. Those of you content with your standing may leave the courtyard. Those of you who are unhappy should stay."

Wu Ying nodded slowly and pulled the sect stamp from within his robes. With just over two thousand outer sect members, the bottom ten percent would be sent home. More than two hundred members. Wu Ying pulled out the sect stamp and stared at the glowing lines of information, illuminated via the chi contained within.

"One thousand, nine hundred, three!" Wu Ying exclaimed, anger flashing upward and flushing his face. "What in the thousand hells?"

"What kind of trash are you to get so low?" a nearby cultivator scoffed, looking at Wu Ying. The man stood with his feet akimbo, arms bulging out of a set of robes that had somehow lost its sleeves.

"I'm no trash."

"That's what they all say." The cultivator smirked at Wu Ying, who growled back.

However, while the pair were facing off, various sect members within the courtyard were moving. Some decided to leave the courtyard, content with their placing. Others stayed—preferring to risk the tournament than to be ejected immediately.

"Not leaving, trash? You think you can do well?"

"Better than this false ranking," Wu Ying said.

He looked up, twisting his head to the side, and spotted Elder Mo standing nearby the Outer Sect Master, staring directly at Wu Ying and smirking. Wu Ying's teeth pulled into a snarl before he looked down, not wanting to confront the Elder. Not yet at least. Anything he could do to the Elder would be like a toddler complaining about an adult—all sound and fury but without any real effect.

"Hah! You overreaching fools will all say that. I'll be your first opponent then." The cultivator grinned, flexing his biceps again.

"Really?" Wu Ying said with a roll of his eyes. Idiot. Even Wu Ying could tell, especially from how slim his waist and legs were, that the cultivator had spent all of his time working on his upper body. Once upon a time, a caravan guard had come by who looked much like this cultivator—all bluster and proud of how strong he was. Then he challenged Old Yi, who had grown a little fat since his back injury. The pair spent the next hour chopping wood to see who was stronger and fitter. At first, the guard had done well, splitting logs with a single blow. But soon enough, he ran out of steam while Old Yi chugged on, splitting log after log. The simple fact was that Old Yi knew how to split the logs from long years of practice, knew how to use all of his body. "If we are so lucky, I'll accept the challenge."

"Good. It seems all those who are content with their places have left," Elder Khoo said, cutting off further discussion. "For those who have stayed, I commend you. It should not be a cultivator's place to be content with their placing. We challenge the gods with our very actions. Settling is not for us!"

Even if Elder Khoo said that, Wu Ying knew that human nature would see most individuals more than happy to "settle." At a certain point, struggling was not worth the effort—especially if one was already limited by one's talent. Still, Wu Ying was there, waiting, just as much because of the trick played on him by Elder Mo as for any desire to upgrade his status.

"Now, since there seems to be more of you than normal, we shall have a quick elimination round. Fight honorably and with care. Remember, these are still your fellow sect members. Intentionally killing one another is not allowed. Now, pick your partner."

The sleeveless cultivator smirked at Wu Ying, who eyed him up before returning the nod. For a second, Wu Ying touched the sword at his side—a practice sword he had taken out just for this event. Thankfully, due to the Sense of the Sword, he had not needed to practice for hours beforehand to get used to the weapon.

"Hey! No weapons," the muscled cultivator said, eyes bulging at Wu Ying's motion.

"Why?" Wu Ying cocked his head to the side as he waited for the Elder's start signal.

Unlike the pair of them, it seemed others were having trouble finding a suitable partner.

"It's not manly," the cultivator said, though the nervous glances he kept giving Wu Ying's weapon told another story.

"That's a good point," Wu Ying said, relaxing and letting his hand move away from the hilt of his sword.

At that point, the gong that signaled the start of the fight rang out. The muscled cultivator sprang into motion, throwing himself in an overhead leap while cocking a hand back to throw a powerful punch. Wu Ying stepped forward, his hand dropping to his sword even as his other hand tilted the scabbard to allow for the quick draw that was part of the Long family style. Dragon unsheathes his claws.

The blow cut across the cultivator's body, cracking ribs and bruising muscle even as Wu Ying completed the form and turned. A quick cut to the back finished the spasming, over-muscled cultivator before Wu Ying sheathed his blade.

"But I don't care."

Chapter 22

"Tou He!" Wu Ying said, finding his friend seated after having rounded nearly the entire courtyard.

After his initial fight, Wu Ying had watched the other fights, expecting the next stage to happen immediately. That expectation had been dashed, so he had taken the free time to search for his friend. Tou He waved to Wu Ying and gestured to an empty patch of ground, where Wu Ying sat gratefully.

"Thanks!" Wu Ying said as he took a steamed meat bun from Tou He. "You brought food, eh?"

"You didn't?" Tou He asked, and Wu Ying shook his head. For all his preparations, eating had not been high on the list.

"I thought we'd have a chance to eat. Or food would be sent," Wu Ying said.

"True. I doubt anyone expected that," Tou He said with an inclination of his head.

Wu Ying followed his gaze to where two giants among the outer sect members continued to battle it out, the cause of their current predicament. It had already been a half hour, but both contestants refused to budge. They were so evenly matched and of high enough cultivation that the deadlocked wrestling match they had undertaken had put a stop to the entire event.

"I wonder why they don't just move on. Or call it done. I'm certain we've been trimmed down enough," Wu Ying said. Of the initial few hundred, less than a hundred were left in the courtyard. Surely they could start the simple elimination rounds now.

"Oh, that's because the Elders have been betting on the result," Tou He said.

Wu Ying blinked, not having heard that. Then again, Tou He had made more friends than Wu Ying, since he had neither directly annoyed an Elder nor left for a month and a half like Wu Ying. In truth, an ex-monk might be considered below a noble, but he was still better than a farmer.

"Hey, how come you're here? I thought you were looking to take it easy," Wu Ying said, recalling Tou He's professed goals.

Tou He chuckled ruefully and scratched his head. "Well, it seems the Elder who sponsored me heard about my plans and was quite irate. He threatened me with expulsion if I did not take part and do well in the tournament."

Wu Ying took another bite from the bun to hide a smile. Served him right. The damn ex-monk was entirely too gifted and content. Even now, among all those who looked worried, excited, and nervous, the ex-monk sat, serenely eating a steamed bun. Only someone so carefree could think of something like food at a time like this.

A loud crack brought the pair's attention to the wrestling match. Somehow, somewhere, the deadlock had been broken. So had an arm. Groaning, the loser cradled his arm while the winner helped him up, clapping his ex-opponent on the shoulder while grinning.

"Good. Now we can begin," Elder Khoo's voice rang out, drawing the group's attention to him.

At the Elder's gesture, a stream of inner sect members appeared, moving down the stairs. In a few minutes, the inner sect members had split the tournament contestants into five mostly even groups. Along with Tou He, there were twenty-one other individuals in Wu Ying's group, with just above a third who looked like peasants. In truth, Wu Ying knew he was guessing—with everyone in sect robes, it was hard to tell, beyond a certain difference in bearing, the darkness of their skin, and the weapons they held. Commoners like him often wielded spears, if they wielded any weapon at all. After all, every family had at least one, if not more, spear at home.

"Each of you will pair up within your groups. After the first match, you will be matched with those of equal wins in the other groups, allowing us to better assess your prowess," Elder Khoo said, sweeping his gaze over the sect members. "While we admire those who are willing to strive for greatness, one must also be aware of their limits. Those of you who fail to do well face a much higher chance of being banished from the sect.

"May the heavens smile on you."

***

Of course, the matches did not start immediately. Firstly, they had to make enough space for the chosen pair to fight. Thankfully, the inner sect members in charge of the matter were efficient, and opponents were quickly paired up. Wu Ying found himself part of the circle around the chosen fighters, watching with avid interest as he assessed his potential opponents.

After four fights, Wu Ying had a clear understanding of the significant difference in skill shown among the remainder members. Through luck or stubbornness, a portion of those who stood in the courtyard were from the bottom ten percent, and it showed in their martial styles. Few lasted more than a few blows against the upper ten percent, those who had stayed in hopes of showcasing their talent to the Inner Sect Elder.

"Wu Ying. Yin Tse."

Wu Ying shook his head free from his thoughts and walked into the middle of the ring, turning his head to look at his opponent. He frowned a bit, noting the slight female before him who wielded a heavy, three-ringed dao[29].

Clasping his hands, Wu Ying bowed to Yin Tse, who followed suit. At the attendant's signal, the pair readied themselves. The small girl took a modified back-weighted stance with the sabre held overhead threateningly. Wu Ying cocked his head to the side as he drew his own sword, tempted to drag out the fight, as that particular pose was tiring on one's arms. Then again, she seemed to be at least Body Cleansing 9, maybe even 10. That would give the slim lady much greater strength than what was directly apparent.

All the while, Wu Ying was circling the dao-wielder, staying just outside of her range. Other than slight shifts in her position to keep Wu Ying lined up, the young lady seemed content to wait.

"Boring!"

"No stalling. We have a lot of fights to get through today. If you two do not begin being active, I will rule this a loss on both your sides," the referee snapped, growing tired of the two.

"Damn it," Wu Ying cursed.

Wu Ying's momentary distraction provided the female cultivator an opening, which she took by exploding forward. Her sword stayed still until the last moment before it swirled, cutting down so fast that it left sword mirages in Wu Ying's eyes. The technique of sword mirages was derived not only from the movement speed of the sword but also the angles, with each cut in a pre-determined order to create a false impression of a net of unbreakable attacks.

---

[29] The three-ringed dao is a sabre with three iron rings set in the back. This adds to the weight of the weapon and allows blocking and locking of weapons, but it is generally considered a brutal weapon.

Eyes wide, Wu Ying could only hold up his sword and launch a series of blocks in an attempt to avoid being struck.

The clash of jian and dao, of sword and sabre rang through the courtyard in a rising crescendo. By the third strike, Wu Ying's hand was trembling, the shock of blocking the heavy weapon passing through to his hand. The fourth strike sneaked past Wu Ying's desperate defense, leaving a shallow wound on his arm. The fifth, blocked, the sixth missed. On and on, the young cultivator's attacks built up, growing stronger with every moment. Of particular concern was that, unlike him, his opponent had chosen not to use a blunted weapon, instead relying on her technique to ensure she did not kill.

Realizing the peril he was in, Wu Ying threw himself forward into the attack. It was not a risk he would have taken before his recent adventures, but now, he understood—there was no holding back within a fight. It was either win or die. In the center of the storm, blood flowed, but Wu Ying entered within the range of her attacks even as he covered his vitals. As suddenly as the storm of sabres had erupted, it ended.

For a moment, the entire group stared at the tableau before them. In one hand, Wu Ying held the cultivator's arm, stopping her sabre from moving. The other pressed his jian against her lower body, ready to disembowel her.

"Winner—Wu Ying," the referee intoned flatly.

Seeing the cultivator relax, Wu Ying let go of her hand and stepped backward, exiting her reach before he returned her bow.

"Thank you for your guidance," the pair recited the ritual words before they moved aside, allowing another pair to take part.

"You scared me on that one," Tou He said as he pulled bandages from his waist pouch. "Are you going to be able to continue?"

"Yes. It's just surface wounds mostly," Wu Ying said. Mostly. One cut along his side had gotten deep enough to tear up some muscles.

Breathing slowly, Wu Ying circulated his chi to speed up the healing process and stem the bleeding while he watched the other fights. A healing pill went into his mouth too, as he worked to reduce the damage. After his experience fighting the sabre-wielder, Wu Ying could only be certain of one thing—winning wouldn't be easy.

***

"Wu Ying, go to group three."

Standing, Wu Ying nodded to the referee before he took off for his assigned group. There, he had the chance to watch another two battles. In particular, the second battle was an eye-opener.

The combatants were a jian-wielder and axe-wielder, both of them in the Energy Gathering stage. As they fought, they flashed from one corner of the ring to another, each attack so sharp and crisp that it raised a wind. Yet for all their speed, Wu Ying was surprised when, seemingly by an unspoken command, the pair began to truly fight.

First came soaring pressure as the pair released the locks around their dantians. Their opened Energy Meridians thrummed with power as the pair pushed the newly released chi into the meridians, giving themselves greater strength and speed. The increased pressure was, of course, a side-effect of the increased flow of chi. Part of Wu Ying was somewhat amused, seeing the sudden increase in pressure not so much as an intimidation tactic but a failure in cultivation. But…

Next came the dome. The referee, seeing the upcoming fight, raised her hands, forming a clear dome between the spectators and the fighters. Not a moment too soon, for the pair threw themselves at each other, blades of compressed chi erupting from the ends of their bladed weapons as they fought, torn apart only by the strikes of their opposition. Yet for all the fury of the fight, it did not last long. The pair exhausted their chi stores within seconds, leaving one cultivator to stare at the axe blade hovering over his face.

As the pair staggered off to rest and gather more chi and the cultivators digested the fight, Wu Ying was called into the now-empty circle. This time, Wu Ying's opponent was a ji-wielder. The ji was a common polearm weapon that had a spear tip and an axe blade at its end. Like the spear, it was a popular weapon for commoners—mostly because it was also a common weapon in the army. In fact, entire regiments were made up of ji-wielders as an effective counter to heavily armed and armored swordsmen or the occasional particularly stubborn spear regiment.

"Ready?"

The pair gave a nod to the referee, having already paid their respects to their opponent. Wu Ying stepped back, giving himself more room, rather than hang just outside the longer weapon's reach as he assessed his opponent.

Probably a military brat, part-scholar, part-soldier. Broad shoulders that wielded the weapon as though he was born to it. Another who had gained Sense of the weapon. Strong, fast, perceptive, with a subdued killing intent. This was someone who had done more than fight in the sparring ring. Face tight, Wu Ying darted in with his sword held upward, ready to block.

The ji stabbed out quickly, only to be deflected by the dragon's greeting to the rising sun. As Wu Ying took another step in, his opponent drew the blade back toward his body, twisting the ji around and swinging the axe head. A cross-body block—covering the clouds with the tail—protected Wu Ying from the attack, but sent him skittering backward as he absorbed the shock.

In seconds, Wu Ying was back on the outskirts of his opponent's range. A clash of ji and jian occurred as his opponent pushed his advantage, the weapon darting forward like a swallow. Wu Ying's breathing quickened, his wrist twisting and curling continuously as he fought to regain the battle's momentum.

"Now." Wu Ying darted down using the cat stretching in the morning, letting the blade skim right above his head. He recovered using dragon steps, attempting to close the distance, but was smashed aside by the haft of the ji, sent sprawling to the ground.

As Wu Ying rolled back up, the ji-wielder recovered from his own hasty retreat and defense.

Long reach. Better cultivation. Sense of the ji and refined killing intent. Wu Ying stared at his opponent, mentally judging his options before he sighed.

"I concede."

Silence spread the moment everyone realized what Wu Ying had said. His opponent's hand slackened slightly, even more so when Wu Ying sheathed his sword and turned to the referee.

"That's allowed, yes?" Wu Ying said.

"Yes. It's highly unusual," the referee said, turning her head back to the opponent. "But it's acceptable. Are you sure?"

"I already said it, haven't I?" Wu Ying said.

"Then I declare this fight over. Please return to your original group for details of your next fight."

Wu Ying bowed to the referee, ignoring the derisive comments that had erupted when everyone realized he was serious. As he walked away, Wu Ying rotated his neck to loosen tight muscles. One win, one loss. Not good, but it could be worse.

"Hey."

"Yes?" Wu Ying turned, seeing his former opponent trotting over to him.

"Why did you do that?"

"Because I was going to lose anyway. You had better reach, as good—if not better—form than me. And better cultivation."

"There is no guarantee in combat. In a fight, anyone can win!" His opponent snapped the words, clutching his weapon tightly. "One should never give up in combat!"

"But this wasn't a fight, was it?" Wu Ying said, fixing his gaze on his opponent. "This was just a sparring match. And after this, we have three more battles. If I fought you all-out, win or lose, I'd be even more injured. I can't always sacrifice my body for a point or else I'll lose completely. In a real fight, you must risk it all to win, but this isn't a real fight. I had little chance of winning, so I'd rather give up and save my strength for the next match."

His opponent fell silent, staring at Wu Ying, gauging his words and weighing the look in his eyes. After a moment, he grinned. "You have seen real battles, haven't you?"

Wu Ying nodded dumbly while the man turned and waved goodbye.

"Fight well. Do not let yourself leave the sect, for we need those whose swords have tasted blood!"

"Sure…" Wu Ying said doubtfully, shaking his head as he walked off.

Army brats were truly strange sometimes. But it was better for them to be friends than enemies.

***

On his way back, Wu Ying realized he was done earlier than normal. As he craned his head around, he spotted Tou He walking into the ring, staff held over his shoulder. The ex-monk was smiling at his dual-wielding sabre opponent, saying something Wu Ying could not catch. Rather than miss the fight, Wu Ying moved toward that group, curiosity aroused.

After the attendant called for the fight to begin, Tou He's opponent charged forward. The ex-monk swung his staff in defense, using both ends of the weapon to occupy his opponent's weapons. The ex-monk rarely shifted his feet, only occasionally moving to a better position as he fought. Wu Ying knew, from previous experience, that that was a hallmark of Tou He's style—the Mountain Resides. An immovable defense that required little footwork changes, but extremely flexible hands and arms as the staff swirled in defense all around him. No surprise that Tou He had reached the Sense of the staff. In fact, Wu Ying believed that Tou He might already be on the precipice of reaching the Heart.

But just as impressive was the way his opponent moved. To have achieved the Sense with not just one hand but both hands, and to be able to wield both weapons with equal familiarity, was stunning.

In moments, the battle between the pair of outer sect members had drawn the attention of everyone nearby. A quick look around showed Wu Ying that even the Elders were pointing and watching the fight as the pair continued to fight at a stalemate. Again and again, the dual-wielding cultivator threw himself at Tou He, only for his attacks to bounce off the staff, and eventually, his momentum was robbed of all strength. At that point, he jumped back, barely avoiding a return strike.

"Go, Tou He!" Wu Ying cheered softly.

But something nagged him. Well, beyond the placid way Tou He took the entire thing, barely bothering to do more than counter once in a while. It took Wu Ying one more pass before he realized what it was.

Tou He's staff had begun to chip and scar. Even when Tou He was blocking by pushing away the incoming edges, it was insufficient to entirely rob the attacks of their momentum and edge. Each block weakened his staff. As the sword-wielding cultivator rushed in once again, the staff finally gave way, shattering in the middle. Tou He swayed aside, dodging the adjusted blow, and hopped backward, staring at the two pieces of his staff with pursed lips.

"Give up," his opponent said, raising his swords as he waited for Tou He's confirmation of his defeat.

"If you dare, I'll have you kicked out myself!" a loud voice cut through the square before Tou He could speak.

All eyes were drawn to an older woman, hunched over and leaning against her walking stick as she glared at Tou He.

"Yes, Elder," Tou He said, bowing slightly to her.

His movement took his immediate gaze off his opponent, who jumped forward to finish the attack. Almost contemptuously, Tou He raised one piece of his broken staff to block the attack, swirling the blade around and locking it with his elbow and stick before he shoved forward, trapping his opponent.

Spinning around his opponent, Tou He pulled his opponent off balance while dodging a missed cut. Then, with his body nearly parallel to his opponent, Tou He smacked his opponent across the temple with the other piece of his staff. Soundlessly, his opponent fell to the ground, the precisely placed attack dropping him.

"Winner, Tou He!"

Wu Ying sighed, shaking his head as Tou He looked embarrassed at his sudden win. After all this time, Wu Ying knew that letting Tou He have the time to grasp your timing and tactics was a bad idea. The damn prodigy just built up a mental library of your attacks then used it against you.

***

"Are you sure you don't want to give up?" Wu Ying asked as he batted aside the spear thrust with ease.

When his opponent stabbed forward again, Wu Ying grabbed the body of the spear, holding it still. As hard as the other cultivator strained, he wasn't able to remove it from Wu Ying's grip.

"No! I won't... fail!" Straining, the cultivator kept on yanking on the spear.

"You've barely even improved your cultivation in the time we've been here," Wu Ying said then twisted his body, rotating from his hip as he pulled his opponent toward him before slamming the hilt of his sword into the cultivator's face. The blow—tightly controlled—sent his opponent staggering back, holding his broken nose. "You haven't even learned to use your hips. What the hell were you thinking?"

The foppish cultivator moaned, holding his nose. When Wu Ying looked at the referee, she looked between the pair before she nodded.

"Wu Ying is the winner!"

"Thank you," Wu Ying said before tossing down the spear and walking away.

Yeesh. And that man had managed to win a single fight. Who was poor enough to lose to him?

***

His next opponent was a fellow jian-user. Wu Ying exhaled as he drew his weapon and fell into his stance. This should be interesting. With one loss and two wins, the individual in front of him was overall considered better than average. Certainly not a complete loser. After so many fights, those who had won more than one would normally be better than normal. Though none were as stellar as those few who had only victories.

"Wu Ying. Long family style," the swordsman in front of him said, twirling the jian absently. "I have always wanted to test out your family's style. It was once considered one of the five great styles of Shen. Too bad your family never amounted to much."

Wu Ying's teeth ground together, the insult stabbing deep into his pride. While the progenitor of their style had been a great martial artist, it was true that few of his descendants had ever reached the same heights. Worse, because there were often large gaps between each notable ancestor, his family had slowly fallen further and further till they became nothing but farmers. Even then, they still kept the style, trained in it.

"Red Lotus Sword Style," Wu Ying said softly as he recalled the other's introduction, idly waving his sword before he nodded. "Is that not for women?"

"You hún dàn!" Incensed, the cultivator threw himself at Wu Ying.

Not bothering to hide his smirk, Wu Ying moved, utilizing the footwork of the Long family style to deal with the sudden rush. Red Lotus Style was a strange style of swordsmanship, one that Wu Ying had heard of only due to their infamous founder. A rare lady scholar of Hakka descent, she had been known for her hot temper and her gift at martial arts. One lucky day, the lady had been enlightened and created the style on a field of white lotuses, dyed red with the blood of her enemies. Her style was reputed to be infected with her temperament, and all her stylists were known to be somewhat impetuous.

Fast. Furious. Never-ending changes in direction with the sword twisting and circling constantly. The style was all about forward momentum and constant impetus, the attacks meant to cut and cut, forcing the opponent to bleed. Some had described the jian in the stylist's hands as a paintbrush, with the paint the opponent's blood.

To combat that, Wu Ying used dragon steps that focused on quick, circling movements to ensure that his opponent would always be at his optimum attack range. Fast strikes at angles, short stabs directed not at the body but the arms.

Wu Ying shifted and fought, the pair dancing around the encirclement at ever-increasing speed, the ting of their blades a symphony of metallic death.

A hit, then another. But the problem was, Wu Ying was using a blunted weapon, and enraged as his opponent was, he was shrugging off blows that would have crippled him with a sharp. Wu Ying's lips compressed as he spun away once again, a stinging blow landing across his shoulders as he did so. Dangerous to stay out there so long when his opponent showed no intent of slowing down.

Then...

Dragon stretches in the morning sent Wu Ying sliding into a low lunge, ducking beneath an attack to suddenly appear within the charging cultivator's reach. Shen Kicking style, a quick wrist lock and upset, then a kick to throw over one's hip. In a second, Wu Ying had the opponent's free arm locked out, his foot wrapped around it, and stretched straight as he put pressure on the elbow and shoulder joint.

"Yield," Wu Ying commanded.

"Never!"

"Yield or I break your elbow and shoulder."

"I will see you eat dirt, you hun dan."

Wu Ying looked at the referee. At the referee's slight nod, Wu Ying sighed and extended his leg fully even as he rotated his body. A loud crack ensued, along with a muffled pop that Wu Ying felt in his body as the opponent's shoulder gave way. Grunting, Wu Ying stepped back and away from the waving sword and the injured cultivator.

"The peasant injured him," one of the other noblemen spoke up, pointing at Wu Ying. "He should be disqualified. The Outer Sect Elder told us to not injure one another."

"He did." Wu Ying tensed before the referee pointed at the moaning cultivator being helped to his feet. "But his opponent was allowed the chance to give up and refused. As he had no other choice to end the fight, his actions are acceptable. Respect must flow both ways. If you refuse to give up when you have lost, you are not respecting your opponent. Do not expect them to respect you either."

There was a pregnant pause after the referee's words.

When no one contradicted or objected, the referee turned to Wu Ying and pointed Wu Ying back to his original group. "You may leave."

Wu Ying bowed to the referee and sheathed his sword before pushing through the crowd, enduring the cold shoulder the rest of the group gave him. Obviously having a commoner injure one of their kind, even if it was fair and right, was still not acceptable. As he limped back, he rubbed at the growing bruises on his body. Three out of four was good enough, was it not?

***

"Why won't you give up?" the other cultivator snarled, the paired shields on his arm blocking and striking Wu Ying in the chest once again.

An explosion of blood and spit erupted from Wu Ying's mouth, coating his opponent in viscera and revulsion as Wu Ying staggered back. Holding his injured chest with one hand, feeling the grate of broken bone as he breathed, Wu Ying took his guard again as he stared at his opponent. Good news—the shield rims were not sharpened. Bad news—dual-wielded shields were a pain to get through. It was the first time Wu Ying had ever fought such a combination, and the turtled defenses were a pain.

"You're good training," Wu Ying replied.

No need to hold back much. If he lost here, he might still be on the bubble. If he won, he was certain even Elder Mo could do nothing to him. After that… well, he would worry about after if he won. And unlike earlier, Wu Ying knew that he had a chance to win here. A small chance perhaps, but small was enough.

"You!" Growling, the cultivator dashed forward, one shield forward and the other a little behind and angled to cover his body or lash out as needed.

Once again, the pair clashed, Wu Ying doing his best to stay out of range while his opponent closed in. With two shields, feints and threats to the body were difficult to enforce, the range of exposed parts fleeting. With only a single sword, Wu Ying often found his attacks hampered by one shield while the second threatened him, forcing Wu Ying to constantly move. Except that within the confines of the fighting circle, Wu Ying could only run so far. Cornered again, Wu Ying dropped low.

"Not this time," the shield cultivator said, gloating as he dropped as well, having seen Wu Ying use this form before.

Even as his opponent dropped, Wu Ying's bunched legs exploded, throwing him up and over the suddenly shorter cultivator. A reflexive raising of the shield allowed Wu Ying to grab hold of one edge, giving the cultivator a pivot point in mid-air. Pain coursed through his body as his injured chest and shoulder muscles strained at the sudden shifts and twists. Yet the movement also pulled the shield stylist off balance and arched his back. As Wu Ying landed, he lashed out with his sword, hammering the blade's edge into the exposed area of his opponent's arm, numbing it. Another twist of the shield with his body pulled his opponent off balance again before he thrust through the exposed gap, the blow taking the fighter in the dantian.

As the shield cultivator finally pried his shield free, Wu Ying rotated at full speed and threw a sidekick directly into the newly regained shield. The opponent, caught unprepared, was thrown backward as the shield slammed him into the center of the ring.

"Got you," Wu Ying said with a grin then clutched his chest as the pain finally caught up with him. He let out a stifled groan as he hurriedly pushed his chi through his chest region, healing and blocking off the frantic nerves.

His opponent stood, his nose bloodied and one arm seriously bruised. "This is not over yet."

"Of course not," Wu Ying said despairingly.

Stubborn idiot. Raising his jian, Wu Ying walked forward. At least he had begun to understand the style before him. Now all he had to do was put his understanding to work.

***

"Winner, Wu Ying!" the referee announced, looking at the pair of beaten, bloody, and bruised cultivators.

Wu Ying gratefully collapsed, cradling his injured leg that was already swelling. That last kick with the already cracked shin bone had been painful but necessary. It was the only opening he had managed to create.

"Should have known you'd punch my leg," Wu Ying said as he slowly channeled more chi into his leg. The process helped alleviate some of the swelling and, just as importantly, helped him assess the full extent of the damage. Wu Ying reached into his robes, pulled forth the pill bottle, and swallowed one, circulating his chi through his stomach to speed up the absorption of the medicine.

"I don't believe you kicked me with that leg." The shield cultivator sat up, talking to Wu Ying friendlily.

As the last match, the scores had to be all tallied before the next stage was announced, so the little circle they had been fighting in was no longer required. All around, groups of cultivators were breaking apart, some despairingly and others with barely concealed hope.

"Why wouldn't I?" Wu Ying said. "I needed to win."

"Yeah, but you didn't even hesitate. If you had…"

"You'd have gotten your shield back into place and broken my knee," Wu Ying said, recalling the last few moments of their fight. "That's why I didn't hesitate."

"For someone who gave up after a single pass, you're nothing like what I thought you'd be," his ex-opponent said, staring at Wu Ying with a puzzled expression.

Around him, a few of his friends who had arrived with water were nodding in agreement. Wu Ying could not help but roll his eyes at how fast the gossip had traveled.

"You do realize he was my second fight," Wu Ying said as he slowly stood, testing his leg. Better to head over to the healing station where more pills, poultices, and acupuncture needles awaited. Perhaps they could speed up his healing further. "If I'd fought him like I did you, I would have been too injured to go on."

After Wu Ying's explanation, a few of the cultivators continued to frown while others relaxed as the mystery was solved. Ignoring both groups, Wu Ying limped over to the healing station in search of a doctor. He continued to flush his chi through his body while absorbing the ambient chi in the surroundings. A slight frown crossed Wu Ying's face as he felt how stifled the chi in the region was—probably from having so many cultivators doing the very same thing. Hopefully they would extend the rest period before they began the next stage.

Four wins. That should be enough. Even Elder Mo could not have him kicked out of the sect now. Having achieved his first goal, Wu Ying realized that he was dissatisfied with the thought of achieving a "good enough" result. No. He had come this far. Maybe the chance of winning, of achieving a position within the inner sect was impossible—but he would try. He owed it to himself.

**

"Thank you for your patience," Elder Khoo said, sweeping his gaze over the participants.

Wu Ying looked up as the Elder's voice pierced the air, splitting his attention to listen as he continued to cultivate and heal.

"The wins and comments have been tallied. Those of you who have been chosen to have an opportunity to win a spot in the Inner sect will be informed in person.

"The next stage of the tournament begins now!"

Chapter 23

"Long Wu Ying?"

"Yes?" Wu Ying said carefully, turning to the attendant. It was probably time to get off the field, though he wondered why they felt the need to tell him directly.

"Please proceed to the front of the courtyard," the attendant said, gesturing in the direction she wanted him to go. Wu Ying's nodded, a part of him wondering why she looked so familiar. "Please, Junior."

"Yes. Of course," Wu Ying said as he stood and winced as pain ran through him. Cracked shin bone, two broken ribs, torn and strained left arm muscles, and so many bruises he could not even count them. Not to mention the cuts he had gained earlier in his first fight.

"Junior Long? Please change your weapon to a proper one," the attendant added.

When Wu Ying's eyes widened at the change in rules to one that enforced sharps, the attendant only offered him a slight, pitying smile.

"Yes, Senior."

"Good." She turned away, searching for and finding her next victim. Before she left, she gave Wu Ying a quick smile. "Good luck, Junior Long."

That smile. Wu Ying realized that the lady attendant was one who had served him before, that first time Elder Mo had shown his displeasure. Shaking his head, Wu Ying walked toward the temporary weapons stands that had been placed around the courtyard and returned his training jian to it. He quickly moved past the various other weapons, finding the stand that displayed the loaner jians available. One after the other, Wu Ying tested weapons, hoping to find one of better quality. In the end, under the attendant's disapproving gaze,

Wu Ying gave up and picked a slimmer and slightly longer blade and went to join the other "chosen" ones.

Wu Ying swept his gaze over the sparse group of individuals who had been brought forward, finding few whom he recognized. Most of the participants were scuffed and slightly dirty, a few even having their clothes torn or sporting bruises and bandages. Still, most had taken the time to clean themselves up, and a few had even changed into spotless robes. After his initial assessment, Wu Ying realized that not a single other participant looked as beaten as he did.

Among those gathered, Wu Ying noted that Tou He was not present, but surprisingly, Yin Xue had advanced. Eyes narrowing, Wu Ying stretched out his senses, feeling for Yin Xue's presence, only to be staggered by the result. Body Cleansing *10*? How? Why? Head spinning, Wu Ying was caught staring at Yin Xue by the very person who sneered at Wu Ying.

"Really? They even let a dog like you this far?" Yin Xue taunted.

His words drew the attention of others to Wu Ying's battered and bloody form, their gazes raking over his disheveled clothing before they assessed his cultivation. More than one sneered like Yin Xue. Between his clothing, his injuries, and the faint presence that he released, Wu Ying knew he was not an imposing sight, especially compared to the Energy Gathering cultivators among them.

"Just like they let you in," Wu Ying said.

"I won four of my fights," Yin Xue said with a snarl and touched his sword's hilt. Drawn by the movement, Wu Ying blinked as he realized that Yin Xue had upgraded his weapon. "That's right. My father passed the family sword to me."

As a villager, Wu Ying knew the stories. It was a fabled sword—at least in their village. Said to be sharp enough to cut a dropping silk scarf, light enough for a child to wield, and durable enough that it never chipped. Of course, a lot of those were from children's stories, but it was without a doubt a very good weapon.

"That's… nice," Wu Ying replied, trying hard to suppress the flare of jealousy and anger. Jealousy over the fine weapon used by an inconsiderate, privileged child, and anger that his own parents were unable to provide him such a gift. It was irrational, but then, emotions were.

"Pray you do not meet me," Yin Xue taunted once more.

"I could say the same for you," Wu Ying said then bit his tongue. Damn it. Why was he acting so juvenile?

Shaking his head, Wu Ying turned away from Yin Xue. He ignored the mocking laugh behind him, lips pressed together as he waited for the next announcement. Before it could happen though, a commotion erupted from the sidelines as an attendant walked out of the crowd, pulling a reluctant Tou He by the ear.

"Ow! Ow! Ow! Please stop. Please!" Tou He complained.

When the female attendant finally made it most of the way into the courtyard, she tugged Tou He forward in front of her before launching him the rest of the way with a well-aimed push-kick. The monk flew forward, tucking himself into a perfect recovery roll to end up crouched and clutching his ear, still complaining.

"Tou He?" Wu Ying said as he stared at his friend.

"Hi!" Tou He waved, still rubbing his ear as he walked over.

"What happened? How are you here?" Wu Ying was sure that Tou He had said he'd lost his other fight, so he must have lost two already. There was no way he should be part of this group.

"I got added." Tou He made a face. When Wu Ying stared at him, the ex-monk dropped his voice as he said, "I think they realized I let myself lose the second fight."

"You…" Wu Ying clamped his mouth shut before he said anything further. Damn the monk. A slight burning rage appeared in Wu Ying's chest once again as he contemplated the genius martial artist of a friend before him. If he wasn't so immune to hard work…

Silence descended over the group. Together, the pair turned toward the stairs where, instead of Elder Khoo, another Elder stood, his presence sending a chill through the courtyard. This Elder was one Wu Ying knew only from rumor—the Inner Hall Master, Elder Khoo's equivalent. Of course, Elder Shin was of greater seniority than Elder Khoo, his position more secure. But the cold gaze he swept over the gathered hopeful outer sect members quieted even the bravest among them.

When pin-drop silence finally held, Elder Shin spoke up. "Those of you standing here have some hope of becoming high-standing members of the sect, of learning stronger techniques, advancing your cultivation, and earning the right to the greater secrets of our sect. But the opportunity to do so is much in demand. This year, we only have eight spaces available."

The Elder's words shocked the group, the open slots being lower than normal. Wu Ying looked around the now-tense group, doing a quick count. Just over twenty hopeful applicants and most of them stronger than him.

"To make this simple, there are seven who did not lose a single battle. Step forward," Elder Shin commanded.

From the group, the seven swaggered forward, looking at the others with a smirk.

Then Elder Shin looked over the group, his gaze falling on Wu Ying, a slight smirk crossing his face. "And you, Wu Ying, can be the eighth."

Wu Ying twitched, the malice clear in Elder Shin's intention. But still, the cultivator had no choice. He walked forward, joining the group, and tried not to listen to the muttered comments around him.

"Him? Why him?"

"He has no sense of propriety. He didn't even clean himself!"

"Don't you know? Elder Mo's group wants him gone."

"Is he *that* cultivator? A disgrace."

Wu Ying's lips tightened as he stood with his back to the group, staring at Elder Shin, who made no move to silence the talk. When the other Elders moved slightly, growing restless at the delay, only then did Elder Shin continue.

"The eight individuals standing here have earned a place in the inner sect," Elder Shin said. When the collective intake from the competitors and audience had subsided, he continued with barely concealed malicious glee. "But any of the other competitors may challenge any of the eight to a battle."

Immediately, all the remaining contestants focused on Wu Ying, their gazes boring into the injured and bedraggled cultivator.

"The winner will, of course, have gained the loser's place. Understand that you will only have one opportunity to win your fight. Choose your opponent well."

Wu Ying drew a deep breath, Elder Shin's words weighing him down further, the pressure almost making his knees buckle. But a memory came of a blade flying at his chest, and Wu Ying found himself straightening, meeting the expectant gazes around him with a half-smile. Could any of them be more dangerous than what he had faced? He had already escaped death twice. And this—this was just a spar.

"Elder Shin." A voice, one that Wu Ying recognized. His eyes tracked over, surprised to see Elder Ko of the library speaking up. "This test seems to be potentially flawed."

"Elder Ko," Elder Shin said, dissatisfaction tingeing his voice. Still, he stared at the other Elder before he inclined his head. "To clarify. No cultivator may be challenged more than twice."

Elder Ko stepped back, retreating into the throng. Wu Ying stared at the group one last time before he turned back to Elder Shin, who detailed further rules, minor clarifications about the upcoming battle. In the time given, he circulated his chi and waited. Two fights. And then he would win.

At least, Wu Ying consoled himself, those he fought would be like him— one-time losers. Not the towering geniuses who stood beside him. So. He had a chance. Maybe.

***

"Of course it's you," Wu Ying said when the speeches were finally done and he turned around. If he had been a betting man, Wu Ying could have won some serious coin. Well, if anyone was willing to take his money.

Across from Wu Ying, Yin Xue smirked. "Well, I guess you didn't have a chance to escape me."

"No. I didn't," Wu Ying said, letting his hand rest on his borrowed blade. Wu Ying found himself smiling slightly in satisfaction. If he had to fight someone, Yin Xue was a good choice. Injuring the lord's son, inadvertently or on purpose, would make Wu Ying lose little sleep.

From the corner of his eyes, Wu Ying was surprised to see Tou He matched up against a slim gentleman wielding a pair of hooked swords. Tou He himself carried his staff, propping the weapon on one shoulder, looking way too casual for the fight he was about to engage in.

"We could just exchange a few blows and I'll call it my defeat," Tou He tried wheedling his opponent, who stared at him impassively.

Wu Ying's attention was torn back to his own stage, where a new cultivator had appeared, staring down at Yin Xue. The new cultivator was attired like the rest of them, but instead of wielding a more common weapon, he had a pair of tong fas slipped into his belt. The simple wooden weapons were basically a stick with a handle a third of the way in on the slimmer side, offering the martial artist a location to hold and wield the weapon. It was an interesting weapon that Wu Ying had never actually fought before. Curiously, Wu Ying cocked his head to the side to listen to the conversation between the pair of cultivators.

"Senior Lin Tsui, I was here first," Yin Xue whined.

"And I do not care. You can stay and suffer afterward, or you can leave," Lin Tsui said, staring straight at Yin Xue fearlessly.

Yin Xue paled slightly, staring between Lin Tsui and the referee who made no move to help. Finally, Yin Xue shook his head and backed away, allowing the other cultivator to take his place on the fighting platform. Wu Ying watched the incident silently, amusement dancing in his eyes. Yin Xue snarled slightly, fist clenching around his sword's hilt when he saw Wu Ying's smile, but eventually he shook his head.

The referee looked between the pair still on the combat stage. "Are we ready?"

***

Wu Ying spat to the side, clearing his mouth of blood and torn skin as he glared at Lin Tsui, who stood up slowly too, favoring his left ankle. Once more, the pair circled one another, Wu Ying carefully probing Lin Tsui's defenses. Of course, since his opponent wielded two weapons that exceled at blocking, Wu Ying made sure to never overextend himself. In turn, Lin Tsui probed Wu Ying's footwork and defense, attempting to find the appropriate time to enter Wu Ying's measure. Because of Wu Ying's reach and his ability to fade away with dragon steps, Lin Tsui had to gauge his timing appropriately. After all, rushing in was the most dangerous time for him.

All this—and Lin Tsui's fighting style with the tong fas—was hard-earned knowledge, gained from significant bruises, a newly re-cracked pair of ribs, and a swelling eye. The damn tong fas were fast, highly manipulable, and perfect for close-in fighting. If Lin Tsui got into Wu Ying's measure, Wu Ying's only chance was to retreat as quickly as possible.

"Why did you learn the Shen style anyway?" Lin Tsui asked conversationally, eyes narrowed as he casually batted away a quick probe of the sword.

"For people like you."

Wu Ying had to smile slightly. That last sweep had done exactly what he wanted—injured his opponent and forced him back. The Shen kicking style, integrated into his Long family style, had been a surprise and the only reason Wu Ying was still in the fight. Every time Lin Tsui closed in, he had to worry about being grappled and kicked away. Though Wu Ying's last attack had done nothing to stop Lin Tsui from smashing him across the face with his tong fa, leading to the fast-growing swelling on his face and bloodied mouth.

"Smart," Lin Tsui said. "Most people try to emphasize their strengths without ever shoring up their weaknesses."

"Thank you."

Wu Ying stopped moving for a second then shifted direction, trying to cut the circle of Lin Tsui's defense. Once again, Wu Ying failed, his quick tip cut easily deflected. However, rather than springing forward, Lin Tsui waited. For the next few minutes, the pair feinted and parried. Occasionally one or the other would step in to attempt a more significant attack. Those attempts were ineffective at everything but exhausting the pair.

Around them, Wu Ying idly noted that the other fights had finished. Some of the other contestants had chosen to pick on one of the winners, leaving only a few contestants waiting. Most of those had gathered around his combat stage, eyeing the pair of them.

"How do you expect to win, injured as you are?" Lin Tsui said.

Wu Ying stood just outside of his lunge distance, catching his breath and circulating his chi to slowly fix his injuries. Wu Ying dared not send too much of his chi in case he was interrupted, but even a little was helping dull the pain.

"It's impressive enough that someone with such a low cultivation level has come so far, but you cannot expect to win. I am at least a half-dozen levels higher than you."

Wu Ying frowned, his exhausted mind unable to understand why Lin Tsui would think there was such a large discrepancy. Sure, he was at Body Cleansing 8, but Lin Tsui himself was only at 11. Maybe 12. There were no levels after that—not without entering Energy Storage. And if he had managed to achieve that, this fight would have been over.

As the pair completed another tired pass, Wu Ying realized the reason. Even if he was cultivating, drawing energy into his body and passing it through weary muscles to give himself strength and speed, to heal and clear fatigue, his strengthened aura was hiding his cultivation. It was likely that the added stress of cultivating and fighting had increased the amount that leaked, giving Lin Tsui a slightly better idea—but not enough.

Could he use that? Wu Ying landed lightly from a skip to the side, swinging his sword in a cut then reversing the rebound to threaten his opponent. As he retreated, Wu Ying felt his thigh want to give out, exhaustion and injuries catching up to him. Except this time, on instinct, Wu Ying let himself collapse.

As if he had been waiting, Lin Tsui exploded forward. Even the injured ankle no longer seemed to impair his movement. Wu Ying found Lin Tsui bearing down on his collapsed form, the lead tong fa sweeping toward his head and the other held low and close, ready to block his sword. Except this time around, Wu Ying ignored his jian, dropping it to catch Lin Tsui's arms. While the other cultivator might be stronger and faster due to his cultivation, the unexpected change caught Lin Tsui by surprise. Even more so when Wu Ying used Lin Tsui's momentum to roll the both of them backward and pinned his opponent.

For a brief second, Wu Ying realized he had not thought of what to do next. He had Lin Tsui pinned cross-body, hands on both arms, a throbbing in his shoulders from a slipped block. But with both hands busy holding his opponent down, Wu Ying had no other weapons. For a second, Wu Ying paused. Then recollections of rolling around in the dirt, fighting and wrestling with his friends in the village, came back.

Wu Ying reared back and slammed his forehead into the surprised nobleman's face, making blood burst from a broken nose. His head throbbed a little from the sudden impact, but it didn't stop Wu Ying from repeating the attack. And again. And once more, before the referee pulled him away, the weakly struggling noble covered in blood.

"What was that?" the referee snarled, pointing at the injured noble.

"Winning," Wu Ying replied blearily, offering the referee a half-smile as he tottered on his feet.

When the referee growled, Wu Ying could only shrug and wipe at the blood on his face. Thankfully, none of the cuts he had gained were wide or bleeding too freely, unlike the smashed lips, nose, and orbital bone of his opponent. After the referee called the fight, Wu Ying moved aside, and the cultivators took his opponent off the stage.

"That was different," Tou He said to his friend, handing Wu Ying a waterskin. "A bit less sophisticated than your usual style."

"It worked, didn't it?" Wu Ying said, splashing water onto a cloth to finish cleaning his injuries. He drew a deep breath, forcing himself to breathe around the pain of his ribs even as he channeled his chi through his body. Even with its aid, the bone-deep weariness in his body was making him sway slightly. "Did you lose?"

"Won actually," Tou He said with a grimace. "I was told I had to fight. Then my opponent tried to cut me up when I tried to give up. Ended up accidentally beating him."

"You accidentally beat your opponent."

"Yes."

"I hate you," Wu Ying said without heat. He was too tired to deal with the damn ex-monk.

As the stage was cleared and the blood hastily washed off, Wu Ying spotted Yin Xue already waiting on the stage, eager to begin. He was pushing the attendants to move faster, intending to give Wu Ying as little of a break as possible.

"Don't lose. I don't want to be the only one in the inner sect," Tou He said to Wu Ying as the referee gestured for the cultivator to take his place.

"Because that's what I'm worried about," Wu Ying said, rolling his eyes as his friend. Still, the words brought a slight smile to his face and took his attention away from the upcoming fight. A good enough result.

As he limped toward his spot, Wu Ying cast one last glance about the courtyard. As the sun set, the courtyard was basked in a pinkish-red glow, creating a slightly surreal view as the attention of the Elders and waiting cultivators turned to his stage. Not that there were many cultivators left—only the most bored or curious still stayed. The rest had left at some point, their interest guttering out like the sunset. After all, the upcoming battle had little to do with them.

Drawing another pain-filled breath, Wu Ying considered his options as he stared at Yin Xue, who smirked right back. Wu Ying was tired, injured, and of lower cultivation than the noble. His opponent had had time to rest, to study his moves, and to plan his attack. This fight should be over in a second.

***

"Are you both ready?"

The referee's voice cut through Wu Ying's exhaustion, pulling his attention back to his situation. Drawing his sword, Wu Ying nodded to the referee. As Yin Xue had already offered his acknowledgement, the battle began almost immediately.

Rather than waiting for Wu Ying to settle into a distance battle, Yin Xue exploded forward, crossing the distance between the pair. Wu Ying's breath hastened, his perception of time slowing as adrenaline and chi coursed through his body, jolting him awake. In the time-dilated moment, Wu Ying found himself with all the time in the world to spot the sneer, the rabid craving to inflict pain in Yin Xue's eyes as he thrust his weapon forward. Wu Ying had all the time to note that the tip was aimed at his heart, but the hand behind it was already angling higher.

A feint for his heart.

Immediately, Wu Ying understood. Yin Xue expected Wu Ying to use dragon stretches in the morning to avoid the blow. It was Wu Ying's—the Long family's—response to a sudden charge, dropping the body beneath the attack while offering their own sword for sheathing in their opponent's body. It was the ingrained response.

In the moment of clarity, Wu Ying saw this all and something shifted in him. He understood, and because he understood, he could act. Rather than dragon stretches, Wu Ying took a drop step to the side, a precursor to the kick that came in under Yin Xue's already dropping tip. Falling rocks in a rainstorm.

Even as Yin Xue folded around the foot that crushed his chest, deforming under the pressure of both cultivators' momentum, Wu Ying was moving. For the form was not a single kick but a series of light attacks with palms, elbows, knees, and then finally another full-body axe kick. The rain of blows, following a dropping rock.

Yin Xue, caught unaware and staggering beneath the initial attack, ate the majority of blows. Blood flowed from a crushed nose, the only spot of color on an otherwise deathly pale face. Only a hastily formed block with his free hand stopped Wu Ying's final kick from crushing his shoulder blade. Weapon waving, Yin Xue forced Wu Ying back. As Wu Ying raised his weapon, readying himself to finish the battle, the referee stepped between the two.

"Wen Yin Xue, can you continue?" the referee asked, his thin body blocking Wu Ying from his opponent.

When no answer came, the referee continued to wait while Wu Ying tried to edge around to see his opponent. Unsurprisingly, Yin Xue was rubbing his chest, drawing tentative breaths as he attempted to make his chest work again.

"Wen Yin Xue. I ask again. Can you continue?"

"He can't answer you. He's obviously injured. Let me finish this or call this my win," Wu Ying said, pointing his sword at Yin Xue as he spoke to the referee.

"Long Wu Ying, do not attempt to influence the referee. Do it again and I will declare this match your loss," the referee replied.

Wu Ying's jaw dropped open in surprise before his eyes narrowed. Of course. Thin. Snobby. Another damn noble son.

"Wen Yin Xue?"

"I can. Continue." Yin Xue said, finally getting the words out.

"Then both contestants, return to your starting positions," the referee commanded the pair.

Wu Ying hastened to his spot, growling softly, especially when the referee said nothing to the slow-moving Yin Xue. By the time Yin Xue had managed to return to his starting spot, the lord's son had recovered most of his color and breath.

"Begin."

This time, Yin Xue did not charge forward. Wu Ying covered the distance between the two immediately, stopping just outside of Yin Xue's range. However, his feinted charge drew no overextended or hasty response, forcing Wu Ying to give up on his plan.

Settling into a longer fight, Wu Ying tested Yin Xue's defenses with simple probes, shifting stances as he focused on the essence of the Long family style. Long-range attacks, probing wrist-cuts, and stabs at full measure that forced his opponent to constantly shift and deal with his weapon. Sudden and quick movement of the feet to open new opportunities and lines of attack. Pass after pass, the pair spun and dueled as sweat grew on Wu Ying's brow. As he fought, Wu Ying's focus grew sharper and tighter, the nagging pain from his injuries fading to the back of his mind.

Yin Xue was faster than him, if only barely, but there was a jerkiness to his motion, as if he had not grown entirely comfortable with the increased strength and speed of his body. It was most apparent when Yin Xue was transitioning from one technique to the next, though it also cropped up whenever Yin Xue had to deal with sudden changes in direction.

Something. Wu Ying knew something was different, something had changed. It nagged at him, as he blocked a thrust then riposted. It distracted him as he twisted his body sideways, throwing a quick tip cut to drive back Yin Xue. It puzzled him as he circled his opponent. And then, it came to him.

"You're scared," Wu Ying said as he pulled outside of Yin Xue's range and shook out his hand. His opponent's attacks had grown stronger, harder. Each block hurt his hand, the stronger weapon and his opponent's greater cultivation sending jarring shocks through his body, wearing away at his endurance.

"Garbage," Yin Xue snarled.

He threw a sudden lunge then a cut to punctuate his words, but Wu Ying did not even bother blocking the attack, instead taking the opportunity to side-step and nick Yin Xue's arm. The hiss of pain and the sudden blood along Yin Xue's arm made Wu Ying smile slightly. But it was not enough. Not yet.

"I'm not afraid of a commoner like you. You only got the Sense of your sword recently. Even with your vaunted heritage," Yin Xue said with a sneer as he tapped his arm, sealing off some of the blood vessels with chi and acupressure points.

Wu Ying blinked, surprised at Yin Xue's unexpected knowledge, but then double-checked the distance between the two of them. Just in case. Acupoint knowledge meant that Yin Xue might be able to deal out acupoint attacks. Dangerous—since such an attack could freeze and block movement. But using it on oneself for such a minor wound... it was foolish. An overreaction.

"Yes, you are," Wu Ying said, his voice growing in confidence. "Because you only have one chance. And I'm winning." A reaction at that, but not a huge one. So. Not that. "You don't want to get hurt again. You don't like the pain." A twitch, just the smallest dip in the tip of the sword before it sprung back up immediately. Yin Xue was shaking his head, denying Wu Ying's words, but Wu Ying had seen the dip. "You're afraid of the pain."

"*No!*" Yin Xue roared, his face flushed as he threw himself forward, desperately rushing to cover the ground, to hack and slash and cut.

But the Long family style was all about staying at a distance, fighting at the outer ranges with reverse lunges and quick circles. A rushing opponent was exactly the kind Wu Ying had trained for all his life.

Dragon steps first, to circle and turn. Covering the clouds with the tail to attack while retreating. And then, as the wounds from the cuts and stabs blossomed, when Yin Xue's desperate rush failed, as fear took control again, the Sword's Truth. A single lunge that covered more ground than any single attack should—that focused all the intent, all the knowledge and force of an individual's chi-empowered body into one attack. In a second, that moment of eternity that is combat time, Wu Ying saw his sword fly forward past the ineffective, waving defenses of his opponent. Ready to end this. End all the taunting, all the anger, all the doubt.

A last-second twitch of his sword shifted the blade from Yin Xue's heart to his shoulder, and the blade stabbed deep within, carrying the cultivator back. Wu Ying's blade erupted from Yin Xue's back. When his momentum finally finished, Wu Ying stopped, straightening and drawing his sword back out with a jerk and a flick of his wrist. Quick steps to move out of reach of his opponent's weapon, though only then did Wu Ying realize it had been dropped.

Then sound returned. Or perhaps, more specifically, his recognition of the noises around him. The gasps, the shouts of dismay and surprise, the screaming and crying from Yin Xue. The thundering beat of his heart in his ears. Wu Ying turned and stared at the referee, whose mouth snapped shut before he shouted for medical aid.

"Junior Long, you purposely injured your opponent!" the referee scolded Wu Ying, pointing at Yin Xue being led off the stage. "You heard the Elder. Injuries should not be inflicted on fellow sect members. That attack could have crippled Lord Wei! I will register your offense immediately!"

Wu Ying blinked slowly as his adrenaline-fueled mind slowly cooled. He found himself baring his teeth, stepping toward the referee even as his hand clenched around his blood-stained sword. "Go ahead. And while you do that, I'll register my complaint about how you interrupted our fight to allow him to heal. The fight would have been over earlier, with fewer injuries, if you had not done so."

"You dare threaten your Senior! You have no respect for the proper order of things!"

"Wrong. I have great respect for the rules and morals of our society. When they're broken, I have no respect for those who break them," Wu Ying replied, his lips pulling into a wolfish grin. Pain and adrenaline rode his sense, robbing him of his usual caution. Even now, he weaved from side to side while standing still.

"You dare!"

The referee was vibrating in anger before Wu Ying shook his head, turning aside and looking around. He spotted Elder Shin staring at him, his lips compressed tightly, but the Elder made no move to stop the altercation. Wu Ying turned away from him, searching for and finding Elder Khoo. Meeting the Elder's gaze, Wu Ying swept his gaze back to the referee continuing to harangue him, sending a silent plea. Elder Khoo looked between the pair before he turned to Elder Shin, raising a single eyebrow.

"Enough. Long Wu Ying has won the match." Elder Shin's lips curled up in disdain. "Both matches. With little grace or nobility, but what can you expect from a peasant?"

Wu Ying exhaled in relief, shaking out his sword and pulling another cloth from his robe to begin the laborious process of cleaning off the blood. He managed to make it mostly off the stage before the adrenaline rush finally ended, his control over his cultivation and his body crashing. He groaned as his chi ran rampant through his body, making Wu Ying stumble and fall.

"Rest, friend. You did well." Tou He's strong arms caught the exhausted cultivator, helping his friend down as the nobles and Elders watched the pair. Marking them in their minds.

Chapter 24

Days later, Wu Ying was sat cross-legged in the courtyard of his new villa. His new sanctum was the smallest, meanest, and least desired accommodation offered to a member of the inner sect. It was also three times the size of the home Wu Ying had resided in with his parents in the village and at least ten times as luxurious. Mother-of-pearl furniture, marble flooring, and beautiful scrollwork filled the building, set there as if each piece was not worth more than the entire contents of his parents' house.

For this reason, Wu Ying found the inner courtyard the most comfortable location in his new residence. After he had moved aside the few stone benches, the center of the courtyard was empty of everything but training dummies, scattered pebbles, and soft grass. Even his well-appointed bedroom was too rich to allow Wu Ying to rest easily.

As he cultivated, memories of the last few days passed through Wu Ying's mind. The days of rest in bed, aided via the lowest-grade recovery pills in the sect. Zhong Shei arriving to congratulate him about his winnings, then bidding farewell as he returned home, a new gleam of motivation in his eyes. The fights in the tournament had set the fire of ambition burning in the guard, giving Zhong Shei direction and a standard to aim for.

Liu Tsong and Tou He had both spent time with the invalid Wu Ying, one to chastise him for pushing himself so hard, the other to bemoan his new status in the sect. Just a day ago, Tou He had taken leave too—forced to join a sect expedition by his sponsoring Elder to "make him take things more seriously." The ex-monk had only brightened at the prospect of getting to eat some of the spirit meat they were likely to acquire during the expedition.

Liu Tsong was also busy, working on her own areas of improvement. The female cultivator was an alchemist, researching the combination of alchemical potions with normal cooking. Her ultimate goal was to improve the taste of potions, making it possible for cultivation resources to be eaten as part of a daily meal, allowing the slow and careful build-up of an individual's cultivation. It was because of this interest that Liu Tsong had been at the kitchen on the day they first met. Since Wu Ying had been injured, Liu Tsong had used the invalid cultivator as a test subject for her latest recipes, an act that had helped Wu Ying's damaged meridians heal all the way.

Chi from the surroundings drew into him, the cleaner and higher air, along with the minor chi-gathering formations in the villa, making cultivating significantly faster. In fact, Wu Ying felt that he was nearing a breakthrough to the next level already.

A knock on his front door interrupted Wu Ying's meditative cultivation, causing the cultivator to open his eyes. A thready exhalation sent out turbid air filled with the corruption and poison of the material world. Standing swiftly, Wu Ying took hold of the laid-out towels and dried himself, cleaning off the majority of the foul-smelling sweat that had accumulated on his body. A glance down showed that black blood had seeped out from his wounds, marring the whiteness of his bandages again.

Wu Ying's servant appeared at the courtyard's entrance, treading around the barrier that hid it. "Senior Long, Elder Cheng and Elder Yang are here."

The servant was another addition, an old woman who few wanted but whose presence Wu Ying found great gratitude for. Without her, he would have to clean and visit the communal dining halls for meals, inconveniences that would have taken even more time from his cultivation.

"Thank you. Let them know I'll be a few minutes."

As the servant bowed and moved to relay his words, Elder Cheng strode in, ignoring proper manners. Behind him, Elder Yang—the newly promoted Fairy Yang—followed docilely. The recently promoted Elder looked resplendent in her new robes, her newly formed Core exerting a subtle pressure on Wu Ying even as he bowed to the pair.

"Elder Cheng. Elder Yang."

Only at Elder Cheng's gesture did Wu Ying dare raise his head. Unlike outer sect members, the rules and formalities binding those in the inner sect were more rigid.

"I thought I sent word for you to rest and not cultivate. Why did you ignore the warning?"

"I… I… I was bored, Elder. And I did not want to waste time."

"There is no waste if you spent the time studying your manuals normally. Pushing yourself is good. Pushing until you injure yourself from your stubbornness is foolish. Learn the difference."

"Yes, Elder."

"Good," Elder Cheng said, walking forward. "I wanted to congratulate you in person. Your victory was unexpected and unusual in its methods."

"Thank you, Elder."

"But you understand what you did, right? You are the peasant who not only beat your noble peers, but did so in an unsightly, undignified manner. You showcased once again that those with discipline, talent, and will can progress. To those diehard nobles, your presence is an insult, a reminder that they are indulgent children," Elder Cheng said, his heavy gaze boring into Wu Ying. "They will not let you go. Not you, or those you are close with." Wu Ying grimaced, and seeing his reaction, Elder Cheng said, "Speak freely."

"Why does the sect let them? It's obvious that if they do not take their studies seriously, they won't progress further. If they push us down—"

"Us being the commoners?" Elder Cheng shook his head. "Politics hampers everything. There are factions that believe that commoners should be treated equally, given equal chances. Then there are nobles who consider themselves above all. It matters not. Those who are fated to ascend in this life will do so."

Wu Ying stared at Elder Cheng, his eyes narrowing. Of course. Elder Cheng was one of those who believed in karma and fate. Absurdly so, it seemed, especially to those who did not believe as strongly. Even if karma and the threads of fate that bound each soul in the cycle of reincarnation were known facts, those who held so strongly to the beliefs and allowed them to influence their everyday lives were rare.

"I came here to offer my congratulations and my warnings. Your time in the inner sect will be more difficult. Especially as I must leave soon to advance my own training. Elder Yuan will be staying behind. She may provide you additional assistance at her discretion."

Wu Ying sighed slightly. In truth, he was uncertain how much more difficult life could get—it was not as if the Elder had provided any significant help in the beginning. But Wu Ying could not help but admit that the man had aided him in his training. Without the intensive hours of training over the last few months, Wu Ying would have never won the fights.

Before Wu Ying could think of anything further to say, the Elder departed, his quiet disciple trailing behind him. In the silence left after their departure, Wu Ying found himself standing in his new residence, opulent and decadent, with enemies all around. He had been left alone for now, but Wu Ying knew that the coming months would only bring more challenges.

Still, as he stood in his own residence, staring down the mist-covered mountains, Wu Ying could only smile. Let them challenge him. He had come this far. He would go further. The path to immortality was a journey of a thousand li, and he had only taken his first steps. Heaven or hell, he would not bow.

###

The End

End of First Steps: Book 1 of the Thousand Li Series

Author's Note

Thank you for reading The First Step, the first book in the A Thousand Li series. As per the saying, a journey of a thousand li begins with a single step and this is Wu Ying's and my first step in writing a novel in a genre that I've loved since been a kid. I grew up watching movies like Once Upon a Time in China, the Swordsman, Return of the Condor Heroes, Stormriders and more. More lately, I've been reading the new works by web novellists translated from China and been impressed by some of the silliness (Library of Heaven's Path) and scope (I Shall Seal the Heavens) of the authors. All this inspired me to try my hand at my own xanxia story.

I hope, by this point, that you have enjoyed the book as much as I had writing it. Wu Ying's journey has just begun, and I hope that with your support, to continue writing more novels for him. If you enjoyed reading the book, please do leave a review and rating. Not only is it a big ego boost, it also helps sales and convinces me to write more in the series!

In addition, please check out my other series, Adventures on Brad (a more traditional LitRPG fantasy), Hidden Wishes (an urban fantasy GameLit), and the System Apocalypse (a post-apocalyptic LitPRG)..

To support me directly, please go to my Patreon account:
- https://www.patreon.com/taowong

For more great information about LitRPG series, check out the Facebook groups:

- GameLit Society

https://www.facebook.com/groups/LitRPGsociety/

- LitRPG Books

https://www.facebook.com/groups/LitRPG.books/

And join my Cultivation Novel Group for more recommendations and to talk about the Thousand Li series (https://www.facebook.com/groups/cultivationnovels/).

About the Author

Tao Wong is an avid fantasy and sci-fi reader who grew up in Malaysia before immigrating to Canada after getting his degrees in the UK. He was the owner of the Vancouver based game store Starlit Citadel and now spends his time working and writing in the cold north of Canada. He's spent way too many years doing various martial arts and, having broken himself too often, now spends his time writing about fantasy worlds.

For updates on the series and other books written by Tao Wong (and special one-shot stories), please visit the author's website:

http://www.mylifemytao.com

Subscribers to Tao's mailing list will receive exclusive access to short stories in the Thousand Li and System Apocalypse universes:

https://www.subscribepage.com/taowong

Or visit his Facebook Page: https://www.facebook.com/taowongauthor/

About the Publisher

Starlit Publishing is wholly owned and operated by Tao Wong. It is a science fiction and fantasy publisher focused on the LitRPG & cultivation genres. Their focus is on promoting new, upcoming authors in the genre whose writing challenges the existing stereotypes while giving a rip-roaring good read.

For more information on Starlit Publishing, visit our website!
https://www.starlitpublishing.com/

You can also join Starlit Publishing's mailing list to learn of new, exciting authors and book releases.
https://starlitpublishing.com/newsletter-signup/

Glossary

Body Cleansing – First cultivation stage where the cultivator must cleanse their body of the impurities that have accumulated. Has twelve stages.

Cao – Fuck

Catty - Weight measurement. One cattie is roughly equivalent to one and a half pounds or 604 grams. A tael is 1/16th of a catty

Chi (or Qi) – I use the Cantonese pinyin here rather than the more common Mandarin. Chi is life force / energy and it permeates all things in the universe, flowing through living creatures in particular.

Chi points (a.k.a. acupuncture points) – Locations in the body that, when struck, compressed, or otherwise affected, can affect the flow of chi. Traditional acupuncture uses these points in a beneficial manner.

Core formation – Third stage of cultivation. Having gathered sufficient chi, the cultivator must form a "core" of compressed chi. The stages in Core formation purify and harden the core.

Dao – Chinese sabre. Closer to a western cavalry sabre, it is thicker, often single-edged, with a curve at the end where additional thickness allows the weapon to be extra efficient at cutting.

Dantian – there are actually three dantians in the human body. The most commonly referred to one is the lower dantian, located right above the bladder and an inch within the body. The other two are located in the chest and forehead, though they are often less frequently used. The dantian is said to be the center of chi.

Energy Storage – Second stage of cultivation, where the energy storage circulation meridians are opened. This stage allows cultivators to project their chi, the amount of chi stored and projected depending on level. There are eight levels.

Huài dàn – Rotten egg

Hún dàn - Bastard

Jian – A straight, double-edged sword. Known in modern times as a "taichi sword." Mostly a thrusting instrument, though it can be used to cut as well.

Li – Roughly half a kilometer per li. Traditional Chinese measurement of distance.

Long family jian style – A family sword form passed on to Wu Ying. Consists of a lot of cuts, fighting at full measure, and quick changes in direction.

Meridians – In traditional Chinese martial arts and medicine, meridians are how chi flows through the body. In traditional Chinese medicine, there are twelve major meridian flows and eight secondary energy flows. I've used these meridians for the stages in cultivation for the first two stages.

Northern Shen Kicking Style – Kicking form that Wu Ying learned at the sect library. Both a grappling and kicking style, meant for close combat.

Qinggong – Literally "light skill." Comes from baguazhang and is basically wire-fu – running on water, climbing trees, gliding along bamboo, etc.

Sect – A grouping of like-minded martial artists or cultivators. Generally, Sects are hierarchical. There are often core, inner, and outer disciples in any sect, with Sect Elders above them and the Sect patriarch above all.

Seven Diamond Fist – Verdant Green Water's Sect most basic fist form taught to outer sect members.

State of Shen – Location in which the first book is set. Ruled by a king and further ruled locally by lords. The State of Shen is made up of numerous counties ruled over by local lords and administered by magistrates. It is a temperate kingdom with significant rainfall and a large number of rivers connected by canals.

State of Wei – The antagonistic kingdom that borders the State of Shen. The two states are at war.

Tael – System of money. A thousand copper coins equals one tael.

Tai Kor – Elder brother

Verdant Green Waters Sect – Most powerful sect in the State of Wen. Wu Ying's current sect.

Preview my other series: the System Apocalypse

Life in the North (Book 1)
Chapter 1

Greetings citizen. As a peaceful and organised immersion into the Galactic Council has been declined (extensively and painfully we might add), your world has been declared a Dungeon World. Thank you. We were getting bored with the 12 that we had previously.

Please note that the process of developing a Dungeon World can be difficult for current inhabitants. We recommend leaving the planet till the process is completed in 373 days, 2 hours, 14 minutes and 12 seconds.

For those of you unable or unwilling to leave, do note that new Dungeons and wandering monsters will spawn intermittently throughout the integration process. All new Dungeons and zones will receive recommended minimum levels, however, during the transition period expect there to be significant volatility in the levels and types of monsters in each Dungeon and zone.

As a new Dungeon World, your planet has been designated a free-immigration location. Undeveloped worlds in the Galactic Council may take advantage of this new immigration policy. Please try not to greet all new visitors the same way as you did our Emissary, you humans could do with some friends.

As part of the transition, all sentient subjects will have access to new classes and skills as well as the traditional user interface adopted by the Galactic Council in 119 GC. Thank you for your co-operation and good luck! We look forward to meeting you soon.

Time to System initiation: 59 minutes 23 seconds

I groan, freeing my hand enough to swipe at the blue box in front of my face as I crank my eyes open. Weird dream. It's not as if I had drunk that much either, just a few shots of whiskey before I went to bed. Almost as soon as the box disappears, another appears, obscuring the small 2-person tent that I'm sleeping in.

Congratulations! You have been spawned in the Kluane National Park (Level 110+) zone.
You have received 7,500 XP (Delayed)

As per Dungeon World Development Schedule 124.3.2.1, inhabitants assigned to a region with a recommended Level 25 or more above the inhabitants' current Level will receive one Small perk.

As per Dungeon World Development Schedule 124.3.2.2, inhabitants assigned to a region with a recommended Level 50 or more above the inhabitants' current Level will receive one Medium perk.

As per Dungeon World Development Schedule 124.3.2.3, inhabitants assigned to a region with a recommended Level 75 or more above the inhabitants' current Level will receive one Large perk.

As per Dungeon World Development Schedule 124.3.2.4, inhabitants assigned to a region with a recommended Level 100 or more above the inhabitants' current Level will receive one Greater perk

What the hell? I jerk forwards and almost fall immediately backwards, the sleeping bag tangling me up. I scramble out, pulling my 5' 8" frame into a sitting position as I swipe black hair out of my eyes to stare at the taunting blue message. Alright, I'm awake and this is not a dream.

This can't be happening, I mean, sure it's happening, but it can't be. It must be a dream, things like this didn't happen in real life. However, considering the rather realistic aches and pains that encompass my body from yesterday's hike, it's really not a dream. Still, this can't be happening.

When I reach out, attempting to touch the screen itself and for a moment, nothing happens until I move my hand when the screen seems to 'stick' to it, swinging with my hand. It's almost like a window in a touchscreen which makes no sense, since this is the real world and there's no tablet. Now that I'm concentrating, I can even feel how the screen has a slight tactile sensation to it, like touching plastic wrap stretched too tight except with the added tingle of static electricity. I stare at my hand and the window and then flick it away watching the window shrink. This makes no sense.

Just yesterday I had hiked up the King's Throne Peak with all my gear to overlook the lake. Early April in the Yukon means that the peak itself was still covered with snow but I'd packed for that, though the final couple of kilometers had been tougher than I had expected. Still, being out and about at least cleared my mind of the dismal state of my life after moving to Whitehorse. No job, barely enough money to pay next month's rent and having just broken up with my girlfriend, leaving on a Tuesday on my junker of a car was just what the doctor ordered. As bad as my life had been, I'm pretty sure I wasn't even close to breaking down, at least not enough to see things.

I shut my eyes, forcing them to stay shut for a count of three before I open them again. The blue box stays, taunting me with its reality. I can feel my breathing shorten, my thoughts splitting in a thousand different directions as I try to make sense of what's happening.

Stop.

I force my eyes close again and old training, old habits come into play. I bottle up the feelings of panic that encroach on my mind, force my scattered thoughts to stop swirling and compartmentalise my feelings. This is not the time or place for all this. I shove it all into a box and close the lid, pushing my emotions down until all there is a comforting, familiar, numbness.

A therapist once said my emotional detachment is a learned self-defence mechanism, one that was useful during my youth but somewhat unnecessary now that I'm an adult with more control over my surroundings. My girlfriend, my ex-girlfriend, just called me an emotionless dick. I've been taught better coping mechanisms but when push comes to shove, I go with what works. If there's an environment which I can't control, I'm going to call floating blue boxes in the real world one of them.

Calmer now, I open my eyes and re-read the information. First rule – what is, is. No more arguing or screaming or worrying about why or how or if I'm insane. What is, is. So. I have perks. And there's a system providing the perks and assigning levels. There's also going to be dungeons and monsters. I'm in a frigging MMO without a damn manual it looks like, which means that at least some of my misspent youth is going to be useful. I wonder what my dad would say. I push the familiar flash of anger down at the thought of him, focusing instead on my current problems.

My first requirement is information. Or better yet, a guide. I'm working on instinct here, going by what feels right rather than what I think is right since the thinking part of me is busy putting its fingers in its ears and going 'na-na-na-na-na'.

"Status?" I query and a new screen blooms.

Status Screen			
Name	John Lee	Class	None
Race	Human (Male)	Level	0

Titles			
None			
Health	100	Stamina	100
Mana	100		
Status			
Twisted ankle (-5% movement speed)			
Tendinitis (-10% Manual Agility)			
Attributes			
Strength	11	Agility	10
Constitution	11	Perception	14
Intelligence	16	Willpower	18
Charisma	8	Luck	7
Skills			
None			
Class Skills			
None			
Spells			
None			

Unassigned Attributes:

1 Small, 1 Medium, 1 Large, 1 Greater Perk

Would you like to assign these attributes? (Y/N)

The second window pop's up almost immediately on top of the first. I want more time to look over my Status but the information seems mostly self-explanatory and it's better to get this over with. It's not as if I have a lot of time. Almost as soon as I think that, the Y depresses and a giant list of Perks flashes up.

Oh, I do **not** have time for this. I definitely don't have time to get stuck in character creation. Being stuck in a zone that is way out of my Level when the System initializes is a one-way ticket to chowville. The giant list of perks before me is way too much to even begin sorting through, especially with names that don't necessarily make sense. What the hell does Adaptive Coloring actually mean? Right, this system seems to work via thought, reacting to what I think so, perhaps I can sort by perk type – narrow it down to small perks for a guide or companion of some form?

Almost as soon as I think of it, the system flashes out and only the word Companion appears. I nod slightly to myself and further details appear, providing two options.

AI   *Spirit*

I select AI but a new notice flashes up

AI Selection unavailable. *Minimum requirements of: Mark IV Processing Unit not met*

I grunt. Yeah, no shit. I don't have a computer on me. Or... in me? No cyberpunk world for me. Not yet at least, though how cool would that be with a computer for a brain and metallic arms that don't hurt from being on the computer too much. Not the time for this, so I pick Spirit next and I acknowledge the query.

System Companion Spirit gained

Congratulations! World Fourth. As the fourth individual to gain a Companion Spirit, your companion is now (Linked). Linked Companions will grow and develop with you.

As I dismiss the notifications, I can see a light begin to glow to my right. I twist around, wondering who or what my new companion is going to be.

***

"Run, hide or fight. Ain't hard to make a choice boy-o."

Look, I'm no pervert. I didn't need a cute, beautiful fairy as my System Companion Spirit. Sure, a part of me hoped for it, I'm a red-blooded male who wouldn't mind staring at something pretty. Still, practically speaking, I would have settled for a Genderless automaton that was efficient and answered my questions with a minimum of lip. Instead, I get... him.

I stare at my new Companion and sigh mentally. Barely a foot tall, he's built like a linebacker with a full, curly brown beard. Brown hair, brown eyes and olive skin in a body-hugging orange jumpsuit that's tight in all the wrong places completes the ensemble. Ali my new companion has been here for all of 10 minutes giving me the lowdown and I'm already partly regretting my choice.

Partly, because for all of his berating, he's actually quite useful.

"Run," I finally decide, pulling apart the chocolate bar and taking another bite. No use fighting, nothing in the store that could scratch a Level 110 monster is going to be usable by me according to Ali and while there's no guarantee one of them will spawn immediately, even the lower level monsters that will make up its dinner would be too tough for me.

Hiding just delays things, so I have to get the hell out of the park which really, shouldn't be that hard. It took me half-a-day of hard hiking to get up this far in the mountain from the parking lot and the parking lot is just inside the new zone. At a good pace, I should be down in a few hours which if I understand things properly means there aren't that many monsters. Once I'm out, it seems Whitehorse has a Safe Zone, which means I can hunker down and figure out what the hell is going on.

"About damn time," grouses Ali. A wave of his hands and a series of new windows appear in front of me. Shortly after appearing he demanded full access to my System which has allowed him to manipulate the information I can see and receive. It's going a lot faster this way since he just pushes the information to me, letting me read through things while he does the deeper search. The new blue windows

- System messages according to him - are his picks for medium and large perks respectively.

Prodigy: Subterfuge

You're a natural born spy. Intrepid would hire you immediately.

Effect: All Subterfuge skills are gained 100% quicker. +50% Skill Level increase for all Subterfuge skills.

"Why this?" I frown, poking at the Subterfuge side. I'm not exactly the spying kind, more direct in most of my interactions. I've never really felt the need to lie too much and I certainly don't see myself creeping around breaking into buildings.

"Stealth skills. It gives a direct bonus to all of them which means you'll gain them faster. A small perk would allow us to directly affect the base Stealth skill but at this level, we've got to go up to its main category." Ali replies and continues, "If you manage to survive, it'll probably be useful in the future anyway."

Quantum Stealth Manipulator (QSM)

The QSM allows its bearer to phase-shift, placing himself adjacent to the current dimension

Effect: While active, user is rendered invisible and undetectable to normal and magical means as long as the QSM is active. Solid objects may be passed through but will drain charge at a higher rate. Charge lasts 5 minutes under normal conditions.

"The QSM – how do I recharge it?"

"It uses a Type III Crystal Manipulator. The Crystal draws upon ambient and line specific..." Ali stares at my face for a moment before waving his hand. "It recharges automatically. It'll be fully charged in a day under normal conditions."

"No Level requirements on these?"

"None."

I picked Ali because he knows the System better than I do, so I can either accept what he's saying or I can do it myself. Put that way, there's really not much of a choice. It's what we talked about, though that Perk Subterfuge isn't really going to be that useful for me. On the other hand, any bonuses to staying out of sight would be great and the QSM would let me run away if I was found out. Which just left my Greater Perk.

Advanced Class: Erethran Honor Guard

The Erethran Honor Guard are Elite Members of the Erethran Armed Forces.

Class Abilities: +2 Per Level in Strength. + 4 Per Level in Constitution and Agility. +3 Per Level in Intelligence and Willpower. Additional 3 Free Attributes per Level.

+90% Mental Resistance. +40% Elemental Resistance

May designate a Personal Weapon. Personal Weapon is Soulbound and upgradeable.

Honor Guard members may have up to 4 Hard Point Links before Essence Penalties apply.

Warning! Minimum Attribute Requirements for the Erethran Honor Guard Class not met. Class Skills Locked till minimum requirements met.

Advanced Class: Dragon Knight

Groomed before birth, Dragon Knights are the Elite Warriors of the Kingdom of Xylargh.

Class Abilities: +3 Per Level in Strength and Agility. + 4 Per Level in Constitution. +3 Per Level Intelligence and Willpower. + 1 in Charisma. Additional 2 Free Attributes per Level.

+80% Mental Resistance. +50% Elemental Resistance

Gain One Greater and One Lesser Elemental Affinity

Warning! Minimum Attribute Requirements for the Dragon Knight Class not met. Class Skills Locked till minimum requirements met.

"That's it?"

"No, you could get this too."

Class: Demi-God

You sexy looking human, you'll be a demi-god. Smart, strong, handsome. What more could you want?

Class Abilities: +100 to all Attributes

All Greater Affinities Gained

Super Sexiness Trait

"That's not a thing."

"It really ain't," smirking, Ali waves and the last screen dismisses. "You wanted a class that helps you survive? That means mental resistances. Otherwise, you'll be pissing those pretty little Pac-Man boxers the moment you see a Level 50 monster. You wanted an end-game? The Honor Guard are some mean motherfuckers. They combine magic and tech making them one of the most versatile groups around, and their Master class advancements are truly scary. The Dragon Knights fight Dragons. One on one and they sometimes even win. Oh, and neither, and I quote 'makes me into a monster'.

"If these are Advanced Classes, what other classes are there?" I prod at Ali, still hesitating. This seems like a big choice.

"Basic, Advance, Master, Grandmaster, Heroic, Legendary," lists Ali and he shrugs. "I could get you a Master Class with your perk, but you'd be locked out of your Class Skills forever. You'd also take forever to level because of the higher minimum experience level gains. Instead, I've got you a rare Advanced Class - it'll give you a better base stat gain per level and you won't have to wait forever to gain access to your Class Skills. Getting a Basic Class, even a rarer Basic Class would be a waste of the Greater Perk. So, what's it going to be?"

As cool as punching a dragon in the face would be, I know which way I'm going the moment he called it up. I mentally select the Guard and light fills me. At first, it just forces me to squint but it begins to dig in, pushing into my body and mind, sending electric, hot claws into my cells. The pain is worse than anything I've felt and I've broken bones, shattered ribs and even managed to electrocute myself before. I know I'm screaming but the pain keeps coming, swarming over me and tearing at my mind, my control. Luckily, darkness claims me before my mind shatters.

Printed in Great Britain
by Amazon